FROM BLUES TO BOP

FROM BLUES TO BOP

A COLLECTION OF JAZZ FICTION

EDITED BY

RICHARD N. ALBERT

Louisiana State University Press
Baton Rouge and London

Manufactured in the United States of America
First printing
99 98 97 96 95 94 93 92 91 90 5 4 3 2 1
Designer: Amanda McDonald Key
Typeface: Sabon
Typesetter: G&S Typesetters, Inc.
Printer and binder: Thomson-Shore, Inc.

Library of Congress Cataloging-in-Publication Data

From blues to bop : a collection of jazz fiction / edited by Richard
N. Albert.
p. cm.
ISBN 0-8071-1616-5 (alk. paper)
1. Jazz music—Fiction. 2. Jazz musicians—Fiction. 3. Short
stories, American. 4. American fiction—20th century. I. Albert,
Richard N.
PS648.J33F76 1990
813′.5080357—dc20 90-31352
CIP

The general editor gratefully acknowledges the authors and publishers who granted permission to reprint the selections herein:

Publication of this book has been supported by a grant from the National Endowment for the Arts in Washington, D.C., a federal agency.

The paper in this book meets the guidelines for permanence and durability of the Committee on Production Guidelines for Book Longevity of the Council on Library Resources. ∞

To the memory of
John Clellon Holmes, whose *The Horn*
inspired my interest in jazz fiction,
and to the jazz musician, whom Holmes called
"the most indigenous American artist"

CONTENTS

INTRODUCTION

Over thirty years ago in *Giants of Jazz* (1957), Studs Terkel proclaimed jazz as "America's most original music. Other lands have given us the opera, the symphony, the concerts, the sonata—classical forms of music. America has given the world jazz." But at about the same time, Nat Hentoff bemoaned the fact that jazz, "one of the most unmistakable strains of American culture—both as a musical language and as a way of life—has been almost entirely overlooked" by the intellectuals. Sadly, even today most Americans don't appreciate it as much as they should. The British, French, and Japanese, among many others worldwide, acclaim jazz much more vigorously than we do.

Yes, jazz is America's most original art form, and since its notorious beginnings as what many referred to as "good time music," it has gained the respect of, indeed has even been played by, "classical" musicians, composers, and conductors such as Gunther Schuller, Leonard Bernstein, and Andre Previn. It is part of the cultural fiber of this country, and though not realized by many, it has contributed to and served as an inspiration for some other areas of modern music, such as rock, fusion, and new wave. Perhaps we're finally beginning to recognize jazz as something in which we can take pride, a viable musical art form that demands critical attention and respect.

Jazz has touched our lives in another way: it has been the inspiration for a body of fiction that, as such, has been pretty much ignored, perhaps because no one has noticed or perhaps because it has not been easy to find. What is jazz fiction? It is novels and short stories, foreign as well as American, that are infused with the spirit of jazz music and jazz musicians and the jazz ambience created by the music and its participants (players and listeners) to the degree that jazz becomes more than a secondary or tertiary element. The theme of a jazz story must depend heavily on the music, the musician, and/or the jazz atmosphere. The story must do more than simply have a scene in a jazz club, or a secondary character who happens to be a musician, or references to jazz musicians or jazz tunes. Rather, the story must have a plot line that depends heavily on the jazz setting or a theme that evolves from the jazz musician characters—their lifestyles, their involvement in the jazz scene, the difficulty of the music and their dedication to mastering it and extending it, their struggles to promote their art, their struggles to cope with all of the complications that life as a jazz musician presents (for instance, how the demanding nature of the art can affect marital relationships, or how it can involve fighting the drug scene). On the other hand, jazz can also produce its own humor and may have a lighter side, though it is less frequently revealed (see, for instance, the pieces by Steve Allen, Marshall Brickman, and Donald Barthelme). I have chosen the stories for this anthology using these guidelines, though perhaps a bit loosely in some cases.

Jazz fiction is uniquely American, and the jazz musician, its central character, is frequently a distinctively American example of alienated man: the artist as rebel. In both life and fiction, the jazz artist's alienation is manifold. He plays a style of music that he has struggled to have recognized and judged as art, especially in the past fifty years. He has been shut out by "respectable society" because of the association of his music in the early years with the brothels and gambling houses of New Orleans' Storyville district. Through the various periods and styles of jazz, he has frequently become alienated from fellow-musicians by virtue of his competitive spirit and his creative desire to present new ideas or a totally new style. Often, the lifestyle of a significant number within his subculture and their seeming penchant for drugs, alcohol, and illicit sex have shut him off from society at large. Also, he is at times alienated because of his color, even though most concede that the great innovators in jazz have been black. Indeed, black and white musicians have often become alienated from one another within the confines of a racially mixed band (I refer here generally to pre-1970 jazz fiction). Finally, the jazz musician is sometimes alienated from himself; his rejections by the establishment (both listeners and critics) confuse him with respect to who he really is or whom he should become. Should he compromise his musical principles for his audience and for the sake of making money? Should he, perhaps unhappily, force himself into the organized and disciplined scheme of a band that plays stock arrangements and allows little or no opportunity for improvisation? Or should he assert himself as a free spirit and face a meager existence? The complexity of the jazz musician as alienated, rebel artist offers writers a wealth of material for inspiration.

Although it is not my purpose here to recount the history of jazz fiction, let me briefly mention in somewhat chronological fashion some of the more prominent jazz stories. Although both Claude McKay in *Home to Harlem* (1928) and Langston Hughes in *Not Without Laughter* (1930) show the great importance of jazz in black culture, theirs are not, strictly speaking, jazz-*inspired* novels. I would start with Dorothy Baker's immensely popular prize-winning *Young Man With a Horn* (1938), the first strongly jazz-oriented story to initiate the figure of the jazz musician as an artist who must struggle with his own aspirations to be the greatest as he seeks to promote his individuality in a world of popular music, where conforming to the discipline of reading and sticking to big band charts is demanded. Bix Beiderbecke inspired Baker's Rick Martin, a jazz rebel who fights the big-band setting in favor of small-group jazz, where priority is given to improvisation. Baker's Rick Martin searches for his personal "truth"—in most jazz literature, that one definitive solo that no one else has ever achieved and which no one will ever repeat. Baker also gives the reader an acute awareness of the importance of the black influence in jazz and some of the problems inherent in 1930s' bands with black and white players.

Henry Steig's *Send Me Down* (1941) was probably the next novel most heavily infused with the jazz spirit. A highly romantic novel with many references to jazz greats, it depicts the life of big band musicians in the 1930s and addresses the problems of crooked agents, the difficulties of blacks getting into white bands, and, of course, drugs. The central character is a piano player who goes the big-band route, becoming an unhappy but successful leader, while his brother, a clarinet player, makes a name for himself via the small group, though with fewer financial rewards.

The 1940s produced a number of little-known novels: Dale Curran's *Piano in the Band* (1940) and *Dupree Blues* (1948); Annemarie Ewing's *Little Gate* (1947); Ernest Borneman's *Tremolo* (1948); Sinclair Traill's *Way Down Yonder* (1949); and George Willis' *Tangleweed* (1945), *The Wild Faun* (1945), and *Little Boy*

Blues (1948). But it was in the 1950s and early 1960s that there was a proliferation of jazz novels, and the generating force was an alto saxophone player out of Kansas City named Charlie Parker—a man who was to change the course of jazz.

Parker was the most frequently used model for the alienated jazz musician. His genius is generally accepted today, but when he lived, he and other exponents of the new jazz called bebop were viewed as musical rebels, except by fellow bop musicians and jazz aficionados who made up a small clique of bop lovers. Parker was an idol of the 1950s' Beat Generation because his individualism in both his lifestyle and his music reflected the Beat love of freedom seen in their lives and writings. Beat writers were rejected and alienated in much the same way that Parker was because they lived (and described in their works) a hedonistic way of life that was in conflict with the more conventional attitudes of the general public and the literary establishment after World War II.

It was in this atmosphere during the 1950s and early 1960s that a significant number of jazz novels were published. Many of these were generated by the popularity of bebop, especially among Beat Generation writers, most notably Jack Kerouac and John Clellon Holmes. Although not regarded as jazz fiction, much of Kerouac's work, particularly *On the Road* (1957), has prominent jazz references and jam session scenes. Holmes, on the other hand, besides having written what many term the first Beat novel, *Go* (1952), wrote the jazz novel *The Horn* (1958), in which the legend of Charlie Parker began to be perpetuated in our literature. Holmes's novel is unusual in that it quite neatly ties together characters loosely based not only on familiar bop jazz musicians (Parker, Lester Young, Dizzy Gillespie, Thelonious Monk, and others) but also on nineteenth-century literary greats noted for their individuality (Herman Melville, Walt Whitman, Emily Dickinson, Henry David Thoreau, and others) and held in esteem by the Beat writers.

Other novels with Parker-like characters are Ross Russell's *The Sound* (1961) and John A. Williams' *Night Song* (1961). Russell is best known as the producer of the Parker Dial recording sessions and as the author of the highly regarded biography of Parker, *Bird Lives!* (1973). His first-hand knowledge of the jazz scene during the bop period is prominent in *The Sound,* which is a veritable catalog of jazz musicians and styles and a lexicon of jazz jargon, though his descriptions are at times a bit too technical for the layman. Russell's central character, Red Travers, does not play alto sax, but rather trumpet. In tracing Red's career, Russell gives the reader an education in bop by describing the small coterie of jazz fans, the conflict between the 1930s'- and 1940s'-style swing bands and the new bop style, the late-night jam sessions during which the musicians challenged one another's inventiveness and technique, the conflicts between whites and blacks both within the bands and without, the exhausting series of one-night stands, the late and missed dates, and the seemingly incessant use of drugs. Red's death is different from Parker's; nevertheless it is the result of his insatiable appetite for sensual pleasures.

Williams' *Night Song* uses the jazz milieu primarily to make a political statement. The alienation of whites and blacks is dramatically highlighted in this story, but a significant character in the story is bop saxophonist Richie "Eagle" Stokes, an obvious allusion to "Bird" Parker. His overindulgence in drugs leads to his death, soon after which signs begin to appear: "Eagle Lives" and "The Eagle Still Soars." Another character says of Eagle, "He symbolizes the rebel in us."

William Melvin Kelley's *A Drop of Patience* (1965) is another possibly Bird-inspired novel, because the dominant character in this story, Ludlow Washington, is a blind-from-birth black man who seems to play alto saxophone (his instrument is never specifically mentioned in the novel). His role in the story is that of an innovator of a new style of jazz in the 1940s (evidently bebop), and his archetypical fight for artistic integrity is the most important aspect of the story's theme.

Two other novels from this period, though not Parker-inspired, deserve some attention: Garson Kanin's *Blow Up a Storm* (1959) and Herbert Simmons' *Man Walking on Eggshells* (1962). Although Kanin is best known for one of his plays, *Born Yesterday,* he at one time played saxophone in jazz bands and used his experiences to produce a story with many knowledgeable references to jazz styles and jazz players. The jazz musician he focuses on is a trumpeter from a common mold: he works hard, pays his dues, achieves prominence, seeks to regain his former glory, and dies tragically. Simmons also has a fine feel for the jazz milieu, and in *Man Walking on Eggshells,* he presents a Miles Davis–type character who has a reputation for turning his back on his audience and not speaking to them through a whole performance. The novel is divided into three parts, each of which bears the title of a famous jazz tune associated with Davis: "Walking," "So What?" and " 'Round Midnight."

Many other novels (of varying quality) were published during the 1950s and 1960s: Harold Sinclair's *Music Out of Dixie* (1952), Stanford Whitmore's *Solo* (1955), Douglass Wallop's *Night Light* (1955), Duke Osborn's *Sideman* (1955), Evan Hunter's *Second Ending* (1956), George Lea's *Somewhere There's Music* (1958), Roland Gant's *World in a Jug* (1961), John Wain's *Strike the Father Dead* (1962), Malcolm Braly's *Shake Him Till He Rattles* (1963), and Gene Lees's *And Sleep Until Noon* (1966). One of the more recent jazz novels is Michael Ondaatje's *Coming Through Slaughter* (1976), a story that builds on the mystery and myth of Buddy Bolden.

The importance of jazz in our culture is further attested to by the number of different authors (besides those represented in this anthology) who have at times been inspired by jazz: Terry Southern ("You're Too Hip, Baby"), Frank London Brown ("McDougal" and "Singing Dinah's Song"), James Jones ("The King"), J. D. Salinger ("Blue Melody"), Rudolph Fisher ("Common Meter"), Malcolm Lowry ("A Forest Path to the Spring"), Albert Murray ("Train Whistle Guitar"), and Ann Petry ("Solo on the Drums"), among scores of others. Jazz has even found its way into science fiction. Two excellent examples are Robert Tilley's short stories, "Something Else" and "Willie's Blues." Readers may wish to refer to my "Bibliography of Jazz Fiction," *Bulletin of Bibliography* (June, 1989) for a comprehensive listing of jazz novels, short stories, and selected criticism.

The jazz novels I have mentioned certainly do not make up a complete list. Others are out there somewhere, but they are difficult to locate. Most of those I have briefly commented on have had single printings and have not been reissued (except *Young Man With a Horn* and *The Horn*). When it comes to short stories, the situation is about the same. Many have been published through the years, but often in obscure periodicals and little magazines. The two *most* accessible stories are Eudora Welty's "Powerhouse" and James Baldwin's "Sonny's Blues," principally because these authors' works are readily available (both stories are often found in college literature anthologies because of their acknowledged literary excellence). Finding jazz short stories is time-consuming but rewarding.

Not every reader may agree that these selections accurately describe all aspects of jazz. It was not my intention that they should. I chose stories that I as a jazz enthusiast enjoy and can relate to based on my knowledge of jazz. Above all, I hope most selections will help to affirm that jazz has been, and possibly will continue to be, an important generating force in fiction. But, more important, I want readers to have some pleasant hours. May I suggest you play some Bird, Diz, Miles, Lady Day, Prez, *et al.* as you read?

Richard N. Albert
Illinois State University

LANGSTON HUGHES

A leading figure of the 1920s' Harlem Renaissance, Langston Hughes wrote prolifically from 1921 until his death in 1967. He traveled worldwide and used his many experiences to promote his ideas in fiction, poetry, drama, nonfiction, and even musical theater.

His love of jazz and the blues manifests itself especially in his poetry, from *The Weary Blues* (1926) down through the bop era with *Montage of a Dream Deferred* (1951), where he describes bop in the preface as being "marked by conflicting changes, sudden nuances, sharp and impudent interjections, broken rhythms, and passages sometimes in the manner of the jam session, sometimes the popular song, punctuated by the riffs, runs, breaks, and distortions of the music of a community in transition"—a neat definition of jazz indeed! So prominent is Hughes's indebtedness to jazz and blues that their influence on his writing has become subject matter for numerous scholarly articles.

Hughes felt that jazz was a commonly shared medium that could promote harmony and understanding among all people. In this excerpt from his first novel, *Not Without Laughter* (1930), jazz is depicted as an important part of black culture and dances as a favorite form of release—a way of giving free rein to one's emotions. Hughes emphasizes the blues—"the plain old familiar blues, heart-breaking and extravagant, ma-baby's-gone-from-me blues"—and the individuality shown by both the dancers and the musicians.

DANCE

MRS. J. J. RICE and family usually spent ten days during the August heat at Lake Dale, and thither they had gone now, giving Annjee a forced vacation with no pay. Jimboy was not working, and so his wife found ten days of rest without income not especially agreeable. Nevertheless, she decided that she might as well enjoy the time; so she and Jimboy went to the country for a week with Cousin Jessie, who had married one of the colored farmers of the district. Besides, Annjee thought that Jimboy might help on the farm and so make a little money. Anyway, they would get plenty to eat, because Jessie kept a good table. And since Jessie had eight children of her own, they did not take Sandy with them—eight were enough for a woman to be worried with at one time!

Aunt Hager had been ironing all day on the Reinharts' clothes—it was Friday. At seven o'clock Harriett came home, but she had already eaten her supper at the restaurant where she worked.

"Hello, mama! Hy, Sandy!" she said, but that was all, because she and her mother were not on the best of terms. Aunt Hager was attempting to punish her youngest daughter by not allowing her to leave the house after dark, since Harriett, on Tuesday night, had been out until one o'clock in the morning with no better excuse than a party at Maudel's. Aunt Hager had threatened to whip her then and there that night.

"You ain't had a switch on yo' hide fo' three years, but don't think you's gettin' too big fo' me not to fan yo' behind, madam. 'Spare de rod an' spoil de chile,' that's what de Bible say, an' Lawd knows you sho is spoiled! De idee of a young gal yo' age stayin' out till one o'clock in de mawnin', an' me not knowed where you's at. . . . Don't you talk back to me! . . . You rests in this house ever' night this week an' don't put yo' foot out o' this yard after you comes from work, that's what you do. Lawd knows I don't know what I's gonna do with you. I works fo' you an' I prays fo' you, an' if you don't mind, I's sho gonna whip you, even if you is goin' on seventeen years old!"

Tonight as soon as she came from work Harriett went into her mother's room and lay across the bed. It was very warm in the little four-room house, and all the windows and doors were open.

"We's got some watermelon here, daughter," Hager called from the kitchen. "Don't you want a nice cool slice?"

"No," the girl replied. She was fanning herself with a palm-leaf fan, her legs in their cheap silk stockings hanging over the side of the bed, and her heels kicking the floor. Benbow's Band played tonight for the dance at Chaver's Hall, and everybody was going—but her. Gee, it was hard to have a Christian mother! Harriett kicked her slippers off with a bang and rolled over on her stomach, burying her powdery face in the pillows. . . . Somebody knocked at the back door.

A boy's voice was speaking excitedly to Hager: "Hemorrhages . . . and papa can't stop 'em . . . she's coughin' something terrible . . . says can't you please come over and help him"—frightened and out of breath.

"Do Jesus!" cried Hager. "I'll be with you right away, chile. Don't worry." She rushed into the bedroom to change her apron. "You Harriett, listen; Sister Lane's taken awful sick an' Jimmy says she's bleedin' from de mouth. If I ain't back by nine o'clock, see that that chile Sandy's in de bed. An' you know you ain't to leave this yard under no circumstances. . . . Po' Mis' Lane! She sho do have it hard." In a whisper: "I 'spects she's got de T.B., that what I 'spects!" And the old woman hustled out to join the waiting youngster. Jimmy was leaning against the door, looking at Sandy, and neither of the boys knew what to say. Jimmy Lane wore his mother's cast-off shoes to school, and Sandy used to tease him, but tonight he didn't tease his friend about his shoes.

"You go to bed 'fore it gets late," said his grandmother, starting down the alley with Jimmy.

"Yes'm," Sandy called after her. "So long, Jim!" He stood under the apple-tree and watched them disappear.

DANCE

Aunt Hager had scarcely gotten out of sight when there was a loud knock at the front door, and Sandy ran around the house to see Harriett's boy friend, Mingo, standing in the dusk outside the screen-door, waiting to be let in.

Mingo was a patent-leather black boy with wide, alive nostrils and a mouth that split into a lighthouse smile on the least provocation. His body was heavy and muscular, resting on bowed legs that curved backward as though the better to brace his chunky torso; and his hands were hard from mixing concrete and digging ditches for the city's new water-mains.

"I know it's tonight, but I can't go," Sandy heard his aunt say at the door. They were speaking of Benbow's dance. "And his band don't come here often, neither. I'm heart-sick having to stay home, dog-gone it all, especially this evening!"

"Aw, come on and go anyway," pleaded Mingo. "After I been savin' up my dough for two weeks to take you, and got my suit cleaned and pressed and all. Heck! If you couldn't go and knew it yesterday, why didn't you tell me? That's a swell way to treat a fellow!"

"Because I wanted to go," said Harriett, "and still want to go. . . . Don't make so much difference about mama, because she's mad anyhow . . . but what could we do with this kid? We can't leave him by himself." She looked at Sandy, who was standing behind Mingo listening to everything.

"You can take me," the child offered anxiously, his eyes dancing at the delightful prospect. "I'll behave, Harrie, if you take me, and I won't tell on you either. . . . Please lemme go, Mingo. I ain't never seen a big dance in my life. I wanta go."

"Should we?" asked Harriett doubtfully, looking at her boy friend standing firmly on his curved legs.

"Sure, if we got to have him . . . damn 'im!" Mingo replied. "Better the kid than no dance. Go git dressed." So Harriett made a dash for the clothes-closet, while Sandy ran to get a clean waist from one of his mother's dresser-drawers, and Mingo helped him put it on, cussing softly to himself all the while. "But it ain't your fault, pal, is it?" he said to the little boy.

"Sure not," Sandy replied. "I didn't tell Aunt Hager to make Harrie stay home. I tried to 'suade grandma to let her go," the child lied, because he liked Mingo. "I guess she won't care about her goin' to just one dance." He wanted to make everything all right so the young man wouldn't be worried. Besides, Sandy very much wanted to go himself.

"Let's beat it," Harriett shrilled excitedly before her dress was fastened, anxious to be gone lest her mother come home. She was powdering her face and neck in the next room, nervous, happy, and afraid all at once. The perfume, the voice, and the pat, pat, pat of the powder-puff came out to the waiting gentleman.

"Yo' car's here, madam," mocked Mingo. "Step right this way and let's be going!"

> Wonder where ma easy rider's gone—
> He done left me, put ma new gold watch in pawn!

Like a blare from hell the second encore of *Easy Rider* filled every cubic inch of the little hall with hip-rocking notes. Benbow himself was leading and the crowd moved like jelly-fish dancing on individual sea-shells, with Mingo and Harriett somewhere among the shakers. But they were not of them, since each couple shook in a world of its own, as, with a weary wail, the music abruptly ceased.

Then, after scarcely a breath of intermission, the band struck up again with a lazy one-step. A tall brown boy in a light tan suit walked his partner straight down the whole length of the floor and, when he reached the corner, turned leisurely in one spot, body riding his hips, eyes on the ceiling, and his girl shaking her full breasts against his pink silk shirt. Then they recrossed the width of the room, turned slowly, repeating themselves, and began again to walk rhythmically down the hall, while the music was like a lazy river flowing between mountains, carving a canyon coolly, calmly, and without insistence. *The Lazy River One-Step* they might have called what the band was playing as the large crowd moved with the greatest of ease about the hall. To drum-beats barely audible, the tall boy in the tan suit walked his partner round and round time after time, revolving at each corner with eyes uplifted, while the piano was the water flowing, and the high, thin chords of the banjo were the mountains floating in the clouds. But in sultry tones, alone and always, the brass cornet spoke harshly about the earth.

Sandy sat against the wall in a hard wooden folding chair. There were other children scattered lonesomely about on chairs, too, watching the dancers, but he didn't seem to know any of them. When the music stopped, all the chairs quickly filled with loud-talking women and girls in brightly colored dresses who fanned themselves with handkerchiefs and wiped their sweating brows. Sandy thought maybe he should give his seat to one of the women when he saw Maudel approaching.

"Here, honey," she said. "Take this dime and buy yourself a bottle of something cold to drink. I know Harriett ain't got you on her mind out there dancin'. This music is certainly righteous, chile!" She laughed as she handed Sandy a coin and closed her pocketbook. He liked Maudel, although he knew his grandmother didn't. She was a large good-natured brown-skinned girl who walked hippishly and used too much rouge on her lips. But she always gave Sandy a dime, and she was always laughing.

He went through the crowd towards the soft-drink stand at the end of the hall. "Gimme a bottle o' cream soda," he said to the fat orange-colored man there, who had his sleeves rolled up and a white butcher's-apron covering his barrel-like belly. The man put his hairy arms down into a zinc tub full of ice and water and began pulling out bottles, looking at their caps, and then dropping them back in the cold liquid.

"Don't seem like we got no cream, sonny. How'd a lemon do you?" he asked above the bedlam of talking voices.

"Naw," said Sandy. "It's too sour."

On the improvised counter of boards the wares displayed consisted of cracker-jacks, salted peanuts, a box of gum, and Sen Sens, while behind the counter was a lighted oil-stove holding a tin pan full of spare-ribs, sausage, and fish; and near it an ice-cream freezer covered with a brown sack. Some cases of soda were on the floor beside the zinc tub filled with bottles, in which the man was still searching.

"Nope, no cream," said the fat man.

"Well, gimme a fish sandwich then," Sandy replied, feeling very proud because some kids were standing near, looking at him as he made his purchase like a grown man.

"Buy me one, too," suggested a biscuit-colored little girl in a frilly dirty-white dress.

"I only got a dime," Sandy said. "But you can have half of mine." And he gallantly broke in two parts the double square of thick bread, with its hunk of greasy fish between, and gravely handed a portion to the grinning little girl.

"Thanks," she said, running away with the bread and fish in her hands.

"Shame on you!" teased a small boy, rubbing his forefingers at Sandy. "You got a girl! You got a girl!"

"Go chase yourself!" Sandy replied casually, as he picked out the bones and smacked his lips on the sweet fried fish. The orchestra was playing another one-step, with the dancers going like shuttles across the floor. Sandy saw his Aunt Harriett and a slender yellow boy named Billy Sanderlee doing a series of lazy, intricate steps as they wound through the crowd from one end of the hall to the other. Certain less accomplished couples were watching them with admiration.

Sandy, when he finished eating, decided to look for the wash-room, where he could rinse his hands, because they were greasy and smelled fishy. It was at the far corner of the hall. As he pushed open the door marked GENTS, a thick grey cloud of cigarette-smoke drifted out. The stench of urine and gin and a crowd of men talking, swearing, and drinking liquor surrounded the little boy as he elbowed his way towards the wash-bowls. All the fellows were shouting loudly to one another and making fleshy remarks about the women they had danced with.

"Boy, you ought to try Velma," a mahogany-brown boy yelled. "She sure can go."

"Hell," answered a whisky voice somewhere in the smoke. "That nappy-headed black woman? Gimme a high yaller for mine all de time. I can't use no coal!"

"Well, de blacker de berry, de sweeter de juice," protested a slick-haired ebony youth in the center of the place. . . . "Ain't that right, sport?" he demanded of Sandy, grabbing him jokingly by the neck and picking him up.

"I guess it is," said the child, scared, and the men laughed.

"Here, kid, buy yourself a drink," the slick-headed boy said, slipping Sandy a nickel as he set him down gently at the door. "And be sure it's pop—not gin."

Outside, the youngster dried his wet hands on a handkerchief, blinked his smoky eyes, and immediately bought the soda, a red strawberry liquid in a long, thick bottle.

Suddenly and without warning the cornet blared at the other end of the hall in an ear-splitting wail: "Whaw! . . . Whaw! . . . Whaw! . . . Whaw!" and the snare-drum rolled in answer. A pause . . . then the loud brassy notes were repeated and the banjo came in, "Plinka, plink, plink," like timid drops of rain after a terrific crash of thunder. Then quite casually, as though nothing had happened, the piano lazied into a slow drag, with all the other instruments following. And with the utmost nonchalance the drummer struck into time.

"Ever'body shake!" cried Benbow, as a ribbon of laughter swirled round the hall.

Couples began to sway languidly, melting together like candy in the sun as hips rotated effortlessly to the music. Girls snuggled pomaded heads on men's chests, or rested powdered chins on men's shoulders, while wild young boys put both arms tightly around their partners' waists and let their hands hang down carelessly over female haunches. Bodies moved ever so easily together—ever so easily, as Benbow turned towards his musicians and cried through cupped hands: "Aw, screech it, boys!"

A long, tall, gangling gal stepped back from her partner, adjusted her hips, and did a few easy, gliding steps all her own before her man grabbed her again.

"Eu-o-oo-ooo-oooo!" moaned the cornet titillating with pain, as the banjo cried in stop-time, and the piano sobbed aloud with a rhythmical, secret passion. But the drums kept up their hard steady laughter—like somebody who don't care.

"I see you plowin', Uncle Walt," called a little autumn-leaf brown with switching skirts to a dark-purple man grinding down the center of the floor with a yellow woman. Two short prancing blacks stopped in their tracks to quiver violently. A bushy-headed girl threw out her arms, snapped her fingers, and began to holler: "Hey! . . . Hey!" while her perspiring partner held doggedly to each hip in an effort to keep up with her. All over the hall, people danced their own individual movements to the scream and moan of the music.

"Get low . . . low down . . . down!" cried the drummer, bouncing like a rubber ball in his chair. The banjo scolded in diabolic glee, and the cornet panted as though it were out of breath, and Benbow himself left the band and came out on the floor to dance slowly and ecstatically with a large Indian-brown woman covered with diamonds.

"Aw, do it, Mister Benbow!" one of his admirers shouted frenziedly as the hall itself seemed to tremble.

"High yallers, draw nigh! Brown-skins, come near!" somebody squalled. "But black gals, stay where you are!"

"Whaw! Whaw! Whaw!" mocked the cornet—but the steady tomtom of the drums was no longer laughter now, no longer even pleasant: the drum-beats had become sharp with surly sound, like heavy waves that beat angrily on a granite rock. And under the dissolute spell of its own rhythm the music had got quite beyond itself. The four black men in Benbow's wandering band were exploring depths to which mere sound had no business to go. Cruel, desolate, unadorned was their music now, like the body of a ravished woman on the sun-baked earth; violent and hard, like a giant standing over his bleeding mate in the blazing sun. The odors of bodies, the stings of flesh, and the utter emptiness of soul when all is done—these things the piano and the drums, the cornet and the twanging banjo insisted on hoarsely to a beat that made the dancers move, in that little hall, like pawns on a frenetic checker-board.

"Aw, play it, Mister Benbow!" somebody cried.

The earth rolls relentlessly, and the sun blazes for ever on the earth, breeding, breeding. But why do you insist like the earth, music? Rolling and breeding, earth and sun for ever relentlessly. But why do you insist like the sun? Like the lips of women? Like the bodies of men, relentlessly?

"Aw, play it, Mister Benbow!"

But why do you insist, music?

Who understands the earth? Do you, Mingo? Who understands the sun? Do you, Harriett? Does anybody know—among you high yallers, you jelly-beans, you pinks and pretty daddies, among you sealskin browns, smooth blacks, and chocolates-to-the-bone—does anybody know the answer?

"Aw, play it, Benbow!"

"It's midnight. De clock is strikin' twelve, an' . . ."
"Aw, play it, Mister Benbow!"

During intermission, when the members of the band stopped making music to drink gin and talk to women, Harriett and Mingo bought Sandy a box of cracker-jacks and another bottle of soda and left him standing in the middle of the floor holding both. His young aunt had forgotten time, so Sandy decided to go upstairs to the narrow unused balcony that ran the length of one side of the place. It was dusty up there, but a few broken chairs stood near the railing and he sat on one of them. He leaned his arms on the banister, rested his chin in his hands, and when the music started, he looked down on the mass of moving couples crowding the floor. He had a clear view of the energetic little black drummer eagle-rocking with staccato regularity in his chair as his long, thin sticks descended upon the tightly drawn skin of his small drum, while his foot patted the pedal of his big bass-drum, on which was painted in large red letters: "BENBOW'S FAMOUS KANSAS CITY BAND."

As the slow shuffle gained in intensity (and his cracker-jacks gave out), Sandy looked down drowsily on the men and women, the boys and girls, circling and turning beneath him. Dresses and suits of all shades and colors, and a vast confusion of bushy heads on swaying bodies. Faces gleaming like circus balloons—lemon-yellow, coal-black, powder-grey, ebony-black, blue-black faces; chocolate, brown, orange, tan, creamy-gold faces—Sandy's eyes were beginning to blur with sleep—colored balloons with strings, and the music pulling the strings. No! Girls pulling the strings—each boy a balloon by a string. Each face a balloon.

Sandy put his head down on the dusty railing of the gallery. An odor of hair-oil and fish, of women and sweat came up to him as he sat there alone, tired and a little sick. It was very warm and close, and the room was full of chatter during the intervals. Sandy struggled against sleep, but his eyes were just about to close when, with a burst of hopeless sadness, the *St. Louis Blues* spread itself like a bitter syrup over the hall. For a moment the boy opened his eyes to the drowsy flow of sound, long enough to pull two chairs together, then he lay down on them and closed his eyes again. Somebody was singing:

St. Louis woman with her diamond rings . . .

as the band said very weary things in a loud and brassy manner and the dancers moved in a dream that seemed to have forgotten itself:

Got ma man tied to her apron-strings . . .

Wah! Wah! Wah! . . . The cornet laughed with terrible rudeness. Then the drums began to giggle and the banjo whined an insulting leer. The piano said, over and over again: "St. Louis! That big old dirty town where the Mississippi's deep and wide, deep and wide . . ." and the hips of the dancers rolled.

Man's got a heart like a rock cast in de sea . . .

while the cynical banjo covered unplumbable depths with a plinking surface of staccato gaiety, like the sparkling bubbles that rise on deep water over a man who has just drowned himself:

Or else he never would a gone so far from me . . .

then the band stopped with a long-drawn-out wail from the cornet and a flippant little laugh from the drums.

A great burst of applause swept over the room, and the musicians immediately began to play again. This time just blues, not the *St. Louis,* not the *Memphis,* nor the *Yellow Dog*—but just the plain old familiar blues, heart-breaking and extravagant, ma-baby's-gone-from-me blues.

Nobody thought about anyone else then. Bodies sweatily close, arms locked, cheek to cheek, breast to breast, couples rocked to the pulse-like beat of the rhythm, yet quite oblivious each person of the other. It was true that men and women were dancing together, but their feet had gone down through the floor into the earth, each dancer's alone—down into the center of things—and their minds had gone off to the heart of loneliness, where they didn't even hear the words, the sometimes lying, sometimes laughing words that Benbow, leaning on the piano, was singing against this background of utterly despondent music:

When de blues is got you,
Ain't no use to run away.
When de blue-blues got you,
Ain't no use to run away,

'Cause de blues is like a woman
That can turn yo' good hair grey.

Umn-ump! . . . Umn! . . . Umn-ump!

Well, I tole ma baby,
Says baby, baby, babe, be mine,
But ma baby was deceitful.
She must a thought that I was blind.

De-da! De-da! . . . De-da! De-da! Dee!

O, Lawdy, Lawdy, Lawdy,
Lawdy, Lawdy, Lawd . . . Lawd . . . Lawd!
She quit me fo' a Texas gambler,
So I had to git another broad.

Whaw-whaw! . . . Whaw-whaw-whaw! As though the laughter of a cornet could reach the heart of loneliness.

These mean old weary blues coming from a little orchestra of four men who needed no written music because they couldn't have read it. Four men and a leader—Rattle Benbow from Galveston; Benbow's buddy, the drummer, from Houston; his banjoist from Birmingham; his cornetist from Atlanta; and the pianist, long-fingered, sissyfied, a coal-black lad from New Orleans who had brought with him an exaggerated rag-time which he called jazz.

"I'm jazzin' it, creepers!" he sometimes yelled as he rolled his eyes towards the dancers and let his fingers beat the keys to a frenzy. . . . But now the piano was cryin' the blues!

Four homeless, plug-ugly niggers, that's all they were, playing mean old loveless blues in a hot, crowded little dance-hall in a Kansas town on Friday night. Playing the heart out of loneliness with a wide-mouthed leader, who sang everybody's troubles until they became his own. The improvising piano, the whanging banjo, the throbbing bass-drum, the hard-hearted little snare-drum, the brassy cornet that laughed, "Whaw-whaw-whaw. . . . Whaw!" were the waves in this lonesome sea of harmony from which Benbow's melancholy voice rose:

You gonna wake up some mawnin'
An' turn yo' smilin' face.
Wake up some early mawnin'

Says turn yo' smilin' face,
Look at yo' sweetie's pillow—
An' find an' empty place!

Then the music whipped itself into a slow fury, an awkward, elemental, foot-stomping fury, with the banjo running terrifiedly away in a windy moan and then coming back again, with the cornet wailing like a woman who don't know what it's all about:

Then you gonna call yo' baby,
Call yo' lovin' dear—
But you can keep on callin'
'Cause I won't be here!

And for a moment nothing was heard save the shuf-shuf-shuffle of feet and the immense booming of the bass-drum like a living vein pulsing at the heart of loneliness.

"Sandy! . . . Sandy! . . . My stars! Where is that child? . . . Has anybody seen my little nephew?" All over the hall. . . . "Sandy! . . . Oh-o-o, Lord!" Finally, with a sigh of relief: "You little brat, darn you, hiding up here in the balcony where nobody could find you! . . . Sandy, wake up! It's past four o'clock and I'll get killed."

Harriett vigorously shook the sleeping child, who lay stretched on the dusty chairs; then she began to drag him down the narrow steps before he was scarcely awake. The hall was almost empty and the chubby little black drummer was waddling across the floor carrying his drums in canvas cases. Someone was switching off the lights one by one. A mustard-colored man stood near the door quarrelling with a black woman. She began to cry and he slapped her full in the mouth, then turned his back and left with another girl of maple-sugar brown. Harriett jerked Sandy past this linked couple and pulled the boy down the long flight of stairs into the street, where Mingo stood waiting, with a lighted cigarette making a white line against his black skin.

"You better git a move on," he said. "Daylight ain't holdin' itself back for you!" And he told the truth, for the night had already begun to pale.

Sandy felt sick at the stomach. To be awakened precipitately made him cross and ill-humored, but the fresh, cool air soon caused him to feel less sleepy and not quite so ill. He took a deep breath as he trotted rapidly along on the sidewalk beside his striding aunt and her boy friend. He watched the blue-grey dawn blot out the night in the sky; and the pearl-gray blot out the blue, while the stars faded to points of dying fire. And he listened to the birds chirping and trilling in the trees as though they were calling the sun. Then, as he became fully awake, the child began to feel very proud of himself, for this was the first time he had ever been away from home all night.

Harriett was fussing with Mingo. "You shouldn't've kept me out like that," she said. "Why didn't you tell me what time it was? . . . I didn't know."

And Mingo came back: "Hey, didn't I try to drag you away at midnight and you wouldn't come? And ain't I called you at one o'clock and you said: 'Wait a minute'—dancin' with some yaller P.I. from St. Joe, with your arms round his neck like a life-preserver? . . . Don't tell me I didn't want to leave, and me got to go to work at eight o'clock this mornin' with a pick and shovel when the whistle blows! What de hell?"

But Harriett did not care to quarrel now when there would be no time to finish it properly. She was out of breath from hurrying and almost in tears. She was afraid to go home.

"Mingo, I'm scared."

"Well, you know what you can do if your ma puts you out," her escort said quickly, forgetting his anger. "I can take care of you. We could get married."

"Could we, Mingo?"

"Sure!"

She slipped her hand in his. "Aw, daddy!" and the pace became much less hurried.

When they reached the corner near which Harriett lived, she lifted her dark little purple-powdered face for a not very lingering kiss and sent Mingo on his way. Then she frowned anxiously and ran on. The sky was a pale pearly color, waiting for the warm gold of the rising sun.

"I'm scared to death!" said Harriett. "Lord, Sandy, I hope ma ain't up! I hope she didn't come home last night from Mis' Lane's. We shouldn't've gone, Sandy . . . I guess we shouldn't've gone." She was breathing hard and Sandy had to run fast to keep up with her. "Gee, I'm scared!"

The grass was diamond-like with dew, and the red bricks of the sidewalk were damp, as the small boy and his young aunt hurried under the leafy elms along the walk. They passed Madam de Carter's house and cut through the wet grass into their own yard as the first rays of the morning sun sifted through the trees. Quietly they tiptoed towards the porch; quickly and quietly they crossed it; and softly, ever so softly, they opened the parlor door.

In the early dusk the oil-lamp still burned on the front-room table, and in an old arm-chair, with the open Bible on her lap, sat Aunt Hager Williams, a bundle of switches on the floor at her feet.

DOROTHY BAKER

A good case might be made for Dorothy Baker's *Young Man With a Horn* (1938) being the genesis of jazz fiction. Inspired by Otis Ferguson's piece on Bix Beiderbecke in the *New Republic,* Mrs. Baker's novel won a Houghton Mifflin Literary Fellowship Award. She felt comfortable writing about jazz and said, "Jazz music was one of the very few things I knew much about, and the only thing, except writing, that I had had a consistent, long-term interest in."

Baker projects the jazz milieu of the 1930s very well. In his review of her novel, Ferguson (from whom she took, with his permission, the title of her novel) notes that she "writes like a man, with the easy habits of men among their kind." She also gives the reader a fine awareness of the importance of the black influence in jazz and some of the problems inherent in orchestras with both black and white players.

In *Young Man With a Horn,* Beiderbecke becomes Rick Martin, a white jazz musician who grows up as a truant, befriending a black drummer, Smoke Jordan, and listening to black musicians. Teaching himself to play piano, he is soon inspired by Art Hazard, black trumpet player, and switches to trumpet. At the early age of fifteen, he is playing professionally at a small local club; a short five years later he is a member of a respected dance band but is displeased with being tied down to playing scored arrangements. Eventually, he becomes a member of the Phil Morrison Orchestra (obviously modeled on Paul Whiteman) and achieves national prominence. Like Beiderbecke, Rick succumbs to alcohol and dies before age thirty of pneumonia while trying to take a cure.

The excerpt included here is from the latter portion of the novel and makes reference to Rick Martin's alcoholism and impending death. Hollywood's rendition of Baker's story, with Kirk Douglas playing Martin and Harry James providing the trumpet expertise, was, as might be expected, romantically mawkish and substituted a happier ending.

Baker died in 1968, having written four novels and a variety of short stories, two of which also have a jazz setting ("The Jazz Sonata" and "Keeley Street Blues").

FROM *YOUNG MAN WITH A HORN*

THEY drove through the tube and five miles into New Jersey to a road-house off the highway, a place known as Silver's. Silver's was always the first place the law looked into when a round-up was called, but that didn't hurt business any. A woman named Olga Vogel ran it; it was called Silver's for someone no longer there.

The three white ones and the three black ones stomped into the house and got a greeting. The players are come to Elsinore and they're of a mind to play. 'Lookit the jig-men,' Olga said. 'I thought you'd give us the go-by. How are you, Rick Martin? Hi, Art; Hi, Jeff, Smoke, Miltyboy. Who's your little friend here? So? A Mr. Cohen? Glad to see you, Mr. Cohen; there's always room here for a countryman. You boys want to stay down here, or do you want to be alone? There's a piano both places.'

'We don't want to play,' Smoke said. He had drums hanging all over him. 'We just come out to see how everything's getting along out here.'

'You'd better go upstairs,' Olga said. 'Lou Marble's up there. She was singing awhile ago. I don't know what she's doing now.'

Olga pushed them through the room and into a door that opened on some stairs. Rick was the last one, and she linked an arm through his on the way upstairs.

'They tell me you married a society girl, Rick,' she said. 'Is she pretty?'

'No,' Rick said, 'she looks like a coal miner.'

'What's her name?' Olga said.

'North.'

'Sort of an odd name for a girl, isn't it?'

They went into a big room. There was a fireplace at one end of it and a bar at the other and ten or fifteen empty tables scattered around.

'Name it and take it,' Olga said at the bar. 'This one's on the house.'

They named it. Gin straight down the line. Six golden fizzes.

Olga said, 'My God, not only do I set up drinks but also a half-dozen eggs. Why don't you ever come out any more?' she said to Art Hazard. 'Did I do something to annoy you boys?'

'You didn't annoy me,' Art said. 'Rick got married, and none of us seen anything of him. And anyhow it's been too cold to get out of town. You say Lou Marble was here? I don't see anything even looks like her in here.'

'She left,' the barman said. 'She got sick and her friend took her out back.'

Rick was at the end of the line, next to Jeff, saying: 'We'd just call it the barrelhouse eight or some name and we could make records that would split them all wide open, make them sit up. Do up a lot of old ones, "Twelfth Street Rag," "China Boy," "Dinah," "Limehouse," "Bugle Call," all the ones we used to play; make a regular thing of it, same bunch all the time under the same name.'

'They wouldn't do it,' Jeff said. 'No record company would want it, because it wouldn't sell enough records. The only records that pay for themselves are the new ones with a vocal. People buy them to learn the words.'

'We could get Josie in and give them vocals, or else Cromwell from Morrison's; he knows how to sing.'

'Yah, but they already know the words to the old ones. They buy records to learn new words. They don't care how you play it. You and Art on the same record wouldn't matter a damn to more than two hundred people in the whole country. Who buys records is the high-school girls. You know that? Talk to that man Brown and he'll tell you. I had the same idea myself once. But the really good stuff doesn't sell records. Oh, in two three years it does, but they don't like to wait that long. They like to make them and sell them the same day. Guys that gang around the music stores to buy Morrison's records as soon as they're released get to hear some damned good horn playing, but they don't know it. They just want to learn the words.'

'I never thought of it that way,' Rick said. He drank with a sad look on his face.

'It's true,' Jeff said. 'Nobody knows what we're doing but us, the guys that do it. I've heard them say they like our record of "Melancholy Baby," and I say thanks, what did you like about it? and they say it's sort of catchy or some damn thing. And that's about the best record we ever made, some ways. The way Jimmy slides out of Davis's solo there and runs up eight bars enough to drive a man crazy, best piece of trambone playing I ever heard in my life, absolutely the best piece of trambone, and they say catchy; cute tune. I never heard anybody except you and two or three others even mention Jimmy on that record. It's a long time ago now, but with Jimmy playing like that I think it's maybe our best record.'

There was depth in his voice. He was talking about the thing, not the people.

'Hell,' Rick said, 'maybe we're all lucky to have jobs, one way you look at it. Maybe we're lucky to get tunes like "Melancholy Baby" that get so popular they'll sell no matter how good you play them.'

'We couldn't sell "Twelfth Street," or "Dinah," all over again, I know that, if we had Gabriel himself sitting in,' Jeff said, 'unless we had the money to do it on our own hook, pay the cost ourselves.'

'What would it cost?'

'Plenty; more than we could get together in ten years.'

'Maybe we could get some rich bastard that likes good jazz to stake us.'

'*You* get him.'

'I guess you're right,' Rick said. 'Let's go sit down.'

They broke away from the line at the bar and sat down at a table. They were something to look at, the two of them there: Jeff, the thoughtful, the Latin-featured, and Rick, the tight-drawn Northman, saying what they thought, knowing that art is long and life is a moment.

'If we'd just get a good bunch together, though,' Rick said one more time, 'get Barrow to play sax, and this kid Cohen I brought tonight, and La Porte that plays fiddle for Morrison, he can play it really *hard,* so that it sounds as good as any instrument in the band.

Funny thing, you should have heard him up at Jameson's one night; you wouldn't think a man could do that with nothing but a fiddle, but he sure was. It was just as *hard,* just as . . . I don't know; he's *good,* that's all; you wouldn't think a damned old vi'lin . . .'

'I know it,' Jeff said. 'I heard him on the record he was in with Deane's. He's the best thing on the record. It doesn't matter so much what a man plays, if he knows how. Take whatshisname, guy that plays the marimba at Moss's . . .'

'Roland.'

'Yeah. The way he plays it it sounds like a piano, only different, better than a piano. And there's nothing I hate, usually, like a marimba.'

'Me too,' Rick said. 'I can smell them a mile. And then here's this boy Roland, that knows something to do to it, and I get so I really *like* the thing.'

'Ain't it the truth? Same way with me. Remember in "Muddy Water" the way he comes in there, three notes over and over like he can't get off it, and then it breaks over and he's going, remember? Goes sort of like this.'

Jeff got up and went to the piano, hit a note or two, and then sat down and played single notes with his right hand as if he were hammering them out. Rick went over and watched him.

'That's it,' he said. 'That sounds exactly like it. It sounds like a piano all right; I mean you make it sound like that marimba.'

He opened his trumpet case, wiped off his trumpet and put the mouthpiece in, and stood there a minute listening to Jeff before he began to play. Then they were playing 'Muddy Water' and Rick was driving it straight ahead, not doing anything in particular, just playing the simple tune one note after the other, and making each single note a shining, fresh thing. He stopped at the end of one chorus, and Jeff took it while he listened, and when Jeff's chorus was complete, he tilted his trumpet up and took his turn, fulfilling the promise that was in the restraint of his first playing. Jeff looked up at him, squinting his eyes to give more knowledge to his ears. The four men at the bar turned around and listened, their heads twisted sharply up for the sound. It was pure Martin, unmistakable. He stood, one foot hooked over the rung of a chair, and he blew the breath of life into that lean, whip-like trumpet.

The four at the bar drifted up toward him, and Olga stayed where she was, leaning against the bar smoking a brown cigarette. Smoke pulled a couple of metal tubes out of his vest pocket, shot the brushes out of them, and began to drum lightly against the sides of his legs. Les Cohen's eyes were popped out a little watching Rick, and every little while he'd shake his head and whisper boy. He was only nineteen then, and it was the first time he'd ever been asked out with any of the great ones.

Rick stopped playing, drew his sleeve across his mouth, and said, 'I thought we were going to do some drinking.' He put the trumpet on top of the piano and went to the bar, but the others didn't follow; they found their cases and got ready to play.

Rick came back with a glass for Jeff and sat it on the piano—can't be playing piano around here on mush and milk, try this one. You like that? Pink; it's got grenadine in it; I'd better ask the General over there to make us up a bowl of this and put it where we can get to it easy. He went back to the bar and asked and it was done. A full pitcher of it, pink lemonade of a sort. Rick drank a tumbler full of it at a shot, just as a thirst-quencher. Playing made him thirsty. It burns a man to tear music out of himself for a long time; it dries him out, leaves salt in his mouth, dust in his throat. He has to keep it wetted down, keep everything moving easily, not let anything grate against anything else.

—General, fill up the jug, but not with any more of that pink wash; fill it up, dear General, with some of that French cognac out of the bottle with the stars on it.

They played music, then; piano, drums, two reeds, two brass. Smoke marked out the boundaries for them and led them wherever they went with a beat that pulled them along, a sensitive, infinitely various, but uncompromising beat—the core, the pumping heart of music.

It was an all-star show that night at Silver's. The only unproven man in it was young Les Cohen, and he proved himself twenty times before the night was out, playing clarinet that was a wild, sweet thing. He had them raising their eyebrows at each other.

'When'd you start playing that clair'net?' Smoke said to him, and Les said:

'Oh, papa took it on a loan and the guy never paid, and I got to blowing around on it so much that papa got me a teacher for a couple of weeks. I guess I was twelve.'

'You'd be sure out of luck if the guy'd come back and pay up now, and take it away, now you've put yourself to so much trouble learning to play it,' Milt Barrow said.

'That would be all right,' Les said. 'I'd just go and buy another one.'

'You would? Well, ain't you the kid, though!'

'What are you guys doing, trying to kid me?' Les said. The liquor and the excitement had him pretty vague.

Rick said, 'You play that clarinet of yours, boy, and none of them can kid you; nobody in the band business can tell you anything when you're playing that thing that way, don't you know that?'

The boy blushed all the way up, and Rick poured him another drink. 'Here, toss that down and see if you can do any worse or better.'

He looked across at Art Hazard, that great black ball bouncing on the edge of a little chair. 'What would you care to play now, Mr. Hazard?"

'I don't care much *what* we play, Mr. Martin,' Art said, 'just so we get playing it while I can still hold on to this here iron horn of mine. Keeps slipping out of my hand like nobody's business. I don't know what's ailing it tonight.'

'Funny,' Rick said. 'I've got just the other trouble. I can't seem to keep mine from sticking to my hand. Can't shake it off. Like that damned cat.'

'What damned cat?'

'Oh, just a damned cat. Keeps walking on my face, sticking to my hand.'

'I used to know a guy that got toads,' Hazard said. 'They'd hop all over everything. Hop hop. He tried to stab one once and got himself in the leg, right in the shin. Never did heal up.'

'But this cat,' Rick said, 'I've really got this cat. It sort of belongs to me. It's a Siamese cat, and they're the worst kind.'

'So did this other guy I was telling you about. He was in bad shape with those toads.'

'But this cat—oh hell . . .' Rick picked up his trumpet and played the opening bars of 'Bugle Call' good and loud, and the rest of them were ready for it with a terrific blare at the end of the opening bars; they kicked it back and forth among them, twenty choruses, taking turns at solo variations on the actual bugle call and then jamming through the rest of the thing all together; then reversing the process and doing the bugle call all together and laying off and letting one man solo it through to the end, which was never the end but simply a return to the bugle call. Never-ending bugle call; endless belt of bugle call.

They played hard and they played well and it wasn't all solo either. Toward daylight they had built up a blend of melody and harmony that was older and emotionally deeper than the brave virtuosity of the first hours. It was the music of men who look backward with wisdom rather than forward with faith. They were tired now, and dependent on each other, not so ruggedly individualistic. They brought the dawn in with sad and mellow music.

> Woke up this morning when chickens were crowing for day,
> And on the right side of my pillow my man had gone away.

'What time's it getting to be?' Milt said, and Rick looked at his watch, but he couldn't make much of it, it moved too fast for him. He looked at it, held it this way, held it that way, and then he knew that something was wrong. He felt waves of intense heat come up his spine and rise to his head, one after the other, and he tried to get his coat off, but then it was all over and he was on the floor with Smoke and Jeff bending over him and telling each other to go get some water. Their faces came into focus and he sat up and looked around.

'I remember falling off the chair,' he said, 'just as plain, I was sitting there looking at my watch; then I was falling and falling; it felt like a mile.'

'It wasn't no mile,' Smoke said, as if to a child; 'it was only from there to there. Get up. You're all right.'

'Sure,' Rick said, 'All I need is a drink. And not any of that fancy French dope, either. What I need is some liquor.'

He got up, made a pass at his knees, put his hand on Smoke's shoulder, and they walked to the bar, which was no longer attended by a keeper. Smoke smelled at two or three bottles, and then poured three fingers of whiskey into a tumbler and shoved it at Rick.

EUDORA WELTY

A native of Jackson, Mississippi, and chronicler of life in the small southern town, Eudora Welty is best known for her novels *Delta Wedding* (1946) and *The Ponder Heart* (1954); but many college students who take general literature courses also know her for some of her short stories: "Petrified Man," "Why I Live at the P.O.," "A Worn Path," and "Powerhouse," among others.

The character Powerhouse is based on the inimitable Fats Waller, whom Welty had listened to on records. One evening, however, she had the chance to hear him in person at a dance in Jackson. So overwhelmed and inspired was she by his performance that she went home and quickly wrote the story we have here—her *own* improvisatory response to Waller's musical and oral improvisations. She claims to have done no revising of the story. She said, "I was not in a position to revise that story, because how could I do it? You know, I didn't know enough to have started it to begin with." However, it is interesting to note that the *Atlantic Monthly,* which eventually published the story, insisted on one change. The final song in the story was originally "Hold Tight," and Welty changed it to "Somebody Loves Me" to mollify the editors who obviously did not like the nonsense lyrics of "Hold Tight," even though they were more suited to a Waller performance than were the lyrics of "Somebody Loves Me."

Beyond having written a wonderfully accurate portrait of Waller in performance, Welty has produced what she calls "my idea of the life of the traveling artist and performer . . . in the alien world." Knowledgeable readers will agree that her perception of that life in the 1930s is uncannily accurate.

POWERHOUSE

POWERHOUSE is playing!

He's here on tour from the city—"Powerhouse and His Keyboard"—"Powerhouse and His Tasmanians"—think of the things he calls himself! There's no one in the world like him. You can't tell what he is. "Negro man"?—he looks more Asiatic, monkey, Jewish, Babylonian, Peruvian, fanatic, devil. He has pale gray eyes, heavy lids, maybe horny like a lizard's, but big glowing eyes when they're open. He has African feet of the greatest size, stomping, both together, on each side of the pedals. He's not coal black—beverage colored—looks like a preacher when his mouth is going every minute: like a monkey's when it looks for something. Improvising, coming on a light and childish melody—*smooch*—he loves it with his mouth.

Is it possible that he could be this! When you have him there performing for you, that's what you feel. You know people on a stage—and people of a darker race—so likely to be marvelous, frightening.

This is a white dance. Powerhouse is not a show-off like the Harlem boys, not drunk, not crazy—he's in a trance; he's a person of joy, a fanatic. He listens as much as he performs, a look of hideous, powerful rapture on his face. When he plays he beats down piano and seat and wears them away. He is in motion every moment—what could be more obscene? There he is with his great head, fat stomach, and little round piston legs, and long yellow-sectioned strong big fingers, at rest about the size of bananas. Of course you know how he sounds—you've heard him on records—but still you need to see him. He's going all the time, like skating around the skating rink or rowing a boat. It makes everybody crowd around, here in this shadowless steel-trussed hall with the rose-like posters of Nelson Eddy and the testimonial for the mind-reading horse in handwriting magnified five hundred times. Then all quietly he lays his finger on a key with the promise and serenity of a sibyl touching the book.

Powerhouse is so monstrous he sends everybody into oblivion. When any group, any performers, come to town, don't people always come out and hover near, leaning inward about them, to learn what it is? What is it? Listen. Remember how it was with the acrobats. Watch them carefully, hear the least word, especially what they say to one another, in another language—don't let them escape you; it's the only time for hallucination, the last time. They can't stay. They'll be somewhere else this time tomorrow.

Powerhouse has as much as possible done by signals. Everybody, laughing as if to hide a weakness, will sooner or later hand him up a written request. Powerhouse reads each one, studying with a secret face: that is the face which looks like a mask—anybody's; there is a moment when he makes a decision. Then a light slides under his eyelids, and he says, "92!" or some combination of figures—never a name. Before a number the band is all frantic, misbehaving, pushing like children in a school-room, and he is the teacher getting silence. His hands over the keys, he says sternly, "You-all ready? You-all ready to do some serious walking?"—waits—then, STAMP. Quiet. STAMP, for the second time. This is absolute. Then a set of rhythmic kicks against the floor to communicate the tempo. Then, O Lord! say the distended eyes from beyond the boundary of trumpets, Hello and good-by, and they are all down the first note like a waterfall.

This note marks the end of any known discipline. Powerhouse seems to abandon them all—he himself seems lost—down in the song, yelling up like somebody in a whirlpool—not guiding them—hailing them only. But he knows, really. He cries out, but he must know exactly. "Mercy! . . . What I say! . . . Yeah!" And then drifting, listening—"Where that skin beater?"—wanting drums, and starting up and pouring it out in the greatest delight and brutality. On the sweet pieces such a leer for everybody! He looks down so benevolently upon all our faces and whispers the lyrics to us. And if you could hear him at this moment on "Marie, the Dawn is Breaking"! He's going up the keyboard with a few fingers in some very derogatory triplet-routine, he gets higher and higher, and then he looks over the end of the piano, as if over a cliff. But not in a show-off way—the song makes him do it.

He loves the way they all play, too—all those next to him. The far section of the band is all studious, wearing glasses, every one—they don't count. Only those playing around Powerhouse are the real ones. He has a bass fiddler from Vicksburg, black as pitch, named Valentine, who plays with his eyes shut and talking to himself, very young: Powerhouse has to keep encouraging him. "Go on, go on, give it up, bring it on out there!" When you heard him like that on records, did you know he was really pleading?

He calls Valentine out to take a solo.

"What are you going to play?" Powerhouse looks out kindly from behind the piano; he opens his mouth and shows his tongue, listening.

Valentine looks down, drawing against his instrument, and says without a lip movement, "'Honeysuckle Rose.'"

He has a clarinet player named Little Brother, and loves to listen to anything he does. He'll smile and say, "Beautiful!" Little Brother takes a step forward when he plays and stands at the very front, with the whites of his eyes like fishes swimming. Once when he played a low note, Powerhouse muttered in dirty praise, "He went clear downstairs to get that one!"

After a long time, he holds up the number of fingers to tell the band how many choruses still to go—usually five. He keeps his directions down to signals.

It's a bad night outside. It's a white dance, and nobody dances, except a few straggling jitterbugs and two elderly couples. Everybody just stands around the band and watches Powerhouse. Sometimes they steal glances at one another, as if to say, Of course, you know how it is with *them*—Negroes—band leaders—they would play the same way, giving all they've got, for an audience of one. . . . When somebody, no matter who, gives everything, it makes people feel ashamed for him.

Late at night they play the one waltz they will ever consent to play—by request, "Pagan Love Song." Powerhouse's head rolls and sinks like a weight between his waving shoulders. He groans, and his fingers drag into the keys heavily, holding on to the notes, retrieving. It is a sad song.

"You know what happened to me?" says Powerhouse.

Valentine hums a response, dreaming at the bass.

"I got a telegram my wife is dead," says Powerhouse, with wandering fingers.

"Uh-huh?"

His mouth gathers and forms a barbarous O while his fingers walk up straight, unwillingly, three octaves.

"Gypsy? Why how come her to die, didn't you just phone her up in the night last night long distance?"

"Telegram say—here the words: Your wife is dead." He puts 4/4 over the 3/4.

"Not but four words?" This is the drummer, an unpopular boy named Scoot, a disbelieving maniac.

Powerhouse is shaking his vast cheeks. "What the hell was she trying to do? What was she up to?"

"What name has it got signed, if you got a telegram?" Scoot is spitting away with those wire brushes.

Little Brother, the clarinet player, who cannot speak, glares and tilts back.

"Uranus Knockwood is the name signed." Powerhouse lifts his eyes open. "Ever heard of him?" A bubble shoots out on his lip like a plate on a counter.

Valentine is beating slowly on with his palm and scratching the strings with his long blue nails. He is fond of a waltz. Powerhouse interrupts him.

"I don't know him. Don't know who he is." Valentine shakes his head with the closed eyes.

"Say it agin."

"Uranus Knockwood."

"That ain't Lenox Avenue."

"It ain't Broadway."

"Ain't ever seen it wrote out in any print, even for horse racing."

"Hell, that's on a star, boy, ain't it?" Crash on the cymbals.

"What the hell was she up to?" Powerhouse shudders. "Tell me, tell me, tell me." He makes triplets, and begins a new chorus. He holds three fingers up.

"You say you got a telegram." This is Valentine, patient and sleepy, beginning again.

Powerhouse is elaborate. "Yas, the time I go out, go way downstairs along a long cor-ri-dor to where they puts us: coming back along the cor-ri-dor: steps out and hands me a telegram: Your wife is dead."

"Gypsy?" The drummer like a spider over his drums.

"Aaaaaaaa!" shouts Powerhouse, flinging out both powerful arms for three whole beats to flex his muscles, then kneading a dough of bass notes. His eyes glitter. He plays the piano like a drum sometimes—why not?

"Gypsy? Such a dancer?"

"Why you don't hear it straight from your agent? Why it ain't come from headquarters? What you been doing, getting telegrams in the *corridor,* signed nobody?"

They all laugh. End of that chorus.

"What time is it?" Powerhouse calls. "What the hell place is this? Where is my watch and chain?"

"I hang it on you," whimpers Valentine. "It still there."

There it rides on Powerhouse's great stomach, down where he can never see it.

"Sure did hear some clock striking twelve while ago. Must be *midnight.*"

"It going to be intermission," Powerhouse declares, lifting up his finger with the signet ring.

He draws the chorus to an end. He pulls a big Northern hotel towel out of the deep pocket in his vast, special-cut tux pants and pushes his forehead into it.

"If she went and killed herself!" he says with a hidden face. "If she up and jumped out that window!" He gets to his feet, turning vaguely, wearing the towel on his head.

"Ha, ha!"

"Sheik, sheik!"

"She wouldn't do that." Little Brother sets down his clarinet like a precious vase, and speaks. He still looks like an East Indian queen, implacable, divine, and full of snakes. "You ain't going to expect people doing what they says over long distance."

"Come on!" roars Powerhouse. He is already at the back door, he has pulled it wide open, and with a wild, gathered-up face is smelling the terrible night.

Powerhouse, Valentine, Scoot and Little Brother step outside into the drenching rain.

"Well, they emptying buckets," says Powerhouse in a mollified voice. On the street he holds his hands out and turns up the blanched palms like sieves.

A hundred dark, ragged, silent, delighted Negroes have come around from under the eaves of the hall, and follow wherever they go.

"Watch out Little Brother don't shrink," says Powerhouse. "You just the right size now, clarinet don't suck you in. You got a dry throat, Little Brother, you in the desert?" He reaches into the pocket and pulls out a paper of mints. "Now hold 'em in your mouth—don't chew 'em. I don't carry around nothing without limit."

"Go in that joint and have beer," says Scoot, who walks ahead.

"Beer? Beer? You know what beer is? What do they say is beer? What's beer? Where I been?"

"Down yonder where it say World Cafe—that do?" They are in Negrotown now.

Valentine patters over and holds open a screen door warped like a sea shell, bitter in the wet, and they walk in, stained darker with the rain and leaving footprints. Inside, sheltered dry smells stand like screens around a table covered with a red-checkered cloth, in the center of which flies hang on to an obelisk-shaped ketchup bottle. The midnight walls are checkered again with admonishing "Not Responsible" signs and black-figured, smoky calendars. It is a waiting, silent, limp room. There is a burned-out-looking nickelodeon and right beside it a long-necked wall instrument labeled "Business Phone, Don't Keep Talking." Circled phone numbers are written up everywhere. There is a worn-out peacock feather hanging by a thread to an old, thin, pink, exposed light bulb, where it slowly turns around and around, whoever breathes.

A waitress watches.

"Come here, living statue, and get all this big order of beer we fixing to give."

"Never seen you before anywhere." The waitress moves and comes forward and slowly shows little gold leaves and tendrils over her teeth. She shoves up her shoulders and breasts. "How I going to know who you might be? Robbers? Coming in out of the black night right at midnight, setting down so big at my table?"

"Boogers," says Powerhouse, his eyes opening lazily as in a cave.

The girl screams delicately with pleasure. O Lord, she likes talk and scares.

"Where you going to find enough beer to put out on this here table?"

She runs to the kitchen with bent elbows and sliding steps.

"Here's a million nickels," says Powerhouse, pulling his hand out of his pocket and sprinkling coins out, all but the last one, which he makes vanish like a magician.

Valentine and Scoot take the money over to the nickelodeon, which looks as battered as a slot machine, and read all the names of the records out loud.

"Whose 'Tuxedo Junction'?" asks Powerhouse.

"You know whose."

"Nickelodeon, I request you please to play 'Empty Bed Blues' and let Bessie Smith sing."

Silence: they hold it like a measure.

"Bring me all those nickels on back here," says Powerhouse. "Look at that! What you tell me the name of this place?"

"White dance, week night, raining, Alligator, Mississippi, long ways from home."

"Uh-huh."

"Sent for You Yesterday and Here You Come Today" plays.

The waitress, setting the tray of beer down on a back table, comes up taut and apprehensive as a hen. "Says in the kitchen, back there putting their eyes to little hole peeping out, that you is Mr. Powerhouse. . . . They knows from a picture they seen."

"They seeing right tonight, that is him," says Little Brother.

"You him?"

"That is him in the flesh," says Scoot.

"Does you wish to touch him?" asks Valentine. "Because he don't bite."

"You passing through?"

"Now you got everything right."

She waits like a drop, hands languishing together in front.

"Little-Bit, ain't you going to bring the beer?"

She brings it, and goes behind the cash register and smiles, turning different ways. The little fillet of gold in her mouth is gleaming.

"The Mississippi River's here," she says once.

Now all the watching Negroes press in gently and bright-eyed through the door, as many as can get in. One is a little boy in a straw sombrero which has been coated with aluminum paint all over.

Powerhouse, Valentine, Scoot and Little Brother drink beer, and their eyelids come together like curtains. The wall and the rain and the humble beautiful waitress waiting on them and the other Negroes watching enclose them.

"Listen!" whispers Powerhouse, looking into the ketchup bottle and slowly spreading his performer's hands over the damp, wrinkling cloth with the red squares. "Listen how it is. My wife gets missing me. Gypsy. She goes to the window. She looks and sees you know what. Street. Sign saying Hotel. People walking. Somebody looks up. Old man. She looks down, out the window. Well? . . . *Sssst! Plooey!* What she do? Jump out and bust her brains all over the world."

He opens his eyes.

"That's it," agrees Valentine. "You gets a telegram."

"Sure she misses you," Little Brother adds.

"No, it's nighttime." How softly he tells them! "Sure, it's the nighttime. She say, What do I hear? Footsteps walking up the hall? That him? Footsteps go on off. It's not me. I'm in Alligator, Mississippi, she's crazy. Shaking all over. Listens till her ears and all grow out like old music-box horns but still she can't hear a thing. She says, All right! I'll jump out the window then. Got on her nightgown. I know that nightgown, and her thinking there. Says, Ho hum, all right, and jumps out the window. Is she mad at me! Is she crazy! She don't leave *nothing* behind her!"

"Ya! Ha!"

"Brains and insides everywhere, Lord, Lord."

All the watching Negroes stir in their delight, and to their higher delight he says affectionately, "Listen! Rats in here."

"That must be the way, boss."

"Only, naw, Powerhouse, that ain't true. That sound too *bad*."

"Does? I even know who finds her," cries Powerhouse. "That no-good pussyfooted crooning creeper, that creeper that follow around after me, coming up like weeds behind me, following around after me everything I do and messing around on the trail I leave. Bets my numbers, sings my songs, gets close to my agent like a Betsy-bug; when I going out he just coming in. I got him now! I got my eye on him."

"Know who he is?"

"Why, it's that old Uranus Knockwood!"

"Ya! Ha!"

"Yeah, and he coming now, he going to find Gypsy. There he is, coming around that corner, and Gypsy kadoodling down, oh-oh, watch out! *Ssssst! Plooey!* See, there she is in her little old nightgown, and her insides and brains all scattered round."

A sigh fills the room.

"Hush about her brains. Hush about her insides."

"Ya! Ha! You talking about her brains and insides—old Uranus Knockwood," says Powerhouse, "look down and say Jesus! He say, Look here what I'm walking round in!"

They all burst into halloos of laughter. Powerhouse's face looks like a big hot iron stove.

"Why, he picks her up and carries her off!" he says.

"Ya! Ha!"

"Carries her *back* around the corner. . . ."

"Oh, Powerhouse!"

"You know him."

"Uranus Knockwood!"

"Yeahhh!"

"He take our wives when we gone!"

"He come in when we goes out!"

"Uh-huh!"

"He go out when we comes in!"

"Yeahhh!"

"He standing behind the door!"

"Old Uranus Knockwood."

"You know him."

"Middle-size man."

"Wears a hat."

"That's him."

Everybody in the room moans with pleasure. The little boy in the fine silver hat opens a paper and divides out a jelly roll among his followers.

And out of the breathless ring somebody moves forward like a slave, leading a great logy Negro with bursting eyes, and says, "This here is Sugar-Stick Thompson, that dove down to the bottom of July Creek and pulled up all those drownded white people fall out of a boat. Last summer, pulled up fourteen."

"Hello," says Powerhouse, turning and looking around at them all with his great daring face until they nearly suffocate.

Sugar-Stick, their instrument, cannot speak; he can only look back at the others.

"Can't even swim. Done it by holding his breath," says the fellow with the hero.

Powerhouse looks at him.

"I his half brother," the fellow puts in.

They step back.

"Gypsy say," Powerhouse rumbles gently again, looking at *them,* "'What is the use? I'm gonna jump out so far—so far. . . .' *Ssssst—!*"

"Don't, boss, don't do it agin," says Little Brother.

"It's awful," says the waitress. "I hates that Mr. Knockwoods. All that the truth?"

"Want to see the telegram I got from him?" Powerhouse's hand goes to the vast pocket.

"Now wait, now wait, boss." They all watch him.

"It must be the real truth," says the waitress, sucking in her lower lip, her luminous eyes turning sadly, seeking the windows.

"No, babe, it ain't the truth." His eyebrows fly up, and he begins to whisper to her out of his vast oven mouth. His hand stays in his pocket. "Truth is something worse, I ain't said what, yet. It's something hasn't come to me, but I ain't saying it won't. And when it does, then want me to tell you?" He sniffs all at once, his eyes come open and turn up, almost too far. He is dreamily smiling.

"Don't, boss, don't, Powerhouse!"

"Oh!" the waitress screams.

"Go on git out of here!" bellows Powerhouse, taking his hand out of his pocket and clapping after her red dress.

The ring of watchers breaks and falls away.

"*Look* at that! Intermission is up," says Powerhouse.

He folds money under a glass, and after they go out, Valentine leans back in and drops a nickel in the nickelodeon behind them, and it lights up and begins to play "The Goona Goo." The feather dangles still.

"Take a telegram!" Powerhouse shouts suddenly up into the rain over the street. "Take a answer. Now what was that name?"

They get a little tired.

"Uranus Knockwood."

"You ought to know."

"Yas? Spell it to me."

They spell it all the ways it could be spelled. It puts them in a wonderful humor.

"Here's the answer. I got it right here. 'What in the hell you talking about? Don't make any difference: I gotcha.' Name signed: Powerhouse."

"That going to reach him, Powerhouse?" Valentine speaks in a maternal voice.

"Yas, yas."

All hushing, following him up the dark street at a distance, like old rained-on black ghosts, the Negroes are afraid they will die laughing.

Powerhouse throws back his vast head into the steaming rain, and a look of hopeful desire seems to blow somehow like a vapor from his own dilated nostrils over his face and bring a mist to his eyes.

"Reach him and come out the other side."

"That's it, Powerhouse, that's it. You got him now."

Powerhouse lets out a long sigh.

"But ain't you going back there to call up Gypsy long distance, the way you did last night in that other place? I seen a telephone. . . . Just to see if she there at home?"

There is a measure of silence. That is one crazy drummer that's going to get his neck broken some day.

"No," growls Powerhouse. "No! How many thousand times tonight I got to say No?"

He holds up his arm in the rain.

"You sure-enough unroll your voice some night, it about reach up yonder to her," says Little Brother, dismayed.

They go on up the street, shaking the rain off and on them like birds.

Back in the dance hall, they play "San" (99). The jitterbugs start up like windmills stationed over the floor, and in their orbits—one circle, another, a long stretch and a zigzag—dance the elderly couples with old smoothness, undisturbed and stately.

When Powerhouse first came back from intermission, no doubt full of beer, they said, he got the band tuned up again in his own way. He didn't strike the piano keys for pitch—he simply opened his mouth and gave falsetto howls—in A, D and so on—they tuned by him. Then he took hold of the piano, as if he saw it for the first time in his life, and tested it for strength, hit it down in the bass, played an octave with his elbow, lifted the top, looked inside, and leaned against it with all his might. He sat down and played it for a few minutes with outrageous force and got it under his power—a bass deep and coarse as a sea net—then produced something glimmering and fragile, and smiled. And who could ever remember any of the things he says? They are just inspired remarks that roll out of his mouth like smoke.

They've requested "Somebody Loves Me," and he's already done twelve or fourteen choruses, piling them up nobody knows how, and it will be a wonder if he ever gets through. Now and then he calls and shouts, "'Somebody loves me! Somebody loves me, I wonder who!'" His mouth gets to be nothing but a volcano. "I wonder who!"

"Maybe . . ." He uses all his right hand on a trill.

"Maybe . . ." He pulls back his spread fingers, and looks out upon the place where he is. A vast, impersonal and yet furious grimace transfigures his wet face.

". . . Maybe it's you!"

SHELBY FOOTE

Shelby Foote was born in Greenville, Mississippi, in 1916 and has used the Mississippi Delta as the backdrop for his novels and short stories. Foote created a mythical county, Jordan County, similar to William Faulkner's Yoknapatawpha County, populating it with recurring characters and covering about 150 years of its history. His first novel was *Tournament* (1949). *Jordan County: A Landscape in Narrative* (1954) comprises seven interlocking stories, one of which is "Ride Out," a story that originally appeared in *Saturday Evening Post* under the title "Tell Them Good-by" (1947). Foote has been the recipient of several Guggenheim Fellowships and a Ford Foundation grant. His most ambitious work is the three-volume *The Civil War: A Narrative* (1958, 1963, 1974).

Foote believes that jazz is, most importantly, communication. He told John Graham in a 1970 interview, "There's something about the very basic best of jazz, something about the blues, that communicates from one person to another." He also acknowledges that Louis Armstrong was part of the inspiration for Duff Conway, and that his "love for the music is very great."

RIDE OUT

THE state executioner had set up the portable electric chair in a cell on the lower floor; now he was testing his circuits. Whenever the switch clicked there was a pulsing hum and an odor of heated copper. The turnkey, who had helped with the installation, watched the rubber-insulated cable that ran like a long dusty blacksnake from a connection at the back, through the window bars, to the generator in a truck parked in the cool predawn darkness of the jail-yard. He watched as if he expected it to writhe like a pressure hose with every surge of current—as if any force with that much power must have body, too—but it lay in loose coils without motion. Low and wide, with heavy arms and legs, the chair had an unfinished look; the workman, a clumsy copyist of Louis Seize pieces, might have dropped his tools, dissatisfied, and walked away. It had been invented and built six months before, on order from the Mississippi legislature, by a New Orleans electrician who stipulated that he was to receive no profit from the job. Luke Jeffcoat, the executioner, was not so squeamish. He called it "my old shocking chair."

Deep creases extended from the wings of his nose to the corners of his mouth. Under the glare from the unshaded bulb, they appeared to have been carved there, exaggerated like the lines on a tragedy mask. Tall and thin, about forty, he worked in a sleeveless undershirt. Tattooed snakes ran down his arms and spread their heads on the backs of his hands. Other, more intimate designs were hidden under his clothes—a three-bladed marine propeller on each cheek of his fundament, for instance, and a bee in a particular place, which he called "my old stingaree." He hummed as he worked. It was low and within a narrow range, curiously like the hum of the generator.

Presently three men came into the cell. The first two, the sheriff and myself—I am county physician—were required by law to be there. But the third, the district attorney, came of his own accord: "to see this thing I'll be sending them to," he had said that afternoon, for he was young and recently elected; this had been his first death-penalty conviction. Entering, the sheriff jerked his thumb toward the window. "Who's that out there?" he asked the turnkey. We had seen them as we came in, a man and a woman on the seat of a wagon under a bug-swirled arc light fifty yards down the alley, both of them hunched with waiting. Two mules dozed in the traces, knees locked, ears slanted forward, and a long box of unpainted pine lay like a pale six-sided shadow in the bed of the wagon.

"It's his mamma," the turnkey said. His name was Jeffcoat too; he and the executioner were cousins. "She rented a dray and bought herself a box to carry him home in. I told her the county would furnish him one, but she said she wanted her own. Yair. They been there since before midnight, sitting like that; theyve got so they dont even slap at the bugs. Just after they got here I went up and took the horn away from him."

"How is he?"

"I think he's sleeping. Anyhow he's quiet. Hoskins is up there with him."

The sheriff took out his watch, a big one in a silver hunting case. He opened it, then snapped it shut with a sound like a pistol shot. "Three thirty," he said morosely. "Where's Doc Benson?"

I said, "He told me he'd be here by three fifteen. But it dont really matter, does it?"

"The law says two doctors, we'll have two doctors." He shook his head, red-faced, with bulging eyes. This was Jordan County's first electrocution and he didnt like it. "Damn these new-fangled inventions anyhow. The old rope and trapdoor method suited me fine."

We heard the sudden tearing sound of tires on gravel, an automobile door being slammed; then Dr Benson came in. He was rubbing his palms and his spectacles glinted fiery in the glare. "Sorry I'm late," he said. "I got held up."

"We arent ready anyhow," I told him.

Just then, however, Jeffcoat threw the switch for the final test, and again there was that pulsing hum, almost a throb, and the faint odor of heated copper. He smiled, then went to the washstand in the corner, soaped his hands, rinsed them under the tap, and dried them carefully on his undershirt.

"All right, sheriff," he said: "I'm ready if he is."

It may be I had seen him before. It seems likely, even. But so far as I know—since, with his shaved head and slit trousers and the fear and sickness in his face, he probably did not resemble himself much anyhow—my first sight of him was when they brought him into the cell a few minutes later. During the past twelve years I have learned his story and I intend to set it down, from beginning to end. I saw only the closing scene, as I said, but four people who knew him well have given me particulars. These were his mother, Nora Conway, a cook here in Bristol; Oscar Bailey, called Blind Bailey, a pianist in a local Negro dancehall; Pearly Jefferson, the New Orleans jazz musician, and Harry Van, the New England composer. In many cases I have merely transcribed notes of conversations with these four, or letters from them, and I want to state my obligations at the outset. There was also a young woman, Julia Kinship, but I have been unable to find her; I understand she went North. At any rate, if ever this gets printed I hope she sees it.

He was born in a time of high water, the stormy May of 1913, in a Red Cross tent on the levee at the foot of the main street of Bristol, Mississippi. His mother was fifteen the month before. The birth was not due until six weeks later, but in the excitement of being herded, along with three or four hundred other Negroes, onto the only high ground within seventy miles, Nora became alarmed and the pains came on her. In a steady drizzle of rain, while water purled up the slope toward where she lay on a strip of salvaged awning, she moaned and bellered through five hours of labor. Between whiles she heard the rain murmur against the canvas, a spooky sound. When the flood reached the level of the river on the opposite side, and therefore ceased its advance up the levee, the child was born. Someone among the white refugee families in the adjoining camp sent her a paper sack of candy. The midwife swaddled the child and placed it beside her. She was content, holding her son against her breast and dissolving a lemon drop in her cheek; but she wished the father was there.

His name was Boola Durfee; originally he was from the lower

delta, down around Nitta Yuma, son of a freedwoman and a half-breed Choctaw blacksmith. Nora was with him less than two weeks, in September of the year before, when the big warm moon of late summer glazed the fields and gilded the corrugated metal roofs of the churches and barrelhouses where he played engagements while she waited outside, too young to enter. A gaunt, high-cheekboned man, he had no home; he roamed the country, tall and flat-chested, with his guitar and his songs. He had warned her at the outset.

"I got a itchy heel," he said. "Some morning, doll baby, youll wake up and find me gone."

That was the way it turned out. The following week she woke with the sun in her eyes and found herself alone on the pallet bed. She had expected this; she had not needed the warning, but at the time she told herself it was worth it. Later she was not so sure. For the next ten years she would hear people mention having seen him, sometimes in far places, Arkansas and Alabama and up in Tennessee, sometimes nearby, Moorhead and Holly Knowe and Midnight, still playing for what he called sukey jumps. But Nora never saw him again. She made it a point never to ask about him or even show an interest when his name came up. At first this indifference was a pretense. Later it was a habit, and quite real. Then she heard that he had been killed in a cutting fight, over near Itta Bena, when some man got jealous.

She gave the child its father's name, Durfee, for a first name, and attached her family name, Conway, for a surname. By pronunciation, Durfee became Duffy, which later was shortened to Duff, and that was how he came to be called Duff Conway.

After the water went down she got a job as maid in a cotton factor's house, and when the cook left three years later Nora took her place. She lived alone with her child in a two-room cabin in a section of Bristol known as Lick Skillet. When she had saved twelve dollars out of her weekly salary of three-fifty, she bought herself a mailorder pistol, a big one, nickel plated, which she kept in a bureau drawer in the front room, near her bed, so that she could turn to it in a time of trouble, as other women would turn to a man.

Aborted thus into a flooded world, Duff was undersized and sickly, cocoa-colored and solemn as a papoose. The red in his skin was like a warning sign to Nora. If the boy could inherit the Choctaw pigment and the pointed cheekbones, she reasoned that he might also inherit the guitar-calloused thumb and the itchy heel. So she kept him by her, in her cabin, at church, and at the cotton factor's house, where at first she put him in a crib on the back porch and later propped him on a chair in one corner of the kitchen. Perched on the tall straight-back chair he passed the waking hours of early childhood amid a clatter of pots and pans in an atmosphere of flour and frying food, his feet suspended ten inches clear of the floor, then six inches, then two inches, then touching it; then he was six and his mother enrolled him in school. Young enough herself to be mistaken for one of the girls in the upper grades, she would take him there every morning and call for him every afternoon.

"You going to mount to something," she told him. "Study hard and stay away from riffraff."

That was how it went; she sought to come between him and whatever shocks might be in store. Then on an April afternoon when Duff was in the fifth grade she missed him among the children trooping out of school. She went by the cabin, thinking perhaps he would get there before her, but he was not there. When she had waited as long as she could, muttering alternate imprecations and prayers, she went back to the cotton factor's house to fix supper, and when she came home that night Duff was in bed, asleep. She stood over him for a moment, watching. Then she shook him. "Where you been?" she shouted while he rubbed his eyes with his fists.

"Lemmy lone."

"Where you been all day?"

"Lemmy lone, mamma. I'm sleepy."

"Sleepy!" She shook him further awake. "Where you been, boy, till all hours of the night? Answer me when I'm talking to you!"

She whipped him. But he cried himself back to sleep without telling her anything, and four days later it happened again.

This time she went looking for him. On Bantam Street, in Bristol's redlight district, she found a crowd gathered around something on the sidewalk. Mostly silk-shirted bucks and their bright-dressed women, they were standing so closely packed that Nora could not see what they were watching but she heard strange music. She elbowed her way toward the center. There she saw four small boys performing on four outlandish instruments, including a jug, a banjo made from a cigar box and a length of lath, a jew's harp, and a set of drums invented from a battered suitcase top and a sawhorse with three stove lids suspended from the crosspiece.

Duff was the drummer. He sat on an upended cracker box, drumming steadily with a pair of chair rungs. Oblivious, he was entering a solo break, a caricature of a real full-sized drummer—head turned sideways down near one shoulder, eyes tight shut, lower lip sucked between his teeth—when Nora caught him by the arm, hauled him off the box, and snatched him through the crowd.

"Wait up, mamma," he wailed, straining back and waving the chair rungs; "I got to get my drums!"

Nora shook him until his teeth rattled above the laughter of the crowd. "Wait till I get you home," she said. "I'll drum you."

He was twelve the following month. For nearly two years after the Bantam Street incident it was a contest between mother and son, she trying in the only way she knew to keep him from becoming what his father had been, and he revolting against being tied to her apron strings. The four-piece band had been organized at school by the boy who played the cigarbox banjo. At first they had practiced only during the noon recess, but after a while that was not enough. They began to cut school, and then they went professional, playing on street corners for nickels and dimes and an occasional quarter. Thus Duff had already come closer to being a part of what Nora hated than she had even allowed herself to fear. He had received not only money but also applause, and from an audience of strangers. Nor was that all. Late at night, after his mother was asleep, he would slip away to Bantam Street, drawn there because something in the music answered something in himself.

At the largest of the places, a two-story frame building called the Mansion House, there was music every night by a blind pianist famous all over the delta. His name was Bailey—Oscar Bailey, called Blind Bailey—an enormous old man built on the lines of a hippo; he had played on showboats until vaudeville and the motion pictures drove them off the river. Duff liked him best, but in time he came to know them all. He would sit under barrelhouse windows, listening to ragtime piano and rare three- and four-man groups, and next day he would teach the songs to the other members of the sidewalk band, drumming the rhythm, humming or whistling the melody, perhaps even singing snatches of the words, if any:

Blow your whistle, freight train,
Care me on down the line!

In this way he developed a sizable repertory of the songs which remained his favorites always, the old riverboat and New Orleans classics, Eagle Rock Rag and Creole Belles and Ostrich Walk, Hilarity Rag and San and High Society. Just before dawn he would slip back into the cabin and creep into bed without waking Nora.

The contest between mother and son ended with an event that took him beyond her control. He was indicted by the grand jury for burglary and larceny, arraigned by the district attorney, and tried by the district court. On a plea of guilty, while Nora wept into her handkerchief and sometimes into the hem of her petticoat, he was sentenced to be placed in reform school for an indefinite period, to be released at the discretion of the authorities. It really happened that suddenly, and here was how it came about.

His three sidewalk-performing partners spent their share of the coins as fast as they made them, but Duff had been saving his fourth ever since the day he saw a set of drums in the window of an uptown music shop. When he had accumulated almost four dollars in loose change, which he carried in a Bull Durham sack worn on a string around his neck, he felt qualified to price the drums. He did not believe that it was enough but at least he felt financial.

He chose a quiet time; there was only the proprietor in the store. When Duff said abruptly, "Captain, how much you aks for them drums in the window?" the proprietor looked up from his newspaper, startled. He had been sitting with his feet on the desk, reading the comics, and had not heard Duff come in.

"Dont sneak up on me like that, boy," he said, loose-jointed, with gold-rim spectacles and a receding chin. His eyes, watching Duff over the edge of the paper, seemed to bulge and spin behind the heavy lenses. "Thats a fine set of drums," he added.

"Yes sir. Sho is."

"You want to buy them, or are you just looking and asking?"

"I want to buy them," Duff said. He unbuttoned his shirt and took out the tobacco sack, beginning to pluck at the knot with his teeth, the way he did every night when he added the day's receipts and counted the total.

"They are seventy-eight dollars and fifty cents," the proprietor said, still watching over the edge of the newspaper.

"Thank you sir." Duff returned the sack, still knotted, and buttoned his shirt. "I be back."

He was seventy-four dollars and thirty-two cents short. Using what little arithmetic he had managed to absorb in class while looking forward to the noon rehearsals, he computed that at the present rate he would require six years to earn that much. But three nights later he got what he believed was a chance to do something about it, a chance to increase his earning power in another direction. At the Mansion House—he had graduated from crouching under the side windows; now he came onto the porch to listen—he encountered a boy about four years older than himself. Duff had never seen him before. The boy asked if he wanted to make some easy money.

"How?" Duff said.

"Take it."

"Take it how?"

"Through a window, man. How you reckon?"

It would be easy, the boy told him. All Duff had to do was stand outside the house and whistle if anyone happened along, particularly the law. They would split the take. "Fifty fifty," the stranger said.

"Will it come to seventy-five dollars?"

"Ought to, easy."

"Then I'm game," Duff said.

"Come on—"

But when he turned and saw the policeman walking toward him, his mouth went dry and all he could manage was a faint low moan. It was enough, however; the stranger got away through a window on the opposite side of the house. A neighbor had seen them and telephoned the police.

At the arraignment the district attorney gave Duff what he called "every chance," but all Duff could do was repeat what he had told the police. He did not know who the stranger was; he had seen him only in the gloom and could not even give them a description. "Dark, I think, and taller than me," was the best he could do. They did not believe him.

"All right, boy," the district attorney said. He was fair and pink cheeked, with hard eyes. "If thats the way you want it."

In circuit court he recommended that Duff be placed in the state reform school until such time as the warden and the parole board would declare it safe to return him to society. The judge so ordered.

Traveling in the custody of a white deputy, Duff and four other Negro youths rode across the dark flat delta and into the brown loam and loess hills where scrub pine grew and knee-high cotton stalks stood bare in the rain. This was his first ride on a train, his first sight of hills. He enjoyed it, up to a point. When they arrived at the reform school that afternoon, standing in the bed of the open truck which had met them at the depot, it was still raining, a slow steady drizzle that ran down their faces like tears. The school was an all-Negro institution, visited yearly by a group of white politicians on an inspection tour for the legislature. It was a low, gray building of weathered clapboard—a short dogrun with a narrow gallery connecting two deep ells: one the prisoners' dormitory, with swinging oil lamps and three-decked bunks along the walls, so that it resembled the fo'c'sle of an oldtime sailing ship; the other the prisoners' mess and an apartment for the warden and his family, the kitchen being shared—set back from a gray, hard-packed, grassless yard like a surface of zinc, and surrounded by a high wire fence which in the dull light of a rainy afternoon had the flat, deadly glint of gunmetal. All this combined to give it the look of an enormous torture machine.

The boys stood in the truck bed, looking, and said nothing. "Well, here you are," the deputy told them, turning on the seat to look at them through the rear window of the cab as the truck pulled up to the gate. "You can call it home for a while. Hey?" None of the boys said anything. They stood looking and the rain ran down their faces.

Then gradually, after the nightmare introduction, they discovered that their fears had been largely of their own invention. It was not as they had supposed from that early look. They were left in the dormitory their first full day, but the following morning they went to the field. Duff learned to run a straight furrow behind the straining crupper of his mule, to wear the lines looped around his neck like a long necklace as he walked, and to reverse the plow with a quick, lifting motion at the end of the row. The hours were long—from dawn to dark during the busy season; "kin til kaint" the inmates called it—but he enjoyed the work and the queer, trembly feeling of fatigue which came when he lay in his bunk after lights-out. He had never known it before.

Sundays were best, however. Five of the prisoners had formed an orchestra. They had real instruments, and every Sunday afternoon they would play a gallery concert from two oclock till sundown. Duff became friendly with the drummer, a light-skinned boy from the piney hills, and was allowed to sit in on an occasional number, reviving the technique of his Bristol sidewalk performances. It involved a good deal more motion than sound, for he flailed his arms and rolled his head, hunching his shoulders like a victim of Saint Vitus.

"You pretty good," the drummer told him; "yair. But you dont hold the sticks right. Look at here." He tore off a long, pulsing snare passage. "Try it." Duff tried it. "Yair," the drummer said. He nodded approval. "Thats more like it, sure enough. But looky. Keep your wrists up. Like this here." He rolled another passage that rose quickly to crescendo, then died to a whisper, as if a mouse had scurried across the drum.

"Something must be wrong with me," Duff said. "I get it, all right, but it dont seem to come out right on the skin. I keep wanting something I can pick up on."

It was six months before he got what he wanted. Then the cornetist died of tuberculosis, a sad-eyed boy who had not been required to work in the field. Apparently he had no people in the outside world; all he ever cared about was music. He was not quite right in the head, and while the others were out working he would lounge around the dormitory, breathing sad, almost tuneless songs into the silver horn. He was sick a long time. Toward the end, though he could no longer play the instrument, he kept it with him in the bed, holding on to it even while unconscious. Then he died. There was no one to claim his effects, so the warden divided them among the prisoners as far as they went, which wasnt far.

"Ive seen you watching him," he said to Duff. "Here"—handing him the dead boy's cornet "—see can you learn to blow it."

Duff took it with both hands. It was heavier than he had expected, the dull gray of old silver, pewter-colored, nicked and battered along the column and at the bell. He held it close to his chest, walking back to the dormitory. This was Sunday and he sat sideways on his bunk all afternoon, learning to blow it. He found that he could control the sound by pushing down on the valves, but this made it doubly difficult because they would stick and he also had to learn to pull them up again. He was still there, and he was still trying, when the others came in for supper and began to undress for lights-out. "Give it a rest, man," someone said from down the line. So he lay quiet in the dark, lips pursed, imagining he was practicing.

Two Sundays later he joined the musicians on the gallery. At first he merely blared the horn, backing up the other players as if the cornet were a rhythm instrument, more or less like a trombone. They gave him strange looks, turning in their chairs, but the drummer said, "Let him blare. Everybody got to learn."

Soon he was able to follow the musical line. By the end of the month he was beginning to lead the way, the horn riding rough and loud above the other instruments, gravelly, sclerotic, and by the end of the year there would be large groups in the reform-school yard, their faces lifted toward the gallery and the five musicians. They came from miles around, their wagons and dusty automobiles parked hub to hub in a field across the road, and sat or stood from soon after the midday meal until well past sundown and into the gathering dusk, when the supper bell would clang, strident and insistent, and the breakup would follow, the boy prisoners going into the low, rambling building and the visitors dispersing to their wagons and cars across the road. They spoke in admiration of the music, their voices floating back through the fading light:

"That was *playing,* warnt it now?"

"It sho was. How about that horn?"

"That boy mortally plays that thing!"

"*He* sho does."

The warden arranged Saturday night engagements for them, loading them into the truck, drums and all, to drive to Jackson and nearby communities for dances and barbecues; whatever money they received went into a recreation fund administered by themselves though with considerable cross-checking to discourage peculation. Within a year of the time Duff was committed, the reform school band had become well known throughout the central portion of the state. On Catfish Row and down Ramcat Alley, wherever people collected who were followers of such music, Duff's cornet began to be talked about. "I heard me a *horn* last week," a voice would say at a fishfry. He was beginning to amount to something in a way his mother never intended when she told him to study hard and stay away from riffraff.

Soon they were being offered more engagements than they could fill. The drummer was nominal leader of the group—they called themselves the Noxubee High Hat Rhythm Kings in memory of the dead cornetist, who had been sentenced from Noxubee County—but Duff was leader once the music got underway. There was no doubt about that; it had been true almost from the outset. The others followed his loud, blary horn on every number. They had no other style; apparently it had never occurred to them that any other style existed. They played the things Duff had learned while crouching under Bantam Street windows, the old songs that had been great before some of the boys were born, things never set down on paper but kept alive in places and in memories such as these. Thump: the drum would beat once and the others would go immediately into it. If anyone got left behind he caught up on his own. There was no vamping, no announcement of theme, no quiet introduction to set a mood. It came out full and uninhibited, the cornet riding high and wide, the other instruments falling in behind its lead like leaves sucked into the rearward vacuum of a speeding truck.

"Man, man," the drummer said once between pieces. "Wherebouts you get all that power?"

Duff looked down at the horn in his lap. He seemed not to have thought of it before. "I dont know," he said. "In my thoat, I reckon."

When he came home to Bristol in the early fall, nearly two years after the trainride with the deputy, there were chocolate bands on houses and trees from the great flood of 1927. In some of the cabins in Lick Skillet, which was in a sort of shallow natural basin, there was powdery soft yellow silt on the rafters, left when the water went down. An abandoned skiff bleached in the adjoining yard, derelict, its painter still tied to an upright. Two children sat in it, a boy and a girl, their faces grave with pretense, playing Steamboat. It was late afternoon, the sun three-quarters down the southwest sky. Waiting for Nora to come home, Duff sat on the steps with a paper-wrapped parcel in his lap. When he lay back on the porch floor the children's voices faded, as if the skiff were indeed bearing them away. Then they passed completely out of hearing, and when he opened his eyes the sun was gone and bullbats were flying. He was looking up into his mother's face.

"Hello, mamma," he said. "I fell to sleep waiting here on you."

"Get up, boy, before you catch your death of cold." She watched him quietly; he had not written to let her know he was coming home. "You had your supper?"

"Noam. I aint eat since I left Moorhead this morning."

He rose, carrying the parcel, and as he limped across the porch toward the door Nora saw that the fronts had been cut out of his shoes. "Whats the matter with your feet?"

"Corns," he said. "I got them plowing."

"Plowing. Well." She followed, watching him walk gingerly through the front room. "Maybe that place done you some good after all."

"Yessum."

"Leastways you aint apt to go breaking into people's houses again real soon, are you?" Duff said nothing. She said, "Are you?"

"Noam," he said.

He sat at the kitchen table, the parcel again in his lap. Nora went to the cupboard and began putting biscuits and cold sidemeat on a plate. Over her shoulder she asked, "What you got in the package?"

"My horn," he said. "The warden give it to me."

"Horn? What kind of horn?"

"A *horn,* mamma, that you blow in to make music. A cornet, they call it. Like in a band."

Nora halted, the plate in her hand. Then she came forward and put the food on the table in front of him. "I'll shake up the stove and perc you some coffee," she said.

He was fifteen that spring, five feet eight inches tall and weighing a hundred and thirty pounds—within half an inch and five pounds of all the height and weight he would ever have, though in later years the wedged shoes and padded suits would raise and broaden him and the perfumed grease would straighten the kinky hair which now fitted his head like a wooly skullcap. His eyes were black, the whites somewhat yellowed as if by jaundice, and his mouth was broad, with regular, white teeth and bluish lips and gums. Though his arms and legs were thin and gangling, his hands and feet were small. His voice was habitually low and he spoke so softly that people often had to ask him to repeat what he had said.

When he went out that evening after supper he took the horn with him, still in its newspaper wrapping. Nora watched him go. Again there was that impulse to restrain him, then to follow and bring him home. But she resisted it now; he was too big. Instead she waited, counting the hours by the courthouse clock, and at midnight when he still had not returned she went to bed. Finally she even went to sleep. At four in the morning—the clock was striking—she heard footsteps on the porch and then a hand fumbling at the door. Rising on one elbow out of sleep she reached automatically for the bureau drawer where she kept her pistol. Then the door came open; it was Duff. She lay and watched him, and as he passed her bed on the way to his cot in the kitchen, she saw that he still carried the horn. Unwrapped, it glinted silver where light struck it from a street lamp down the block.

"You act like that thing was part of you," she said suddenly out of the darkness. Duff turned in the kitchen doorway. "Where you been, boy, till all hours of the night?"

"I got me a job, mamma."

"What doing?"

"Playing this." He did not raise the cornet or glance down at it or indicate it in any way; he did not need to, for he knew she would know what he meant and he also knew how she felt about it. "At the Mansion House, seven nights a week," he said. "They give me a dollar a night."

This time the contest had been brief, was over, indeed, before she had time to plan; he had outgeneraled her so quickly that before she even became aware that an engagement was in progress it had ended in her defeat. The fourth stroke of the courthouse clock vibrated in the room; it was that darkest final hour before dawn. Nora lay back and pulled the covers over her face. Presently, as he stood waiting, she spoke from under the quilt, her voice muffled. "Go on to bed," she told him.

So now at last it was Duff who was on the inside, screened by whirling dancers and curtained by swirling smoke, making the wild Mansion House music while other boys, his age and younger, crouched outside under the windows where he had crouched two years before, to hear the music they were too young to approach. It was a new world to him, with a new population. Blind Bailey was there every night, but the other musicians were transients. Guitar or clarinet, saxophone or banjo, they seldom stayed longer than a week and there were never two of them together. Like Boola Durfee they traveled alone and they never stayed anywhere long; they were independent-minded men, troubadors who thought as highly of their freedom as they did of their music; they played for money and then spent it and moved on, and none of them had the least thought for tomorrow.

Usually Duff and the enormous old pianist were alone, a study in contrast. Blind Bailey was gray-haired and wore blue-lensed spectacles and a boxback blue serge coat, double-breasted but always left ajar; he said it gave him "room to move around in." He affected a high celluloid collar and a narrow tie like a preacher, but he kept a flat pint of corn whiskey on the upright. Weighing just under three hundred pounds, with skin so black it glistened with purple highlights, he sat straight-backed, punching the keyboard with big hands whose fingers were dark and apparently boneless. He was said to be older than God. Duff, by contrast, was years younger than anyone else in the house. He wore denim trousers, an open neck shirt, and shoes with the fronts cut away to accommodate his corns. Sitting with his legs crossed and his body hunched over the silver horn, he kept his eyes tightly closed against the hard yellow glare of the lightbulb suspended on a cord from the ceiling. His manner was mild and gentle, incongruous with what came out of the horn, which was wild and blary and would almost deafen anyone who nudged up too close to the bandstand.

When the whiskey was good and the music went to suit him, Blind Bailey would sing. Then the dancers would stop and watch, for it was well worth seeing. Except by suggestion the songs were meaningless, without connected thought and sometimes even without words. He would begin bouncing on the oversized bench which had been especially constructed for his weight, cross-braced with two-by-fours and baling wire, then throw back his head and holler from down deep in his throat:

Shake it up, break it up,
Throw it on the wall!
Hug it up, lug it up,
Dont *let it fall!*

and then go off into a language all his own, composed mostly of shouts and moans, punctuated with growls and hisses, like an enraged sea lion—which, indeed, he managed to resemble at such a time. Duff learned to conform to these voice improvisations, obbligato, and they were the basis for much of the spectacular art of his later years.

He played at the Mansion House for nearly three years, by the end of which time he had learned all it had to offer him. He was not restless; he was never restless about his work; but he knew that it was nearing the time for him to be moving on. Then one cold February morning, a little after two oclock, a group of young Negroes, bandsmen off an excursion steamer that had stopped at the Bristol wharf for a moonlight dance, came in wearing unseasonal white flannel trousers, blue and white striped blazers with big pearl buttons, and two-tone shoes. The steamer was lying over until morning because of ice and debris on the river, and the musicians had come ashore to make the rounds on Bantam Street. They danced with the girls and listened to the music for an hour—both with an air of conscious superiority, bringing as they did into the dance room a cosmopolitan atmosphere of the wide outside world—then moved on, taking half a dozen of the best girls with them. They had been gone about twenty minutes when Blind Bailey began to strum the Farewell Blues, winding up with a few fast bars of Home Sweet Home; that was how he finished off each evening. Duff held the spit valve open and blew out the cornet, and Blind Bailey rapped with the piano lid to waken the boy who slept in the corner behind the upright every night until time to take the old man by the coat sleeve and guide him home to the Chinaman's store, Joe Toy's, where he had a room in the back.

The moon had risen late. As Duff came down the Mansion House steps he saw it shining bright and cold on the bell-bottom flannel trousers and gaudy jacket of one of the steamer bandsmen. "How do," the stranger said. He stood on the sidewalk, holding out his hand. "Ive been waiting to catch you, see you. I'd have seen you inside there but I make it a practice never to talk business with regards to hiring a musician while he is actually engaged in performing for someone else, for pay I mean. Excuse my glove."

"How do," Duff said. He had never heard such a speech before;

it was like hearing a foreign language, one that required no breathing pauses. He felt soft, cold suede against his palm. Suddenly it was withdrawn.

"The name is Jefferson," the bandsman said. "Pearly, they call me in the trade." He paused.

"Glad to meet you," Duff said, like a prompted actor.

"Likewise. Would you join me in a drink somewhere where we can talk?"

"I generally get me a cup of coffee at the All Nite Café. It's just up the street a piece."

"That will be congenial," Jefferson said.

Over the coffee, and employing the same highflown garrulity with which he had performed the greeting outside the Mansion House, he explained that his orchestra—he was the leader—had lost a horn man on Beale, two nights ago in Memphis. "A woman," he said sadly. He paused; he shook his head. Then suddenly he returned to the business at hand. "I like your tone," he said. "With a little polish I think youll fit right in."

There were barely two hours before the steamer would take in her stageplank. When Duff woke Nora and told her he was leaving, she sat up clutching the edge of the quilt under her chin.

"I declare, boy, *I* cant make you out." She shook her head. "How come you want to be running off with strangers? Last time you got mixed up with a stranger you wound up in reform school for two years. Is that what you want, some more of that? Because this time itll be Parchman and lots longer."

Duff kept his eyes down, hearing her through. "I want to make something out of myself, mamma."

"Hump. You want to make that wild scandalous music: thats all you want. Why cant you stay here and play it? I aint stopping you."

"They going to pay me twenty dollars a week, mamma."

"A week?"

"Yessum."

This was impressive; Nora paused. But having paused she hurried on. "And whats the good in that?" she said. "Youll just spend it on riotous living—canned peaches, cigars, sardines, and suchlike."

"I got to go."

"You aint got to nothing."

"Yessum I have; I got to."

She waited perhaps five seconds, watching him. It seemed long, and she knew she was defeated again. Then she said quietly, "All right. If you got to, you got to. I aint holding you. When did I ever, once you took a notion?"

The stageplank was taken in on schedule. The paddle blades thrashed water, backing the steamer away from the wharf; the whistle screamed and rumbled, precipitating steam, and the paddles reversed, driving the boat ahead on the forward slope of a churning wave. From the rail Duff watched Bristol shrink and fade in the pale light of the winter dawn. When he was a mile downriver the sun rose big and scarlet, and as the steamboat rounded the lower bend he looked back and saw the town gleam blood-red for an instant, house roofs and church spires, smoke stacks and water towers burgeoning in flame. Then, apparitionlike, as the trees along the Arkansas bank swept a curtain of green across it, it was gone.

That night they played Vicksburg. In the course of another week they played Natchez and Baton Rouge, and within a third week they were in New Orleans. Duff made two trips on the excursion steamer, to and from Saint Louis and fifty river towns along the way. He was learning, playing and listening in all those different places flanking the river where this kind of music was born. What was more, Jefferson—who, Duff soon discovered, had a good deal more genuine friendliness than the garrulous façade had indicated—taught him to read musical notation and featured him on a share of the songs.

"Look here now," Pearly said, spreading a sheet of music. "It's easy as Baby Ray. All those squiggles and dots and dashes, theyre not there to mix you up, they are there to help you. Look what I mean. Here's this fellow with a round white face—he goes slow. Give him a leg, like this one here, and he goes twice as fast. Then black his face and he goes twice as fast again, like Jesse Owens outrunning all those white men. Put him a tail on the end of his leg and he doubles speed, eight times as swift as the round-face white one. Another tail, that makes it a flipper; he goes doubling up again. All the time doubling, however many. Comprehend?"

"Two tails and he goes sixteen times as fast?"

"Co-rect. You catching on."

"That does seem mighty swift."

"Well, you got to remember—that white-face fellow, he goes awful slow. We'll get to sixty-fourths before we're done. And look at this. Where he sits on the ladder, high or low, shows how he sounds, how shrill or rumbly. F, A, C, E, between the rungs: spells face. The higher he goes, the higher you go with him. Here. Play me this line by the notes, and take it easy. All I'm trying to do is teach you something on paper that you already know in your mind."

Duff had the flannel trousers now and the coat of many colors, but he could not wear the two-tone shoes because they were only lent for the duration of the job. Like the jacket and trousers they belonged to the boat, and the owner would not allow him to slit them for his corns. But that was all right; he had other compensations. In Memphis, on the trip back downriver, he bought a new cornet, a golden horn with easy valves and a glitter like new money. He wrapped the old one carefully in burlap and mailed it back to the warden. *Here and thanks,* he wrote in a note he inclosed. *Give it to some other boy to learn on. I am fine.*

Jefferson played piano. After the second trip he persuaded Duff to join him on a job in a New Orleans riverfront dancehall near the Quarter. With four other musicians, drums, trombone, clarinet, guitar, they formed a combination known as Pearly Jefferson's Basin Six. As a group—though they made no recordings by which to prove or disprove it at this late date, or even to argue or rave over—the Basin Six were probably not as good as the cultists nowadays declare. They were late in the tradition, too late for the "carving" contests held on street corners in the days when rival bands played to attract the public to their dancehalls and cafés, too late also for the days when a band advertised its music by driving around town in a mule-drawn wagon, the musicians hunched in the bed between the pianist, who faced forward against the driver's seat, and the trombone man, who faced rear and moved his slide out over the tailgate. There was none of that left by the time Duff Conway reached New Orleans. But late or early, he was in the tradition. He played the same songs for people who had heard them in the early days and he got to know musicians who had grown old in the trade, who had sat on the same rostrum with Buddy Dubray and Cleaver Williams and were willing to talk about it: as for instance, how

Buddy would lean out of a window, pointing the bell of his cornet toward the city, and "call his children home," meaning that he would signal the customers to come on out, the dance was getting started; he hadnt needed to go downtown to advertise. Duff's four years in New Orleans were not the years of his greatest music, but they did more than any other years to develop his final tone and style. Backed by the example of Blind Bailey—who had never presumed to "teach" him anything—they were the years that made him what he was when, later, musicians who were supposed to know called him the best horn man of his time.

In March of 1935 he accepted a job with Rex Ingersoll in New York. Tall, handsome, light-skinned, with sideburns and a hairline mustache, Ingersoll was billed as "the crown prince of swing" in billboard and newspaper advertisements for the motion pictures and radio programs which featured him. In New Orleans two weeks before, he had heard Duff play and had talked with him for half an hour. He was interested in the Basin Six treatment of Maple Leaf Rag and had paid Pearly a hundred dollars for what he called the "arrangement." Pearly spent ten dollars of it on a wreath for Cleaver Williams' grave (Williams had played the Rag that way, twenty years ago), gave another twenty to beggars on the street (that was the way Williams had wound up, begging on the street after he lost a hand in a shooting scrape) and blew the rest on a beer bust for the band. From New York Ingersoll telegraphed Duff an offer of eighty dollars a week. Duff packed a cardboard suitcase and caught the first train north.

Ingersoll was waiting for him at Pennsylvania Station. From there he took Duff straight to a tailor who measured him for half a dozen orchestra suits. "We'll get that out of the way first," he said. Then he took him to rehearsal. Afterwards he told him, "Duff, you really blow that thing. It's great, kid, really great. But it's a little different up here. On those passages that belong to you, go right on and ride it out; it's great. But other times you have to hold back on it, sort of melt in with the others. See what I mean?"

"Play it soft?"

"Yes, kid, background it. Tacet."

"All right, Rex."

He tried to do as he was told, but two days later Ingersoll spoke to him again about it. "We've got to take out some of the blare," he said. "Not that it's not great. It's really great. But you know, kid, we got to keep the icks happy, not go breaking their eardrums."

Duff tried this time, too. He kept on trying, right up to the day when he couldnt even try any longer; he had to give it up. Later he explained it this way:

"He told me to hold back on it, and I tried. But I couldnt. So Rex put a mute in the horn and hung a derby over the bell. That was all right, then—Rex said it was fine." Duff wagged his head. "Maybe it was, to listen to, but my wind backed up on me. What was suppose to be coming out the other end got choked back down my throat. I like to bust. Rex said it was great, kid, great, but it got me so wrought-up I couldnt sleep. I'd sit up mornings, trying to woodshed it out of me, but that didnt help any whole lot. So finally one night I stayed home.

"Next afternoon when Rex come round I told him how it was. 'I cant,' I told him. But he said I was wrong. He said music wasnt only for the ones that played it; it was for the ones that listened to it, too. He said it was up to us to give it to them the way they wanted it, and let the longhairs take care of the other and go hungry." Duff nodded gravely. "That sounded reasonable, you know. I figured he was right, being top man in the big time and all that. I figured he wasnt clearing any hundred thousand a year without knowing what he was talking about. And Lord knows I wanted to stay. All that money and high living, fine clothes and good food and smooth women—I like it well as the next man, all of it. But I couldnt; I couldnt even go back and try any more. I would have if I could have but I couldnt."

The following day a drummer he had worked with in New Orleans came to see him. The drummer said, "I heard you took off from Rex. What you planning now?"

"I dont know. Go back home, I reckon."

"Aint no sense to that, man; you just got here. Look. This friend of mine is opening a place right here in Harlem—a gin mill affair, nothing special; youd be playing for cakes at first. But come on in with us and we'll make us some music the way it ought to be made."

"I dont know, Juny. Seems like my horn dont suit this town. Rex ought to know."

"Itll suit this place. Come on."

There were no tin derbies at the Black Cat, no mutes, no music stands spelling R E X in blinking neon; there were no music stands at all, in fact. Opening night, the following Saturday, everything that had been pent up inside him for the past ten days came out loud and clear. From that first night it got better. Six months later he hit his stride.

"I dont know how it happened," he told Harry Van afterward, looking back. "It seem like the horn kind of opened up and everything I ever learnt come sailing out."

Harry Van had never heard jazz before, to listen to. It was something he accepted much as a person might accept Joyce or Brancusi, admitting there might be something there and even admitting it was probably sincere, but never caring to study it or give it any real attention. Van was twenty-seven, only beginning to compose the things he had always worked toward, music that was intellectual in concept and highly organized, with a good deal more stress on form than content. There were plenty of interesting ways to put notes together, and this way was the safest—meaning that it was the one least likely to lead to disappointment; the less you ventured, emotionally, the less you stood to lose. He was aware of the shortcomings of this approach but he excused them on the grounds that what he had done so far was student work, preparation; he was learning his craft, one of the most difficult in the world, and when the time came for what he called the breakthrough (he was anti-romantic, but he was romantic enough to believe in this) he believed he would find his material proceeding naturally from his studies; that is, he would find 'himself,' as so many others had done before him. After all, he told himself, there were plenty of interesting ways to put notes together if 'themes' were what you were after. Nothing had interrupted or even disturbed this belief until the night his harmony instructor took him to a Harlem nightclub.

Over the doorway there was an arched cat with green electric eyes and a bristling tail. The instructor rapped and a panel opened inward upon a face so black that the eyeballs glistened unbelievably white. The Negro showed an even row of gold teeth when he recognized the harmony instructor. "Evening, professor," he said, and the door swung open, revealing a dingy anteroom and another door. From beyond it came a pulse of music, like something under pressure in a bell jar. When this second door was opened they were struck by a violent wave of sound, the ride-out finish of China Boy, followed by one thump of the drum and an abrupt cessation, a silence so empty that, in its turn, it too seemed to strike them across their faces like an open palm, a slap.

On a low dais in the opposite corner there was a five man group—drums, piano, cornet, trombone, clarinet—seen dimly through smoke that hung like cotton batting, acrid and motionless except when it divided to let waiters through and closed again immediately behind them as they moved among the small round tables where people sat drinking from undersized glasses. Van looked for other instruments, unable to believe that all that sound had come from five musicians. As he and the instructor were being seated the drum set a new beat, pulsing unvaried; the clarinet began to squeal, trilling arpeggios with the frantic hysteria of a just-castrated pig; the trombone growled; the cornet uttered tentative notes; the piano brought out *One Hour* for sixteen bars (Van knew it as *If I Could Be With You,* from college dances) and subsided into a general rhythm of sustained chords. Then it happened.

The cornet man, whose skin had the reddish tint of cocoa, took a chorus alone. Wearing a pale blue polo shirt, high-waisted light tan trousers, and shoes with the fronts hewn out to expose white cotton socks, he sat with his legs crossed, the snub horn bunched against his face. His eyes were closed and he held his head so determinedly down that through the early measures he appeared to be blowing the notes deliberately into the floor, driving them there like so many silver nails, a lick to each. His playing was restrained; it sounded almost effortless; but, seeing him, Van got an impression that the cornetist was generating a tremendous pressure only to release a small part of it. Apparently this was the case, for near the end of the chorus, as if the pressure had reached that point he was building toward, the player lifted his head, the cornet rising above his face, and the leashed energy seemed to turn loose all at once, riding powerfully over what had gone before. It approached the limit at which hearing would renege, that farthest boundary of the realm of sound, soaring proud and unvanquishable beyond the restraint of all the music Van had ever known. "No! No!" and "Hey!" people cried from adjoining tables. Van just sat there looking, knowing that his life had reached a turning.

The harmony instructor left soon after midnight but Van was there when dawn began to pale the hanging smoke. He left when the musicians did. He went home, ate breakfast, walked the early morning streets for an hour, and went to class. Afterwards, looking back, it seemed to him that this day had the unreal quality of a dream not quite remembered, partly no doubt because of the lack of sleep (he had always followed a healthy regimen) but mostly because of his state of mind, his reaction to what he had heard. He was confused. Something had happened beyond his will, and he could not call it back or comprehend. It was not until three hours after dark, after a restless four-hour sleep, when he passed through the tandem doors of the Black Cat for the second time, that the dream state ended and he returned to the actual living world.

Knowing nothing of the schedule, he was early. The tables were empty and last night's smoke had dispersed. Four of the musicians were there, two of them with their instrument cases, cornet and trombone, on the floor beside their chairs. The crowd began to arrive. Presently, when the room was about one-third filled, the pianist mounted the dais and took his seat. Again it was like no music Van had ever heard; again it was without melody or, seemingly, even tempo—a vague tinkling in which the black keys seemed to predominate, a strumming such as might have been done by a performing animal, ape or seal, except that there was a certain intelligence to the touch, a tonal sentience beyond Van's comprehension. Then the clarinetist arrived. White, about forty, with a neat pale tonsure exposed when he removed his Homburg, he resembled a successful dentist or a haberdasher's clerk. As he crossed the room, the air already beginning to thicken with smoke, he took the instrument from the flat, booksized case beneath his arm and began assembling its five sections. He stepped onto the rostrum without breaking his stride, halted at the far end of the piano—an upright with its front removed to show the busy hammers capped with felt—and began to play the shrill, sliding runs of the night before. The other three members came forward together, as if this were some sort of muster signal, and during the trombone break Van recognized the melody and realized that he had been hearing it all along. It was *I Never Knew,* which had been popular at dances in his Yale undergraduate days.

He was there for the closing this second night as well, sitting alone at one of the back tables, the steel-gray smoke matting thicker and thicker between him and the bandstand. The following day he cut classes, but he stayed away from the Black Cat that night. He was dazed, like a survivor of some disaster, a dancehall fire or a steamboat explosion. 'All I have done adds up to nothing,' he told himself as he lay in bed unable to sleep after the day's idleness; 'now I'll have to start all over again.' He kept remembering the tone of the cornet, recalling whole passages of improvisation by the cocoa-colored Negro. 'Maybe he cant even read music,' Van thought. 'Maybe he came here from a cornfield somewhere, dropped the hoe and took up the horn and played what his grandfathers played in the jungle a hundred years ago.'

The following night he found that some of this was wrong. The cornetist could read notes, for one thing, anyhow after a fashion. His name was Conway; he had come up from New Orleans two years before and had already made a name for himself. Van learned all this from an enthusiastic young man who sat at an adjoining table. He wore a crew haircut and a hound's tooth jacket and explained off-hand, though with an edge of pride, that he was a writer for *Platter,* a trade magazine published by a record manufacturer. "Thats the most horn in the world," he said. "I thought everybody interested in music knew Duff Conway." He spoke a racy jargon which Van could not always follow, and he had a habit of pacing the music by patting the table with his palms and humming du-duh du-duh through his teeth with a rhythm which Van, at any rate, thought did not always conform to that of the musicians on the bandstand. The gold-toothed manager seemed impressed, however; he kept dropping by to ask how things were going and sent the writer a fresh drink every fifteen minutes without charge.

During a break the young man brought the cornetist to Van's table. "You been asking so I thought I'd bring him round," he said by way of introduction. He spread his arms and put his head back like a prize-ring announcer. "Comb them all—52nd Street, the Loop, 12th Street in K.C., anywhere—you wont find a horn like this one. Mind what I'm telling you."

"I'm pleased to meet you," Van said.

"How do," Duff said, shaking hands.

He was twenty-four that month. His manner with strangers was nearly always awkward, but soon after meeting Harry Van he lost this awkwardness, at least in Van's direction. They became friends and were seen together in such diverse places as Swing Row and Carnegie Hall, the Village and the Metropolitan—one the son of a New England choir master and a sea captain's daughter, advanced student at one of the nation's leading music institutions, already composing music which even the conservative officials of the school called "promising" with considerable more enthusiasm than usually hid behind the word; the other the son of an itinerant guitarist and a Mississippi servant girl, horn man in a Harlem gin-mill, whose name spoken casually was enough to evoke superlatives from his followers and whose recordings were beginning to be collectors' items. For two years this relationship grew, Van being drawn steadily away from the music he had known and into the orbit—or maybe vortex—of the music Duff represented, until finally he was composing things like those he formerly had believed were without melody or harmony or sometimes even rhythm. At first his friends at the institute talked against it; it didnt make sense, they said. But now he seldom saw them. He was at work on a four-part composition made up of jazz themes with variations based on Duff's improvisations. Later he was to abandon this. Indeed, the jazz influence is hardly apparent in his work today. But he had got what he wanted by then; he had made the breakthrough, and the influence remained, if not the signs. What he wanted was an approach, and jazz had shown him that. An inferior art by virtue of its limitations, it involved great drive and marvelous technique and little else, but jazz men—anyhow the good ones, and where the emotions were so naked, thrown out in such a spendthrift fashion, it was obvious from the outset which were good and which were not—never let technique be anything but a means to an end. This was what he mainly got; this was what had struck him that first night in Harlem (though he did not know it then, or at least could not identify it) and this was what stayed with him after he left jazz behind.

Van had completed about two-thirds of this four-part composition, almost as far as he was to go with it, when Duff began to admit a weariness in his arms and legs. He had felt it for some time, but now he began to admit it, at least to himself; he had lost weight, and some nights he was so tired he could barely hold the horn up to his face. So he began drinking to fight it, keeping a waiter on the move between the bandstand and the bar. This took away some of the weariness, or seemed to. But toward the middle of August, 1939, something happened.

It was near closing time and he was just entering the chorus of *Body and Soul,* one of his best numbers. As the horn mounted toward the final, unbelievable note he felt something rise at the back of his throat, an insistent tickling like a feather against his pharynx. He fell off the note. There was a moment of flat silence; waiters froze in midstride, and here and there about the smoky room people sat with glasses halfway raised. "Fluffed," someone said, dismayed and loud against the sudden quiet. Duff coughed and there was a taste of salt at the base of his tongue. He stood there on the platform, looking over the cornet at the crowd, and wiped his mouth with the back of one hand, still holding the horn. When he saw the darker red against the flesh he coughed again, harder, and a bright bubble of blood broke from his lips, running down his chin, onto the horn and onto the front of his shirt.

Van took him home and sat feeding him cracked ice until morning. At the clinic, when the examination was over and the x-ray had been taken, the doctor said: "Come back at five and we'll see what there is to this. Go back to bed till then."

He was a mild, gray-haired man with beautifully laundered cuffs and a collar like mother-of-pearl; he prided himself on never being hurried. When Duff and Van returned, late afternoon sunlight lay in soft yellow bars across the doctor's desk, filtered through a slatted blind. The doctor held the negative against the light. "Here you are," he said, indicating the x-ray like a portrait at a private showing, himself the painter.

At first Duff could not see what he meant. Then, as the doctor's finger moved among the smoky branches of the ribs, he discerned a gray smudge about the size and color of a tarnished silver dollar. He had been watching it for a good while before he became conscious that the doctor was still speaking.

". . . prescribe in a case like this. What you need is bed rest. I cannot tell how long it will take to cure you, if at all, but I can tell you anyhow it will take less than six months to kill you if you stay in that airtight smoke-filled room blowing your lungs out on a trumpet every night."

"It's a cornet," Duff told him.

"Cornet, then. Isnt that worse?" Duff did not answer. The doctor said, "Do you want me to arrange accommodations at a sanitorium for you?"

"No, thank you, doctor." Duff rose, holding his hat, and Van rose with him. "I'm going home."

Every morning, on her way out, Nora would set the pitcher of milk and the glass on the bedside table. Duff would lie there watching them through the long quiet day. Just before sundown he would tilt an inch of milk into the glass, sloshing it around to stain the glass to the brim. When he had drunk it—painfully, sip by finicky sip—he would set the glass back on the table, take the still-full pitcher to the kitchen, and being careful not to spatter any drops his mother might discover on the sink, pour the remainder down the drain. Then he would compose himself in bed for her return.

He took the inactivity fairly well. Some days, however, a speculative expression would come on his face as he lay there, and after a while he would get up and cross the room to the bureau. The cornet lay in the drawer beside Nora's pistol. He would not touch it; sometimes he would not even open the drawer, for he could see it clearly in his mind, thus juxtaposed, the dull shadowed gleam of gold beside the brighter glint of nickel. He had been in the room for three months now, hearing newsboy voices cry Hitler and the ruin of Poland while the tree outside the window, like something in a hackneyed movie interlude, turned from dusty green to the hectic flare of Indian summer and then stood leafless in the steady rain of late November; winter came early that first war year. Christmas Day he took up the horn for the first time since he put it away, four months ago. He carried it back to bed with him and played it for an hour as a sort of self-given Christmas present, holding the quilt over the bell to deaden the sound.

After that he began to play it for an hour every afternoon, and by the end of January he was playing it mornings too, without the quilt. But it was March, the tree budding in the abrupt Mississippi springtime, before he left the cabin with the horn. Except that now he left by the front door—Nora slept on the cot in the kitchen, having surrendered the front-room bed to Duff—it was like the nights a dozen years ago, when he would steal away to hear forbidden music on Bantam Street.

That was where he went, this time, too. As he walked up the steps of the Mansion House he heard the piano going strong on *Deed I Do*. Looking across the dance room, through the smoke and around the heads and shoulders of the dancers, he saw Blind Bailey's broad blue back and his gray head bobbing in time to the music. A young man in overalls sat wooden-faced beside him, strumming a guitar. Duff crossed the room and stood behind the piano, watching the heavy hands move over the keyboard. Some of the keys were dead or badly out of tune, from stretched strings or missing hammers, but Blind Bailey knew how to avoid them; he only struck them for special effects. Duff raised the cornet, waiting, then came in on the beat, carrying it wide open for sixteen bars before fading for the piano break, and they took it together for a ride-out finish, the guitarist straggling along as best he could.

"Lord, Lord, Duff, it's good to hear you," Blind Bailey said, lifting his head. The spectacle lenses were blue disks, flat and opaque as target centers in the glare of the lightbulb. "How you been so long?"

"Fine as fine," Duff told him, smiling. "Just you play me some more of that mean piano."

At the cabin four hours later the lamp was burning and Nora was waiting. This was like the old days too. As was her custom, she had got up in the night to see if there was anything he needed. Finding the bed empty, she dressed and went straight to Bantam Street. From the sidewalk outside the Mansion House, along with a crowd of others who could not afford the twenty cents admission, she heard the cornet. Then she came home, lighted the lamp, and waited.

When Duff had closed the door and turned to face her with the horn in his hands, she said calmly: "I aint going to try and reason with you, because you grown now and besides I learnt better long ago. But aint you got no more sense than to be at that place, blowing that thing with them wore-out lungs that the doctor his own self's done told you wouldnt last a half a year that way?" She waited for him to answer, then said again, "Aint you?"

"Noam."

"All right. Go on to bed. Satan can call you his own where I'm concerned."

At first he went to the Mansion House twice a week, rationing his pleasure. By the middle of April he was there every other night, and before the end of May he was not missing a session. But by that time, with spring an actuality, not a promise, and the long hot days of summer drawing in, the trees and flowers in full leaf and bloom before the press of heat made them wilt, there was more to draw him than the music. There was a girl.

Her name was Julia, a light brown girl with a wide mouth, sloe eyes, and a boisterous manner. She had the loveliest laugh he'd ever heard. Nineteen, slim, high-bosomed, she had come to Bristol from Vicksburg when her parents opened a café on Bantam Street; their name was Kinship. She had her faults and Duff saw them from the beginning—a capacity for cruelty, for example, in any connection that clashed with her self-interest—but they were the faults of youth and were therefore not only correctible but were also as charming as her virtues, at least in his eyes. With his New York clothes and haircut and his aura of fame, Duff attracted her from the start, but the first time he noticed her was one night when he had just finished a fast chorus of *Wish I Could Shimmy.* She was wearing a knee-length red silk dress and suddenly, out of nowhere, she leaned forward and threw her arms around his neck.

"Oh people, people!" she cried. "Look here at my horn-blowing man!"

"Back up, gal," Duff told her, almost gruffly. "Back up and I'll blow one just for you."

This kind of thing had happened before—on the river, in New Orleans, and up in Harlem—but this time something in him answered. He played the *Corn Crib Blues,* and for the rest of the night, on into morning, whenever he looked out over the dance floor he saw Julia either watching him or performing for him, switching the red dress and preening like a bird. When the last number was over and the room emptied, she was waiting for him. After coffee at the All Nite Café he walked her home, and from the porch swing they watched the dawn come through. There appeared to be two sources of light, one descending from the sky, one rising from the earth; when they touched, joined, it was broad open daylight. He had never noticed this before.

In the three weeks that it lasted Duff experienced much else that he had never known before. Except for his music and his illness he had never been involved in anything he could not walk away from. His mother had not held him, for all her wiles, and even at the reform school he could look forward to a time when he would be released. But there was no such assurance here. Sick as he was, his system upset by coughing fits that were growing more frequent and more violent all the time, he was conscious of his inability to hold her. Within a week of the night she threw her arms around his neck and called him her horn-blowing man, Julia began letting him know his shortcomings. Wherever they were he was always aware that he did not satisfy her wants, whether at the All Nite Café, where she expected raucous talk to impress her friends—and even strangers—with his life in the big time, or in the high back room of the Mansion House, where she would rail at him with all the passion he was unable to assuage.

There were really only two considerations that kept her by him even for the short three weeks it lasted. One was her wanting to get full benefit of the reflected fame, which was there whether he would boast of it or not; the other was a lack of anyone to take his place. Two weeks were enough to exhaust the first, and the second was filled by the end of the third week. But Julia could not be satisfied with just leaving Duff for another man. She wanted to be won, preferably after a contest that would display her as the object of contention. The man she chose was likely to furnish whatever violence she desired.

He was Chance Jackson, a gambler well known in the region for his instant willingness to bet on almost anything, as well as for his loud clothes, his pearl-gray derby, and the big yellow diamond studs he wore in place of buttons on his shirtfront. Born and raised in Oxford, where his mother worked in the home of the president of the University of Mississippi, he had been given his mother's employer's official title, Chancellor, as a first name. Faculty members and townspeople thought it a ludicrous name, until he began growing up and it was shortened to Chance. Then they realized how apt it was. While still in knee breeches he became known as a master at dice, coon-can, pitty pat, and all the other Negro gambling games. When he had cleaned out his section of the state he widened his field, and now he went from town to town, staying no longer than the winnings were good; 'pickings' he called them. He was nearing forty. There were men who had saved between visits for more than twenty years, awaiting an opportunity to skin him, not so much for the money—though it would have been considerable, by their standards—as for the prestige, the sake of being able to boast about it later. It had been known to happen, but the satisfaction was shortlived; they either had to face him when he returned, or decline the contest, or move outside the circle of his glory. All the same, they kept waiting, hoping, trying, and they kept losing.

Bristol was on his itinerary; he came here twice a year. A section at the rear of the Mansion House dance room was partitioned off by an old theater curtain nailed along its top edge to the ceiling, thus forming an alcove in which two blanketed card tables and a canvas-bottomed dice table stood under steel-blue cones of down-funneled light. Whenever there was a hush on the dance floor, which was rare, the rattle of dice and the cries of gamblers came through the curtain. Foot-high letters across its center spelled ASBESTOS and there were faded advertisements of harness shops and restaurants, gunsmithies and clothing stores, whose dead proprietors had never guessed the final room their names would grace.

Duff was resting on one of Blind Bailey's special numbers when he saw the gray derby above the red silk dress. He watched, brooding, for Chance had a reputation for handling women that almost equaled his reputation for handling cards and dice; it was a bad sign that he had forsaken the gambling alcove for the dance floor. But when the piano stopped, Julia came to the rostrum. "Make him leave me lone," she said. "I'm scared of that man."

"Whats he doing?"

"Nothing. But I'm scared. He *holds* me funny."

"Stay away from him then," Duff told her.

Half an hour later he saw them together again. He could see that they were talking while they danced, Julia with her head tilted back, looking up at Chance, who was looking toward Duff on the bandstand. Though he could not hear what they were saying, Julia was telling the gambler that Duff had said he would beat her if she danced with him again. "He'll do it, too," she added.

"Him?" Chance peered through the smoke at Duff. "He aint going to bother *no*body. Watch here." He danced toward the rostrum. "Hey, boy," he said. "Was you wanting to beat on somebody?"

It was between pieces; Blind Bailey had just finished the special, and Duff sat with the cornet in his lap. The gambler's diamonds flashed yellow as he leaned forward, one arm around Julia's waist. His face was close; his nose was large, fleshy and powerful-looking. "Was you?" he insisted. Duff did not answer. Chance leaned closer and spoke again. His voice was soft, almost caressing, his face less than six inches away. "I said *was* you?"

"Move on and let that girl alone," Duff told him.

What followed happened so quickly that he was not aware of any sequence of events until it had ended. Without taking his arm from around Julia's waist, Chance raised the other hand. Then—not making a fist, not even using the flat of his palm—he touched Duff under the chin with the tips of his fingers, lifted him gently clear of the chair, and toppled him over backward. There was a loud thump as his head hit the floor, and then, his ears still ringing, Duff heard a clang as the cornet struck.

"Watch out there, whoever!" Blind Bailey cried. "Quit that horseplay round the bandstand."

Looking up, Duff saw the pearl-gray derby haloing the smiling chocolate face. "Just who was you going to give that beating to?" Chance asked.

The cornet, on the planks beside Duff's head, had an ugly dent in the column, just behind the bell. He saw this first; then he saw Julia. The gambler's hand, still clasping her waist, showed dark against the red silk of her dress. She was smiling now, and Duff realized that he had heard her laugh as he went over, a laugh that had been a cry, a squeal almost, not only of nervous excitement but of delight.

Afterwards he was to tell himself that the smile had caused what followed; the smile stayed in his mind even more than the laugh, for the smile was in cold blood. He had expected to look up and find her striking at the gambler with one of her high-heeled shoes. Instead he found her smiling. There were other factors, too. His nerves were upset from knowing the girl would not stay with him, and his music had been getting worse because he had been holding back to stave off coughing fits. All this combined and contributed, so that when he went over backward, sent sprawling not by a blow from a fist or even a slap from an open palm, but by the almost gentle lift and nudge of fingertips, when he saw the scarred cornet and then looked up to find Julia smiling approval of what had been done to him, he reached the end of misery and he knew already what he was going to do. Curiously enough, however, he felt no particular hatred toward Chance; hating the gambler would have been like hating the car with which a careless or spiteful driver had run him down. He went out, carrying the dented horn, and behind him the crowd was laughing.

He walked fast, went up the cabin steps and into the room, crossed straight to the bureau, and opened the drawer. For a moment the cornet and the pistol lay side by side, nickel and gold, as they had done through the months he spent in bed. Then he turned with the gun in his hand and heard the canvas cot squeak in the kitchen. "Duff?" Closing the front door behind him he heard his mother's voice again, sharper this time: "Duff!" He left, walking fast, the pistol heavy in his pocket.

Blind Bailey was banging out *Tin Roof Blues* as he came up the steps and into the dance room. Chance and Julia were dancing in a far corner. Duff shouldered his way through the crowd until he was within ten feet of them. Then he took out the pistol and waited. The other couples faded toward the walls; the room was hushed except for the loud piano and the cries from the dice table beyond the curtain; "Come on, *eight!*" a voice shouted with all the fervency of prayer. Chance and Julia, cheek to cheek in a slow turn, did not notice any of this. The gambler's head continued to revolve until beneath his lowered lids he saw the glint of the pistol: whereupon, the gyral movement half completed, he stopped, still clasping his partner. He moved Julia slowly aside, never taking his eyes off the pistol. It was as stylized as ballet.

Chance had time to raise one hand, the palm showing pink in a gesture of protest; "Wait a minute, boy," he said, maneuvering for time to reach for the pistol everyone knew he carried under his waistband. Then the gun went off—louder, Duff thought, then anything he had ever heard; he had never been that close to a shot before. The piano stopped like a dropped watch as the gambler went back against the theater curtain and slid down it to the floor. The bullet had passed through his outstretched palm, ranging upward; it entered his forehead, just above one eyebrow, and came out high at the back of his head. The gray derby rose, and now it fell, spinning on its crown to show a new red lining matching the red of Julia's dress.

There were hurried patters and scrabbling sounds as dancers and gamblers went out through the two doorways and the windows. For a moment the curtain billowed like a sail in a strong wind; then it hung straight, becalmed. There was silence again, and Duff and Julia and Blind Bailey were alone in the room with the body of Chance Jackson, who appeared to muse profoundly upon his shoetips. Forgotten cigarettes raised their plumes among overturned chairs and half-empty beer bottles. Julia began to back away, eyes bulged, one hand against her mouth. "Dont," she said, looking into the muzzle of the pistol. "Dont . . ." Duff watched her until the end of the curtain lifted and she was gone.

Alone on the bandstand, under the steady glare of the naked bulb, Blind Bailey sat with his hands suspended above the keyboard, the flat blue disks of his spectacles reflecting no light. "Whoever you are, God bless you," he said. "And please dont shoot a blind old man."

Then there were footsteps on the porch and at the door. Dropping the pistol, Duff turned and saw the policeman at the end of the room. A sand-colored snapbrim hat cast a parabola down the top half of his face. Beneath this shadow the mouth moved steady and thin-lipped.

"Dont try nothing, boy," the white face said. "Just stand there."

He was in jail three months awaiting trial for having done violence against the peace and dignity of the State of Mississippi. It was held in early September, the hottest weather of the year. The judge sat behind his high bench, an old man who wore a black alpaca jacket and a string tie, despite the heat, and had a habit of clearing his throat with a rattle of phlegm to signal his displeasure as he watched the opposing lawyers around the stem of a bulldog pipe. The jury was out less than half an hour; the district attorney had made much of the fact that Duff had left the dancehall for the pistol and returned; here was premeditation indeed, he said, and here was the chance for right-thinking people to show the lawless element whether they intended to put up with all these barrelhouse killings or not. Duff's lawyer, a young man just out of law school and appointed by the court, sat there helpless though he tried to earn his fifty dollars by objecting as often as possible. When the jurors had filed back into the box and the foreman had reported ("Guilty as charged," he said, without recommendation of mercy) the judge leaned forward and peered at the prisoner over the swoop of his pipe. This was the last case of the term; tomorrow he would make another halt on the circuit.

"Do you have anything to say before sentence of the court is passed upon you?"

No one heard Duff say anything but those on the forward side of the rail saw his lips form the words No Sir. Overhead the paddle-blade fans made a creaking. The judge paused, leaning forward, forearms flat along the bench. He watched the prisoner intently. Then, seeming to gather his strength for some particularly energetic pleasure, he spoke slowly like an actor measuring up to his big speech:

"I sentence you to be committed to a felon's cell, and there to be safely kept until the tenth day of October in the year of our Lord nineteen hundred and forty, at which time you shall suffer death by electrocution, and may God have mercy on your soul."

There was a sigh, a collective suspiration; then the spectators rose and filed for the door. They showed an unaccustomed politeness toward each other, having been in the presence of death, though once they were out in the hall they threw it off. A deputy led Duff down the stairway, across the rear lawn of the courthouse, and back to his upstairs cell in the county jail. The door closed behind him with an iron clang like the final stroke of a clock. But that was all right; he was used to it by now, after three months in the cell; today was not much different from yesterday. He sat looking up at the barred window, the high hot bright blue September sky.

Next morning when Nora came to see him she carried a bundle

wrapped in freshly laundered flour-sacking, the creases still crisp from ironing. Even before he unwrapped it he could feel the familiar, compressed shape of the cornet. There was no instrument repair man closer than Memphis, so Nora had taken it to a local gunsmith to have the dent smoothed out; it was her way of asking her son's pardon for having told him Satan could call him his own. Duff played the horn whenever the turnkey would let him. The other prisoners didnt mind. They liked it, the white ones in their individual cells and the Negroes in the bull-pen. The notes were less blary now, for his lungs were worse, but the tone was as clear as ever. Every day there would be a sizable group in the yard below the cell window, sitting under trees or leaning against the weathered concrete wall of the jail itself, listening.

When Harry Van first heard the horn he was halfway to the county jail. It caught him in midstride, as if he had crossed an exact circumference into a circle of sound which had for its center the golden bell of the cornet, and though it grew louder as he drew near, the tone was no clearer beneath the cell window than it had been a block away.

He had taken the midnight train out of Memphis—the one natives called the Cannonball, in derision—south through the fields that were white as if with incongruous snow in the warm October moonlight. The trip was one hundred and fifty miles and it lasted beyond eight hours; the coach bucked and rattled, halting at every hamlet along the way and even backing onto spur tracks to make those stops that were off the main line. During the final two hours he could see the countryside quite clearly, first in the pale, misty dawn which came through slowly, like a scene on a photographic print in the process of being developed, and then in sunlight, the corrugated metal gins whining soprano with queues of mule-drawn wagons lined up for the sucker pipe, the slow willow-bordered creeks and drainage ditches with their rackety bridges, the flat, ash-gray fields where pickers moved down the rows dragging nine-foot sacks that bulged at their lower ends with the fiber which had resembled snow in the moonlight.

Van had never before seen cotton growing, and in fact, though he had made two European crossings, had never been south of Philadelphia. In rumpled tweed, with his soft hat and careful collar, Scotch-grained shoes and black knit tie, juxtaposed among salesmen sleeping on their sample cases and excursionists returning from two-day flings in the city, he was like a visitor from a future generation or even another planet; the other passengers looked at him once and then let him strictly alone. When at last the conductor passed down the aisle announcing Bristol, Van took his pigskin bag from the overhead rack and went out on the platform. He stepped down onto a graveled quay, deserted except for an old Negro who wore a dusty tailcoat and a frayed white panama.

"Pardon," Van said, and to him his voice sounded rusty from not having used it for such a long time, "but could you direct me to the county jail?" The old man watched him curiously, puzzled by the Eastern syntax and vocabulary. "The county jail," Van said again. "Where is it?"

The old man raised one arm, pointing. "Yonder ways," he said at last. "Two blocks twill you sees the soldier: thats the cyote-house. Hit's in back, behindside."

Now it was Van's turn to be puzzled. However, he took up the bag again and began walking down the sidewalk in the direction the old man had indicated. Behind him what was obviously the main street, lined with store fronts, ran westward into a steep, grassy sort of earthwork which he did not recognize as the levee. He had known the river was there, having heard Duff speak of it and having seen it on the map, but 'river' to him meant the rivers of New England, France, and Italy; he had expected to find a village sprawled along its bank, all green and peaceful, with white church spires and cottages in ordered rows, each with its brass knocker. Instead the town looked gimcrack, characterless with its false storefronts, unclean with its litter of trash and dust. He would have been even more dismayed, and perhaps alarmed, if he had known that instead of the town overlooking the river, the river—from behind its earthwork, which he did not recognize; he saw no sign of the river at all—overlooked the town. What was worse, he had left the bright, hazy riot of Indian summer, with a tinge of woodsmoke in the air, but now it was as if he had traveled not only southward through space but also backward through time. It was summer indeed, and the clothes he wore were too heavy for the weather; he was sweating, wilting the careful collar which gripped him now like a damp hand at his throat.

All this was forgotten, however, even the press of heat, when he crossed the circumference of the music. He paused for an instant, then continued forward, moving now within the rich circle of sound, hearing again after all those months the proud, soaring tone of the cornet known to jazz musicians and their followers everywhere. But to Van it did not seem that he was hearing it again. It seemed, rather, that he had never stopped hearing it since a night almost three years ago, when his harmony instructor took him up to Harlem, under the arched back of that green-eyed cat.

When Duff left New York, the morning after the interview in the doctor's office, he said he would be back within a year. Perhaps he even believed it, at the time. But eleven months later a waiter at the Black Cat told Van that Duff had been tried for a roadhouse shooting and would be executed in October. That was in late September. Van wrote and waited ten days for an answer. Then he took the train for Memphis. And now, walking along the southern street, hearing again the cornet which had become for him the ultimate expression of all music, he thought in a kind of rage: 'There ought to be two sets of laws, one for us and another for the few like him. It's enough that they carry the burden and the anguish of their talent and their genius; it's not right to expect them to follow something set down and codified in books for men who dont even think the way they do, if they think at all.'

He crossed the intersection toward a wooded lawn where a marble column gleamed pale among oaks and sycamores, magnolias and elms, still wearing their dusty summer foliage. Surmounting the shaft, the Confederate faced south, his blanket-roll tied neatly across his left shoulder to leave his shooting arm unencumbered; he stood with one foot a bit advanced, both hands clasping the muzzle of his musket, and his eyes were bland, impervious, the pupils dimpled into the stone eyeballs, under the shadow of a hat-brim as stiff and unyielding as if it had just been lifted from the stamping machine; he seemed not to have gotten word of the surrender. This was the soldier the old Negro at the depot had told Van to watch for, and the ugly brownstone structure with its new cupola was the courthouse. Behind it there was a square two-story building of harsh concrete, bars slatting the windows and a heavily grilled door blocking the entrance.

It was the jail, and a man sat on the stoop. He wore khaki trousers and a faded denim shirt with half-moons of darker blue beneath the armpits. As Van approached, carrying the pigskin bag, the man looked up. His eyes were a pale green, as if they had been washed in too-strong soap and the color had not held, and there was a lax, mobile expression about his mouth. He held a knife and a whittling stick. Van halted in front of him, looking more out-of-place than ever in his city tweeds. "May I see Duff Conway?"

The man dropped his glance. Without looking up, he shaved a long curl of pine from the stick. "From up his way?" he asked. There was a big ring of keys at his belt.

"Yes."

"Figured you were." He looked up. Van, whose knowledge of such things was limited to what he had seen in the papers and magazines, wondered what would happen next; he had no taste for being involved in one of those 'southern' incidents. The man rose, brushing shavings from his lap. "Sho now. You can see him." He swung the iron door ajar and led the way. "Put your suitcase there," he said. "Wont nobody bother it." His voice was not strong but it had a staminal quality. "I understand he got sick up there or something, and come down here to get well. But it dont matter now. My cousin Luke Jeffcoat is going to give him the big treatment tonight."

"Treatment?"

"The chair—the 'lectric chair. He comes around and sets it up; calls it his old shocking chair. Sick or well wont make any nevermind then. Were you acquainted with him up the country?"

"Yes."

"Lawyer?"

"No: friend."

"Ah?" The turnkey looked back over his shoulder. They were climbing a steep circular staircase. "Then maybe you can bring it home to him. I'm a religious man, myself; I always have been. But I cant talk to him, seems like." He toiled ahead, speaking over his shoulder with the same unflagging volubility. "I can talk to most of them, bring them round before the end, but not this boy. He listens but it dont get through. So you tell him. Tell him to lay that horn aside and get right with his Maker."

'Oral personality,' Van thought, remembering the term out of a far-off psychology classroom as he followed the faded broad blue back, the shifting khaki hams just at eye level. 'Does he ever stop?'

"Most of them we have to kind of put the damper on, they get so wrought-up and sanctified with all their kinfolks there in the cell and two or three jackleg preachers yelling about salvation at the top of their voice. But this one cant seem to get it through his mind the time aint long. Wont see a preacher, wont even pay his mamma any mind: just sits there all day long with that durn horn, playing them honky-tonk songs like his soul depended on it. He'd be blowing it all night too, I reckon, if I'd let him."

They had reached the second story by now; the turnkey led Van down a corridor flanked with cells. Convicts in striped trousers and sleeveless undershirts watched through the bars, the eyes of the Negroes rolling white in the gloom of the bull-pen. "Full house," the turnkey said. "But thats all right. The long-chain man will be here a week from Monday to take them up to Parchman." Van felt the need for a guide book and a two-way dictionary. There was a combined odor of creosote and mildew, of perspiration and urine, of rust and sweating iron and much else, anonymous and myriad. The sound of the cornet filled the jail; it was *Tailgate Ramble,* near the finish.

"Well," the turnkey continued, unwearied, against the soar of the horn, "he can blow it tonight if he wants. Most of them ask for a quart of corn and a woman, but I reckon he'll want the horn. The sheriff always gives them what they want. If it's possible I mean, because we had one to ask us for a hacksaw. He could joke at a time like that. Last January we had a boy wanted watermelon; wouldnt nothing do but that, he said. In January, mind you. And we got it for him out of the cooler at the icehouse. Fellow that owned it had been saving it for something special, a wedding or an election, some such rumpus, but he didnt begrudge it. No sir. He never begrudged it a-tall, since that was the one thing the poor boy wanted. I think youll find the folks round here are like that, by and large, with some exceptions."

While he told about the watermelon he stood at the cell door with the keyring in his hand like a badge of office. Finally he selected one of the big keys and fitted it into the lock. It turned with a clanking of tumblers. Then he swung the door ajar, performing a gesture of presentation with one hand. "Company, son," he said.

Duff did not hear him. In fact he appeared too busy, too concentrated on what he was doing, to hear anything but the music. Riding out the coda of *Tailgate Ramble,* he was jackknifed into the lower section of the double bunk, hunched against the wall with his knees drawn up and his heels against the bed frame. The cornet was lifted toward the window, catching the light as in a golden bowl. While the final note died away he turned and saw Van standing in the doorway. He did not seem surprised. He lowered the horn and smiled, and his teeth were white and even against his cocoa-colored face.

"Hello, Harry," he said then. "You a long ways from home."

At first, in the dim light from the high window, Van thought that Duff had changed very little. He did not wear convict stripes as Van had expected; he had on the peg-top trousers and polo shirt of his Harlem days. The skin fitted closer to his skull; that was all, Van thought at first. Then—either because his eyes had become accustomed to the light, or else because his mind was recovering from the shock—he saw the difference, and once he had seen it he saw little else. The skin did indeed fit close; the face was like one of those African masks, the lines of suffering and sickness grooved deep into the wood with all the exaggeration of the primitive, wherein the carver pits the force of his emotion against his lack of tools and training. Duff's voice had sounded even lower than usual, a hoarse whisper, and now Van saw that this was because the lungs were almost gone; he breathed with difficulty, high in his throat. His arms and legs were thin as famine. Only the eyes and teeth remained unchanged, yet even so they had a terrible kind of beauty, frightening by contrast.

Van had come twelve hundred miles but there was little he could find to say. He was too conscious of the haunted mask, the sticklike arms and legs, the shallow breathing. Smalltalk was an effort, like a constant lifting of weights, yet anything but smalltalk would have been outrageous; death was like a presence in the cell. Also, though he was patient and polite, Duff was obviously waiting for them to leave so that he could return to his music. Within nineteen hours of the chair, he belonged to another world already, and now Van understood why Duff had not answered his letter. He had known it would be like this.

The three men sat in the cell for about twenty minutes, the turnkey doing most of the talking. At last, when Van got up to leave, Duff looked at him quietly and said in a hoarse whisper: "Dont be feeling bad about all this. There wasnt anything anybody could do, Harry. It's just I ought not ever have left home. Going off like that I lost touch with everything I was born to be with. I been thinking about it, some. I ought to stayed at home where I belong."

Standing in the corridor while the turnkey locked and tested the door, Van said, "I'll tell them hello for you when I get back."

"Thanks," Duff said, and still it was as if he had to make an effort to be a part of the world. He looked down at his hands, holding the cornet; they were thinner, too. "But you better not make it hello. Make it goodbye."

He raised the horn toward the glittering eyes and teeth. Van turned, following again the broad, faded back of the turnkey. Halfway down the corkscrew staircase he heard the first note. This made him hurry. He took up the pigskin bag and stepped out into the sunlight.

"So long," the turnkey said.

"Goodbye," Van said in a choked voice, not looking back.

Crossing the lawn he could hear the cornet, well into *Didnt He Ramble.* The vivid, brilliant waves of sound swept over him, surging past the dusty trees and the ugly brownstone courthouse, past the pale Confederate, undefeated on his marble shaft, and into the street beyond, where people on the way to work were pausing to listen, their heads cocked toward the high cell window. The power behind the music was gone yet the clarity and sweetness were still present. There was more than an hour before time for the northbound train, but Van walked fast, wanting to be out of range of the horn.

The sheriff and Hoskins brought him into the cell, walking on either side of him, their hands supporting his elbows. His shaved head glistened like mahogany. He was thin, slight and frail between the florid sheriff and the husky deputy, and his slit trouser-legs flapped about his ankles. His eyes glittered, the pupils contracted in the sudden light. His teeth looked false, too white to be true and too large for his mouth, which was drawn in what appeared to be a grimace or even a smile though it was neither; it was fright. Roscoe followed them into the cell; Dr Benson and I and the district attorney watched from the rear wall. Luke Jeffcoat, who had stood beside the chair and watched them come in, stepped forward now and took over, beginning the running commentary, the oration he supplied with every job. He spoke with the full-mouthed accent of the old-time stump orators, sometimes addressing the condemned man, sometimes the witnesses.

"All right," he said. "Here you are for that last fast ride they promised you in court. Dont be troubled in your mind; youre in good, professional hands." He led him to the chair. "Have a seat," he said with grave formality; he even made a shallow bow, one hand out, palm up. Then he secured the straps at the wrists and ankles, going onto his knees for these last, and the larger strap across the chest. "Now dont you be trembling, son. Sit up straight and tall and take it cool, so when I tell all your friends how you stood it theyll be proud. Do you have anything to say?"

He stepped back, waiting, but there was nothing. Then he secured the plated cap and the hood. As he worked, the snakes tattooed on his arms seemed to writhe. "Ive had them all kinds," he said. "Some moaned and groaned. Some didnt. But they all went, every man jack of the lot, the way youre going. So dont you fight it; dont fight back . . . Hey there!"

The switch clicked and for a moment there was that deep, pulsing hum and that odor of burning.

"Yair!" the executioner cried. "One quick bump on the road to glory and he rode right out of this world never knowing what hit him. Yair. Steady, folks; we'll hit him again. Not because he needs it, no, but because the law says do it and the law's almighty. Yair!"

There were footsteps hurrying through the door of the cell, and as I came forward with the stethoscope we heard the young district attorney being sick in the hall. I leaned over the chair, then straightened up and pronounced the prisoner dead.

J. F. POWERS

J. F. Powers was born in Jacksonville, Illinois, in 1917 and currently resides in Collegeville, Minnesota. He is the author of the National Book Award novel *Morte d'Urban* (1962), *Wheat That Springeth Green* (1988), and three collections of short stories: *Prince of Darkness and Other Stories* (1947), *The Presence of Grace* (1956), and *Look How the Fish Live* (1975). He has shown special interest in the conflicts between whites and blacks in northern urban areas (seen in "He Don't Plant Cotton") and has explored the problems of modern Catholic clergy facing the temptations of commercial materialism (most effectively expressed in his satirical *Morte d'Urban*).

Regarding jazz, Mr. Powers says, "I must have heard jazz from the time I was born, but it wasn't until after high school that it *took*, that I realized what jazz musicians were doing when they weren't playing the tune. Recently, I mentioned this to someone in the presence of a young person who, with heartbreaking curiosity, asked, 'What were they doing?' I spent many long short nights at the old Three Deuces Club in Chicago where I sat at the feet—the bandstand behind the bar was slightly elevated—of Baby Dodds, Lonnie Johnson, Darnell Howard, and Gladys Palmer. What gave me the idea for 'He Don't Plant Cotton' happened elsewhere, though, where Jimmie Noone played."

"He Don't Plant Cotton" was first published in 1943 and must be read in the context of a pre–civil rights Chicago setting. The story portrays the tiredness of black musicians who have to restrain their desire to play "the music [they] were born to, blue or fast, music that had no name" while catering to the tastes of white audiences who demanded "Mickey Mouse sound effects, singing strings, electric guitars, neon violins, even organs and accordions and harmonica teams."

HE DON'T PLANT COTTON

SPRING entered the black belt in ashes, dust, and drabness, without benefit of the saving green. The seasons were known only by the thermometer and the clothing of the people. There were only a few nights in the whole year when the air itself told you. Perhaps a night in April or May might escape the plague of smells, achieve a little of the enchantment, be the diminished echo of spring happening ardently in the suburbs, but it was all over in a night and the streets were filled with summer, as a hollow mouth with bad breath, and even the rain could not wash it away. And winter . . .

The beginning snow swirled in from the lake, dusting the streets with white. Baby squinted down the lonesome tracks. The wind twisted snow into his eyes, the flakes as sharp as sand, grinding, and his eyeballs were coated with cold tears. Baby worked his hands in his overcoat pockets to make heat. He saw a woman cross the street to catch the Big Red, which was coming now, but the woman refused stiffly to run for it. The wind went off hooting down the tracks ahead. Baby got on. The conductor held out one hand for the fare and yanked a cord twice with the other, prodding the red monster into motion.

Baby sat down inside. A cold breeze swept the floor, rattling old transfers and gum wrappers. Baby placed his feet uneasily on the heater to make the meager warmth funnel up his pants' legs. The dark flesh beneath the tuxedo was chilled to chalky gray at the joints. He listened to the wheels bump over the breaks in the track, and the warmth from the heater rose higher on his legs. He became warm and forgetful of the weather, except as scenery. The streets were paved evenly with snow twinkling soft and clean and white under the lights, and velvet red and green from the neon signs.

New York may be all right, he hummed to himself, but Beale Street's paved with gold. That's a lie, he thought; I been down on Beale. And Chicago, same way. All my life playing jobs in Chicago, and I still got to ride the Big Red. And that's no lie. Jobs were getting harder and harder to find. What they wanted was Mickey Mouse sound effects, singing strings, electric guitars, neon violins, even organs and accordions and harmonica teams. Hard to find a spot to play in, and when you did it was always a white place with drunken advertising men wanting to hear "a old song"—"My Wild Irish Rose" or "I Love You Truly." So you played it, of course, and plenty of schmaltz. And the college kids who wanted swing—any slick popular song. So you played that, too. And always you want to play the music you were born to, blue or fast, music that had no name. You managed somehow to play that, too, when there was a lull or the place was empty and you had to stay until 4 A.M. anyway.

Baby got off the streetcar and walked the same two blocks he saw every night except Tuesday. The wind had died down almost entirely and the snow whirled in big flakes end over end. Padding along, Baby told himself he liked winter better than summer. Then he came to the place, said, "How's it, Chief?" to the doorman, an Indian passing for Negro, went down three steps, and forgot all about winter and summer. It was always the same here. It was not so much a place of temperatures as a place of lights and shades and chromium, pastel mirrors, the smell of beer, rum, whisky, smoke—a stale blend of odors and shadows, darkness and music. It was a place of only one climate and that was it.

Baby's overcoat, hat, and scarf went into a closet and settled familiarly on hooks. His old tuxedo walked over to the traps. Its black hands rubbed together briskly, driving out the chill. One hand fumbled in the dark at the base of the big drum, and a second later a watery blue light winked on dully and flooded the drumhead, staring like a blind blue eye. Immediately the tuxedo sat down and worked its feet with a slight rasping noise into the floor. The fingers thumped testingly on the hide, tightened the snare. They knew, like the ears, when it was right. Gingerly, as always, the right foot sought the big drum's pedal. The tuxedo was not ready yet. It had to fidget and massage its seat around on the chair, stretch out its arms, and hug the whole outfit a fraction of an inch this way and that. Then the eyes glanced at the piano player, signaling ready. The drumsticks paused a moment tensely, slid into the beat, barely heard, accenting perfectly the shower of piano notes. Everything worked together for two choruses. Then the piano player tapered his solo gently, so that at a certain point Baby knew it was his. He brought the number to a lifeless close, run down. Too early in the evening.

"Dodo," Baby said to the piano player, "Libby come in yet?"

Dodo sent a black hand up, slow as smoke, toward the ceiling. "Upstairs," he said, letting the hand fall to the keyboard with a faint, far-off chord. It stirred there, gently worming music from the battered upright. Notes drew nearer, riding on ships and camels through a world of sand and water, till they came forthright from the piano, taking on patterns, as the other black hand came to life on the bass keys, dear to Dodo. Baby picked up his sticks, recognizing the number. He called it "Dodo's Blues," though he knew Dodo called it nothing. Every night about this time, when there was no crowd and Dodo hadn't yet put on the white coat he wore servicing the bar, they would play it. Baby half closed his eyes. With pleasure he watched Dodo through the clouds of rhythm he felt shimmering up like heat from his drums. Baby's eyes were open only enough to frame Dodo like a picture; everything else was out. It was a picture of many dimensions; music was only one of them.

Here was a man, midgety, hunchbacked, black, and proud—mostly all back and music. A little man who, when he was fixing to play, had to look around for a couple of three-inch telephone directories. Piling them on top of the piano bench, he sat down, with all their names and streets and numbers and exchanges under him. He had very little of thighs and stomach—mostly just back, which threw a round shadow on the wall. When he leaned farther away from the piano, so the light slanted through his hands, his shadow revealed him walking on his hands down the keyboard, dancing on the tips of fingery toes. Sometimes it seemed to Baby through half-closed eyes, when Dodo's body was bobbing on the wall and his hands were feet dancing on the keyboard, as though the dim light shaped him into a gigantic, happy spider. When he became a spider you could forget he was a man, hunchbacked, runtish, black; and he, too, could forget perhaps that he had to be careful and proud.

Perhaps he could be happy always if his back and size and color and pride were not always standing in the way. The piano made him whole. The piano taught him to find himself and jump clean over the moon. When he played, his feet never touched the pedals.

People were beginning to fill the place. They finished off the number, Baby smiling his admiration, Dodo scrupulously expressionless.

"For a young man . . ." Baby said.

Dodo got down off the telephone directories and threw them under the piano at the bass end, beyond the blue glow of the big drum. He had seen Libby come down the steps from the dressing room—a red dress, a gardenia. Dodo went behind the bar and put on his white service coat. Libby sat down at the piano.

Helplessly attracted, several men came over from the bar and leaned on the piano. They stared, burdening Libby's body with calculations. Singly at first and then, gathering unity, together. Libby sang a popular song. The men went back to the bar to get their drinks, which they brought over and set on top of the upright. Libby sang the words about lost love, and the men licked their lips vacantly. At the end of the song they clapped fiercely. Libby ignored them with a smile.

"Say, that was just fine," one man said. "Where you from anyhow?"

With a little grin Libby acknowledged Baby. Baby, beaming his veteran admiration of a fine young woman, nodded.

"Where you from? Huh?"

"New Orleans."

"Well, you don't say!" the man blurted out joyfully. "We're from down South, too . . . Mississippi, matter of fact!"

Icily, Libby smiled her appreciation of this coincidence. She looked at Baby, who was also registering appropriately. Just think of that! Small world! And welcome to our city!

"Well, what do you know!" crowed the gentleman from Mississippi. "So you're from down South!" He was greatly pleased and already very drunk. He eyed his friends, four or five of them, distributing his discovery equally among them.

"You never know," he explained. Then he appeared to suffer a pang of doubt. He turned quickly to Libby again, as though to make sure she was still there. His eyes jellied blearily and in them an idea was born.

"I know," he said. "Sing . . . sing—sing 'Ol' Man River' for the boys. They all'd sure like that."

Without responding, Libby looked down at her hands, smiling. She measured chords between her thumbs and little fingers, working her amusement into the keys. Baby stared at the mottled hide of his snare drum, at the big one's rim worn down from playing "Dixieland." The gentleman from Mississippi got worried.

"Aw, sing it," he pleaded. So Libby sang a chorus. The gentlemen from Mississippi were overwhelmed. They loved the song, they loved the South, the dear old Southland. Land of cotton, cinnamon seed, and sandy bottom. Look away! Look away! They loved themselves. Look away! Look away! There was the tiniest touch of satire in Libby's voice, a slightly over-ripe fervor. Baby caught it and behind the bar Dodo caught it, but the gentlemen did not. Dodo had put down the martini glass he was polishing and look away! look away!—good.

At the bridge of the second chorus, Libby nodded "Take it!" to Baby. He stood up, staggering from the heat of the fields, clenching his black, toilworn fists. In profound anguish, he hollered, giving the white folks his all, really knocking himself out.

"Tote dat barge!"
"Lift dat bale,"
Git a little drunk . . .

Baby grimaced in torment and did his best to look like ol' Uncle Tom out snatchin' cotton.

Behind the bar, unnoticed, Dodo's sad black face had turned beatific. "—And you land in jail!" Dodo could not see the other faces, the big white ones, but he could imagine them, the heads fixed and tilted. It was too dark in the place, and he could make out only blurrily the outlines of the necks. Ordinarily he was capable only of hating them. Now he had risen to great unfamiliar heights and was actually enjoying them. Surprised at this capacity in himself, yet proud he could feel this way, he was confused. He went further and started to pity them. But his memory stood up outraged as his forgetfulness and said, Kill that pity dead. Then he remembered he was really alone in the place. It was different with Libby and Baby, though they were black, too. He did not understand why. Say their skin was thicker—only that was not why. Probably this was not the first time they had jived white folks to death and them none the wiser. Dodo was not like that; he had to wait a long time for his kicks. From his heart no pity went out for the white men. He kept it all to himself, where it was needed. But he had to smile inside of him with Libby and Baby. Only more. Look at that fool Baby! Jam up!

Bend yo' knees
An' bow yo' head,
An' pull dat rope
Until yo're dead.

Baby sat down with a thud, exhausted. The gentlemen from Mississippi brayed their pleasure. My, it was good to see that black boy all sweatin' and perspirin' that way. They clapped furiously, called for drinks, gobbled . . .

"And bring some for the darkies!"

Baby swallowed some of his drink. He looked at the beaten rim of the big drum, then at the sticks. He took out his pocketknife and scraped the rough, splintery places smooth. He glanced at Libby and ventured the kind of smile he felt and knew she did. He finished his drink. The gentlemen from Mississippi hung around the piano, getting drunker, shouting in one another's faces. Nervously Libby lighted a cigarette. A college boy tried to make conversation with her while his honey-haired girl assumed an attitude of genuine concern.

"Can you play 'Hot Lips'?" He was the real American Boy.

"Don't know it," Libby lied. She wished she didn't.

"Can you play 'Sugar Blues'?" Right back.

"Don't know it."

One of the Mississippi gentlemen, who had been hanging back, crowded up to the piano, making his move. He drained his drink and pushed closer to the piano so as to brush Libby's left hand with the front of his trousers. Libby moved her hand, sounding a chord that Baby caught. The gentleman, grinning lewdly, tried to follow her hand up the keyboard.

"That's all right," he snickered. "Play lots of bass, honey."

The first gentleman from Mississippi, drink in hand, stumbled over from the bar. He told Libby to play that "Ol' Man River" song some more. Libby hesitated. Then she lit into it, improvising all around it, and it was a pleasure for Baby, but the first gentleman from Mississippi was not happy. He said that if that was the best she could do she had better try singing. Libby sang only one chorus. The gentlemen from Mississippi, though they applauded, were not gratified. There was an air of petulance among them. They remembered another time they heard the song, but it was not clear now what had made it different and better. They saw Baby all right, but they did not remember that he was the one who had sung before, the good one that toted their bars, lifted their bales, and landed drunk in their jails. Something was wrong, but they saw no remedy. Each gentleman suspected the fault was personal, what with him drinking so heavy and all.

Dodo, behind the bar, had not enjoyed the song the last time, hating the coercion the white men worked on Libby and Baby, and feared his advantage was slipping away. In a minute he would be hating them to pieces again.

"Can you play 'Tiger Rag'?" The American Boy was back.

"No." Libby made a face and then managed to turn it into a smile for him. He held his drink up for the world to see on the night before the big game.

The honey-haired girl wrenched her face into a winning smile and hit the jack pot. "Can you play 'St. Louis Blues'?"

"How you want it?" Libby said. She put out her cigarette. "Blues, rhumba . . . what kind a way?"

"Oh, play it low down. The way *you people* play it." So Libby would understand, she executed a ponderous wink, narrowed her eyes, and made them glitter wantonly behind the lashes. "*You* know," she said.

Libby knew. She played "St. Louis," losing herself in it with Baby. She left the college boy and the honey-haired girl behind. She forgot she knew. She gazed at Baby with her eyes dreamy, unseeing, blind with the blue drum, her head nodding in that wonderful, graceful way. Baby saw his old tuxedo in the mirror, its body shimmying on the chair, and he was pleased. The drums, beating figures, rocked with a steady roll. They were playing "Little Rock Getaway" now, the fine, young-woman music.

And Libby was pleased, watching Baby. And then, somehow, he vanished for her into the blue drum. The sticks still danced at an oblique angle on the snare, but there were no hands to them and

Libby could not see Baby on the chair. She could only feel him somewhere in the blue glow. Abandoning herself, she lost herself in the piano. Now, still without seeing him, she could feel him with a clarity and warmth beyond vision. Miniature bell notes, mostly blue, blossomed ecstatically, perished *affettuoso,* weaving themselves down into the dark beauty of the lower keys, because it was closer to the drum, and multiplied. They came back to "St. Louis" again.

"Stop." The first gentleman from Mississippi touched Libby on the arm. "When I do that to you, that means 'Stop,'" he said. Libby chorded easily. "Some of the boys like to hear that 'Ol' Man River' some more." He straightened up, turning to the other gentleman, his smile assuring them it would not be long now.

"Kick off," Baby sighed.

But Libby broke into "St. Louis" again. Baby, with a little whoop, came clambering after, his sticks slicing into the drum rim, a staccato "Dixieland."

The first gentleman frowned, touching Libby's arm, "Remember what that means? Means 'Ol Man River,'" he said calmly, as though correcting a slight error. "Toot sweet. Know what that means? That's French. Means right now." No harm done, however. Just that his friends here, a bunch of boys from down South, were dying to hear that song again—up to him to see that they got satisfaction—knew there would be no trouble about it.

"We'll play it for you later on," Libby said quickly. "We got some other requests besides yours. How many we got now, Baby?"

Baby held up eight fingers, very prompt.

"Coming up," he said.

The first gentleman was undecided. "Well . . ." he drawled. Libby began a popular song. The first gentleman faced his friends. His eyes more or less met theirs and found no agreement. The boys looked kind of impatient, like a bunch of boys out for a little fun and not doing so well. He turned to Libby again.

"We just gotta have that 'Ol Man River' some more. Boys all got their hearts set on it," he said. "Right away! Toot sweet! Toot—away!" There he'd gone and made a joke, and the boys all laughed and repeated it to each other. Libby played on, as though she had not heard. The first gentleman took hold of her arm. She gazed steadily up into his bleary eyes.

"Not now. Later."

"No, you don't. You gotta play it right now. For a bunch of boys from down South. They all got a hankerin' to hear that 'Ol Man River' some more."

"So you best play it," another gentleman said, leaning down hard on the old upright piano. "On account of I'm gonna take and give ear. We kinda like how that old song sounds up North. Whatcha all need. The drummer will sing," he said, and looked at Baby. Baby looked back, unsmiling.

Libby chorded lightly, waiting for the gentlemen from Mississippi to get tired. They could not see how it was with her and Baby—never.

"You ain't gonna play?"

Baby's eyes strained hard in their sockets.

"We ain't comin'," Libby said.

Baby's eyes relaxed and he knew the worst part was over. They felt the same way about it. They had made up their minds. The rest was easy. Baby was even a little glad it had happened. A feeling was growing within him that he had wanted to do this for a long time—for years and years, in a hundred different places he had played.

Secretly majestic, Baby sat at his drums, the goal of countless uplifted eyes—beseeching him. For it seemed that hordes of white people were far below him making their little commotions and noises, asking favors of him, like Lord, please bring the rain, or Lord, please take it away. Lord Baby. Waves of warm exhilaration washed into him, endearing him to himself. No, he smiled, I am sorry, no favors today. Yes, Lord, they all said, if that's the way it is, so be it.

But somebody objected. The manager's voice barked, far below, scarcely audible to Baby in his new eminence. ". . . honoring requests," he heard, and ". . . trouble with the local," and ". . . wanting to get a sweet-swing trio in this place a long time now." And the manager, strangely small, an excited pale pygmy, explaining to the gentlemen from Mississippi, also small, how it was, "That's all I can do in the circumstances," and them saying, "Well, I guess so; well, I guess so all right; don't pay to pamper 'em, to give 'em an inch."

Baby noticed Libby had got up from the piano and put on her coat, the long dress hanging out at the bottom, red.

"I won't change," she said, and handed Baby the canvas cover for the snare drum.

"Huh?" Baby said foggily. He set about taking his traps apart. Dodo, not wearing his white service coat, came over to help.

"You don't have to," Baby said.

Chief, freezing outside in his long, fancy maroon coat, opened the door for them. "You all through, Baby?"

"Yeah, Chief. You told that right."

They walked down the street toward the car line. Baby, going first, plowed a path for Libby and Dodo in the snow. Window sills, parked cars, and trees were padded with it. The wind was dead and buried. Baby bore the big drum on his shoulder and felt the sticks pressing tight and upright in his vest pockets, two on each side. Libby had her purse and street clothes rolled up under her arm. Dodo carried the snare drum.

Softly as snow, Libby laughed. "That's all I can do in the circumstances," she said.

"I got your old circumstances," Baby said.

Then they were silent, tramping in the snow.

At the corner they waited in a store entrance for a southbound streetcar. Libby raised a foot now and then, shuddering with cold. Dead still, Dodo breathed down inside the collar of his overcoat, retarding his breath, frowning at the little smoke trickling out, as though it were the only thing left in the world to remind him he was alive. Baby talked of taking a cab and finally did go out into the street to hail one approaching. It slowed up, pulled over to the curb, hesitated . . . and lurched away, with Baby's hand reaching for the door. Baby watched the cab speed down the snowy street, following it for a few steps, speechless. There was nothing to do. Without looking, he saw Libby and Dodo shivering in the store entrance. They had seen the cab come and go. They had not moved an inch. They waited unfooled, as before, for the Big Red.

"What's wrong with you, Baby?" Libby called out. A tiny moment of silence, and she was laughing, gradually louder, mellow octaves of it, mounting, pluming . . .

Like her piano, it seemed to Baby—that fine, young-woman laughter.

"Why you laugh so much, woman?" he inquired plaintively from the street. Then he moved to join them, a few steps only, dallying at the curb to temper the abruptness of his retreat. Like her piano on "Little Rock"—that fine, young-woman laughter.

ELLIOT GRENNARD

Born in New York City in 1907, Elliot Grennard played piano in dance bands, composed music and wrote lyrics, took a turn at play-writing, and wrote for various magazines and newspapers. "Sparrow's Last Jump" was his first short story and won a 1948 O. Henry Prize; one of the judges noted that the story "is written with authority, and it certainly carries the tones and overtones of the world of jazz musicians." The story was first published in *Harper's Magazine* in May, 1947.

Ross Russell's Dial recording session with Charlie Parker on July 29, 1946, provided the inspiration for the story. Grennard, then a correspondent for *Billboard* magazine, was one of only twelve people there, including the musicians. He told Robert Reisner, "[Parker] couldn't get started on anything. . . . He couldn't tune up. He could just fit the mouthpiece." Russell concluded that the session was a total waste. That same night, oversaturated with the whiskey that he used as a substitute for the heroin he was attempting to kick, Parker set fire to his bed at the Civic Hotel in Los Angeles and shortly thereafter was sent to Camarillo for the cure.

Among jazz buffs, Bird's "Lover Man" session is a well-known episode in the Parker legend. Uninformed readers will find excellent coverage of it in Ross Russell's *Bird Lives: The High Life and Hard Times of Charlie (Yardbird) Parker* (1973).

SPARROW'S LAST JUMP

WE had seen "Specter of the Rose" and the talk got around to Nijinsky and somebody said, "Imagine if they had a camera going when Nijinsky blew his top!"

I wanted to tell them I got Sparrow Jones down on acetate the night he was taken away, but they would have wanted me to play the record for them. They weren't the kind who would say, how can you compare a jazz musician with Nijinsky? They would have said, I want to own that platter, what a collector's item!

Telling me? I guess everyone who read the last *Jazz Year-Book* and saw how Sparrow rated would want a copy of the last record he made. I could probably sell 20,000 in a month, maybe 50,000, once word got around. And don't think I can't use that kind of sale. Hot jazz doesn't sell the way Freddy Martin or Sammy Kaye does, you know. You get a 10,000 copy sale and you think you're doing great.

I even played around with the idea of releasing the record and tossing the dough into the pot to pay for Sparrow's sanitarium. But when a thing like that happens right in front of your eyes! I don't want to see it again every time I hear the record.

I had just got back from New York that morning, and on the way over to my room I thought I might as well stop in at Jackson's Record Shop and see how my disks were going. I release only three records every two months and when you're a little guy in this business, you're smart if you give it that personal touch. That's all I'd been doing for six weeks; dropping in on record dealers between L.A. and New York, giving them a big, well hel-lo.

Jackson is my best customer in Hollywood. He can't afford to—and doesn't want to—stock everything he'd have to if he held Victor, Columbia, and Decca franchises, so Jackson pushes the off-labels. Not a big business but not a bad one, when you figure there are eighty-nine off-labels on the market and most of them wax nothing but hot jazz.

I said, "Hi ya, Jackson," sneaking a quick look at the walls to see if my stickers were up.

"You ain't real, McNeil?" he said. Then he asked me what I heard from the mob and I told him the big news in the East was be-bop. I said, I was thinking of getting hold of Sparrow Jones and cutting me some of this be-bop.

Jackson bared his teeth in what he thought was a grin. "You clowning, Browning? There's a cat spinning your Basin Street album in the booth who'll run you out of town if you tell him you're going to wax be-bop."

Jackson was kidding on the square. "New Orleans" collectors are murder. They swear that jazz died in 1924 and anyone who didn't personally rock the cradle of jazz with his own two beats is strictly commercial. Benny Goodman? A bed-chamber music clarinetist who couldn't shine Jimmy Noone's shoes.

Me, I don't argue. I put my stuff out under three different labels: N'Orleans, Southside, and Hep. That way, nobody gets mad at anybody.

I went back to see this character in the booth, and not only because it's good business. The truth is, I like all kinds of jazz—Louis, Duke, Goodman. Even when I don't exactly like it, or understand it—like be-bop—I respect what the boys are trying to do. What the hell, how many guys collected the Duke before the middle thirties?

When I opened the door of the booth what do I hear but some frantic trumpet that could only be Dizzy Gillespie. Before I can ask myself if I'm hearing things or what, I see it is no character playing the Gillespie record. It's big Hughie Hadliffe.

Hughie is one of my favorite people, and I hadn't seen him since I went East six weeks back. I yelled, "Hughie!" and I pumped his arm.

Hughie always gives you a solid handshake because that's the way he is, solid and serious. With his glasses on, Hughie looks like an interne, which is what he would have been if he hadn't decided after three years of college that being a Negro doctor is pretty tough going. So instead of breaking his back, Hughie stuck to the trumpet that had been paying his way through school.

But he still looked like a medic. No little nanny-goat whiskers for Hughie, even if shaving under the lip was supposed to hurt your playing. And no dark glasses, either. The only thing screwy about Hughie was that he had gone on a be-bop kick and had chucked up a sweet job with Basie, plus a bookful of recording dates every month. That's the trouble with be-bop. Once you start hearing those screwy chords in your ear and get those offbeats in your system, you can't play any other way. The old way is too straight, too on-the-nose.

"How's my boy?" I asked.

Hughie shook his head. "He's not doing so good."

I said, "Huh?" and then realized he thought I was asking about Sparrow.

Jazz musicians have single-track minds. They eat, drink, and sleep their music. They're so hipped, if somebody comes along with something new, they make him God. That's the way it was with Hughie and Sparrow. Hughie had heard Sparrow one night, and when Sparrow asked if he'd like to play with him, Hughie dropped everything. Sparrow was his boy, and the way he saw it, there could be only one boy.

"Doesn't he like it at the Club?" I said.

"He likes it all right, I guess."

I saw he didn't feel like telling me, but I asked anyway. "What's the matter?"

Hughie sort of shrugged. Not indifferently, but like he didn't know what to say.

Jazz musicians don't pop off a lot. Like when you ask them about jazz; they don't trust words to say what they feel, so they dummy up. If they don't like something and you ask them, they kind of turn away and say, "Well. You know." If they like something, they'll grin and say, "That's all right." When they're really gone on someone, they'll say, "Man, he plays fine!"

So when Hughie didn't say anything, I knew this business about Sparrow was something big. That changed my plans.

"Too bad," I said. "I wanted you and Sparrow and the band to make some records for me."

Hughie straightened up. "Gee, that would be great, Harry. No kidding, great. Why don't we do that. We got some fine numbers. Real fine."

I thought, what goes on here? This isn't the Hughie I know. "Take it easy," I said. "You just told me different."

Hughie's shoulders dropped. I knew he couldn't keep up that fast chatter.

"Sparrow's sick," he said quietly. "I don't know how long he's going to hold up. I thought it would be nice if he made some records while he could."

It gave me a stab seeing Hughie like that, but I didn't want to let on. "Forget it," I said. "I'll drop in at the Club one of these nights and we'll talk to Sparrow about a date."

Hughie looked solemn. "If you're going to record Sparrow," he said, "you better do it soon."

Then I knew it was bad.

Jackson's got a loose lip, so I tried to duck him on my way out. He popped up from behind the counter just as I was passing.

"I forgot to tell you about Sparrow," he said. "Man, his wig is really loose. Looks like he's blowing his top for good."

I purposely misunderstood. "Yeah, I hear he's playing fine."

"When he can hold his instrument," Jackson said. "Man, he's got a tic that makes a Holy Roller look like she's holding still!"

That meant it was all over the street.

I couldn't put Sparrow out of my mind. He got this job at the Club about four weeks back, and it should have made him feel good. He'd been laying off for nearly eight months, and that's a long time for a guy who's worked steady since he was fourteen. I decided to look in on him that same night.

The Club was a bottle joint on Central and 38th. Not much of a place for a guy who's played the best locations in the country, but be-bop was too new to have a following and no Los Angeles night club operator with a big overhead was going to take a chance. Especially a white night club.

I know these clubs. They don't get started till one, so I got there a little after two. I took a table next to the bandstand and ordered some setups. The boys were just going on, so while I unwrapped my bottle I watched. When Sparrow sat down in his chair and turned around I nearly caved. He wasn't the same Sparrow.

It was hard to believe this middle-aged man was only twenty-two years old. His dark skin used to be tight, with a shine to it; now it set on his bones like black putty. His eyes were big and round and empty, and the expression on his face was just about the saddest expression I've ever seen. It made you think he wanted to cry inside, only he had tried and found he couldn't.

I remember when his tight little body used to operate like a precision machine. When he used to get set to play, his eyes would narrow down and his body would get taut, as if a spring had been wound up. And then he went. Anybody who heard him those three years with Joe Pepper's Hot Five knows how Sparrow could go. He went so fast and so far that the last year he was with them, Joe and the others couldn't keep up. That's when they began calling him "Sparrow." He was playing just too frantic.

Sparrow never could play with a big band; his tone was too personal, his intonation too full of shadings to blend with other saxophones. That's why Joe Pepper's band was good for him. They played blues, and Sparrow kept them from dragging. Then the band played only jump tunes at a medium tempo, and Sparrow really began to jump.

That's when the trouble between him and Joe started. Joe wanted to keep the beat nice and relaxed, but they just couldn't hold Sparrow down. He kept pushing the beat harder and harder, driving it ahead. It didn't become faster, it just stopped being relaxed. And then Sparrow began playing notes that made Joe uneasy.

When Sparrow quit the band, he found he had no place to go. He was playing in another world. It wasn't until Hughie went with him, and they got Jimmy Brash on piano, Joe Miggs on drums, and Fat Stuff on bass, that Sparrow had someone he could play with. Sparrow would tear loose until Hughie caught it; then they were playing together. The other three just about hung on, but it didn't matter. That's the outfit I had planned to record. Looking at Sparrow sitting there, I didn't think there was a chance.

I didn't want to stare at him but I couldn't help myself. He was twitching and jerking like a machine gone crazy. It was the worst tic I'd ever seen. First his head would snap to the right, then to the left. Then maybe four times to the right. Meanwhile his legs would shoot out at cockeyed angles and a shoulder would jerk. Sometimes one part of him moved, sometimes two or three parts at the same time, but you couldn't anticipate any of it. It had no pattern, no rhythm. And all the time his face didn't show it knew what his body was doing. It just looked sad.

The band was supposed to be Sparrow's, but Hughie was taking care of things. He said what tunes they would play, who would take solos, and they got ready. I looked to see what they were doing about Sparrow, but they acted like he wasn't there. Except that when I saw the way their expressionless eyes passed over him, I knew they were thinking plenty about him. It was just one of those things too big for words, or expressions.

Hughie beat off on "Oh My, Oh My," a crazy, hopped-up be-bopper, and Sparrow stopped twitching. Then his head jerked to the right about twenty times, fast, in time with the music. Suddenly his head stopped jerking, his body went rigid, and his legs performed a nightmarish buck-and-wing step. When he came out of the step, the snap swung his chair clean around while his saxophone flew to his lips—and he was blowing with the first beat of the second chorus, right on cue. Only his chair was facing the back of the bandstand and Sparrow was blowing to the empty wall. On the last beat of the phrase, his chair swung around again and Sparrow was blowing to the room. I mean, really blowing.

It was the old Sparrow again and the band knew it. They didn't look at him, or smile, but they knew it and the way they played proved it.

I must have been holding my breath for thirty seconds. When I let go and sat back in the chair, my body ached as though it had been caught in an ice-crusher. I poured myself a double and tried to relax by concentrating on the music. A lot that helped.

You know what be-bop's like? I don't mean in musical terms; the guys who play it don't even try to explain it. They don't even call it "be-bop." They just say it's "frantic," and maybe that's the best way of describing it when you consider that the dictionary says frantic means: "violently mad or distracted; outrageous; transported by passion." Personally, I don't go that far. I think of be-bop as: "tense, agitated; controlled hysteria."

Sparrow and Hughie had worked out some unison choruses your ear couldn't follow, and when they finished the set, the other three boys were smiling. I could just hear them saying, "Man, that was fine. Real fine."

Hughie joined me for a drink but Sparrow stayed in his chair. He didn't do anything or look at anything. He just sat there like he was asleep, only he had his eyes open. Hughie and I drank without talking. Our eyes didn't let go of Sparrow.

"What goes?" I asked finally.

Hughie shrugged.

"He been drinking too much?" I hesitated. "Or taking anything?"

I could see Hughie making up his mind to tell me. "He's been on morphine lately."

I said, "Oh."

Hughie didn't want to leave it at that. "Sparrow used to take a drink like anyone else, but that last year with Joe Pepper he was beginning to play frantic and he was afraid he couldn't keep up with it. He started drinking heavy, then he began on reefers. When it didn't give him what he was looking for, he tried morphine." Hughie shook his head sadly. "I've tried to tell him that stuff never helped anybody's music."

The old story. I knew how most of the old-timers got started taking things. They'd play some cheap cafe from seven till unconscious, then have to be at a recording studio at nine in the morning. They'd smoke a weed and get a lift from it, then think that's what made them play good. They found out different, but the kids that followed had to learn it for themselves, the hard way. It made me sore.

"How good did he think he could get, for Christ sakes! He's only twenty-two, and there aren't three guys on his instrument who can touch him right now!"

"Sparrow's like that. He's always fussing about his playing, thinking up new ideas, new ways of using his horn." Hughie looked at me, wondering if I'd understand. "Sparrow worries. He meets strange people and they tell him he's a genius, and he feels like a fool not knowing what to say back to them. He never went past the eighth grade, and how much chance has a Neg—" Hughie changed it. "How much chance has Sparrow had to mix and learn about things? He's got a feeling all he knows is how to play. That's why he works so hard on it; it's all he's got to give."

I thought, and I'm shooting my mouth off. What do I know how it's like for a colored guy in a white world, even a guy with Sparrow's talent? He meets other musicians and that's all right; with them it's the way you play your instrument that counts. But the others. The ones who discover jazz and collect records and think that makes it all right for them to go scouting for Negro musicians like on a scavenger hunt. Or the magazine writers looking for stories they can sell, talking so palsy-walsy and making the guy they're interviewing feel like he's something that crawled out from the woodwork. Or the drunk at the bar who thinks it's okay to throw his arm around a colored musician and say "Why don't you and me go out tonight and get us some high yaller gals?"

And Sparrow felt it was up to him; that he had to justify their interest in him. For that he was playing his heart out.

I was thinking of something I could talk about when I saw somebody I hadn't noticed before, sitting at the drums behind Sparrow. He was swishing the wire brushes on the snare drum, and while he wasn't looking right at Sparrow, I got the feeling he was watching him all the time.

"Who's that?" I asked Hughie, pointing with my chin.

"That's Cappy. Sparrow's band boy."

He looked about thirty-five, kind of old to be a band boy. I grinned. "This job must pay better than I thought."

"Cappy doesn't take anything from Sparrow," Hughie said. "He just wants to be around him."

I know how jazz fans worship great musicians. "Sparrow his boy?"

Hughie smiled. "That's his boy."

We watched Cappy for a while. He had a nice smile. He kept a soft rhythm going with the brushes, as if he were caressing Sparrow's back with it. It seemed to keep Sparrow quiet. I got to thinking about Sparrow making some records and the more I thought about it, the more I felt the way Hughie did.

"How about a recording date?" I said after a couple of minutes. "Think Sparrow would be able to make it?"

Hughie got eager again. "He was fine this last set."

I thought, what the hell. "Tomorrow? I'll get the Sunset Studio for seven, so we can eat first."

"Tomorrow'd be fine."

"Want me to talk to Sparrow?"

"I'll tell him," Hughie said.

He stood up and the other boys got up from where they had been sitting. Cappy didn't stop swishing those brushes until Joe Miggs took over the drums. When Cappy passed Sparrow, he made it a point to run his hand accidentally across Sparrow's shoulders. He waited near Sparrow until the boys started the first number, then he stepped back. He smiled an apology when he saw he had almost bumped into my table.

I smiled back. "Have a drink?" I asked.

He said all right, and he pulled out a chair so it faced the bandstand. He took his eyes off Sparrow when I reached for my bottle.

"Make my plain coke," he said in an nice easy way.

I said sure, and I signaled the waiter.

"You play drums?" I asked when we had both taken a drink.

"Uh-uh. I used to play tenor."

"No more?"

"I ain't played in four years," he said in that easy way of his.

I looked at him wondering.

"Maybe you remember me," he said. "Cappy Graystone?"

Then I remembered. "Sure. You were with Webster when he had his big band. And before that, the Rhythm Riders."

Cappy smiled. "You remember. That's nice."

I started to say, "Why'd you stop playing?" when I changed my mind.

Cappy caught it, but he didn't seem to mind. "I was sick," he said. "Like Sparrow."

I steered away from that. "He sure plays that horn," I said.

"Nobody plays like Sparrow," Cappy said. Then he grinned, shyly. "I started him."

I said, "No kidding."

Cappy liked that. "Yeah, I started him. I taught him his first piece. Thirteen years ago. He was nine, and I was playing my first big job. The old Paradise Ballroom."

The band had finished the opening number of the set and was started on the next. Cappy's eyes opened wide.

"That's it! That's the piece I was telling you."

I listened to Jimmy Brash playing a piano intro, and what surprised me was how slow he was playing it. Be-bop bands hardly ever play anything slow. Then I recognized the tune. It was "Sweet Sue," and that was another surprise. They hardly ever play standards. Sparrow came in on the up-beat and Cappy's smile reached from ear to ear.

"Can you beat that man?" he said. "He's playing it for Cappy. He knew I was bragging on him."

I peered at Sparrow but his face had the same dead-pan expression. He didn't know we were alive, let alone talking about him. Then, just when I decided it was all a coincidence, Sparrow's face twitched like he was winking and he honked five notes of the melody right at Cappy. Cappy went crazy.

"I hear you talkin'!" he yelled back. "Play it for Cappy, boy. Play it for Cappy!"

Sparrow proceeded to do things to Sue she never would have believed possible.

The table couldn't hold Cappy after that. He had to get up close where he could almost touch the sad-looking boy with the saxophone.

The next number was a fast one again, and right in the middle of it Sparrow's sax shot up in front of him, over his head, like someone had pulled a string on it. I thought he was clowning for Cappy but I changed my mind fast. Sparrow couldn't bring the instrument down. He kept playing it in that position until Hughie brought the number to an abrupt end.

The boys on the stand shot Hughie a quick look and he motioned, that's all, to them. They walked off the stand and Cappy pried the instrument out of Sparrow's hands.

It was too much for me. I threw some bills on the table and beat it out of there.

At six, I gave up trying to fall asleep. I phoned Hughie, figuring he'd be home by then. Hughie answered the phone himself. "How is he?" I asked.

"Cappy took him home right after you left."

"Jesus," I said. "Is that the way he's been?"

"Last night was the worst."

"Look," I said. "What about it? You think we ought to go through with that date? Put him through the wringer for a lousy couple of records?"

"It might be the last time for a while."

I cursed. "Shall I go get him tonight?" I asked.

"Cappy'll bring him."

I said okay, and banged the phone down in its cradle.

I wondered how smart I was, letting myself in for this. Counting the band, the studio, engineers, and incidentals, my recording sessions set me back a thousand bucks apiece. An awful lot of dough. I cut four tunes on each date and I can generally figure on them selling enough to get me back my costs. But unless one of the four sides turns out to be a real seller, I'm in the hole. You can't stay in business just making back your costs. If Sparrow showed up in the condition I saw him last, I'd be lucky if I got back the price of a pack of cigarettes.

I bought a bottle on the way to the studio and by the time the boys arrived, the bottle was a little less than half full.

When I saw Sparrow I stopped worrying, he looked so much better. He still had that dead-pan look but he wasn't twitching. I said hello, but I guess he didn't hear me. I didn't know what else to say, so I handed him the bottle. He held it for a while without looking at it, then he took a swig. He made a mouth like it was Clorox. It didn't look like he wanted more, so I took the bottle from him and handed it around. Everybody but Cappy took a good slug. Then Hughie got busy laying out the tunes.

Sparrow sat quietly where Cappy put him, puffing a cigarette Cappy put in his mouth. I thought it was going to be all right, but I felt fidgety. I clomped around the big studio, avoiding the group around the piano and drums. Then I looked at Sparrow and saw his eyes weren't blank any more. They were staring, with the same sad expression I remembered from the night before. It began to get me. I told Hughie we'd cut everything and I went back into the mixer's glass booth.

I watched them through the glass window. Cappy handed Sparrow his instrument and I saw the boys waiting for him to tune up. When Sparrow didn't make any motions, I looked at Hughie. He didn't look at me.

"Let's go," I said to the mixer. "It's a take."

The mixer looked at me like I was crazy. "Aren't they going to warm up?"

I didn't answer, so he switched into the engineer and told him it was a take. Then he switched into the studio and told the boys to watch the lights. The white light would go on first, then the red. The red meant play. That's so you can time the number and get your three minutes.

Hughie nudged Sparrow and pointed to the light bulbs on top of the window where I sat. Sparrow put his instrument in his mouth and stood up at the mike. They waited for the lights. The white light went on. That meant ten seconds more. It seemed like a year. Then the red light flashed on. Hughie beat off with a nod of his head and they swung into "Wing Ding."

It was no good. "Wing Ding" has a tricky opening where the sax and trumpet play against each other, accenting different beats. It's got to be right or it sounds like a clambake. Sparrow came in a beat late, fouling it up.

The mixer switched into the studio and told them to try it again. Then he switched over to the engineer's room, telling him to smear it and get ready for another take.

The white light went on again, then the red. This time Sparrow came in a beat too soon.

The third time he was late again.

We tried it twice more but it was no use. Sparrow wasn't focusing. The boys looked embarrassed. Cappy came over to the booth and yelled through the glass window. We would have heard him anyway, the mike was on.

"It's those lights," Cappy pleaded. "They make him tight. He'll play good when he's relaxed. It's those lights."

I pulled the switch and called in to Hughie that we'd try another tune without lights. "Whenever you're ready, tell me."

Cappy put Sparrow back on his chair and lit another cigarette for him. The others stood around for a while, not doing anything. Then Jimmy Brash started playing something on the piano, just anything. The bass and drums picked it up, and Hughie started noodling. After a minute, Sparrow joined in from his chair, nice and easy.

Then Sparrow began to blow hard and the music jumped. They jammed choruses for five minutes before Hughie waved it to a close. He looked at Sparrow.

"How about 'The Sparrow Jumps'?" he asked. He didn't wait for an answer. "No lights this time, Sparrow. You start and we'll come in. Let's make this something, Sparrow. Okay?"

Sparrow blinked and it shocked me. I hadn't realized his eyes had been staring wide open all the time. He stood up, pushing the chair away with the back of his legs, and he stepped up to the mike. His body was tense the way it used to get years ago when he was ready to play. Nobody moved. Then I poked the mixer and he called in, "Ready for a take," to the engineer.

"The Sparrow Jumps" is a showcase piece; no arrangements, nothing. Just Sparrow soloing, with Hughie and the piano playing figures behind him. Sparrow tore off the opening cadenza at a tempo that brought the boys' heads up. They were used to playing the "Jump" at a good clip, but this was, what I mean, fast.

I didn't know what might happen. I crossed my fingers. Then I uncrossed them. The band was playing like it never played before and Sparrow was going like a bat out of hell. But it was more than that, it had an excitement that gave me goose pimples; the kind of excitement that hallmarks all the really great records and still comes through long after the wax has worn thin and what you hear is only an inkling of what it was. I thought, man oh man. The hell with whether I get my four sides. This one's enough. This is for the books. When this hits the record stores—

The music seemed to be getting faster and I looked to see what the hell Joe Miggs was thinking about on his drums. The time is always the same in jazz. If it starts slow, it stays slow. If it starts fast, it stays that way, it doesn't get faster. Only this was. Then I saw Jimmy Brash's face had a funny look. His fingers were flying but that wasn't bothering him. Then my ears caught it. It was the chords. They weren't jibing with what Sparrow was playing. Sparrow was changing keys, sometimes in the middle of a phrase. The bass player had the same worried look. They had been playing together long enough to follow any of Sparrow's changes, but he was getting away from them. Only Hughie couldn't be shaken off. He managed to hang on, and how he did it I'll never know. I guess only a guy who felt about Sparrow the way Hughie did, could. It was the most frantic, wonderful, exciting music I had ever heard.

Sparrow's tic had returned but I didn't catch it right away; I'd watched too many jazz musicians swing their shoulders and shimmy their knees while they played. Even when I knew the tic was there, I couldn't always follow it. Sparrow's head would jerk to one side and notes from his horn would catch the swing back, making the jerk part of the musical phrase. The same thing happened when his body twitched or his legs kicked out. Music caught the spasm at the point it broke off, completing it. It was as if the jerks and twitches were musical sounds Sparrow could hear. That's what made it different from the night before. This had pattern, rhythm; it was so all of a piece you couldn't tell whether you were seeing it or hearing it.

Then you couldn't miss it. His whole body began to twitch crazily, and what he played was crazy in exactly the same way. It had to be, if his jerks and twitches were notes Sparrow could hear. And that's the way he was hearing it.

The other boys kept playing, but they were watching him the way I was. I thought I was losing my mind. I don't know how long I watched it before I got hold of myself. I pressed down on the switch, yelling, "Stop it! Stop it! Stop it! Stop it!"

The boys stopped, gradually, their music sort of trickling away, their eyes still on Sparrow. He was still going, his twisted music and his tortured body all mixed up in one long insane convulsion.

I stumbled out of the booth and grabbed him. I held him tight until the notes from his horn finally petered out. I could feel his tremors in my fingertips. I eased him onto a chair, still holding him.

The other boys were looking at me, like they were expecting me to do something. I didn't know what to do. I only knew we couldn't leave him in whatever crazy world he was inhabiting. We had to bring him back, give him something he could tie onto, something familiar, something rational. I looked for Cappy. He was standing right behind me, but I saw his face and I knew it was up to me.

"Jimmy! 'Sweet Sue'" I snapped my fingers at the piano player. "Play it, for Christ sakes!" Jimmy began playing, good and slow, and distinctly. I held Sparrow's shoulders so they couldn't move. I spoke right into his face. "I want you to play this for Cappy! You hear?" I thought, I've got to get through to him, I've got to. "Play this for Cappy. *For Cappy.*"

I felt Sparrow shiver. Then he looked up slowly. I saw meaning come into his empty eyes. His mouth opened, closed, then opened again, and he whispered, "Cappy?"

I was screaming inside but I kept my voice quiet. "Yes, Sparrow. Cappy." I bent closer. "He wants to hear you play. Will you play this for him, Sparrow? For Cappy?"

I could see him struggling with the idea, then he nodded solemnly, like a little boy saying, "Yes, sir." He wet his lips, fixed his mouth around his instrument, and his toe tapped out a careful 1-2-3-4. Then Sparrow played "Sweet Sue" for Cappy. You know how the neighbor's kid sounds when he's practicing his new lesson, squeaky and screechy but earnest—so damned earnest? That's how Sparrow sounded when he played "Sweet Sue." Exactly as it must have sounded that first time, thirteen years ago.

I left Cappy crying like a baby, and I headed for the nearest bar.

Yeah, Sparrow's last recording would sure make a collector's item. One buck, plus tax, is cheap enough for a record of a guy going nuts.

LEONARD FEATHER

Premier jazz critic and historian Leonard Feather has been contributing to the literature of jazz since the 1930s. His *New Encyclopedia of Jazz* (1960) and *The Encyclopedia of Jazz in the Sixties* (1966) are standard references. Other highly regarded discussions of jazz are his *Inside Bebop* (1949), *From Satchmo to Miles* (1972), and *The Pleasures of Jazz* (1976). Feather has covered all areas of jazz with unparalleled fairness. He continues to contribute jazz criticism and is presently on the staff of the Los Angeles *Times*.

Through the years, Feather has been involved with the Voice of America jazz programming, the BBC, the National Association of Jazz Educators, and the Newport Jazz Festival. He is also an arranger and composer ("I Remember Bird," "Whisper Not," and many other compositions; he also composed the music for the now-rare recording of Langston Hughes's "Weary Blues").

The piece that follows shows another side of Feather: his ability to see humor in an art form that many do not take seriously enough and that many take too seriously. His Professor S. Rosentwig McSiegel appeared with some regularity in the pages of *Down Beat* and *Metronome* in the forties; here he represents the would-be "artist" who takes unto himself the laurels of others.

I INVENTED JAZZ CONCERTS!

by Prof. S. Rosentwig McSiegel

It is evidently known, beyond contradiction, that New Orleans is the cradle of jazz, and I, myself, happened to be the creator in the year 1901.

Jelly Roll Morton

A figure so legendary that he has been called a near-myth, Professor S. Rosentwig McSiegel began his literary career in 1940 in the long-forgotten pages of Swing Magazine. *His byline made medium-rare appearances in* Metronome *in the 1940s, and from the early 1950s was seen with welcome irregularity in* Down Beat. *He is said to have signed a recent agreement with* The Musical Courier *under the terms of which he guarantees to stay out of that publication for five years, with options.*

Professor McSiegel can truly claim that his story is, in essence, the story of jazz itself. As one of the foremost sousaphone players of the 1890s, he was among the first (and despite his innate modesty he will admit it under duress) to do everything. Since he has remained permanently under duress throughout his career as a chronicler of musical Americana, it was not without a considerable lack of diffidence that we approached him to reedit, update and reissue some of his apocalyptic revelations.

(The jazz concert phenomenon was a landmark of the late 1940s and early 1950s. Symbolic of the era were the solos of exhibitionist tenor saxophonists such as Illinois Jacquet and Big Jay McNeely. Jacquet's work on How High the Moon *was a highlight of innumerable concerts presented by Norman Granz at Carnegie Hall, as were the percussion contests involving Buddy Rich and Gene Krupa. In the following memoir, Professor McSiegel relates how the jazz concert idea really began.)*

THERE are two schools of thought concerning the stage as a medium for the presentation of jazz. One school maintains that the concert hall has no place in jazz. The other, with equally valid and well-documented arguments, contends that jazz has no place in the concert hall.

Personally, I take a position squarely halfway between these two (like President Eisenhower, I have always cautioned against extremists on both sides). This places me about three blocks from Carnegie Hall and three blocks from Birdland.

The whole germ of the jazz concert concept germinated in prewar Germany. I was playing a four-hour location (with two two-hour options) at Max Ganzegasser's Konditorei und Brauhaus, just 19 miles from the heart of the Kurfuerstendamm on Route Sechsundsechzig.

The men in the band (I call them men because mankind is a generic term, though we had a girl on second trombone and I was never quite sure about the harpist) held the Konditorei in low esteem and nicknamed it "the Upholstered Sewer" (an irrational allegation, since the Konditorei actually was not upholstered). We used this spot as somewhere to sit down when times were slow, but this was one of our better years and we didn't spend more than about 47 weeks in the joint.

This being shortly after the Civil War, we called the group McSiegel's Illegal Eagles; appropriately, the whole thing began when we went on our first flying trip to Europe. We were operating under considerable transportation handicaps, since this was several decades before the official start of the aviation era; however, as some wag remarked at the time, "Nobody can stay high longer than those McSiegel cats." Our German tour was made under the auspices of the Jazz at the Philharmonic Foundation, on one of its Norman Grants.

Unfortunately communications were poor at the time and after losing contact with the foundation we found the bottom falling out of everything. After bumming around the Continent for a while, Pat O'Lipschitz having long since hocked his final fluegelhorn, we were soon flatter, if I may conjure up a colorful image momentarily, than Pat's high B Natural. So, necessity being the mother of all second rate gigs, that is how we wound up in Max's Konditorei.

Not having any horns, we worked there for a while as waiters, cooks and busboys. Pooling our tips, we then made a mass descent upon Fritz Mendelssohn's Schweinische Hockerei.

When we presented our claims it turned out there had been some sort of mixup in the tickets. Our own instruments had been turned loose; in their place we received an unfamiliar assortment of horns and boxes. On showing them later to a group of more worldly musicians, we were told they consisted of three violins, two violas, a cello, an oboe, a bassoon and other arty artifacts.

"A fine thing!" commented Pat. "Here we are, the most modern jazz outfit west of the Rhine, and we wind up with a trunkful of longhair instruments. What can we," he continued, "do?"

Suddenly signals flashed in my head. One said: "Left turn on red light permitted," another "Right lane must turn left," a third "Do not pass Go." I pieced the signals together and found a brainstorm. "Why not take these longhair instruments into a longhair joint?" I suggested.

This was a crucial moment in jazz history. Only one obstacle presented itself: within a fifty-mile radius in both directions (up and down) there was no concert hall. But good old American know-how knew how to get back of this setback. We all set to work with beaver board, scissors and glue, and within three weeks had expanded the Konditorei into a municipal auditorium the like of which was never seen before or since; it was also the best ventilated (this only lasted a few months, until the roof was added).

We sent out invitations to friends and relations, announcing our opening day. Friends and our relations sent congratulations, but by an odd coincidence had all been called away that evening to an urgent business meeting, a grandmother's fit of gout or a conflicting concert in Cairo. Nevertheless, the word soon spread that we were planning a presentation of "Progressive Music" (a happy phrase coined by Wingy FitzGoldberg, who had just joined us on phallic cymbals). This billing for our brand of music turned out to be singularly apt, since at every concert the group sounded progressively worse.

Nevertheless, we took in enough marks (and don't forget, these were not Confederate marks) to pay our way back home, whereupon we decided to return to a simple, unpretentious small-band jazz format for a while, to play in simple, unattended clubs. But fate decreed otherwise. Somebody up at the Gloe Jazzer Agency got two contracts mixed up—ours and the New York Philharmonic's—and we found ourselves booked into Carnegie Hall, while the New York Philharmonic played an off-night at the Village Gate.

When the truth leaked out, the Carnegie operators were nice about it. They made a few slight new stipulations in our contract (something about guaranteeing to reupholster all torn seats), but this didn't faze us, and as the great day drew near we worked up a promotional campaign second to nothing.

First we blanketed the city with disc jockey plugs. (The night we did this was so stormy that we wound up with a truckload of wet blankets.) Pat arranged to start his own show, 15 minutes every Tuesday from 5:30 to 5:45 a.m. over WWWW in Montauk, Long Island. I personally guested, all in a single day, on *Breakfast with Benny, Brunch in the Bronx, Luncheon at Luchow's, Tea in Teaneck, Dinner with Dinah,* and *Supper with Symphony Sid* (Sid at this time was barely out of his teens and, like radio itself, was in a primitive stage of development). After this round of shows, by midnight I realized that I would need a new tux for the concert, six inches larger around the waist.

Needless to say, with publicity of this magnitude we could hardly miss. Yet the Cassandras of the music business (including even Sam Cassandra, whom I considered a friend) predicted dire results. "Jazz in Carnegie Hall?" they said. "We predict dire results. The hall will be half empty." They had to eat their words, of course, when the curtain rose and revealed that Carnegie was half-*full.*

The sensation of the concert was a young tenor man named Jack Coates who had just breezed in from Chicago. We called him "Chicago" Coates. Since we couldn't expect to fill Carnegie with the type of cats who would patronize us at Kelly's Stable we told Chicago not to play for the cats, but to put on the dog a little. Accordingly, he played notes only a dog could hear, inventing a concerto for steam-whistle entitled *The Firefly and the Gnome,* which later, under the abbreviated title *Fly 'n' Gnome,* was swiped by another tenor player, who shall be gnomeless.

I need hardly tell you that Coates had the audience eating out of his hand (he was selling peanuts, popcorn and candy during intermission). After the break came a somewhat esoteric interlude, a set of quadrilles and French-Canadian folk songs by a pianist we had sneaked across the border, Peter Oscarson; but the limited appeal of Oscarson was happily canceled out as all through his set one of our drummers, the charming Jean Cooper, was fighting for possession of the percussion equipment while our other drum specialist, the belligerent Rudy Beach, was insisting that it was he who was supposed to accompany Oscarson. This custody fight ended with Cooper and Beach each holding one wire brush, one stick, half a bass drum and half a snare. I need hardly add that this was the origin of one of my most-imitated innovations, the drum battle.

Since our first night produced the first and biggest gross ever attracted up to that time by a jazz concert at Carnegie, we decided that a crowd of this kind was too good to lose. Accordingly, we initiated a course in audience manners. After three months of instruction in such niceties as how to spit at the stage, how to talk loud enough to cover up the music, how to tear chairs without leaving fingerprints, and even how to stub out one's cigarette on the neck of the guy in the row in front, our students emerged perfectly equipped to be a jazz audience.

After the success of Chicago Coates had gone to his pants and he had become too big for his britches, we replaced him with "Big Foot" McMealy, originator of the so-called "McMealy Mouthed" school of tenor sax. There may be indignant denials from others who claim the honor, but I can truthfully boast that Big Foot, while working with me, became the first man to take off his shirt during his tenor solo *without* removing his jacket. Later, as his musicianship improved, he learned to take off his socks without removing his shoes, and to take off his mouthpiece while removing his teeth.

Big Foot's big hit was *Hoo Hoo the Moo,* adapted by my old buddy Sing Bum Sing from a tender Chinese folk song. Later he scored an even bigger success with *Perdoodoo,* the first 69 choruses of which he played while standing on his head. When the novelty of

Joe's musical inversion wore off we introduced an extra gimmick: he remained upside down, but his head was on a small record player on the floor, stage left, that revolved at 33⅓, the spindle fitting neatly into the crater in Joe's cranium.

Later, when our audience tired of this, we had the cavity enlarged to accommodate a doughnut sized spindle so that he could revolve at 45 r.p.m. By this time *Perdoodoo* was old hat and he was featuring such novelties as *Voodoo, Hoodoo* and *Yoodoo,* all based on a revolutionary idea that I had dreamed up: the chord changes of *I Got Rhythm.*

I need hardly tell you how our pioneering efforts ended. Within a few years everybody and his brother (including his brother Irving) was making money out of jazz concerts, while here am I, patiently waiting, looking for a gig for New Year's Eve. It's like I always said: originality pays off, but usually to some other guy.

MONTY CULVER

Monty Culver teaches in the writing program at the University of Pittsburgh. He has had stories published in *Four Quarters, Esquire, Saturday Evening Post,* and other periodicals. Culver wrote "Black Water Blues" as a student in his senior year at the University of Pittsburgh; it was originally published in *Atlantic Monthly* and won an Atlantic Award contest in 1949. It was later published in *Prize Stories of 1951: The O. Henry Awards.*

In "Black Water Blues," Culver focuses on the problems associated with the integration of previously all-white bands in the late 1930s and early 1940s and reverses the situation by giving us a white piano player in an otherwise all-black band who must also contend with the jealousy of his bandleader because the leader's flirtatious vocalist wife is playing up to him. Things become more even more complicated when several white men show up at a black dance.

BLACK WATER BLUES

HIS name was Rohrs. They called him the Lion, of course; they could not be expected to do much else. The name was out there with the others, on the big poster by the box office: Bump Roxy and his Famous Blue Band. Featuring Adelia Roxy, Step-Up Tate, "The Lion" Rohrs.

He sat in front of the dimly lighted hall and chorded lightly with long, knobby fingers on eighty-eight keys. The hall was beginning to fill. Couples straggled through the door, circling timidly around the vastness of the bare dance floor, staring at the young white man who sat on the piano stool. A few were young; tall buck Negroes in high-hitched pants and bulging shoulder pads; girls in gay dresses, giggling up at their grinning escorts. But most of the early comers were the older folks, who came to listen only and not to dance. They came before eight o'clock to get the choice seats underneath or at the ends of the footlights. Often they sat without moving for the whole five or six hours, tapping their shoes along with the big bass, flashing grins that gleamed weirdly in their black and brown faces.

The Lion Rohrs sat alone on the big stage, playing gently, quietly, to the early comers. He had learned that it took the Negroes a little time to get used to the idea of a white man playing in a colored man's band. He usually managed to get up on the stage while the others were unpacking the paraphernalia.

He looked up from the keyboard and into the eyes of a staring young couple across the lights. He grinned at them—a savage grin, a grin of joy born of the chords that chortled under the long hand. And the couple grinned back.

He pressed the loud pedal and did a sudden trick in the bass, watching an older couple sitting near the stage. As they jerked their heads up, he winked at them, into their startled faces, and heard their laughter, clear and relieved.

Tonight a few white men were out there to listen. That would be a nuisance. Bump Roxy hated to play to white men. But there was no sense worrying about it now.

Bump strode from the wings, nodding curtly to Rohrs. Stagehands followed him on and began setting up the traps on the platform in center stage.

"Here sits the Lion, warmin' up the audience," said Sam Lester. The others straggled in: Hadley the number-one horn man, LeRoy Bunner with his guitar, Clarence Jackson, the incomparable Step-Up Tate. Tate and Willie Shepherd stopped beside the Lion. He cocked an eyebrow at them and rolled the treble playfully.

"M-mmm," Willie sighed. "That Lion, you just never know what he's gonna do next."

"Lion, he don't know what he'll do his damn self." Step-Up chuckled and touched Rohrs lightly on the arm before moving away.

It was funny, the Lion thought, funny how easy it was to get along—with everybody but Bump, at least. All you had to do was smile most of the time and play music all the time. The music was the thing, of course; it sometimes thawed even Bump Roxy's scowling distrust. He had sold himself to Bump by sitting on a piano stool and touching the keys as he talked.

"Man, it wouldn't work," Bump had said. "It wouldn't work at all. I ain't taking on no white man. . . . Man, play some more. Play that damn thing some more."

Rohrs looked up at Bump, sitting up on the high chair behind the traps, the sticks in his hands. Oh, Lord! thought the Lion, for Bump was glaring across the lights at the little knot of white men in the near corner of the floor. Most of them were all right—kids, college kids maybe, who paid their way into a colored dance hall to hear the music they wore out on records. But a couple of them, big smirking men in sport coats, looked mean. The lights distorted their faces, but Rohrs could see the coats and the sport shirts with the tight-buttoned, long-pointed collars—the uniform of the toughs.

It was bad enough when there were just decent white men out there for Bump to glare at. A couple of mean ones might spoil the whole show. They might make cracks at Adelia, and that would really be something. Bump usually tolerated a white audience, but it was different when his wife came into it. He had raised a lot of sand in St. Louis when a white man had just whistled at his wife. And he had snapped at the Lion for a week afterward.

The Lion watched Bump grip the sticks. Bump Roxy was a great drummer and a great musician. He told them when they overdid it or underdid it; he mapped the order of the solos. He held the band together.

It was worth holding together, the Blue Band. They were one of the few low-down outfits left in the country, perhaps the only great one. To Rohrs they were a way of life. He had left home to play piano against his family's wishes. When he joined the Blue Band, a year ago, he had written of it to his father. There had been no reply.

He watched Bump drop his eyes to the drums, touch the sticks to the snare. The muttering roll grew slowly, rising, fading, then higher still. Rohrs, although he had heard the theme a thousand times, held his breath until he heard the alto wail, the shuddering note of Step-Up's break.

It was a loafer for the Lion, nothing but rhythm and a couple of quick breaks. He glared from Adelia's empty chair to the wings, wondering where she was, what the hell was she doing. Bump always got sore when she was late getting on, and Bump would be sore tonight as it was, with those two nasty-looking white fellows out there. Besides, she had to do "It Ain't Necessarily So" in the first set.

Then, while he worried, Adelia came. She glided out of the shadows of the wings in her bold red gown, dazzling band and audience with her smile. The dance hall sighed.

And she spoiled Bump's big drum break. She walked on and grabbed at the eyes and minds of the audience just when they should have been fixed on the wooden blur over the tomtoms. The Lion thought, I wonder if she did that on purpose.

As she sat down, someone in the white corner whistled. Bump jerked his head up and stared dead-pan over the lights. Rohrs heard Clarence Jackson's fingers stumble on the big fiddle.

They played a couple of pops for the dancers, and it was time for "It Ain't Necessarily So"—the bawl of Hadley's muted trumpet, Lester's slim, clear notes on the clarinet. And Adelia with her head bent a little to one side, Adelia calling to the lovers in her husky voice. When she finished and the band started another dance tune, she came and stood by the piano. As the saxes played, she leaned down and gave the Lion that brilliant smile.

"How was I?" she asked. "Better than usual?"

"There's nothing better than your usual," he replied, and she laughed and touched his shoulder. Even as she did it, as the brown hand rested there for a second, he saw her eyes flicker over his head, up to Bump on the high chair, looking for a reaction.

Damn it, Rohrs thought, I wish she'd cut that out. He gets sore at me often enough as it is. Aloud he said, "Why don't you put that thing away?"

"What thing?"

"That needle you're stickin' in him all the time," Rohrs said. She giggled, and he grinned at her. He went on, "No kidding, you better lay off him. There's a couple guys out front he don't seem to like the looks of."

"He just frets about them on account of me," she said. "If he ain't got sense enough to know better, let him worry."

She walked away and sat down in her chair; it stood at the end nearest the white corner, the Lion noticed. He shook his head, worrying.

He had been warned about that situation when he first joined the band. On the night of his first trip with them, he had ridden alone in the coupe with Sam Lester. He had asked questions by the dozen, anything about the band that came into his head. And naturally he asked about Adelia.

"Bump and Adelia married?"

Lester looked sidewise at him. "Yeah, they're married. That's a good thing for you to remember."

"Jesus! Do I look like forgetting it?"

"Lots of white men do," Lester grinned. "Lots of white men come to hear the band try to make her forget it. Lots of colored men too. We had a horn player once, tried to fool around with Adelia. Bump damn near kill that man. Hard to tell what he'd do to a white man. Damn if I ever want to see."

Rohrs had remembered that. He was friendly when he talked to Adelia, but he only did it when he had to, and he was always careful to avoid giving any impression of talking confidentially to her. Even then, Bump sometimes resented it.

Clarence Jackson once told the Lion that Bump had a sister who ran off with a white man. That would explain a lot. If Adelia knew that, she ought to have more sense than to dog him all the time.

Another time Step-Up Tate had said, "That man crazy about that woman. He ought to tell her so more often." The Lion was still thinking about that as they wound up the fox-trot. Bump Roxy shoved a handkerchief across his scowling face. He sat staring at the drums.

Rohrs was suddenly concerned. Bump always wanted to play loud when he was mad; he liked to hit the drums as he would hit the heads of the whistling white men; he liked to hear the horns open up and blast, maybe blow the leering faces off the floor.

That was all right, but they weren't in shape to blast. It was nine o'clock and they had nothing but a few dance numbers behind them. They would blow their brains out on anything like "High Low Jack" or "Shattered Slumber." . . .

Bump lifted his head and called it. "'Shattered Slumber.'"

The Lion said, "Hold it now." He slid off the stool, grinning, seeing the faces of the band staring up at Bump. When he stood by the drums, he said, "Man, you know better than that."

"Goddamn it, Lion . . ."

"Man, it ain't ready, it ain't ripe," the Lion went on. "We ain't ready and the audience ain't ready. You got to build up to a thing like that. You know that." It was true; the boys would kill themselves and the audience wouldn't give a damn.

"That's right, Bump," Sam Lester said. "You know that."

"I figured it was Lion's time," Bump said lamely. There was a long piano solo in "Shattered Slumber." "I figured it was Lion's time for a big one. Everybody else had one."

"'Crosstown,' then," said the Lion. "'Crosstown,' if it's my time. It's too early for the other."

Bump's face was sullen. Rohrs grinned at him and said confidentially, "Man, we can't all warm up as quick as you do."

He walked away, chuckling at the relief in the faces of Hadley and Step-Up, winking at Willie Shepherd. He wondered how mad Bump would be.

They played the "Crosstown Blues." Nobody would ruin himself on melancholy "Crosstown," but it was something, just the same. The horns started: Hadley, Step-Up, and Lester, in turn, wailing the mournful one-bar phrase, then together. They held one, cut it off.

The Lion broke, with tingling chords. He talked to Step-Up for a while, piano and sax alternating and then mixing in dialogue. There were little appreciative chortles from the faces that crowded each other and peered over the edge of the stage.

The horns swept it up again and carried a chorus, fading, dying into silence. Bump took a rimshot. The Lion rolled one, high on the keyboard, held it, did tricks with it. He broke it, walked his hand down the board. With the left he reached deep down for the boogie bass.

They said that the Lion had it; everyone who knew, who had ever heard him, said so. He had the touch, they said: the touch of the great ones that had gone before; the touch that twitched the muscles and boiled the blood. There is music that can grow only of the love of music, and its greatest and supreme thrill is in its playing. This the Lion knew.

He gave it back to the horns, and the yells at the solo's end drowned even the trumpet. He wiped sweat from the corners of his eyes and swiveled on the stool to watch the boys finish it up. As his head swung, he saw the ugly smiles on the faces of the two white men who stared up at Adelia.

It was midnight, fourth intermission time. The Lion, alone, leaned against the wall outside the stage door and watched the rain drizzling into the alley. It pattered in the puddles and dribbled from the roof's edge over his head. He knew that the puddles were dirty, black with the soot and grime of the mill town, and he grinned, singing his song to himself.

"I wake up in the mornin
Black water drippin from the eaves
I wake up in the mornin
Black water drippin from the eaves
It's runnin in the gutters
Soaking down the grass and leaves"

Bump Roxy said, "Move youh goddamn chair!"

The Lion jerked away from the wall. The voice was so close that he was sure it was spoken to him, but when he looked around the edge of the door he saw Bump and Adelia in the tiny vestibule.

"What you talking about?" said Adelia.

"You hear what I say. I say move that goddamn chair!"

"Why should I?"

"You know why. You know I don't like them men lookin' at you," Bump said. His fingers clenched.

"What harm that do you?"

"That's all right. I don't like the way you look at them, either!"

"How can you tell how I look when you sittin' up there behind me?" Adelia was angry now, Rohrs realized. "You talk like you crazy. In the first place, I move my chair, those men move right with me if they want to. In the second place, I can't move my chair anywhere without sittin' right in front of somebody. You must be out youh head."

She stalked back toward the stage. Bump, following, yelled, "And stay away from that goddamn Lion too!"

Rohrs shook his head. He thought of Step-Up saying, "Crazy about her. Ought to tell her so more often." He shrugged and walked back to the stage, flopping his hands loosely from the wrists, wriggling and drooping the fingers, trying to relax them. The last set was coming up.

The last set was the big one. It was mostly their own stuff, and it was all what they loved to play. The fox-trotters had heard their last ballad, and they knew it; they moved from the edges of the hall and crowded toward the stage.

The last set had "Shattered Slumber"—the shouting horns, the thunder of the drums, the hilarious vocal dialogue between Jackson and Shepherd. The last set had "Basement Stuff," and "High Low Jack," and Delia singing the haunting "Ride On." The crowd gulped it and howled for more. They groped over the edge of the stage with their hands, trying to pull more music from the grinning, sweating players.

Bump did a specialty. Rohrs turned and watched admiringly. That man is great, he thought, great enough that this white-audience business is going to hurt him someday. . . .

It was time for Adelia's last song, "The Man I Love." Hadley stood up and scatted it, and the bawl of the trumpet filled the hall, made the Lion shiver. And Adelia sang.

The guitar carried the accompaniment alone, and the Lion had turned to look. Oh, Jesus! he thought. . . .

She was singing it at the toughs, at the two leering white men who stood directly below her. She swayed her body, and she smiled and flicked her eyes at the two men.

This is going to be bad, the Lion thought as he had to swing back to the piano. This is going to be hell.

And when, at the end of the number, he fearfully turned again, what he saw was so unexpected that he literally rubbed his eyes and looked again. The two men were gone.

He didn't have much time to wonder about it. Bump called them into a huddle. He was wet all over; he wiped his eyes and cheeks as he talked. "Now 'Black Water,'" he said hoarsely. "'Black Water,' and then we got to slack it off. We got to tone it down or they'll never let us out of here."

"Black Water Blues" was the Lion's favorite specialty. He had written it himself, and it was a little poetry, and a lot of sadness, and all the old-time blues scheme and rhythm. It was the only thing he ever sang. He was no Cab Calloway, but he carried a tune well enough, and he could put the mourning in his voice.

"Black water is somethin
Lord that I sure do hate
Black water is somethin
That I sure do hate
Fortune teller told me
Black water gonna be my fate"

He stroked the keyboard and listened to the soft play of the band. The thing was his and theirs at the same time. They had taken it in; they had played it happily, lovingly. And the audience strained forward over the lights.

"I wake up the morning
Black water in my bed
I go to eat my breakfast
Black water in my bread
Well I believe
Believe I better go my way

Black water gonna haunt me
Until my dying day

"I had myself a woman
She liked to dress in red
I found her in black water
Found her lying dead
Well I believe
Believe I'll go far far away
Black water gonna dog me
Until that judgment day"

The crowd yelled and clapped. The boys were grinning. Jackson leaned over and hit him on the back. Rohrs gave LeRoy the flat-hand sign of approval for the guitar solo. It was all good: the joy of playing it and the sadness of hearing it; the way the crowd clapped and the boys grinned.

A stagehand stood in the wings, trying to get Adelia's attention. She heard his whisper and walked to him. He said something, pointing offstage, and she nodded and went off, out of sight. The Lion watched her go out, wondering.

They played three more, quietly and sweetly, tapering-off tunes to calm the audience so that they could quit. Then it was closing time, theme time, and Adelia had not returned. Bump was scowling again. The Lion shook his head in disgust. She was going too far, not being on the stage at theme time.

The drums rolled again, and Step-Up broke. He had finished, and Hadley was standing, when the terrified face of the stagehand appeared over the piano. "Man! Man, there's trouble!" He was almost crying.

"What's wrong?"

"End it! End it, man, quick!"

"Start the curtain down," said the Lion, and called out, in the singsong, syncopated voice that they used for communicating during numbers, "Knock it off, right now! There's trouble brewin'!"

They stared at him, but Hadley cut the solo, and they blew the final blare as the curtain fell.

Then everything happened fast. The stagehand cried out, "I

didn't mean nothin'! I didn't know nothin' was wrong!" and the manager, calmer, said, "Mistuh Roxy, I'm afraid youh wife hurt bad."

They all charged off and were in time to see two stagehands carrying Adelia through the hall backstage—Adelia with her red gown torn mostly off, and what was left smeared and dripping with the dirty water from the alley; Adelia crying in little gasps of amazement and horror. . . .

Bump Roxy roared and the stagehand gibbered and the manager soothed; a doctor followed the bearers into a dressing room, and Bump plunged after them.

"Two white men," the guilty stagehand babbled to the frozen band. "Two white men told me ask Mrs. Roxy come out 'n' autograph . . ."

"You know you hadn't ought to do nothin' like that!"

"I didn't know nothin' was wrong! They gimme five dollars. Jesus, I didn't know nothin' was wrong!" The manager guided him gently away.

There was an old piano in the end of the tiny hallway, near the dressing-room door. The Lion sat heavily on the stool. A stack of folding chairs was heaped against the wall; the band opened them and sat down, lined along the hall, waiting for the door to open.

Rohrs was staring at the keyboard when someone touched his arm. LeRoy Bunner's face was grave. "You better get out of here, man."

The Lion shook his head.

"Lion, you crazy. Don't you know what them men done to Adelia? It ain't gonna be safe out here for no white man."

"You might be right," said the Lion. He touched the keys softly, it a B-flat chord.

"I tell you that man like to kill somebody," LeRoy said. He looked around for support.

"Let him be," Step-Up said. "The Lion, maybe he know what he's doin'."

"Bump gonna go for the first white man he sees!"

"That's all right," the Lion said. "This way he won't have to go out in the street and chase one." Old Step-Up, he thought, he sees it, he sees it like I do. He started to play quietly. He took a simple four-note walking bass figure and worked over it gently, playing sadness. LeRoy looked around, licked his lips, and then sat down.

The Lion played, waiting.

It was for Bump, so that he wouldn't go raging the streets and get arrested. But it was for more than that; Rohrs knew it and Step-Up had seen it. It was for the great Bump Roxy, who might never be able to face another white audience if this wasn't handled right. It was for the music: for "Crosstown" and "Shattered Slumber," and the "Black Water Blues" that might never be played again; for the grins and flat-hand signs when they finished one. It was for Adelia, and for himself. It was for Bump Roxy and his Blue Band.

He did not look up when the door opened and the footsteps came out slowly and then stopped. He heard Bump move toward him, felt him standing directly behind. He made himself stay loose when the huge hand touched his shoulders and the back of his neck.

The hand did not move; it lay there gently. He did not let himself sigh; he sat and played the blues. He did not look up even when the hand began to tremble and he heard the ugly, harsh sobs.

The chords rippled the stillness of the room.

JOHN CLELLON HOLMES

John Clellon Holmes is often referred to as the chronicler of the Beat Generation—an active participant with Kerouac, Allen Ginsberg, William Burroughs *et al.*, but an objective, straightforward writer who kept journals, which he used to produce his strongly autobiographical novel *Go* (1952) and the essays that eventually were gathered together into the volume *Nothing More to Declare* (1967).

His novel *The Horn* (1958) is a jazz classic, but obscure enough to be a rare book. It is a novel that was inspired by many jazz legends—Billie Holiday, Lester Young, and Charlie Parker, among others. Although Holmes's depiction of the complexities of bop jazz may not always be absolutely authentic, the story has an exciting jazz setting and credible pictures of the life of a bop musician in the late 1940s and early 1950s. Of *The Horn,* Holmes said, "I wanted to write a book about the artist as American, or the American as artist, and rather than write about writers . . . I picked out to me the most indigenous American artist, which is the jazz musician."

A gracious and generally unappreciated writer, Holmes told Arthur and Kit Knight in 1980, "I'm suspicious of [fame]—that is, I'm suspicious of taking it seriously; all its gauds are ephemeral, its rewards can't buy you anything of great importance, and I've managed to get most everything I want, and to have most of the work is all. The rest is only ego-massage. To tell the truth, neither to explain or apologize, is a decent and demanding enough endeavor to occupy a serious and honest man. Notoriety, when it comes, is mostly a distraction." Holmes died in March, 1988, at age 62, and as might be expected, the nightly news made no note of his passing.

The following selection is an excerpt from *The Horn* that originally appeared in *Discovery 2* in 1953, five years before the publication of the complete novel.

THE HORN

CONSIDER that it was four o'clock of a Monday afternoon, and under the dishwater-gray shade (just the sort of shade one sees mostly pulled down over the windows of cheap hotels fronting the sooty elevateds of American cities where the baffled and the derelict loiter and shift their feet), under this one shade, in the window of a building off 53rd Street on Eighth Avenue in New York, the wizen September sun stretched its old finger to touch the dark, flutterless lids of Walden Blue, causing him to stir among sheets a week of dawntime lying-down and twilight getting-up had rumpled.

Walden Blue always came awake like a child, without struggle or grimace, relinquishing sleep in accordance with the truce he had long ago worked out with it. He came awake with a sparrow stare, fast dissolving as the world was rediscovered around him, unchanged for his absence. He lay without moving, as a man used to waking beside the bodies of women will most often move either toward them or away, depending on his dream; lay, letting his water-cracked ceiling remind him (as it always did) of the gulleys of shack-roads back home where he would muddy his bare black feet when a child, and where, one shimmering-cicada noon, he had stood and watched a great, lumbering bullock careen toward him, and become a Cadillac-ful of wild zoot-suited city boys, pomaded, goateed, upending labelless pints, singing and shouting crazily at everything: "Dig the pick'ninny! Dig the cotton fiel'! Dig the life here!"; to bump past him, gape-faced there in the ruts, splashing mud over his go-to-meeting britches, and plunging on around the bend of the scrub-pines where he once mused over an ant-hill in the misty Arkansas dawns—for all like some gaudy, led-astray caravan of gypsies, creating a wake of rumor and head-shaking through the countryside.

Walden Blue slid long legs off the bed, and for a moment of waking reflection—that first moment which in its limpid, almost idiotic clarity is nearly the closest human beings come to glimpsing the dimensions of their consciousness—he considered the polished keys, and the catsup-colored neck of the tenor saxophone which, two years before, had cost him $150 on Sixth Avenue, becoming his after an hour of careful scales and haggling, and the gradual ease which comes to a man's fingers when they lose their natural suspicion of an instrument or a machine which is not their own, but must be made to respond like some sinewy, indifferent horse, not reluctant to being owned but simply beautiful in its blooded ignorance of ownership. For on this saxophone Walden Blue made music as others might have made love a kind of fugue on any bed; Walden made music as a business, innocent (because love of it was what kept him alive), just what others might mean by "their business," implying as that did some sacrifice of most that was skilled and all that was fine in them. He considered this saxophone, in this first moment of waking, without pleasure or distaste; noting it with the moody, half-fond stare of a man at the tool he has spent much time, sweat and worry to master, but only so that he can use it.

Looking at it, he knew it also to be an emblem of some inner life of his own, something with which he could stand upright, at the flux and tempo of his powers—as others consider a physical feat an indication of manhood, and, still others, a wound; to Walden the saxophone was, at once, his key to the world in which (always like some mild, slouchy stranger) he found himself; and also the way by which that world was rendered impotent to brand him either failure or madman or Negro or saint. But then sometimes, on the smoky stand between solos, he hung it from his swinging shoulder like one bright, golden wing, and waited for his time.

"Hey, there," he said to himself reproachfully, dandling his feet in an imaginary brook, for it was nearing four-fifteen, which meant the afternoon was slipping by; and so he got up, stretching himself with the voluptuous grace some musicians give to any movement, and went about coffee-making. The electric plate was dead in one coil; the pot itself rusty from weeks of four o'clock makings; and, without troubling his head about it, he used yesterday's soggy grounds. Coffee had no taste or savor to him at that hour; it was merely hot and black. He started his day with it, as though it poured something of its nature into him, by the swirling night-hours, amid smoke and roar, he would be like it; hotter and blacker, if anything. The second scalded cup was as necessary to the beginning of this day as the second shot of bourbon, or the second stick of tea was to its blissful morning end someplace uptown where, for sociability and personal kicks, he would blow one final chorus for himself, with a rhythm section of hardy, sweating souls collected from a scattering of groups around town, and then, packing up, go home empty of it all again. He drank his coffee back on the bed, lean shanks settled down on it, naked as a child; and each gulp re-established him in the world.

His mind was clear; in these first moments, scarcely a man's mind at all, for he had no thoughts, just as he rarely dreamed. One afternoon in L.A.—back four years ago when bop was an odd new sound, and a name for the jazz many of them had been blindly shaping, and something else as well (a miraculous, fecund word because no one then really understood its meaning, only somehow knew)—he sat on a similar bed over his first cup, just like now, and out of the sweet emptiness of his morning-head one thought had come, like cigarette smoke drifting across a shaft of pale sunlight, leaving no visible trace: that he was a saxophone, as bright and shiny and potential as that, and still as well. The night and his life would play upon him. Some afternoons since then, he recalled his thought, and often giggled secretly at its foolish accuracy. But never troubled his head.

Only this afternoon something else was there. That morning—four or five at least, up at Blanton's on 125th Street where, in the back, and after hours, they served coffee and the musicians gathered to listen or play or talk that shop-talk without which any profession in America would be thwarting to Americans—Edgar Pool had been inveigled to sit in with the house-group (nothing more than rhythm upon which visitors could build their fancies), and, as everyone turned to him in the drab, low-ceilinged room, giving him that respectful attention due an aging, original man whom all have idolized in the hot enthusiasm of youth, something had happened. And now Walden remembered.

There are men who stir the imagination deeply and uncomfortably; around whom swirl unplaceable discontents; men self-damned to difference; and Edgar Pool was one of these. Once an obscure tenor in a brace of road-bands, now only memories to those who had heard their crude, uptempo riffs, and managed neither to remember nor forget (their only testament the fading labels of a few records, and these mostly lost, some legendized already, one or two still to be run across in the bins of second-hand jazz record stores along Sixth Avenue), Edgar Pool emerged from an undistinguished and uncertain musical environment by word-of-mouth. He went his own way, and from the beginning (whenever it had been, and something in his face belied the murky facts) he was unaccountable. Middling tall, sometimes even lanky then, the thin mustache of the city Negro accentuating the droop of a mouth at once determined and mournful, he managed to cut an insolently jaunty figure, leaning towards prominent stripes, knit ties, soft shirts and suede shoes. He pushed his horn before him, and, listening to those few records years later when bop was gathering in everyone but had yet to be blown, Walden, striving more with his fingers than his head at that time, first heard the murmur of the sounds they were all attempting. Edgar had been as stubbornly out of place in that era, when everyone tried to ride the drums instead of elude them, as he was stubbornly unchanged when bop became an architecture on the foundation he had laid.

He hung on through fashions, he played his way when no one cared, and made his money as he could, and never argued. One night in 1940, in a railroad bar in Cincinnati, where the gangmen came to drink their pay with their dusky, wordless girls (something in them aching only for dance), he sat under his large-brimmed hat and blew forty choruses of "I Got Rhythm," without pause, or haste, or repetition; staring at a dead wall; then lit up a stick of tea with the piano man, smiled sullenly, packed his horn and caught a train for Chicago and a job in a burlesque pit. Such things are bound to get around, and when Walden met him a year later (on another night at Blanton's) the younger tenors had started to dub him "The Horn," though never (at that time) to his face.

Edgar Pool blew methodically, eyes beady and open, and he held his tenor saxophone almost horizontally extended from his mouth. This unusual posture gave it the look of some metallic albatross, caught insecurely in his two hands, struggling to resume flight. In those early days, he never brought it down to earth, but followed after its isolated passage over all manner of American cities, snaring it nightly, fastening his drooping, stony lips to its cruel beak and tapping the song. It had a singularly human sound—deep, throaty, often brutal with a power skill could not cage, an almost lazy twirl on the phrase-ends: strange, deformed melody. When he swung with moody nonchalance, shuffling his feet instead of beating, even playing down to the crowd with scornful eyes averted, they would hear a wild goose honk beneath his tone—the noise, somehow, of the human body; superbly, naturally vulgar; right for the tempo. And then out of the smearing notes, a sudden shy trill would slip, infinitely wistful and tentative.

But time and much music and going alone through the American night had weakened the bird. Over the years, during which he disappeared and then turned up, blowing here and there; during which, too late, a new and restless generation of young tenors (up from the shoeless deltas and shacklands like Walden, or clawed out of the tangled Harlems and the back-alley gangs) discovered in his music something apt and unnameable—not *the* sound, but some arrow toward it, some touchstone—over the years which saw him age a little and go to fat, which found him more uncommunicative and unjudging of that steady parade of eager pianists and drummers which filed past behind him, the horn came down. Somehow it did not suggest weariness or compromise; it was more the failure of interest, and that strain of isolated originality which had made him raise it in the beginning out of the sax sections of those road-bands of the past, and step solidly forward, and turn his eyes up into the lights. The tilt of his head, first begun so he could grasp the almost vertical slant of the mouthpiece, remained, the mouthpiece now twisted out of kilter to allow it; and this tilt seemed childishly fey and in strange contrast to his unhurried intent to transform every sugary melody he played, and find somewhere within it the thin sweet song he had first managed to extract, like precious metal from a heap of slag.

Walden felt Edgar Pool threaded through his life like a fine black strand of fate, and something always happened. When he first heard him in the flesh—sometime back in 1942, in the dead-center of war, after learning those few records by heart, after finding his own beginnings in "Brahmin" Lightcap's big band that came in with a smashing engagement in Boston, swamped in publicity and champagne parties (because Lightcap was, after all, the Dean of Jazz, the scallawag from New Orleans cat-houses eventually medaled by the governments of France and Belgium for "goodwill spread on a jazz trumpet"), and which went out six months later, a financial bubble, when the trumpet section grumpily enlisted in the Navy and most of the saxes were arrested on narcotics charges; after this, after waiting to hear Edgar, missing him in L.A. by a lost bus connection, getting hung-up in Chicago right after Edgar took up with Geordie Dickson, Walden had come into Blanton's one night, and heard a sound, and there was Edgar, horn at a forty-five-degree angle to his frame, playing behind Geordie as she sang "What Is This Thing Called Love," with a tremble in her voice then that made you wonder. Something settled in Walden that night, and he decided to get out of the big bands, the bus schedules, the dancehalls, the stifling arrangements; off the roads for a while; to stick around New York, which was his adopted pond after all; to give himself his head. It wasn't Edgar actually—just that aura of willful discontent around him; wanting a place, but not *any* place.

Since then Walden dug Edgar whenever he was around, puzzled and disturbed, but not until this morning in Blanton's had anything come out clear. Edgar had played with weary and indifferent excellence, noting neither Cleo, who played piano with Walden at The Go Hole every night but never got enough and, like so many young musicians (he was only 17) seemed to have no substantial, homely life but jazz, no other hours but night, and so hung around Blanton's till dawn with untiring smiles of expectation, nor the others who wandered in and out, listening to every other bar, gossiping, and showing off their latest women. Edgar stood before them, down among the tables for there was no proper stand, sax resting on one thigh, and Walden studied him for an instant with that emotion of startling objectivity that only comes when a man least expects or desires it. And for that moment he forgot his own placid joy at the night narrowing down to an end and to this hour among his own sort, at the sight of someone so inexplicably isolated from it all, though generally accepted as one pivot on which it turned.

Edgar fingered lazily, ignoring Cleo's solid, respectful chords, one shoulder swinging back and forth slightly, his chin pulled in. His hair was long over his large collar, he padded up and down on exaggerated crepe soles, between solos he chewed an enormous wad of gum soaked in benzedrine. They said he had "gone queer," but there was something soft and sexless about him nonetheless. Then he smeared a few notes over a pretty idea—a crooked smile glimmering behind the mouthpiece, all turned in upon himself, all dark; and Walden alone seemed to catch the sinister strain of self-ridicule behind the phrase, behind the sloppy, affected suit, the fairy hip-swinging; and at that moment the presence of a secret in Edgar reached him like a light.

For if jazz was a kind of growing Old Testament of the Negro race—and of all lost tribes in America, too—a testament being written night after night by unknown, vagrant poets on the spot (and so Walden, reared on a strange Biblical confusion, often thought of it), then Edgar had once been a sort of Genesis, as inevitable and irreducible as the beginnings of things; but now, mincing, chewing, flabby, he sounded the bittersweet note of Ecclesiastes, ironical in his confoundment. Then it happened.

Geordie Dickson flounced in with her cocker spaniel under one arm, and two dark, smirking escorts guiding her, half-tipsy, between them. And the sweaty faces around the room pivoted, and someone hoarsely whispered. For this was the first time in the two years since something unknown and awful had separated them that they had been in the same room. Their lives were fatefully, finally intertwined, for Edgar had found her singing in a back-road gin-mill in Tennessee (no more than sixteen then) and, probably with only a clipped word of command, had taken her away, and brought her north: a sturdy, frightened, bitter girl, one quarter white, raped at fourteen on a country lane by two drunken liquor salesmen, thrown into reform school where she was chained to her iron cot when her child was born out of her dead, finally released to find her family vanished, thrown back for pocket-picking in colored churches, released again in the custody of a probation officer who tried to get her into a whorehouse, and trying to keep off the streets with her voice when Edgar saw her first. He taught her some sense of jazz, got her the initial jobs, backed her up on the records that followed, and took money from her, when, all overnight, she became a sensation to that dedicated breed of lonely fanatic which jazz creates. Walden, among the others, had often stood in the vest-pocket clubs on 52nd Street during 1943 as the lights faded away and one spot picked her out—mahogany hair oil-bright, the large gardenia over one ear still wet from the florist's, candle-soft eyes, skin the sheen of waxy, smooth wood—and heard the opening chords, on grave piano, of "I Must Have That Man"; and also heard, with the others, the slur, the sugar, the pulse in the voice and known, without deciding or judging, that it was right; and been dazzled too.

People turned wherever she went (although not anticipating a scene as they did at Blanton's that morning), because she had the large, separated breasts of a woman who has spent hours leaning over her knees, working or praying; breasts that would be tipped with wide, copper-colored nipples; breasts that would not be moored; made for the mouths of children, not of men. In all her finery (off-the-shoulders gown, single strand of small pearls, the eternally just-budded gardenia), her flesh and the heavy-boned grace of her body alone had any palpable reality. There was a breath-catching mobility to her—nothing fragile or well-bred—but that extraordinary power of physicality which is occasionally poured into a body. The deep presence of fecundity was about her like an aroma, something mindless and alive; that touch of moist heaviness (suggestive of savagery, even when swathed in lace) which is darkly, enigmatically female. She was a woman who looked most graceful when her legs were slightly parted, who appeared to move blindly, obediently, from some source of voluptuous energy in her pelvis; whose thighs shivered in brute, incomplete expression of the pure urge inside her.

Edgar did not indicate by even the quaver of a note that the excitement and apprehension in the rest of the room had reached him. He played on, as if in another dimension of time, when she took a seat not ten feet from him, the spanial squatting in her lap, wet nose over the edge of the table, eyes large. Neither did *she* look, but went about settling herself, nodding to acquaintances, chatting with her companions. She was arrogantly drunk, opulently sensual as only a woman, in the candor of dissipation, can be; and beside her Edgar looked pale, delicate, even curiously effeminate. She had always been strangely respectful of him, even when swarms of white men had fidgeted at her elbow, pleading to fasten her bracelets, even when easy money had turned her life hectic and privileged; she had looked at him, even then, with a tawny, resentful respect, like a commoner with a sickly prince. She had sensed that he could *see,* and it always, just for an instant, blurred her picture of herself.

Now she was drinking heavily out of a silver-headed, leather-jacketed pocket flask; her eyes grown flashing and wet. The spaniel lay on her thighs, subdued, with the natural humility dogs often have before the antics of humans, and she poked and patted and cooed to him loudly, as if trying to goad him into a bewildered bark.

Edgar finished his chorus and gave it to Cleo on the piano, who never soloed; for whom the dreadful spaces of thirty-four bars held no terrors, but small interest either; and then he slowly turned his back on her, a dreamy, somehow witless grin weakening his face as he muttered nonsense with the drummer.

His absolute lack of recognition in these first moments was the surest sign to Geordie that he was electrically aware of her movements there in the room, but something in him was indestructible, some merciless pride with which he chose to victimize himself. Only he could smash or break it. Some said, after all, that he had gotten her on the morphine habit she threw only when, at the height of her glittering success, she had been arrested for "possession & addiction"; other rumors went that love between them had been a stunted, hot-house pantomime, always lurching on the shadowy edges of sensations—as queer and deformed as Edgar himself; and certainly he had liberated a gnaw in her that had, ever since, run wild, even amuck, enslaving her to a vision of life he only entertained for himself, an ironical indulgence of whim he had only endorsed, with passion, for a brief season, and then unaccountably drifted away, leaving her stranded in it, gnashing her teeth.

She began to chatter with vicious affectation when he took his reed into his mouth like a thumb and blew a windy yawp—trapped into the chatter as in everything else, because his placid, punishing indifference (not only to her but to all the real world) was yet another symbol of some incalculable superiority. Her mouth, as it snarled and quivered, was (to all the stunned young men like Walden, who, years before, had thirsted after her like an ideal), to them, indescribably, cruelly sensual, as though she were about to faint from some morbid and exhilarating thought. But only her mouth had learned the tricks of contempt, brittleness, and sophistication. Her eyes glowed steadily with something else, and as Walden looked at her, in these first moments that seemed supercharged with tension and thus unendurably long, he saw (as this morning he seemed fated to see everything that had been under his nose for years) the nature of that something else; saw that her long, shapely neck had started to wrinkle; saw she had expensive powder in her armpits where there should have been soft, dark hair; saw some sweet rot in her; and knew there was a flaw now where there had been none before, a flaw developed by a life that had carved a black cross on her forehead; and then sensed the woman in her flesh again, now gone slightly stale, and remembered that some said even the dog had licked it.

Edgar chose this moment to blow sweet, as a final passionless mockery of the auspiciousness or sentiment others might be feeling in that situation. His sound was disarmingly feeble, in earnest; but meant to prove, by some inmost private irony, that he was, if so he chose, a timeless man. The limpid pathos of his song was somehow a denial of the past, a denial of any power over him but his peculiar self-abusive ability, which he had mastered so totally as to be able to ignore it for years if that was his whim. And at that moment, just as Geordie's eyes drifted across him to something else, the saxophone, hanging limp against one thigh, stirred and came up, and there was (for just that second) a corresponding stir of vigor in his sound; and then he fell back into the vapid, thin tone, his horn descending, as if to say (and Walden heard) that he would be a slave to nothing, not even the genius inside him. His obsession (and all men are dominated by something) was his last secret, the note he carefully never blew.

To Walden (for that moment paralyzed, turned outward, willless), Edgar seemed a mask over a mask; all encrusted in an armored soul. Some said, he knew, that Geordie had once stripped the masks away, one by one, with no intent but desire, and had a hint of the inside, and been driven wanton out of helplessness. The secret must have been (as it most always is) that his need was formless, general; a need which persists only because no satisfaction could ever be fashioned for it; an inconceivable thing in a woman, a thing forever mysterious and infuriating to her; but something peculiarly male, the final emblem of imperfection, impotence; but with terrifying power to wound or create, the Jeremiah-like power of a fury at powerlessness.

So they were alone in all that room, absolutely locked together and alone, and yet steadfastly refusing to notice each other, and Walden knew that Edgar would blow all night if necessary, burst a lung, dredge himself to obliterate her—and not because he cared, not for her; but because of himself. Already somebody was thinking about how he could possibly describe it to the "cats in his group" the next night. "Man, it was positively the gonest!" would prove far too thin, and by the time word of it reached L.A., K.C., Chicago, it would be a kind of underground history, one of those nights that, passed from mouth to mouth, year upon year, become, in the alchemy of gossip, fabulous and Homeric.

Cleo, alone of everyone, refused to be drawn into the drama of their wills, but looked from Edgar to Geordie, not casually or with suspense as the others were, but with an expression of trembling, clear-eyed sorrow, his little hands automatically making the sad chords on which Edgar was shaping his humiliation of sadness, his lips saying softly over and over again: "Oh, man, what for. Oh, man, why. Oh, man, no!" Edgar only wiped a phrase across the words and wiggled his hips.

Walden, too, was struck dumb, all eyes, somehow horrified, for now Geordie's mouth was capped with straining avidity around the neck of the flask, the spaniel staring up at her with baffled, dark eyes. Even Edgar watched this over his horn with a half-hidden, secretive smirk; and Walden, at that instant, suddenly thought of him as a Black Angel—something out of the scared, rainy nights of his childhood when his mother had tried to remember the Bible her mother had once, long ago in a bayou town, read to her; and gotten it all mixed and filled it in herself in a droning, righteous whisper—till Satan carried a razor and Babylon was a place in midnight Georgia, and the fallen angels were black bucks run wild through the country like the city-boys in the Cadillac, and even Jehovah wore a Kluxer's sheet, and everyone was forever lost. Edgar was a Black Angel, and half the tug Walden had always heard in his music was right here, clear and unavoidable—the dark-half, the damned-half, the sweet-demon-half. Edgar was a Black Angel all right, and Walden suddenly knew; for like many people brought up on the Bible like a severe laxative, he often thought, without whimsy, about angels and suchlike. Not that he believed, that wasn't necessary; but sometimes when he played and stared up into a rose spotlight so as to concentrate, he thought about some possible heaven, some decent kind of life—and groped blindly like any man.

If he had better understood himself and the inconsolable ambiguity of men's aspirations, the unforgiveable thing he did then might not have stunned him so. But he did not understand, and knew little of the concepts upon which men struggle to define their existence (although down in his heart waited a single note of music that he felt would shatter all discord into harmony), and so when he found himself suddenly beside Edgar, his horn clipped to its swing around his neck, and heard himself break into the pedestrian chorus of "Out of Nowhere" that Edgar was blowing, he was filled with the same sense of terror that had swept over him the first time, ten years ago, that he stood up before live, ominous drums and cut out a piece for himself. Only it was worse, because there was a complex protocol to "after-hours"; unwritten, inarticulate, but accepted by even the most beardless tyro with the taped-up, secondhand horn for which he did not even own a case—certain, in his feverish preoccupation with himself, that he had found *the* idea. There was a protocol and it did not countenance an uninvited intrusion from the watchers, no matter who. Even a man suddenly possessed by an unendurable impulse to blow was expected to wait his time and keep his head. On top of that, Walden (thought of among musicians as a "good, cool tenor," who was reliable, with sweet ideas, and a feel for riffs, but one who had not yet found his way) was presuming upon Edgar Pool, revered from a distance by everyone who came later and blew more; whose eccentricities were accorded the tolerance due to anyone embittered by neglect; and whose lonely eminence as "The Horn," was beyond challenge, a matter of sentimental history. What Walden did, then, was unheard-of.

But he started the next twelve bars nevertheless, keeping a simple tasty line. Edgar, reed still between loose lips, gave him a startled, then slyly amused glance, telling Walden, all in a flash, that for the audacity and the stupidity of the move he would do him the honor of "cutting" him to pieces, bar to bar, horn to horn. But the affront had shocked everyone else; the room was frozen, speechless; and Walden knew he was, in effect, saying to them: "I secede from the protocol, the law," and further (and this he did not know, though it was the truth of what he felt): "What I know must be done cannot be done within it." But thereby he was placing himself outside their mercy and their judgment, in a no-man's-land where he must go alone. Only Geordie was not transfixed; a slow, quivering smile had curled her lips, and her fingers had left the spaniel's ears.

Edgar leaped back easily, satirizing Walden's last idea, playing it three different ways, getting a laugh, horn hung casually out of one side of his mouth. The drums slammed in perfectly on top of Cleo's remonstrative chord, and Walden started to swing one shoulder, playing sweet when it was his turn, knowing they would take only six bar breaks from then on, to tighten the time, and finally only four, where a man had to make himself clear and be concise; the last gauntlet where a misfingered note could be the end.

Edgar slouched there beside him, as if playing with one hand, yawping, honking, aping him; and only his beady eyes were alive, and they were sharp, black points of irony and rage; not, somehow, at the ill-mannered challenge, but at something else, a memory that made him old in the recalling. And Walden looked into those eyes, and blew a moving phrase that once another Edgar might have blown, and was, at last, victim of the naïve core of his heart, the unthoughtout belief that it mustn't be Edgar's way. He looked at Edgar, loving him even in all his savage, smearing mockery, battling not him but the dark side of that black-angel soul; bringing light.

It got hotter, tighter, and Cleo, staring at Walden as at a barefoot man exulting on a street corner, laid down solid, uncritical chords for both of them, that it might be fair and just—all the time his innocent, dewy eyes on the side of sweetness, who ever would speak up for it.

Walden looked at Edgar, sweating now and gloomily intent, and blew four bars of ringing melody, so compelling that Edgar stumbled taking off, unable to remember himself (for "cutting" was, after all, only the Indian-wrestling of lost boyhood summers, and the trick was getting your man off balance). And then Walden came back clear, and suddenly knew (so beyond doubt he almost faltered) that his was the warmer tone, that this was what he had always *meant;* and so experienced a moment of incredible, hairbreadth joy.

The silence in the room came apart, because music was fair contest. The crowd unwillingly shifted the center of their prejudices, acknowledging that "something was happening," and between phrases Walden could hear Geordie crying sharply: "Blow! Blow!" but, looking to find her rocking back and forth, eyes narrowed now to bright wicks, could not tell at whom she cried, and did not, he realized, consider himself her champion; but was only bringing light.

Edgar was shuffling forward and blew four bars of a demented cackle, and, for an instant, they were almost shoulder to shoulder, horn to horn in the terrible equality of art, pouring into each wild break (it felt) the substance of their separated lives—crazy, profound Americans, both! For America, as only they knew it who had wandered like furtive Minnesingers across its billboard wastes to the screaming distances, turned half a man sour, hard-bitten, barren, but awakened a grieving hunger in his heart thereby.

In Edgar's furious, scornful bleat sounded the moronic horn of every merciless Cadillac shrieking down the highway with a wet-mouthed, giggling boy at the wheel, turning the American prairie into a graveyard of rusting chrome junk; the idiot-snarl that filled the jails and madhouses and legislatures; some final dead-wall impact. And in Walden, no sky-assaulter but open-eyed, there was the equally crazy naïveté that can create a new staggering notion of human life and drive some faulty man before it through the cities, to plant an evangelist on every atheist Times Square, a visionary in any godless road-house; the impulse that makes cranks and poets and bargain-drivers; that put up a town at the end of every unlikely road, and then sent someone with foolish curiosity to see what was there. America had laid its hand on both of them.

This time Walden had the last chorus to himself, having earned it. By that same unspoken protocol, it was understood by everyone that he had "cut," and so Edgar stepped back—for though the victor might venture outside the law, the victim, having nothing left, must abide by it. And Edgar accepted. The crowd was on its feet when the drums signified by a final, ecstatic slam that it was over, Geordie standing too, but in all the shouting and heated laughter there, she alone was motionless, grave.

Walden's moment of joy had gone off somewhere, and he felt a chill of apprehension and so swung on Edgar, one hand extended vaguely as if to right himself. But Edgar, unsnapping his horn, half-turned from the room, only glanced at him once—a withering, haunted look, a look he had probably never shown anyone before; and leveled now at Walden, without malice, only as a sort of grisly tribute to his prowess and his belief. It was to be Walden's spoils: that bewildered stare about the eyes of another man, whose effort, even to punish himself out of pride, had been thwarted. It was a look which had a future, from which heavy, fatal consequences must proceed; and with it went a weak, lemonade grin, meant only to cover the wince of nausea; for Walden knew then that Edgar had horrified himself, like a drunk who sees, in the single, focused moment of hangover, the twitching, blotchy ruin of his own face, the shadow across his eyes—knowing all along that the horror will not fight down the thirst, knowing then that he is unalterably damned.

At that, Edgar turned, leaving his horn abandoned there, and limped away, pausing only at Geordie, not to touch her, but only to peer at her for an instant, mutter something almost without moving those stony lips, and disappear into the crowd, making for the exit. Walden's hand still lay, half-spread, on the air, and he felt, for the first waking time, the import of tampering, for whatever the reason, with another man's tussle with fate.

Then Cleo was at his elbow, staring past him after Edgar, eyes moist with alarm, voice choked with shock as he exclaimed in an undertone: "Catch him before he dies! Catch him!" And he, too, ran away through the milling crowd, still on the side of sweetness, knowing where it lay, looking neither to right nor left.

So Walden stood there alone in the light, isolated in his achievement, and by it, breathless and transformed, the way a man feels who has, on an impulse coming up from far down in his soul, totally altered his life all in a moment, and who then looks up, stunned, to discover himself in a new moral position to everything around him. And in that dazzling isolation, only Geordie approached him, coming so close her fragrance swirled thickly through his head, and he saw that she was exhausted, sobered, and somehow resigned. For just a second they were caught in an odd, impersonal affinity, and in that second, she whispered:

"Don't worry. Don't you worry now. You know what he said to

me? He only said: 'He sounded good.' Just that. Don't you worry now, honey."

She gave him a last, wan forgiving half-smile just as her escorts hurried up, one of them snuggling the sleepy spaniel, and Walden knew, for all the smile and for all the words, that *she* was worried nevertheless. But she turned and glided away then, as though she too was going under; leaving him standing there by himself, while people he had known for years clustered and exclaimed around him as though he were a notorious stranger, and he held his head up manfully under their praises.

Sitting on his bed, it all came back with blinding clarity between gulps of coffee; all of a piece, all in an instant, undamaged by sleep. He got up, shivering with the memory, to pour himself the second cup and realize, with dumb acceptance, that this was to be the first afternoon of his life.

He had brought the light all right, but the conflicts in a man's nature were not to be resolved by light alone. Edgar had fled in disgust and despair at what it had revealed, fled from the light because it was not for him anymore; fled, open-eyed anyway, into the murk that had always stood around him. The light had only shown him an inevitable path. Walden was frozen, even now hours later, by the power one man had over another; it sickened something trusting in him, even though he could not disbelieve the clear impulse which had prodded him to stand up. But the consequences of an action were endless, and he could not see the end of this particular one. He had taken a stand for once, and as he had discovered about his tone, so he had, for once and all, damned himself to going his way.

Then he knew that sometime, perhaps in the cramped, second-sax chair of one of those tireless, all-but-forgotten road-bands of the mythical past, this awful moment of human commitment must have been pushed up to Edgar too, and without thought or hesitation, he had leapt in, cutting his road alone; and blown, as himself, for the first time, and started down (for that was his unswervable direction) as he went up, started toward that morning and Walden by finally tapping the sources of himself, and letting his sound out. That was the only secret, and Walden wondered, with all the astonishment of a new idea, what his end would be.

From now on, he realized as he stood before the bed, suddenly amazed by his nakedness, there would be dreams through the mornings when he alone slept in the busy world, and, when he awoke, all the irritations and responsibilities of age and work. The armistice with sleep and discord had been forever broken. From now on he had to fight for his life and his vision like every man.

At that, the quiet loneliness of self-knowledge descended over him like a prophetic hint of the shroud toward which all loves irrevocably progress; and, pulling on his shorts, he remembered what Cleo had said just that morning:

"Catch him before he dies!"

And wondered if that was to be part of it too. But, putting the wondering aside for then, he set himself to dressing methodically. This was his first day in a strange, lonesome country, and one part of it, anyway, was knowing that it could not be postponed any longer.

JACK KEROUAC

Cult-hero of the Beat Generation, Jack Kerouac and the way of life he proclaimed in *On the Road* (1957) continue to be controversial. He has been damned and praised. Martin Seymour-Smith says that his first book, *The Town and the City* (1950), "is his best, and it is poor." John Clellon Holmes, in his prize-winning *Playboy* essay, "The Great Rememberer," says Kerouac is "the kind of writer only America could produce, and that only America could so willfully misunderstand." But today he is being approached more seriously by the critics.

Publication of *On the Road* was not easily achieved, even though Kerouac had already had his first book published. Repeated rejections by publishers made him more and more frustrated. Malcolm Cowley at Viking Press tried to convince Viking to publish it, but to no avail. It was Cowley, however, who helped to get part of the book published in *New World Writing* under the title "Jazz of the Beat Generation." Kerouac made only $120 on the deal. He insisted that the story be by Jean-Louis; presumably this was to avoid having his former wife, Joan Haverty, sue him for support of a child he denied fathering.

The piece stands nicely by itself. It shows Kerouac's affinity for, and understanding of, jazz and its origins. Its style fits the subject perfectly, reflecting the freedom and improvisatory nature of jazz. Holmes says that "modern jazz is almost exclusively the music of the Beat Generation . . . the music of inner freedom, of improvisation, of the creative individual rather than the interpretive group." Charlie Parker and bebop were most dramatically aligned with the Beat credo, but Kerouac in this piece uses his spontaneous prose style to outline and pay tribute to a long line of jazz greats who were a part of the varied American jazz scene in the 1930s, 1940s, and early 1950s.

JAZZ OF THE BEAT GENERATION

OUT we jumped in the warm mad night hearing a wild tenorman's bawling horn across the way going "EE-YAH! EE-YAH!" and hands clapping to the beat and folks yelling "Go, go, go!" Far from escorting the girls into the place, Dean was already racing across the street with his huge bandaged thumb in the air yelling "Blow, man, blow!" A bunch of colored men in Saturday night suits were whooping it up in front. It was a sawdust saloon, all wood, with a small bandstand near the john on which the fellows huddled with their hats on blowing over people's heads, a crazy place, not far from Market Street, in the dingy skid-row rear of it, near Harrison and the big bridge causeway; crazy floppy women wandered around sometimes in their bathrobes, bottles clanked in alleys. In back of the joint in a dark corridor beyond the splattered toilets, scores of men and women stood against the wall drinking wine-spodi-odi and spitting at the stars . . . wine, whiskey and beer. The behatted tenorman was blowing at the peak of a wonderfully satisfactory free idea, a rising and falling riff that went from "EE-yah!" to a crazier "EE-de-lee-yah!" and blasted along to the rolling crash of butt-scarred drums hammered by a big brutal-looking curl-sconced Negro with a bullneck who didn't give a damn about anything but punishing his tubs, crash, rattle-ti-boom crash. Uproars of music and the tenorman *had it* and everybody knew he had it. Dean was clutching his head in the crowd and it was a mad crowd. They were all urging that tenorman to hold it and keep it with cries and wild eyes; he was raising himself from a crouch and going down again with his horn, looping it up in a clear cry above the furor. A six-foot skinny Negro woman was rolling her bones at the man's hornbell, and he just jabbed it at her, "Ee! ee! ee!" He had a foghorn tone; his horn was taped; he was a shipyard worker and he didn't care. Everybody was rocking and roaring; Galatea and Alice with beers in their hands were standing on their chairs shaking and jumping. Groups of colored studs stumbled in from the street falling over one another to get there. "Stay with it man!" roared a man with a foghorn voice, and let out a big groan that must have been heard clear to Sacramento, "Ah-haa!"—"Whoo!" said Dean. He was rubbing his chest, his belly, his T-shirt was out, the sweat splashed from his face. Boom, kick, that drummer was kicking his drums down the cellar and rolling the beat upstairs with his murderous sticks, rattlety-boom! A big fat man was jumping on the platform making it sag and creak. "Yoo!" The pianist was only pounding the keys with spread-eagled fingers, chords only, at intervals when the great tenorman was drawing breath for another blast of phrase, Chinese chords, they shuddered the piano in every timber, chink and wire, *boing!* The tenorman jumped down from the platform and just stood buried in the crowd blowing around; his hat was over his eyes; somebody pushed it back for him. He just hauled back and stamped his foot and blew down a hoarse baughing blast, and drew breath, and raised the horn and blew high wide and screaming in the air. Dean was directly in front of him with his face glued to the bell of the horn, clapping his hands, pouring sweat on the man's keys; and the man noticed and laughed in his horn a long quivering crazy mule's hee-haw and everybody else laughed and they rocked and rocked; and finally the tenorman decided to blow his top and crouched down and held a note in high C for a long time as everything else crashed along skittely-boom and the cries increased and I thought the cops would come swarming from the nearest precinct.

It was just a usual Saturday night goodtime, nothing else; the bebop winos were wailing away, the workingman tenors, the cats who worked and got their horns out of hock and blew and had their women troubles, and came on in their horns with a will, saying things, a lot to say, talkative horns, you could almost hear the words and better than that the harmony, made you hear the way to fill up blank spaces of time with the tune and very consequence of your hands and breath and dead soul; summer, August 1949, and Frisco blowing mad, the dew on the muscat in the interior fields of

Joaquin and down in Watsonville the lettuce blowing, the money flowing for Frisco so seasonal and mad, the railroads rolling, extra-boards roaring, crates of melons on sidewalks, bananas coming off elevators, tarantulas suffocating in the new crazy air, chipped ice and the cool interior smells of grape tanks, cool bop hepcats standing slumped with horn and no lapels and blowing like Wardell, like Brew Moore softly . . . all of it insane, sad, sweeter than the love of mothers yet harsher than the murder of fathers. The clock on the wall quivered and shook; nobody cared about that thing. Dean was in a trance. The tenorman's eyes were fixed straight on him; he had found a madman who not only understood but cared and wanted to understand more and much more than there was, and they began duelling for this; everything came out of the horn, no more phrases, just cries, cries, "Baugh" and down to "Beep!" and up to "EEEEE!" and down to clinkers and over to sideways echoing horn-sounds and horselaughs and he tried everything, up, down, sideways, upside down, dog fashion, horizontal, thirty degrees, forty degrees and finally he fell back in somebody's arms and gave up and everybody pushed around and yelled "Yes, yes, he done blowed that one!" Dean wiped himself with his handkerchief.

Up steps Freddy on the bandstand and asks for a slow beat and looks sadly out the open door over people's heads and begins singing "Close Your Eyes." Things quiet down for a minute. Freddy's wearing a tattered suede jacket, a purple shirt with white buttons, cracked shoes and zoot pants without press; he didn't care. He looked like a pimp in Mecca, where there are no pimps; a barren woman's child, which is a dream; he looked like he was beat to his socks; he was down, and bent, and he played us some blues with his vocals. His big brown eyes were concerned with sadness, and the singing of songs slowly and with long thoughtful pauses. But in the second chorus he got excited and embraced the mike and jumped down from the bandstand and bent to it and to sing a note he had to touch his shoe tops and pull it all up to blow, and he blew so much he staggered from the effect, he only recovered himself in time for the next long slow note. "Mu-u-u-sic pla-a-a-a-a-a-ay!" He leaned back with his face to the ceiling, mike held at his fly. He shook his shoulders, he gave the hip sneer, he swayed. Then he leaned in almost falling with his pained face against the mike.

"Ma-a-a-ke it dream-y for dan-cing"—and he looked at the street outside, Folsom, with his lips curled in scorn—"while we go ro-man-n-n-cing"—he staggered sideways—"Lo-o-o-ove's holi-da-a-a-ay"—he shook his head with disgust and weariness at the whole world—"Will make it seem"—what would it make it seem?—everybody waited, he mourned—"O—kay." The piano hit a chord. "So baby come on and just clo-o-o-o-se your pretty little ey-y-y-es"—his mouth quivered, offered; he looked at us, Dean and me, with an expression that seemed to say "Hey now, what's this thing we're all putting down in this sad brown world"—and then he came to the end of his song and for this there had to be elaborate preparations during which time you could send all the messages to Garcia around the world twelve times and what difference did it make to anybody because here we were dealing with the pit and prune juice of poor beat life itself and the pathos of people in the Godawful streets, so he said and sang it, "Close—your—" and blew it way up to the ceiling with a big voice that came not from training but feeling and that much better, and blew it through to the stars and on up—"Ey-y-y-y-y-y-es" and in arpeggios of applause staggered off the platform ruefully, broodingly, nonsatisfied, artistic, arrogant. He sat in the corner with a bunch of boys and paid no attention to them. They gave him beers. He looked down and wept. He was the greatest.

Dean and I went over to talk to him. We invited him out to the car. In the car he suddenly yelled "Yes! ain't nothing I like better than good kicks! Where do we go?" Dean jumped up and down in the seat giggling maniacally. "Later! later!" said Freddy. "I'll get my boy to drive us down to Jamson's Nook, I got to sing. Man I *live* to sing. Been singing 'Close Your Eyes' for a month—I don't want to sing nothing else. What are you two boys up to?"

We told him we were going to New York tomorrow. "Lord, I ain't never been there and they tell me it's a real jumping town but I ain't got no cause complaining where I am. I'm married you know." "Oh yes?" said Dean lighting up. "And where is the little darling tonight and I bet she's got lots of nice friends . . . man . . ." "What you mean?" said Freddy looking at him half-smiling out of the corner. "I tole you I was married to her, didn't I?"—"Oh yes, Oh yes," blushed Dean. "I was just asking. Maybe she's got a couple of friends downtown, or somethin', you know a man, a ball, I'm only looking for a ball, a gang ball, man."—"Yah, what's the good of balls, life's too sad to be ballin all the time, Jim," said Freddy lowering his eye to the street. "Shee-it," he said, "I ain't got no money and I don't care tonight."

We went back in for more. The girls were so disgusted with Dean and I for jumping around with everybody else that they had left by now, gone to Jamson's Nook on foot; the car we'd come in, and had to push from down Mission, wouldn't run anyway. We saw a horrible sight in the bar; a white hipster fairy of some kind had come in wearing a Hawaiian shirt and was asking the big bull-knecked drummer if he could sit in. The musicians looked at him suspiciously. He sat at the tubs and they started the beat of a blues number and he began stroking the snares with soft goofy bop brushes, swaying his neck with that complacent Reich-analyzed ecstasy that doesn't mean anything but too much T and soft foods and goofy kicks in cafeterias and pads at dawn and on the cool order. But he didn't care. The musicians looked at him and said, "Yeah, yeah, that's what the man does, shh-ee-eet." He smiled joyously into space and kept the beat with butterfly brushes, softly, with bop subtleties, a giggling rippling background for big solid foghorn blues. The big Negro bull-neck drummer sat waiting for his turn to come back. "What that man doing?" he said. "Play the music," he said. "What in hell!" he said. "Shh-ee-eet!" and looked away red-eyed. Freddy's boy showed up at this moment; he was a little taut Negro with a great big Cadillac. We all jumped in. He hunched over the wheel and blew the car clear across San Francisco without stopping once, seventy miles per hour; he was fulfilling his mission with a fixed smile, his destiny we'd expected of the rumors and songs of him. Right through traffic and nobody even noticed he was so good. Dean was in ecstasies. "Dig *this* guy, man—dig the way he sits right in that seat with the feel of the car under his both haunches, a little bit forward, to the left, against the gut of the car and he don't make any outward indication and just balls that jack and can talk all night while doing it, only thing is he doesn't bother with life, listen to them, O man the things, the things, he lets Freddy do that, and Freddy's his boy, and tells him about life, listen to them, O man the things . . . the things I could—I wish—let's not stop, man, we've got to keep going now!" And Freddy's boy wound around a corner and bowled us right in front of Jamson's Nook and was parked. "Yes!" yelled Dean. A cab squeaked to a stop in the street; out of it jumped a skinny seventy-year-old withered little Negro preacherman who threw a dollar bill at the cabby and yelled "Blow!" and ran into the club pulling on his coat (just come out of work) and dashed right through the downstairs bar yelling "Go, go, go!" and stumbled upstairs almost falling on his face and blew the door open and fell into the jazz session room with his hands out to support him against anything he might fall on, and he fell right on Lampshade who was reduced to working as a waiter in Jamson's Nook that summer (the great Lampshade whom I'd seen shout the blues with veins helling in his neck and his overcoat on), and the music was there blasting and blasting and the preacherman stood transfixed in the open door screaming "Blowblowblow!" And the man was a little short Negro with an alto horn that Dean said obviously lived with his grandmother, "Just like my boy Jim!", slept all day and blew all night and blew a hundred choruses before he was ready to jump for fair, and that's what he was doing. "It's Carlo Marx!" screamed Dean above the fury. And it was. This little grandmother's boy with the scrapped up alto had beady glittering eyes, small crooked feet, spindly legs in formal black pants, like our friend Carlo, and he hopped and flopped with his horn and threw his feet around and kept his eyes transfixed on the audience (which was just people laughing at a dozen tables, the room thirty by thirty feet and low ceiling) and he never stopped. He was very simple in his ideas. Ideas meant nothing to him. What he liked was the surprise of a new simple variation of chorus. He'd go from "ta-potato-rup, ta-potato-rup" repeating and hopping to it and kissing and smiling into his horn—and then to "ta-potatola-dee-rup, ta-potatola-DEE-rup!" and it was all great moments of laughter and understanding for him and everyone else who heard. His tone was clear as a bell, high, pure, and blew straight in our faces from two feet away. Dean stood in front of him, oblivious to everything else in the world, with his head bowed, his hands socking in together, his whole body jumping on his heels and the sweat, always the sweat pouring and splashing down his tormented neck to literally lie in a pool at his feet. Galatea and Alice were there and it took us five minutes to realize it. Whoo, Frisco nights, the end of the continent and the end of the road and the end of all dull doubt. Lampshade was roaring around with trays of beer: everything he did was in rhythm; he yelled at the waitress with the beat: "Hey now, baby-baby, make a way, make a way, it's Lampshade coming your way!" and he hurled by her with the beers in the air and roared through the swinging doors in the kitchen and danced with the cooks and came sweating back. Ronnie Morgan, who'd earlier in the evening performed at the Hey Now Club screaming and kicking over the mike, now sat absolutely motionless at a corner table with an untouched drink in front of him, staring gook-eyed into space, his hands hanging at this sides till they almost touched the floor, his feet outspread like lolling tongues, his body shriveled into absolute weariness and entranced sorrow and what-all was on his mind: a man who knocked himself out every night and let the others put the quietus to him at dawn. Everything swirled around him like a cloud. And that little grandmother's alto, that little Carlo Marx hopped and monkey-danced with his magic horn and blew two hundred choruses of blues, each one more frantic than the other and no signs of failing energy or willingness to call anything a day. The whole room shivered. It has since been closed down, naturally.

Dean and I raced on to the East Coast. At one point we drove a 1947 Cadillac limousine across the state of Nebraska at 110 miles an hour, beating hotshot passenger trains and steel wheel freights in one nervous shuddering snapup of the gas. We told stories and zoomed East. There were hoboes by the tracks, wino bottle, the moon shining on woodfires. There were white-faced cows out in the plains, dim as nuns. There was dawn, Iowa; the Mississippi River at Davenport, and Chicago by nightfall. "Oh man" said Dean to me as we stood in front of a bar on North Clark Street in the hot summer night, "dig these old Chinamen that cut by Chicago. What a weird town—whee! And that woman in that window up there, just looking down with her big breasts hanging from her old nightgown. Just big wide eyes waiting. Wow! Sal we gotta go and never stop going till we get there."—"Where we going man?"—"Obvious question say Charley Chan. But we gotta go, we gotta GO." Then here came a gang of young bop musicians carrying their instruments out of cars. They piled right into a saloon and we followed them. They set themselves up and started blowing. There we were. The leader was a slender drooping curly-haired pursy-mouthed tenorman, thin of shoulder, twenty-one, lean, loose, blowing modern and soft, cool in his sports shirt without undershirt, self-indulgent, sneering. Dean and I were like car thieves and juvenile heroes on a mad—with our T-shirts and beards and torn pants—but the bop, the combo! How that cool leader picked up his horn and frowned in it and blew cool and complex and was dainty stamping his foot to catch ideas and ducked to miss others—saying "Wail" very quietly when the other boys took solos. He was the leader, the encourager, the school-maker, the Teshmaker, the Bix, the Louis in the great formal school of new underground subterranean American music that would someday be studied all over the universities of Europe and the world. Then there was Pres, a husky handsome blond like a freckled boxer, like Jackie Cooper, meticulously molded in his sharkskin plaid suit with the long drape and the collar falling back and the tie undone for exact sharpness and casualness, sweating and hitching up his horn and writhing into it, and a tone just like Pres Lester Young himself, blowing round and Lester-like as they all leaned and jammed together, the heroes of the hip generation. "You see man Pres has the technical anxieties of a money-making musician, he's the only one who's expensively dressed, obvious big band employee, see him grow worried when he blows a clinker, but the leader, that cool cat, tells him not to worry and just blow truth." They roll into a tune—"Idaho." The Negro alto high-school broad-gash-mouth Yardbird tall kid blows over their heads in a thing of his own, moveless on the horn, fingering, erect, an idealist who reads Homer and Bird, cool, contemplative, grave—raises his horn and blows into it quietly and thoughtfully and elicits birdlike phrases and architectural Miles Davis logics. The children of the great bop innovators. Once there was Louis Armstrong blowing his beautiful bop in the muds of New Orleans; even before him the mad tuba-players and trombone kings who'd paraded on official days and broke up their Sousa marches into ragtime, on Bourbon, Dauphine and South Rampart and Perdido Street too. After which came swing, and Roy Eldridge vigorous and virile blasting the horn for everything it had in waves of power and natural tuneful reason—"I Want a Little Girl," "I Got Rhythm," a thousand choruses of "Wonderful"—

leaning to it with glittering eyes and a lovely smile and sending it out broadcast to rock the jazz world. Then had come Charlie Parker, a kid in his mother's woodshed in Kansas City, the dirty snow in late March, smoke from stovepipes, wool hats, pitiful brown mouths breathing vapor, faint noise of music from down the way—blowing his tied-together alto among the logs, practicing on rainy days, coming out to watch the old swinging Basie and Bennie Moten band that had Hot Lips Page and the rest—lost names in swingin' Kaycee—nostalgia of alcohol, human mouths chewing and talking in smoky noisy jazzrooms, yeah, yah, yeah, yah, last Sunday afternoon and the long red sunset, the lost girl, the spilt wine—Charlie Parker leaving home and unhappiness and coming to the Apple, and meeting mad Monk and madder Gillespie . . . Charlie Parker in his early days when he was out of his mind and walked in a circle while playing his horn. Younger than Lester, also from K.C., that gloomy saintly goof in whom the history of jazz is wrapped: Lester. Here were the children of the modern jazz night blowing their horns and instruments with belief; it was Lester started it all—his fame and his smoothness as lost as Maurice Chevalier in a stage-door poster—his drape, his drooping melancholy disposition in the sidewalk, in the door, his porkpie hat. ("At sessions all over the country from Kansas City to the Apple and back to L.A. they called him Pork Pie because he'd wear that gone hat and blow in it.") What doorstanding influence has Dean gained from this cultural master of his generation? What mysteries as well as masteries? What styles, sorrows, collars, the removal of collars, the removal of lapels, the crepe-sole shoes, the beauty goof—that sneer of Lester's, that compassion for the dead which Billy has too, Lady Day—those poor little musicians in Chicago, their love of Lester, early heroisms in a room, records of Lester, early Count, suits hanging in the closet, tanned evenings in the rosy ballroom, the great tenor solo in the shoeshine jukebox, you can hear Lester blow and he is the greatness of America in a single Negro musician—he is just like the river, the river starts in near Butte, Montana, in frozen snow caps (Three Forks) and meanders on down across states and entire territorial areas of dun bleak land with hawthorn crackling in the sleet, picks up rivers at Bismarck, Omaha, and St. Louis just north, another at Kay-ro, another in Arkansas, Tennessee, comes deluging on New Orleans with muddy news from the land and a roar of subterranean excitement that is like the vibration of the entire land sucked of its gut in mad midnight, fevered, hot, the big mudhole rank clawpole old frogular pawed-soul titanic Mississippi from the North, full of wires, cold wood and horn—Lester, so, holding, his horn high in Doctor Pepper chickenshacks, backstreet. Basie Yaycee wearing greasy smeared corduroy bigpants and in torn flap smoking jacket without straw, scuffle-up shoes all slopey Mother Hubbard, soft, pudding, and key ring, early handkerchiefs, hands up, arms up, horn horizontal, shining dull, in wood-brown whiskeyhouse with ammoniac urine from broken gut bottles around fecal pukey bowl and a gal sprawled in it legs spread in brown cotton stockings, bleeding at belted mouth, moaning "yes" as Lester, horn placed, has started blowing, "glow for me mother blow for me," 1938, later, earlier, Miles is still on his daddy's checkered knee, Louis' only got twenty years before him, and Lester blows all Kansas City to ecstasy and now Americans from coast to coast go mad, and fall by, and everybody's picking up. Stranger flowers now than ever, for as the Negro alto kid mused over everyone's head with dignity, the slender blond kid from Curtis Street, Denver, jeans and studded belt and red shirt, sucked on his mouthpiece while waiting for the others to finish; and when they did he started, and you had to look around to see where the new solo was coming from, for it came from his angelical smiling lips upon the mouthpiece and it was a soft sweet fairy-tale solo he played. A new kind of sound in the night, sweet, plaintive, cold; like cold jazz. Someone from South Main Street, or Market, or Canal, or Streetcar, he's the sweet new alto blowing the tiny heartbreaking salute in the night which is coming, a beauteous and whistling horn; blown easily but fully in a soft flue of air, out comes the piercing thin lament completely softened, the New Sound, the prettiest. And the bass player: wiry redhead with wild eyes jabbing his hips at the fiddle with every driving slap, at hot moments his mouth hung open; behind him, driving, the sad-looking dissipated drummer, completely goofed, chewing gum, wide-eyed, rocking the neck with that Reich kick, dropping bombs with his foot, urging balloons. The piano—a big husky Italian truck-driving kid with meaty hands and a burly and thoughtful joy; anybody start a fight with the band, he will step down; dropping huge chords like a Wolfean horse turding in the steamy Brooklyn winter morn. They played an hour. Nobody was listening. Old North Clark bums lolled at the bar, whores screeched in anger. Secret Chinamen went by. Noises of hootchy-kootchy interfered. They went right on. Out on the sidewalk came an apparition—a sixteen-year-old kid with a goatee and a trombone case. Thin as rickets, mad-faced, he wanted to join this group and blow with them. They knew him from before and didn't want to be bothered with him. He crept into the bar and meekly undid his trombone case and raised the horn to his lips. No opening. Nobody looked at him. They finished, packed up and left for another bar. The boy had his horn out, all assembled and polished of bell and no one cared. He wanted to jump. He was the Chicago Kid. He slapped on his dark glasses, raised the trombone to his lips alone in the bar, and went "Baugh!" Then he rushed out after them. They just wouldn't let him play with them, like the sandlot baseball gang back of the gas tank. "All these guys live with their grandmothers just like my boy Jim and our Carlo Marx alto!" said Dean and we rushed after the whole gang. They went across the street. We went in.

There is no end to the night. At great roar of Chicago dawn we all staggered out and shuddered in the raggedness. It would start all over tomorrow night. We rushed on to New York. "There ain't nothing left after that," said Dean. "Whee!" he said. We seek to find new phrases; we try hard, we writhe and twist and blow; every now and then a clear harmonic cry gives new suggestions of a tune, a thought, that will someday be the only tune and thought in the world and which will raise men's souls to joy. We find it, we lose, we wrestle for it, we find it again, we laugh, we moan. Go moan for man. It's the pathos of people that gets us down, all the lovers in this dream.

STEVE ALLEN

Steve Allen gives credibility to the notion that for certain people, there are thirty-six hours in a day. His numerous achievements as writer, comedian, television and radio talk-show host, actor, and musician (jazz pianist and composer of more than four thousand songs) are astounding. He was the host of the original *Tonight Show* from 1954 to 1956 and is usually associated with comedy and satire, but he also created and hosted the successful PBS series *Meeting of Minds* from 1977 to 1981. His portrayal of Benny Goodman in the film *The Benny Goodman Story* is probably his best-remembered film role.

"Crazy Red Riding Hood" was originally part of Allen's Coral recording, *Bebop Fables,* a retelling of popular fairy tales "as they might be told by a 'progressive' musician," says Allen. The stories were subsequently published in 1955 with illustrations by George Price.

CRAZY RED RIDING HOOD

GATHER 'round, kiddies, and your old Uncle Steve will tell you another story.

Once upon a time, many many years ago, in the Land of Ooboprshebam, there lived a lovely little girl named Red Riding Hood.

To give you an idea of what a sweet thing she was, children, I'll just say that she was not only a *lovely little girl;* she was a *fine chick.*

One day Red Riding Hood's mother called her into the kitchen and said, "Honey, your grandma is feeling the least."

"What a drag!" said Red. "What's the bit?"

"Hangoversville, for all I know," said her mother. "At any rate, I've fixed up a real wild basket of ribs and a bottle of juice. I'd like you to fall by grandma's joint this afternoon and lay the stuff on her."

"Crazy," said Red, and, picking up the basket, she took off for her grandmother's cottage, going by way of the deep woods.

Little did Red Riding Hood know that a big bad wolf lurked in the heart of the forest.

She had traveled but a short distance when the wolf leaped out from behind a bush and confronted her.

"Baby," he said, grinning affably, "gimme some skin!"

"Sorry, Daddy-o," said Red. "Some other time. Right now I have to make it over to my grandmother's place."

"Square-time," said the wolf. "Why don't you blow your grandmother and we'll have some laughs."

"Man," said Red, "Cootie left the Duke and I'm leaving you. For the time being we've had it."

"Mama, I'm hip, said the wolf. "Dig you later."

So saying, the wolf bounded off through the forest and was soon lost to sight. But his evil mind was at work. Unbeknownst to Red

Riding Hood, he took a short cut through the trees and in a few minutes stood panting before the helpless old grandmother's cottage.

Quietly he knocked at the door.

"That's a familiar beat," said Red Riding Hood's grandmother. "Who's out there?"

"Western Union," lied the wolf. "I have a special invitation to Dizzy's opening at Birdland."

"Wild," said the grandmother, hobbling across the room.

Imagine her horror when, on opening the door, she perceived the wolf! In an instant he had leaped into the house, gobbled her up and disguised himself in her night clothes.

Hearing Red Riding Hood's footsteps on the stones of the garden path, he leaped into the poor lady's bed, pulled the covers up to his chin and smiled toward the door in a grandmotherly way.

When little Red Riding Hood knocked he said, "Hit me again. Who goes?"

"It's me, Gram," said Red Riding Hood. "Mother heard you were feeling pretty beat. She thought you might like to pick up on some ribs."

"Nutty," said the wolf. "Fall in."

Red Riding Hood opened the door, stepped inside and looked around the room. "Wowie," she said. "What a crazy pad!"

"Sorry I didn't have time to straighten the joint up before you got here," said the wolf. "But you know how it is. What's in the basket?"

"Oh, the same old jazz," said Red.

"Baby," said the wolf, "don't put it down."

"I have to," said Red. "It's getting heavy."

"I didn't come here to play straight," said the wolf. "Let's open the basket. I've got eyes."

"I'm hip," said Red, "not to mention the fact that you can say that again. Grandma, what frantic eyes you have!"

"The better to dig you with, my dear," said the wolf.

"And, Grandma," said Red, "I don't want to sound rude, but what a long nose you have!"

"Yeah," said the wolf. "It's a gasser."

"And, Grandma," said Red, "your ears are the most, to say the least."

"What is this," snapped the wolf, "face inspection? I know my ears aren't the greatest, but whadda ya gonna do? Let's just say somebody goofed!"

"You know something?" little Red Riding Hood said, squinting suspiciously at the furry head on the pillow. "I don't want to sound square or anything, but you don't look like my grandmother at all. You look like some other cat."

"Baby," said the wolf, "you're flippin'!"

"No, man," insisted Red. "I just dug your nose again and it's too much. I don't want to come right out and ask to see your card, you understand, but where's my grandma?"

The wolf stared at Red Riding Hood for a long, terrible moment. "Your grandma," he said, "is gone."

"I'm hip," said Red. "She is the swingin'est, but let's take it from the top again. Where is she?"

"She cut out," said the wolf.

"Don't hand me that jazz," said Red, whereupon the wolf, being at the end of his patience, leaped out of bed and began to chase poor Red Riding Hood about the room.

Little did he know that the wolf season had opened that very day and that a passing hunter could hear little Red Riding Hood's frantic cry for help.

Rushing into the cottage, the brave hunter dispatched the wolf with one bullet.

"Buster," said Red gratefully, "your timing was like the end, ya know?"

And so it was.

JAMES BALDWIN

James Baldwin's novels, plays, and short stories are often as polemical as his essays. His best-known novel is the highly controversial *Another Country* (1962). His polemics are most evident in his essay collections, most notably *Nobody Knows My Name* (1962) and *The Fire Next Time* (1963).

Disturbed by prejudice in the United States, he moved in 1948 to Europe, where he felt he could live most comfortably as a black person and take a more objective look at America and its racial problems. He returned in 1957.

"Sonny's Blues" is from Baldwin's short story collection, *Going to Meet the Man* (1965). Readers will note Baldwin's use of Louis Armstrong and Charlie Parker as symbols for the old versus the new—the assimilationist or Uncle Tom versus the free and nonconforming. The story also illustrates the importance of the past in one's life—in this case with reference to the blues, which are a reflection of the past, the past being a past of suffering as a prerequisite for being able to sing or play the blues.

Baldwin was especially fond of Bessie Smith, Empress of the Blues, and he said that it was only in Europe that he could feel comfortable playing her records, because in America doing so had become part of the black stereotype. He also believed that blacks through the years had had their music stolen by whites who then reaped the profits while the blacks struggled to exist. He told Nikki Giovanni, "Look, let us say I'm King Oliver and I'm a pretty good musician. . . . And there is somebody called, let us say, Bing Crosby, who couldn't carry a tune from here to here, right? . . . Right? Now I watch this little white boy become a millionaire many times over. I can't get a job and time goes on. You get older, you get more weary, and since you cannot get a job, your morale begins to be destroyed." The implication in "Sonny's Blues" may be that Sonny will have to face such a life as a jazz musician.

SONNY'S BLUES

I read about it in the paper, in the subway, on my way to work. I read it, and I couldn't believe it, and I read it again. Then perhaps I just stared at it, at the newsprint spelling out his name, spelling out the story. I stared at it in the swinging lights of the subway car, and in the faces and bodies of the people, and in my own face, trapped in the darkness which roared outside.

It was not to be believed and I kept telling myself that, as I walked from the subway station to the high school. And at the same time I couldn't doubt it. I was scared, scared for Sonny. He became real to me again. A great block of ice got settled in my belly and kept melting there slowly all day long, while I taught my classes algebra. It was a special kind of ice. It kept melting, sending trickles of ice water all up and down my veins, but it never got less. Sometimes it hardened and seemed to expand until I felt my guts were going to come spilling out or that I was going to choke or scream. This would always be at a moment when I was remembering some specific thing Sonny had once said or done.

When he was about as old as the boys in my classes his face had been bright and open, there was a lot of copper in it; and he'd had wonderfully direct brown eyes, and great gentleness and privacy. I wondered what he looked like now. He had been picked up, the evening before, in a raid on an apartment downtown, for peddling and using heroin.

I couldn't believe it: but what I mean by that is that I couldn't find any room for it anywhere inside me. I had kept it outside me for a long time. I hadn't wanted to know. I had had suspicions, but I didn't name them, I kept putting them away. I told myself that Sonny was wild, but he wasn't crazy. And he'd always been a good boy, he hadn't ever turned hard or evil or disrespectful, the way kids can, so quick, so quick, especially in Harlem. I didn't want to believe that I'd ever see my brother going down, coming to nothing, all that light in his face gone out, in the condition I'd already seen so many others. Yet it had happened and here I was, talking about algebra to a lot of boys who might, every one of them for all I knew, be popping off needles every time they went to the head. Maybe it did more for them than algebra could.

I was sure that the first time Sonny had ever had horse, he couldn't have been much older than these boys were now. These boys, now, were living as we'd been living then, they were growing up with a rush and their heads bumped abruptly against the low ceiling of their actual possibilities. They were filled with rage. All they really knew were two darknesses, the darkness of their lives, which was now closing in on them, and the darkness of the movies, which had blinded them to that other darkness, and in which they now, vindictively, dreamed, at once more together than they were at any other time, and more alone.

When the last bell rang, the last class ended, I let out my breath. It seemed I'd been holding it for all that time. My clothes were wet—I may have looked as though I'd been sitting in a steam bath, all dressed up, all afternoon. I sat alone in the classroom a long time. I listened to the boys outside, downstairs, shouting and cursing and laughing. Their laughter struck me for perhaps the first time. It was not the joyous laughter which—God knows why—one associates with children. It was mocking and insular, its intent was to denigrate. It was disenchanted, and in this, also, lay the authority of their curses. Perhaps I was listening to them because I was thinking about my brother and in them I heard my brother. And myself.

One boy was whistling a tune, at once very complicated and very simple, it seemed to be pouring out of him as though he were a bird, and it sounded very cool and moving through all that harsh, bright air, only just holding its own through all those other sounds.

I stood up and walked over to the window and looked down into the courtyard. It was the beginning of the spring and the sap was rising in the boys. A teacher passed through them every now and again, quickly, as though he or she couldn't wait to get out of that courtyard, to get those boys out of their sight and off their minds. I started collecting my stuff. I thought I'd better get home and talk to Isabel.

The courtyard was almost deserted by the time I got downstairs. I saw this boy standing in the shadow of a doorway, looking just like Sonny. I almost called his name. Then I saw that it wasn't Sonny, but somebody we used to know, a boy from around our block. He'd been Sonny's friend. He'd never been mine, having been too young for me, and, anyway, I'd never liked him. And now, even though he was a grown-up man, he still hung around that block, still spent hours on the street corners, was always high and raggy. I used to run into him from time to time and he'd often work around to asking me for a quarter or fifty cents. He always had some real good excuse, too, and I always gave it to him, I don't know why.

But now, abruptly, I hated him. I couldn't stand the way he looked at me, partly like a dog, partly like a cunning child. I wanted to ask him what the hell he was doing in the school courtyard.

He sort of shuffled over to me, and he said, "I see you got the papers. So you already know about it."

"You mean about Sonny? Yes, I already know about it. How come they didn't get you?"

He grinned. It made him repulsive and it also brought to mind what he'd looked like as a kid. "I wasn't there. I stay away from them people."

"Good for you." I offered him a cigarette and I watched him through the smoke. "You come all the way down here just to tell me about Sonny?"

"That's right." He was sort of shaking his head and his eyes looked strange, as though they were about to cross. The bright sun deadened his damp dark brown skin and it made his eyes look yellow and showed up the dirt in his kinked hair. He smelled funky. I moved a little away from him and I said, "Well, thanks. But I already know about it and I got to get home."

"I'll walk you a little ways," he said. We started walking. There were a couple of kids still loitering in the courtyard and one of them said goodnight to me and looked strangely at the boy beside me.

"What're you going to do?" he asked me. "I mean, about Sonny?"

"Look. I haven't seen Sonny for over a year, I'm not sure I'm going to do anything. Anyway, what the hell *can* I do?"

"That's right," he said quickly, "ain't nothing you can do. Can't much help old Sonny no more, I guess."

It was what I was thinking and so it seemed to me he had no right to say it.

"I'm surprised at Sonny, though," he went on—he had a funny way of talking, he looked straight ahead as though he were talking to himself—"I thought Sonny was a smart boy, I thought he was too smart to get hung."

"I guess he thought so too," I said sharply, "and that's how he got hung. And now about you? You're pretty goddamn smart, I bet."

Then he looked directly at me, just for a minute. "I ain't smart," he said. "If I was smart, I'd have reached for a pistol a long time ago."

"Look. Don't tell *me* your sad story, if it was up to me, I'd give you one." Then I felt guilty—guilty, probably, for never having supposed that the poor bastard *had* a story of his own, much less a sad one, and I asked, quickly, "What's going to happen to him now?"

He didn't answer this. He was off by himself some place. "Funny thing," he said, and from his tone we might have been discussing the quickest way to get to Brooklyn, "when I saw the papers this morning, the first thing I asked myself was if I had anything to do with it. I felt sort of responsible."

I began to listen more carefully. The subway station was on the corner, just before us, and I stopped. He stopped, too. We were in front of a bar and he ducked slightly, peering in, but whoever he was looking for didn't seem to be there. The juke box was blasting away with something black and bouncy and I half watched the barmaid as she danced her way from the juke box to her place behind the bar. And I watched her face as she laughingly responded to something someone said to her, still keeping time to the music. When she smiled one saw the little girl, one sensed the doomed, still-struggling woman beneath the battered face of the semi-whore.

"I never *give* Sonny nothing," the boy said finally, "but a long time ago I come to school high and Sonny asked me how it felt." He paused, I couldn't bear to watch him, I watched the barmaid, and I listened to the music which seemed to be causing the pavement to shake. "I told him it felt great." The music stopped, the barmaid paused and watched the juke box until the music began again. "It did."

All this was carrying me some place I didn't want to go. I certainly didn't want to know how it felt. It filled everything, the people, the houses, the music, the dark, quicksilver barmaid, with menace; and this menace was their reality.

"What's going to happen to him now?" I asked again.

"They'll send him away some place and they'll try to cure him." He shook his head. "Maybe he'll even think he's kicked the habit. Then they'll let him loose"—he gestured, throwing his cigarette into the gutter. "That's all."

"What do you mean, that's *all?*"

But I knew what he meant.

"I *mean,* that's *all.*" He turned his head and looked at me, pulling down the corners of his mouth. "Don't you know what I mean?" he asked, softly.

"How the hell *would* I know what you mean?" I almost whispered it, I don't know why.

"That's right," he said to the air, "how would *he* know what I mean?" He turned toward me again, patient and calm, and yet I somehow felt him shaking, shaking as though he were going to fall apart. I felt that ice in my guts again, the dread I'd felt all afternoon; and again I watched the barmaid, moving about the bar, washing glasses, and singing. "Listen. They'll let him out and then it'll just start all over again. That's what I mean."

"You mean—they'll let him out. And then he'll just start working his way back in again. You mean he'll never kick the habit. Is that what you mean?"

"That's right," he said, cheerfully. "*You* see what I mean."

"Tell me," I said at last, "why does he want to die? He must want to die, he's killing himself, why does he want to die?"

He looked at me in surprise. He licked his lips. "He don't want to die. He wants to live. Don't nobody want to die, ever."

Then I wanted to ask him—too many things. He could not have answered, or if he had, I could not have borne the answers. I started walking. "Well, I guess it's none of my business."

"It's going to be rough on old Sonny," he said. We reached the subway station. "This is your station?" he asked. I nodded. I took one step down. "Damn!" he said, suddenly. I looked up at him. He grinned again. "Damn it if I didn't leave all my money home. You ain't got a dollar on you, have you? Just for a couple of days, is all."

All at once something inside gave and threatened to come pouring out of me. I didn't hate him any more. I felt that in another moment I'd start crying like a child.

"Sure," I said, "Don't sweat." I looked in my wallet and didn't have a dollar, I only had a five. "Here," I said. "That hold you?"

He didn't look at it—he didn't want to look at it. A terrible, closed look came over his face, as though he were keeping the number on the bill a secret from him and me. "Thanks," he said, and now he was dying to see me go. "Don't worry about Sonny. Maybe I'll write him or something."

"Sure," I said. "You do that. So long."

"Be seeing you," he said. I went on down the steps.

And I didn't write Sonny or send him anything for a long time. When I finally did, it was just after my little girl died, he wrote me back a letter which made me feel like a bastard.

Here's what he said:

> Dear brother,
>
> You don't know how much I needed to hear from you. I wanted to write you many a time but I dug how much I must have hurt you and so I didn't write. But now I feel like a man who's been trying to climb up out of some deep, real deep and funky hole and just saw the sun up there, outside. I got to get outside.
>
> I can't tell you much about how I got here. I mean I don't know how to tell you. I guess I was afraid of something or I was trying to escape from something and you know I have never been very strong in the head (smile). I'm glad Mama and Daddy are dead and can't see what's happened to their son and I swear if I'd known what I was doing I would never have hurt you so, you and a lot of other fine people who were nice to me and who believed in me.
>
> I don't want you to think it had anything to do with me being a musician. It's more than that. Or maybe less than that. I can't get anything straight in my head down here and I try not to think about what's going to happen to me when I get outside again. Sometime I think I'm going to flip and *never* get outside and sometime I think I'll come straight back. I tell you one thing, though, I'd rather blow my brains out than go through this

again. But that's what they all say, so they tell me. If I tell you when I'm coming to New York and if you could meet me, I sure would appreciate it. Give my love to Isabel and the kids and I was sure sorry to hear about little Gracie. I wish I could be like Mama and say the Lord's will be done, but I don't know it seems to me that trouble is the one thing that never does get stopped and I don't know what good it does to blame it on the Lord. But maybe it does some good if you believe it.

Your brother,
Sonny

Then I kept in constant touch with him and I sent him whatever I could and I went to meet him when he came back to New York. When I saw him many things I thought I had forgotten came flooding back to me. This was because I had begun, finally, to wonder about Sonny, about the life that Sonny lived inside. This life, whatever it was, had made him older and thinner and it had deepened the distant stillness in which he had always moved. He looked very unlike my baby brother. Yet, when he smiled, when we shook hands, the baby brother I'd never known looked out from the depths of his private life, like an animal waiting to be coaxed into the light.

"How you been keeping?" he asked me.

"All right. And you?"

"Just fine." He was smiling all over his face. "It's good to see you again."

"It's good to see you."

The seven years' difference in our ages lay between us like a chasm: I wondered if these years would ever operate between us as a bridge. I was remembering, and it made it hard to catch my breath, that I had been there when he was born; and I had heard the first words he had ever spoken. When he started to walk, he walked from our mother straight to me. I caught him just before he fell when he took the first steps he ever took in this world.

"How's Isabel?"

"Just fine. She's dying to see you."

"And the boys?"

"They're fine, too. They're anxious to see their uncle."

"Oh, come on. You know they don't remember me."

"Are you kidding? Of course they remember you."

He grinned again. We got into a taxi. We had a lot to say to each other, far too much to know how to begin.

As the taxi began to move, I asked, "You still want to go to India?"

He laughed. "You still remember that. Hell, no. This place is Indian enough for me."

"It used to belong to them," I said.

And he laughed again. "They damn sure knew what they were doing when they got rid of it."

Years ago, when he was around fourteen, he'd been all hipped on the idea of going to India. He read books about people sitting on rocks, naked, in all kinds of weather, but mostly bad, naturally, and walking barefoot through hot coals and arriving at wisdom. I used to say that it sounded to me as though they were getting away from wisdom as fast as they could. I think he sort of looked down on me for that.

"Do you mind," he asked, "if we have the driver drive alongside the park? On the west side—I haven't seen the city in so long."

"Of course not," I said. I was afraid that I might sound as though I were humoring him, but I hoped he wouldn't take it that way.

So we drove along, between the green of the park and the stony, lifeless elegance of hotels and apartment buildings, toward the vivid, killing streets of our childhood. These streets hadn't changed, though housing projects jutted up out of them now like rocks in the middle of a boiling sea. Most of the houses in which we had grown up had vanished, as had the stores from which we had stolen, the basements in which we had first tried sex, the rooftops from which we had hurled tin cans and bricks. But houses exactly like the houses of our past yet dominated the landscape, boys exactly like the boys we once had been found themselves smothering in these houses, came down into the streets for light and air and found themselves encircled by disaster. Some escaped the trap, most didn't. Those who got out always left something of themselves behind, as some animals amputate a leg and leave it in the trap. It might be said, perhaps, that I had escaped, after all, I was a school teacher; or that Sonny had, he hadn't lived in Harlem for years. Yet, as the cab moved uptown through streets which seemed, with a rush, to darken with dark people, and as I covertly studied Sonny's face, it came to me that what we both were seeking through our separate cab windows was that part of ourselves which had been left behind. It's always at the hour of trouble and confrontation that the missing member aches.

We hit 110th Street and started rolling up Lenox Avenue. And I'd known this avenue all my life, but it seemed to me again, as it had seemed on the day I'd first heard about Sonny's trouble, filled with a hidden menace which was its very breadth of life.

"We almost there," said Sonny.

"Almost." We were both too nervous to say anything more.

We live in a housing project. It hasn't been up long. A few days after it was up it seemed uninhabitably new, now, of course, it's already rundown. It looks like a parody of the good, clean, faceless life—God knows the people who live in it do their best to make it a parody. The beat-looking grass lying around isn't enough to make their lives green, the hedges will never hold out the streets, and they know it. The big windows fool no one, they aren't big enough to make space out of no space. They don't bother with the windows, they watch the TV screen instead. The playground is most popular with the children who don't play at jacks, or skip rope, or roller skate, or swing, and they can be found in it after dark. We moved in partly because it's not too far from where I teach, and partly for the kids; but it's really just like the houses in which Sonny and I grew up. The same things happen, they'll have the same things to remember. The moment Sonny and I started into the house I had the feeling that I was simply bringing him back into the danger he had almost died trying to escape.

Sonny has never been talkative. So I don't know why I was sure he'd be dying to talk to me when supper was over the first night. Everything went fine, the oldest boy remembered him, and the youngest boy liked him, and Sonny had remembered to bring something for each of them; and Isabel, who is really much nicer than I am, more open and giving, had gone to a lot of trouble about dinner and was genuinely glad to see him. And she's always been able to tease Sonny in a way that I haven't. It was nice to see her face so vivid again and to hear her laugh and watch her make Sonny laugh. She wasn't, or, anyway, she didn't seem to be, at all uneasy or embarrassed. She chatted as though there were no subject which had to be avoided and she got Sonny past his first, faint stiffness. And thank God she was there, for I was filled with that icy dread again. Everything I did seemed awkward to me, and everything I said sounded freighted with hidden meaning. I was trying to remember everything I'd heard about dope addiction and I couldn't help watching Sonny for signs. I wasn't doing it out of malice. I was trying to find out something about my brother. I was dying to hear him tell me he was safe.

"Safe!" my father grunted, whenever Mama suggested trying to move to a neighborhood which might be safer for children. "Safe, hell! Ain't no place safe for kids, nor nobody."

He always went on like this, but he wasn't, ever, really as bad as he sounded, not even on weekends, when he got drunk. As a matter of fact, he was always on the lookout for "something a little better," but he died before he found it. He died suddenly, during a drunken weekend in the middle of the war, when Sonny was fifteen. He and Sonny hadn't ever got on too well. And this was partly because Sonny was the apple of his father's eye. It was because he loved Sonny so much and was frightened for him, that he was always fighting with him. It doesn't do any good to fight with Sonny. Sonny just moves back, inside himself, where he can't be reached. But the principal reason that they never hit it off is that they were so much alike. Daddy was big and rough and loud-talking, just the opposite of Sonny, but they both had—that same privacy.

Mama tried to tell me something about this, just after Daddy died. I was home on leave from the army.

This was the last time I ever saw my mother alive. Just the same, this picture gets all mixed up in my mind with pictures I had of her when she was younger. The way I always see her is the way she used to be on a Sunday afternoon, say, when the old folks were talking after the big Sunday dinner. I always see her wearing pale blue. She'd be sitting on the sofa. And my father would be sitting in the easy chair, not far from her. And the living room would be full of church folks and relatives. There they sit, in chairs all around the living room, and the night is creeping up outside, but nobody knows it yet. You can see the darkness growing against the windowpanes and you hear the street noises every now and again, or maybe the jangling beat of a tambourine from one of the churches close by, but it's real quiet in the room. For a moment nobody's talking, but every face looks darkening, like the sky outside. And my mother rocks a little from the waist, and my father's eyes are closed. Everyone is looking at something a child can't see. For a minute they've forgotten the children. Maybe a kid is lying on the rug, half asleep. Maybe somebody's got a kid in his lap and is absent-mindedly stroking the kid's head. Maybe there's a kid, quiet and big-eyed, curled up in a big chair in the corner. The silence, the darkness coming, and the darkness in the faces frightens the child obscurely. He hopes that the hand which strokes his forehead will never stop—will never die. He hopes that there will never come a time when the old folks won't be sitting around the living room, talking about where they've come from, and what they've seen, and what's happened to them and their kinfolk.

But something deep and watchful in the child knows that this is bound to end, is already ending. In a moment someone will get up and turn on the light. Then the old folks will remember the children and they won't talk any more that day. And when light fills the room, the child is filled with darkness. He knows that every time this happens he's moved just a little closer to that darkness outside. The darkness outside is what the old folks have been talking about. It's what they've come from. It's what they endure. The child knows that they won't talk any more because if he knows too much about what's happened to *them*, he'll know too much too soon, about what's going to happen to *him*.

The last time I talked to my mother, I remember I was restless. I wanted to get out and see Isabel. We weren't married then and we had a lot to straighten out between us.

There Mama sat, in black, by the window. She was humming an old church song, *Lord, you brought me from a long ways off*. Sonny was out somewhere. Mama kept watching the streets.

"I don't know," she said, "if I'll ever see you again, after you go off from here. But I hope you'll remember the things I tried to teach you."

"Don't talk like that," I said, and smiled. "You'll be here a long time yet."

She smiled, too, but she said nothing. She was quiet for a long time. And I said, "Mama, don't you worry about nothing. I'll be writing all the time, and you be getting the checks. . . ."

"I want to talk to you about your brother," she said, suddenly. "If anything happens to me he ain't going to have nobody to look out for him."

"Mama," I said, "ain't nothing going to happen to you *or* Sonny. Sonny's all right. He's a good boy and he's got good sense."

"It ain't a question of his being a good boy," Mama said, "nor of his having good sense. It ain't only the bad ones, nor yet the dumb ones that gets sucked under." She stopped, looking at me. "Your Daddy once had a brother," she said, and she smiled in a way that made me feel she was in pain. "You didn't never know that, did you?"

"No," I said, "I never knew that," and I watched her face.

"Oh, yes," she said, "your Daddy had a brother." She looked out of the window again. "I know you never saw your Daddy cry. But *I* did—many a time, through all these years."

I asked her, "What happened to his brother? How come nobody's ever talked about him?"

This was the first time I ever saw my mother look old.

"His brother got killed," she said, "when he was just a little younger than you are now. I knew him. He was a fine boy. He was maybe a little full of the devil, but he didn't mean nobody no harm."

Then she stopped and the room was silent, exactly as it had sometimes been on those Sunday afternoons. Mama kept looking out into the streets.

"He used to have a job in the mill," she said, "and, like all young folks, he just liked to perform on Saturday nights. Saturday nights, him and your father would drift around to different places, go to dances and things like that, or just sit around with people they knew, and your father's brother would sing, he had a fine voice, and play along with himself on his guitar. Well, this particular Saturday night, him and your father was coming home from some place, and they were both a little drunk and there was a moon that night, it was bright like day. Your father's brother was feeling kind of good, and he was whistling to himself, and he had his guitar slung over his shoulder. They was coming down a hill and beneath them was a road that turned off from the highway. Well, your father's brother, being always kind of frisky, decided to run down this hill, and he did, with that guitar banging and clanging behind him, and he ran across the road, and he was making water behind a tree. And your father was sort of amused at him and he was still coming down the hill, kind of slow. Then he heard a car motor and that same minute his brother stepped from behind the tree, into the road, in the moonlight. And he started to cross the road. And your father started to run down the hill, he says he don't know why. This car was full of white men. They was all drunk, and when they seen your father's brother they let out a great whoop and holler and they aimed the car straight at him. They was having fun, they just wanted to scare him, the way they do sometimes, you know. But they was drunk. And I guess the boy, being drunk, too, and scared, kind of lost his head. By the time he jumped it was too late. Your father says he heard his brother scream when the car rolled over him, and he heard the wood of that guitar when it give, and he heard them strings go flying, and he heard them white men shouting, and the car kept on a-going and it ain't stopped till this day. And, time your father got down the hill, his brother weren't nothing but blood and pulp."

Tears were gleaming on my mother's face. There wasn't anything I could say.

"He never mentioned it," she said, "because I never let him mention it before you children. Your Daddy was like a crazy man that night and for many a night thereafter. He says he never in his life seen anything as dark as that road after the lights of that car had gone away. Weren't nothing, weren't nobody on that road, just your Daddy and his brother and that busted guitar. Oh, yes. Your Daddy never did really get right again. Till the day he died he weren't sure but that every white man he saw was the man that killed his brother."

She stopped and took out her handkerchief and dried her eyes and looked at me.

"I ain't telling you all this," she said, "to make you scared or bitter or to make you hate nobody. I'm telling you this because you got a brother. And the world ain't changed."

I guess I didn't want to believe this. I guess she saw this in my face. She turned away from me, toward the window again, searching those streets.

"But I praise my Redeemer," she said at last, "that He called your Daddy home before me. I ain't saying it to throw no flowers at myself, but, I declare, it keeps me from feeling too cast down to know I helped your father get safely through this world. Your father always acted like he was the roughest, strongest man on earth. And everybody took him to be like that. But if he hadn't had *me* there—to see his tears!"

She was crying again. Still, I couldn't move. I said, "Lord, Lord, Mama, I didn't know it was like that."

"Oh, honey," she said, "there's a lot that you don't know. But you are going to find it out." She stood up from the window and came over to me. "You got to hold on to your brother," she said, "and don't let him fall, no matter what it looks like is happening to him and no matter how evil you gets with him. You going to be evil with him many a time. But don't you forget what I told you, you hear?"

"I won't forget," I said. "Don't you worry, I won't forget. I won't let nothing happen to Sonny."

My mother smiled as though she were amused at something she saw in my face. Then, "You may not be able to stop nothing from happening. But you got to let him know you's *there*."

Two days later I was married, and then I was gone. And I had a lot of things on my mind and I pretty well forgot my promise to Mama until I got shipped home on a special furlough for her funeral.

And, after the funeral, with just Sonny and me alone in the empty kitchen, I tried to find out something about him.

"What do you want to do?" I asked him.

"I'm going to be a musician," he said.

For he had graduated, in the time I had been away, from dancing to the juke box to finding out who was playing what, and what they were doing with it, and he had bought himself a set of drums.

"You mean, you want to be a drummer?" I somehow had the feeling that being a drummer might be all right for other people but not for my brother Sonny.

"I don't think," he said, looking at me very gravely, "that I'll ever be a good drummer. But I think I can play a piano."

I frowned. I'd never played the role of the older brother quite so seriously before, had scarcely ever, in fact, *asked* Sonny a damn thing. I sensed myself in the presence of something I didn't really know how to handle, didn't understand. So I made my frown a little deeper as I asked: "What kind of musician do you want to be?"

He grinned. "How many kinds do you think there are?"

"Be *serious,*" I said.

He laughed, throwing his head back, and then looked at me. "I *am* serious."

"Well, then, for Christ's sake, stop kidding around and answer a serious question. I mean, do you want to be a concert pianist, you want to play classical music and all that, or—or what?" Long before I finished he was laughing again. "For Christ's *sake,* Sonny!"

He sobered, but with difficulty. "I'm sorry. But you sound so—*scared!*" and he was off again.

"Well, you may think it's funny now, baby, but it's not going to be so funny when you have to make your living at it, let me tell you *that.*" I was furious because I knew he was laughing at me and I didn't know why.

"No," he said, very sober now, and afraid, perhaps, that he'd hurt me, "I don't want to be a classical pianist. That isn't what interests me. I mean"—he paused, looking hard at me, as though his eyes would help me to understand, and then gestured helplessly, as though perhaps his hand would help—"I mean, I'll have a lot of studying to do, and I'll have to study *everything,* but, I mean, I want to play *with*—jazz musicians." He stopped. "I want to play jazz," he said.

Well, the word had never before sounded as heavy, as real, as it sounded that afternoon in Sonny's mouth. I just looked at him and I was probably frowning a real frown by this time. I simply couldn't see why on earth he'd want to spend his time hanging around nightclubs, clowning around on bandstands, while people pushed each other around a dance floor. It seemed—beneath him, somehow. I had never thought about it before, had never been forced to, but I suppose I had always put jazz musicians in a class with what Daddy called "good-time people."

"Are you *serious?*"

"Hell, *yes,* I'm serious."

He looked more helpless than ever, and annoyed, and deeply hurt.

I suggested, helpfully: "You mean—like Louis Armstrong?"

His face closed as though I'd struck him. "No. I'm not talking about none of that old-time, down home crap."

"Well, look, Sonny, I'm sorry, don't get mad. I just don't altogether get it, that's all. Name somebody—you know, a jazz musician you admire."

"Bird."

"Who?"

"Bird! Charlie Parker! Don't they teach you nothing in the goddamn army?"

I lit a cigarette. I was surprised and then a little amused to discover that I was trembling. "I've been out of touch," I said. "You'll have to be patient with me. Now. Who's this Parker character?"

"He's just one of the greatest jazz musicians alive," said Sonny, sullenly, his hands in his pockets, his back to me. "Maybe *the* greatest," he added, bitterly, "that's probably why *you* never heard of him."

"All right," I said, "I'm ignorant. I'm sorry. I'll go out and buy all the cat's records right away, all right?"

"It don't," said Sonny, with dignity, "make any difference to me. I don't care what you listen to. Don't do me no favors."

I was beginning to realize that I'd never seen him so upset before. With another part of my mind I was thinking that this would probably turn out to be one of those things kids go through and that I shouldn't make it seem important by pushing it too hard. Still, I didn't think it would do any harm to ask: "Doesn't all this take a lot of time? Can you make a living at it?"

He turned back to me and half leaned, half sat, on the kitchen table. "Everything takes time," he said, "and—well, yes, sure, I can make a living at it. But what I don't seem to be able to make you understand is that it's the only thing I want to do."

"Well, Sonny," I said, gently, "you know people can't always do exactly what they *want* to do—"

"*No,* I don't know that," said Sonny, surprising me. "I think people *ought* to do what they want to do, what else are they alive for?"

"You getting to be a big boy," I said desperately, "it's time you started thinking about your future."

"I'm thinking about my future," said Sonny, grimly. "I think about it all the time."

I gave up. I decided, if he didn't change his mind, that we could always talk about it later. "In the meantime," I said, "you got to finish school." We had already decided that he'd have to move in with Isabel and her folks. I knew this wasn't the ideal arrangement because Isabel's folks are inclined to be dicty and they hadn't especially wanted Isabel to marry me. But I didn't know what else to do. "And we have to get you fixed up at Isabel's."

There was a long silence. He moved from the kitchen table to the window. "That's a terrible idea. You know it yourself."

"Do you have a *better* idea?"

He just walked up and down the kitchen for a minute. He was as tall as I was. He had started to shave. I suddenly had the feeling that I didn't know him at all.

He stopped at the kitchen table and picked up my cigarettes. Looking at me with a kind of mocking, amused defiance, he put one between his lips. "You mind?"

"You smoking already?"

He lit the cigarette and nodded, watching me through the smoke. "I just wanted to see if I'd have the courage to smoke in front of you." He grinned and blew a great cloud of smoke to the ceiling. "It was easy." He looked at my face. "Come on, now. I bet you was smoking at my age, tell the truth."

I didn't say anything but the truth was on my face, and he laughed. But now there was something very strained in his laugh. "Sure. And I bet that ain't all you was doing."

He was frightening me a little. "Cut the crap," I said. "We already decided that you was going to go and live at Isabel's. Now what's got into you all of a sudden?"

"*You* decided it," he pointed out. "*I* didn't decide nothing." He stopped in front of me, leaning against the stove, arms loosely folded. "Look, brother. I don't want to stay in Harlem no more, I really don't." He was very earnest. He looked at me, then over toward the kitchen window. There was something in his eyes I'd never seen before, some thoughtfulness, some worry all his own. He rubbed the muscle of one arm. "It's time I was getting out of here."

"Where do you want to *go,* Sonny?"

"I want to join the army. Or the navy, I don't care. If I say I'm old enough, they'll believe me."

Then I got mad. It was because I was so scared. "You must be crazy. You goddamn fool, what the hell do you want to go and join the *army* for?"

"I just told you. To get out of Harlem."

"Sonny, you haven't even finished *school.* And if you really want to be a musician, how do you expect to study if you're in the *army?*"

He looked at me, trapped, and in anguish. "There's ways. I might be able to work out some kind of deal. Anyway, I'll have the G.I. Bill when I come out."

"*If* you come out." We stared at each other. "Sonny, please. Be reasonable. I know the setup is far from perfect. But we got to do the best we can."

"I ain't learning nothing in school," he said. "Even when I go." He turned away from me and opened the window and threw his cigarette out into the narrow alley. I watched his back. "At least, I ain't learning nothing you'd want me to learn." He slammed the window so hard I thought the glass would fly out, and turned back to me. "And I'm sick of the stink of these garbage cans!"

"Sonny," I said, "I know how you feel. But if you don't finish school now, you're going to be sorry later that you didn't." I grabbed him by the shoulders. "And you only got another year. It ain't so bad. And I'll come back and I swear I'll help you do *whatever* you want to do. Just try to put up with it till I come back. Will you please do that? For me?"

He didn't answer and he wouldn't look at me.

"Sonny. You hear me?"

He pulled away. "I hear you. But you never hear anything *I* say."

I didn't know what to say to that. He looked out of the window and then back at me. "OK," he said, and sighed. "I'll try."

Then I said, trying to cheer him up a little. "They got a piano at Isabel's. You can practice on it."

And as a matter of fact, it did cheer him up for a minute. "That's right," he said to himself. "I forgot that." His face relaxed a little. But the worry, the thoughtfulness, played on it still, the way shadows play on a face which is staring into the fire.

But I thought I'd never hear the end of that piano. At first, Isabel would write me, saying how nice it was that Sonny was so serious about his music and how, as soon as he came in from school, or wherever he had been when he was supposed to be at school, he went straight to that piano and stayed there until suppertime. And, after supper, he went back to that piano and stayed there until everybody went to bed. He was at the piano all day Saturday and all day Sunday. Then he bought a record player and started playing records. He'd play one record over and over again, all day long sometimes, and he'd improvise along with it on the piano. Or he'd play one section of the record, one chord, one change, one progression, then he'd do it on the piano. Then back to the record. Then back to the piano.

Well, I really don't know how they stood it. Isabel finally confessed that it wasn't like living with a person at all, it was like living with sound. And the sound didn't make any sense to her, didn't make any sense to any of them—naturally. They began, in a way, to be afflicted by this presence that was living in their home. It was as though Sonny were some sort of god, or monster. He moved in an atmosphere which wasn't like theirs at all. They fed him and he ate, he washed himself, he walked in and out of their door; he certainly wasn't nasty or unpleasant or rude, Sonny isn't any of those things; but it was as though he were all wrapped up in some cloud, some fire, some vision all his own; and there wasn't any way to reach him.

At the same time, he wasn't really a man yet, he was still a child, and they had to watch out for him in all kinds of ways. They certainly couldn't throw him out. Neither did they dare to make a great scene about that piano because even they dimly sensed, as I sensed, from so many thousands of miles away, that Sonny was at that piano playing for his life.

But he hadn't been going to school. One day a letter came from the school board and Isabel's mother got it—there had, apparently, been other letters but Sonny had torn them up. This day, when Sonny came in, Isabel's mother showed him the letter and asked where he'd been spending his time. And she finally got it out of him that he'd been down in Greenwich Village, with musicians and other characters, in a white girl's apartment. And this scared her and she started to scream at him and what came up, once she began—though she denies it to this day—was what sacrifices they were making to give Sonny a decent home and how little he appreciated it.

Sonny didn't play the piano that day. By evening Isabel's mother had calmed down but then there was the old man to deal with, and Isabel herself. Isabel says she did her best to be calm but she broke down and started crying. She says she just watched Sonny's face. She could tell, by watching him, what was happening with him. And what was happening was that they penetrated his cloud, they had reached him. Even if their fingers had been a thousand times more gentle than human fingers ever are, he could hardly help feeling that they had stripped him naked and were spitting on that nakedness. For he also had to see that his presence, that music, which was life or death to him, had been torture for them and that they had endured it, not at all for his sake, but only for mine. And Sonny couldn't take that. He can take it a little better today than he could then but he's still not very good at it and, frankly, I don't know anybody who is.

The silence of the next few days must have been louder than the sound of all the music ever played since time began. One morning, before she went to work, Isabel was in his room for something and she suddenly realized that all of his records were gone. And she knew for certain that he was gone. And he was. He went as far as the navy would carry him. He finally sent me a postcard from some place in Greece and that was the first I knew that Sonny was still alive. I didn't see him any more until we were both back in New York and the war had long been over.

He was a man by then, of course, but I wasn't willing to see it. He came by the house from time to time, but we fought almost every time we met. I didn't like the way he carried himself, loose and dreamlike all the time, and I didn't like his friends, and his music seemed to be merely an excuse for the life he led. It sounded just that weird and disordered.

Then we had a fight, a pretty awful fight, and I didn't see him for months. By and by I looked him up, where he was living, in a furnished room in the Village, and I tried to make it up. But there were lots of other people in the room and Sonny just lay on his bed, and he wouldn't come downstairs with me, and he treated these other people as though they were his family and I weren't. So I got mad and then he got mad, and then I told him that he might just as well be dead as live the way he was living. Then he stood up and he told me not to worry about him any more in life, that he *was* dead as far as I was concerned. Then he pushed me to the door and the other people looked on as though nothing were happening, and he slammed the door behind me. I stood in the hallway, staring at the door. I heard somebody laugh in the room and then the tears came to my eyes. I started down the steps, whistling to keep from crying, I kept whistling to myself, *You going to need me, baby, one of these cold, rainy days.*

I read about Sonny's trouble in the spring. Little Grace died in the fall. She was a beautiful little girl. But she only lived a little over two years. She died of polio and she suffered. She had a slight fever for a couple of days, but it didn't seem like anything and we just kept her in bed. And we would certainly have called the doctor, but the fever dropped, she seemed to be all right. So we thought it had just been a cold. Then, one day, she was up, playing, Isabel was in the kitchen fixing lunch for the two boys when they'd come in from school, and she heard Grace fall down in the living room. When you have a lot of children you don't always start running when one of them falls, unless they start screaming or something. And, this time, Grace was quiet. Yet, Isabel says that when she heard that *thump* and then that silence, something happened in her to make her afraid. And she ran to the living room and there was little Grace on the floor, all twisted up, and the reason she hadn't screamed was that she couldn't get her breath. And when she did scream, it was the worst sound, Isabel says, that she'd ever heard in all her life, and she still hears it sometimes in her dreams. Isabel will sometimes wake me up with a low, moaning, strangled sound and I have to be quick to awaken her and hold her to me and where Isabel is weeping against me seems a mortal wound.

I think I may have written Sonny the very day that little Grace was buried. I was sitting in the living room in the dark, by myself, and I suddenly thought of Sonny. My trouble made his real.

One Saturday afternoon, when Sonny had been living with us, or, anyway, been in our house, for nearly two weeks, I found myself wandering aimlessly about the living room, drinking from a can of beer, and trying to work up the courage to search Sonny's room. He was out, he was usually out whenever I was home, and Isabel had taken the children to see their grandparents. Suddenly I was standing still in front of the living room window, watching Seventh Avenue. The idea of searching Sonny's room made me still. I scarcely dared to admit to myself what I'd be searching for. I didn't know what I'd do if I found it. Or if I didn't.

On the sidewalk across from me, near the entrance to a barbecue joint, some people were holding an old-fashioned revival meeting. The barbecue cook, wearing a dirty white apron, his conked hair reddish and metallic in the pale sun, and a cigarette between his lips, stood in the doorway, watching them. Kids and older people paused in their errands and stood there, along with some older men and a couple of very tough-looking women who watched everything that happened on the avenue, as though they owned it, or were maybe owned by it. Well, they were watching this, too. The revival was being carried on by three sisters in black, and a brother. All they had were their voices and their Bibles and a tambourine. The brother was testifying and while he testified two of the sisters stood together, seeming to say, amen, and the third sister walked around with the tambourine outstretched and a couple of people dropped coins into it. Then the brother's testimony ended and the sister who had been taking up the collection dumped the coins into her palm and transferred them to the pocket of her long black robe. Then she raised both hands, striking the tambourine against the air, and then against one hand, and she started to sing. And the two other sisters and the brother joined in.

It was strange, suddenly, to watch, though I had been seeing these street meetings all my life. So, of course, had everybody else down there. Yet, they paused and watched and listened and I stood still at the window. *"Tis the old ship of Zion,"* they sang, and the sister with the tambourine kept a steady, jangling beat, *"it has rescued many a thousand!"* Not a soul under the sound of their voices was hearing this song for the first time, not one of them had been rescued. Nor had they seen much in the way of rescue work being done around them. Neither did they especially believe in the holiness of the three sisters and the brother, they knew too much about them, knew where they lived, and how. The woman with the tambourine, whose voice dominated the air, whose face was bright with joy, was divided by very little from the woman who stood watching her, a cigarette between her heavy, chapped lips, her hair a cuckoo's nest, her face scarred and swollen from many beatings, and her black eyes glittering like coal. Perhaps they both knew this, which was why, when, as rarely, they addressed each other, they addressed each other as Sister. As the singing filled the air the watching, listening faces underwent a change, the eyes focusing on something within; the music seemed to soothe a poison out of them; and time seemed, nearly, to fall away from the sullen, belligerent, battered faces, as though they were fleeing back to their first condition, while dreaming of their last. The barbecue cook half shook his head and smiled, and dropped his cigarette and disappeared into his joint. A man fumbled in his pockets for change and stood holding it in his hand impatiently, as though he had just remembered a pressing appointment further up the avenue. He looked furious. Then I saw Sonny, standing on the edge of the crowd. He was carrying a wide, flat notebook with a green cover, and it made him look, from where I was standing, almost like a schoolboy. The coppery sun brought out the copper in his skin, he was very faintly smiling, standing very still. Then the singing stopped, the tambourine turned into a collection plate again. The furious man dropped in his coins and vanished, so did a couple of the women, and Sonny dropped some change in the plate, looking directly at the woman with a little smile. He started across the avenue, toward the house. He has a slow, loping walk, something like the way Harlem hipsters walk, only he's imposed on this his own half-beat. I had never really noticed it before.

I stayed at the window, both relieved and apprehensive. As Sonny disappeared from my sight, they began singing again. And they were still singing when his key turned in the lock.

"Hey," he said.

"Hey, yourself. You want some beer?"

"No. Well, maybe." But he came up to the window and stood beside me, looking out. "What a warm voice," he said.

They were singing *If I could only hear my mother pray again!*

"Yes," I said, "and she can sure beat that tambourine."

"But what a terrible song," he said, and laughed. He dropped his notebook on the sofa and disappeared into the kitchen. "Where's Isabel and the kids?"

"I think they went to see their grandparents. You hungry?"

"No." He came back into the living room with his can of beer. "You want to come some place with me tonight?"

I sensed, I don't know how, that I couldn't possibly say no. "Sure. Where?"

He sat down on the sofa and picked up his notebook and started leafing through it. "I'm going to sit in with some fellows in a joint in the Village."

"You mean, you're going to play, tonight?"

"That's right." He took a swallow of his beer and moved back to the window. He gave me a sidelong look. "If you can stand it."

"I'll try," I said.

He smiled to himself and we both watched as the meeting across the way broke up. The three sisters and the brother, heads bowed, were singing *God be with you till we meet again*. The faces around them were very quiet. Then the song ended. The small crowd dispersed. We watched the three women and the lone man walk slowly up the avenue.

"When she was singing before," said Sonny, abruptly, "her voice reminded me for a minute of what heroin feels like sometimes—when it's in your veins. It makes you feel sort of warm and cool at the same time. And distant. And—and sure." He sipped his beer, very deliberately not looking at me. I watched his face. "It makes you feel—in control. Sometimes you've got to have that feeling."

"Do you?" I sat down slowly in the easy chair.

"Sometimes." He went to the sofa and picked up his notebook again. "Some people do."

"In order," I asked, "to play?" And my voice was very ugly, full of contempt and anger.

"Well"—he looked at me with great, troubled eyes, as though, in fact, he hoped his eyes would tell me things he could never otherwise say—"they *think* so. And *if* they think so—!"

"And what do *you* think?" I asked.

He sat on the sofa and put his can of beer on the floor. "I don't know," he said, and I couldn't be sure if he were answering my question or pursuing his thoughts. His face didn't tell me. "It's not so much to *play*. It's to *stand* it, to be able to make it at all. On any level." He frowned and smiled: "In order to keep from shaking to pieces."

"But these friends of yours," I said, "they seem to shake themselves to pieces pretty goddamn fast."

"Maybe." He played with the notebook. And something told me that I should curb my tongue, that Sonny was doing his best to talk, that I should listen. "But of course you only know the ones that've gone to pieces. Some don't—or at least they haven't *yet* and that's just about all *any* of us can say." He paused. "And then there are some who just live, really, in hell, and they know it and they see what's happening and they go right on. I don't know." He sighed, dropped the notebook, folded his arms. "Some guys, you can tell from the way they play, they on something *all* the time. And you can see that, well, it makes something real for them. But of course," he picked up his beer from the floor and sipped it and put the can down again, "they *want* to, too, you've got to see that. Even some of them that say they don't—*some,* not all."

"And what about you?" I asked—I couldn't help it. "What about you? Do *you* want to?"

He stood up and walked to the window and remained silent for a long time. Then he sighed. "Me," he said. Then: "While I was downstairs before, on my way here, listening to that woman sing, it struck me all of a sudden how much suffering she must have had to go through—to sing like that. It's *repulsive* to think you have to suffer that much."

I said: "But there's no way not to suffer—is there, Sonny?"

"I believe not," he said and smiled, "but that's never stopped anyone from trying." He looked at me. "Has it?" I realized, with this mocking look, that there stood between us, forever, beyond the power of time or forgiveness, the fact that I had held silence—so long!—when he had needed human speech to help him. He turned back to the window. "No, there's no way not to suffer. But you try all kinds of ways to keep from drowning in it, to keep on top of it, and to make it seem—well, like *you.* Like you did something, all right, and now you're suffering for it. You know?" I said nothing. "Well you know," he said, impatiently, "why *do* people suffer? Maybe it's better to do something to give it a reason, *any* reason."

"But we just agreed," I said, "that there's no way not to suffer. Isn't it better, then, just to—take it?"

"But nobody just takes it," Sonny cried, "that's what I'm telling you! *Everybody* tries not to. You're just hung up on the *way* some people try—it's not *your* way!"

The hair on my face began to itch, my face felt wet. "That's not true," I said, "that's not true. I don't give a damn what other people do, I don't even care how they suffer. I just care how *you* suffer." And he looked at me. "Please believe me," I said, "I don't want to see you—die—trying not to suffer."

"I won't," he said, flatly, "die trying not to suffer. At least, not any faster than anybody else."

"But there's no need," I said, trying to laugh, "is there? in killing yourself."

I wanted to say more, but I couldn't. I wanted to talk about will power and how life could be—well, beautiful. I wanted to say that it was all within; but was it? or, rather, wasn't that exactly the trouble? And I wanted to promise that I would never fail him again. But it would all have sounded—empty words and lies.

So I made the promise to myself and prayed that I would keep it.

"It's terrible sometimes, inside," he said, "that's what's the trouble. You walk these streets, black and funky and cold, and there's not really a living ass to talk to, and there's nothing shaking, and there's no way of getting it out—that storm inside. You can't talk it and you can't make love with it, and when you finally try to get with it and play it, you realize *nobody's* listening. So *you've* got to listen. You got to find a way to listen."

And then he walked away from the window and sat on the sofa again, as though all the wind had suddenly been knocked out of him. "Sometimes you'll do *anything* to play, even cut your mother's throat." He laughed and looked at me. "Or your brother's." Then he sobered. "Or your own." Then: "Don't worry. I'm all right now and I think I'll *be* all right. But I can't forget—where I've been. I don't mean just the physical place I've been, I mean where I've *been*. And *what* I've been."

"What have you been, Sonny?" I asked.

He smiled—but sat sideways on the sofa, his elbow resting on the back, his fingers playing with his mouth and chin, not looking at me. "I've been something I didn't recognize, didn't know I could be. Didn't know anybody could be." He stopped, looking inward, looking helplessly young, looking old. "I'm not talking about it now because I feel *guilty* or anything like that—maybe it would be better if I did, I don't know. Anyway, I can't really talk about it. Not to you, not to anybody," and now he turned and faced me. "Sometimes, you know, and it was actually when I was most *out* of the world, I felt that I was in it, that I was *with* it, really, and I could play or I didn't really have to *play,* it just came out of me, it was there. And I don't know how I played, thinking about it now, but I know I did awful things, those times, sometimes, to people. Or it wasn't that I *did* anything to them—it was that they weren't real." He picked up the beer can; it was empty; he rolled it between his palms: "And other times—well, I needed a fix, I needed to find a place to lean, I needed to clear a space to *listen*—and I couldn't find it, and I—went crazy, I did terrible things to *me,* I was terrible *for* me." He began pressing the beer can between his hands, I watched the metal begin to give. It glittered, as he played with it, like a knife, and I was afraid he would cut himself, but I said nothing. "Oh well. I can never tell you. I was all by myself at the bottom of something, stinking and sweating and crying and shaking, and I smelled it, you know? *my* stink, and I thought I'd die if I couldn't get away from it and yet, all the same, I knew that everything I was doing was just locking me in with it. And I didn't know," he paused, still flattening the beer car, "I didn't know, I still *don't* know, something kept telling me that maybe it was good to smell your own stink, but I didn't think that *that* was what I'd been trying to do—and—who can stand it?" and he abruptly dropped the ruined beer can, looking at me with a small, still smile, and then rose, walking to the window as though it were the lodestone rock. I watched his face, he watched the avenue. "I couldn't tell you when Mama died—but the reason I wanted to leave Harlem so bad was to get away from drugs. And then, when I ran away, that's what I was running from—really. When I came back, nothing had changed, *I* hadn't changed, I was just—older." And he stopped, drumming with his fingers on the windowpane. The sun had vanished, soon darkness would fall. I watched his face. "It can come again," he said, almost as though speaking to himself. Then he turned to me. "It can come again," he repeated. "I just want you to know that."

"All right," I said, at last. "So it can come again, All right."

He smiled, but the smile was sorrowful. "I had to try to tell you," he said.

"Yes," I said. "I understand that."

"You're my brother," he said, looking straight at me, and not smiling at all.

"Yes," I repeated, "yes. I understand that."

He turned back to the window, looking out. "All that hatred down there," he said, "all that hatred and misery and love. It's a wonder it doesn't blow the avenue apart."

We went to the only nightclub on a short, dark street, downtown. We squeezed through the narrow, chattering, jam-packed bar to the entrance of the big room, where the bandstand was. And we stood there for a moment, for the lights were very dim in this room and we couldn't see. Then, "Hello, boy," said a voice and an enormous black man, much older than Sonny or myself, erupted out of all that atmospheric lighting and put an arm around Sonny's shoulder. "I been sitting right here," he said, "waiting for you."

He had a big voice, too, and heads in the darkness turned toward us.

Sonny grinned and pulled a little away, and said, "Creole, this is my brother. I told you about him."

Creole shook my hand. "I'm glad to meet you, son," he said, and it was clear that he was glad to meet me *there*, for Sonny's sake. And he smiled, "You got a real musician in *your* family," and he took his arm from Sonny's shoulder and slapped him, lightly, affectionately, with the back of his hand.

"Well. Now I've heard it all," said a voice behind us. This was another musician, and a friend of Sonny's, a coal-black, cheerful-looking man, built close to the ground. He immediately began confiding to me, at the top of his lungs, the most terrible things about Sonny, his teeth gleaming like a lighthouse and his laugh coming up out of him like the beginning of an earthquake. And it turned out that everyone at the bar knew Sonny, or almost everyone; some were musicians, working there, or nearby, or not working, some were simply hangers-on, and some were there to hear Sonny play. I was introduced to all of them and they were all very polite to me. Yet, it was clear that, for them, I was only Sonny's brother. Here, I was in Sonny's world. Or, rather: his kingdom. Here, it was not even a question that his veins bore royal blood.

They were going to play soon and Creole installed me, by myself, at a table in a dark corner. Then I watched them, Creole, and the little black man, and Sonny, and the others, while they horsed around, standing just below the bandstand. The light from the bandstand spilled just a little short of them and, watching them laughing and gesturing and moving about, I had the feeling that they, nevertheless, were being most careful not to step into that circle of light too suddenly: that if they moved into the light too suddenly, without thinking, they would perish in flame. Then, while I watched, one of them, the small, black man, moved into the light and crossed the bandstand and started fooling around with his drums. Then—being funny and being, also, extremely ceremonious—Creole took Sonny by the arm and led him to the piano. A woman's voice called Sonny's name and a few hands started clapping. And Sonny, also being funny and being ceremonious, and so touched, I think, that he could have cried, but neither hiding it nor showing it, riding it like a man, grinned, and put both hands to his heart and bowed from the waist.

Creole then went to the bass fiddle and a lean, very bright-skinned brown man jumped up on the bandstand and picked up his horn. So there they were, and the atmosphere on the bandstand and in the room began to change and tighten. Someone stepped up to the microphone and announced them. Then there were all kinds of murmurs. Some people at the bar shushed others. The waitress ran around, frantically getting in the last orders, guys and chicks got closer to each other, and the lights on the bandstand, on the quartet, turned to a kind of indigo. Then they all looked different there. Creole looked about him for the last time, as though he were making certain that all his chickens were in the coop, and then he—jumped and struck the fiddle. And there they were.

All I know about music is that not many people ever really hear it. And even then, on the rare occasions when something opens within, and the music enters, what we mainly hear, or hear corroborated, are personal, private, vanishing evocations. But the man who creates the music is hearing something else, is dealing with the roar rising from the void and imposing order on it as it hits the air. What is evoked in him, then, is of another order, more terrible because it has no words, and triumphant, too, for that same reason. And his triumph, when he triumphs, is ours. I just watched Sonny's face. His face was troubled, he was working hard, but he wasn't with it. And I had the feeling that, in a way, everyone on the bandstand was waiting for him, both waiting for him and pushing him along. But as I began to watch Creole, I realized that it was Creole who held them all back. He had them on a short rein. Up there, keeping the beat with his whole body, wailing on the fiddle, with his eyes half closed, he was listening to everything, but he was listening to Sonny. He was having a dialogue with Sonny. He wanted Sonny to leave the shoreline and strike out for the deep water. He was Sonny's witness that deep water and drowning were not the same thing—he had been there, and he knew. And he wanted Sonny to know. He was waiting for Sonny to do the things on the keys which would let Creole know that Sonny was in the water.

And, while Creole listened, Sonny moved, deep within, exactly like someone in torment. I had never before thought of how awful the relationship must be between the musician and his instrument. He has to fill it, this instrument, with the breath of life, his own. He has to make it do what he wants it to do. And a piano is just a piano. It's made out of so much wood and wires and little hammers and big ones, and ivory. While there's only so much you can do with it, the only way to find this out is to try; to try and make it do everything.

And Sonny hadn't been near a piano for over a year. And he wasn't on much better terms with his life, not the life that stretched before him now. He and the piano stammered, started one way, got scared, stopped; started another way, panicked, marked time, started again; then seemed to have found a direction, panicked again, got stuck. And the face I saw on Sonny I'd never seen before. Everything had been burned out of it, and, at the same time, things usually hidden were being burned in, by the fire and fury of the battle which was occurring in him up there.

Yet, watching Creole's face as they neared the end of the first set, I had the feeling that something had happened, something I hadn't heard. Then they finished, there was scattered applause, and then, without an instant's warning, Creole started into something else, it was almost sardonic, it was *Am I Blue*. And, as though he commanded, Sonny began to play. Something began to happen. And Creole let out the reins. The dry, low, black man said something awful on the drums, Creole answered, and the drums talked back. Then the horn insisted, sweet and high, slightly detached perhaps, and Creole listened, commenting now and then, dry, and driving, beautiful and calm and old. Then they all came together again, and Sonny was part of the family again. I could tell this from his face. He seemed to have found, right there beneath his fingers, a damn brand-new piano. It seemed that he couldn't get over it. Then, for awhile, just being happy with Sonny, they seemed to be agreeing with him that brand-new pianos certainly were a gas.

Then Creole stepped forward to remind them that what they were playing was the blues. He hit something in all of them, he hit something in me, myself, and the music tightened and deepened, apprehension began to beat the air. Creole began to tell us what the blues were all about. They were not about anything very new. He and his boys up there were keeping it new, at the risk of ruin, destruction, madness, and death, in order to find new ways to make us listen. For, while the tale of how we suffer, and how we are delighted, and how we may triumph is never new, it always must be heard. There isn't any other tale to tell, it's the only light we've got in all this darkness.

And this tale, according to that face, that body, those strong hands on those strings, has another aspect in every country, and a new depth in every generation. Listen, Creole seemed to be saying, listen. Now these are Sonny's blues. He made the little black man on the drums know it, and the bright, brown man on the horn. Creole wasn't trying any longer to get Sonny in the water. He was wishing him Godspeed. Then he stepped back, very slowly, filling the air with the immense suggestion that Sonny speak for himself.

Then they all gathered around Sonny and Sonny played. Every now and again one of them seemed to say, amen. Sonny's fingers filled the air with life, his life. But that life contained so many others. And Sonny went all the way back, he really began with the spare, flat statement of the opening phrase of the song. Then he began to make it his. It was very beautiful because it wasn't hurried and it was no longer a lament. I seemed to hear with what burning he had made it his, with what burning we had yet to make it ours, how we could cease lamenting. Freedom lurked around us and I understood, at last, that he could help us to be free if we would listen, that he would never be free until we did. Yet, there was no battle in his face now. I heard what he had gone through, and would continue to go through until he came to rest in earth. He had made it his: that long line, of which we knew only Mama and Daddy. And he was giving it back, as everything must be given back, so that, passing through death, it can live forever. I saw my mother's face again, and felt, for the first time, how the stones of the road she had walked on must have bruised her feet. I saw the moonlit road where my father's brother died. And it brought something else back to me, and carried me past it, I saw my little girl again and felt Isabel's tears again, and I felt my own tears begin to rise. And I was yet aware that this was only a moment, that the world waited outside, as hungry as a tiger, and that trouble stretched above us, longer than the sky.

Then it was over. Creole and Sonny let out their breath, both soaking wet, and grinning. There was a lot of applause and some of it was real. In the dark, the girl came by and I asked her to take drinks to the bandstand. There was a long pause, while they talked up there in the indigo light and after awhile I saw the girl put a Scotch and milk on top of the piano for Sonny. He didn't seem to notice it, but just before they started playing again, he sipped from it and looked toward me, and nodded. Then he put it back on top of the piano. For me, then, as they began to play again, it glowed and shook above my brother's head like the very cup of trembling.

ALSTON ANDERSON

A native of Panama educated in Kingston, Jamaica, Alston Anderson came to the United States and earned a degree from North Carolina College after a stint from 1943 to 1946 in the U.S. Army. He did graduate work in philosophy at Columbia University, then studied eighteenth-century German metaphysics at the Sorbonne in Paris. It was there that he began to write after being inspired by William Faulkner and Franz Kafka.

Anderson told Robert Graves that he wrote *Lover Man* (from which "Dance of the Infidels" is taken) "—first called *Darn that Dream*, . . . to the accompaniment of Harold Land's beautiful tenor-saxophone solo in the song." "Dance of the Infidels," titled after Clifford Brown's composition, shows Anderson's knowledge of the bop era, its musicians and tunes, and, as seems almost inevitable in so many jazz pieces, the drug scene.

DANCE OF THE INFIDELS

I used to listen to jazz all day and most of the night. I'd go to bed by it and wake up with it. Look like nobody else in town was as crazy about it as me; they all said I was 'music happy.' But that was OK by me. They live their life and I live my own.

I used to go to a little cafe on Davis Street a whole lot. There was a big old juke box in the place, and I'd stoop over and put my ear right up against the speaker and listen. That way all I could hear in the whole wide world was music, and that was fine with me. So this night when I walked in the cafe and seen a man doing the same thing—leaning down with his ear against the speaker—I went over and tapped him on the shoulder.

He looked up. I hadn't never seen him before. 'I got that record at home,' I said.

'Oh, yeah?'

'Yeah.'

'Well, that's crazy,' he said, and put his ear to the speaker again. Even while he was stooped over I could tell he was taller than me. When the record was finished and he stood up I noticed that his eyes had a real far-away look in them, like he was used to looking at mountains from a distance.

'You want to go over to my place and listen to records?' I said. He just looked at me, real blank. Then he said 'Crazy,' and we went outside to the street. He walked like he had springs in the toes of his shoes; like every step he took was going to be a long one, so that you were always surprised at how short they were. All the way to my place he didn't say a word. Most times we walked with enough room between us for a growed woman to walk through. Then one time a man passed us and we had to move together to let him by.

Our coat sleeves touched, and he jumped like he'd been burnt. 'What the hell is this?' I thought to myself. I got to thinking right then of how to get rid of him without hurting his feelings.

When we got to my place I offered him a seat, but he didn't sit down. I don't mean to say nothing derogatory about him, but he acted just like a dog acts when he gets to a place he ain't never been in before: he walked all around and sniffed at things. You could almost hear him sniffing out loud.

'You want a drink?' I said.

'You got wine?'

'I ain't got nothing but whisky.'

'No thanks.'

'I can go get some wine, if you want.'

'I'll go get it,' he said.

'No, I'll get it. Make yourself at home.'

I went out and got the wine and when I got back he was sitting in a chair with his legs crossed. I still couldn't figure him out. He looked like he was in a world all his own.

'You blow?' he said.

'Blow?'

'Yeah. You play anything?'

'No. No, I don't play nothing. You?'

'I blow box.'

'You blow what?'

'Piano.'

He sounded irritant because I couldn't understand everything he said.

'You from around here?'

'I'm from The Apple,' he said. Then he knew right off I didn't get it so he said, 'New York. I'm down here visiting my people.'

I poured myself a drink and turned on the record player. Then I remembered that I hadn't opened the wine bottle, so I opened it and poured him a drink. While the record player was warming up I got to leafing through the records. He came over and stood beside me, so I held the records so's he could read the labels. Our coat sleeves touched again and he moved away a little. I handed the records to him and said, 'Here. Why'nt you play what you want?' I said it real soft so's not to offend him and went over and sat on the couch.

He got to looking through the records, and every once in a while he'd say, 'Solid!' Then he got to laughing. Not at me or anything in particular; just laughing.

'Where'd you pick up on these, man?'

'I gets them from a store in New York,' I said. I meant to say The Apple instead of New York, and I was sorry I didn't. He turned around and looked at me, half-smiling, like *he* was the one that was trying to figure *me* out.

He put a record on the player. It was 'Salt Peanuts' by Dizzie Gillespie, with Don Byas on tenor sax. I thought to tell him that that was the first one I bought, that I got it while I was in the Army in New Orleans; but I didn't. He turned the volume up real loud and sat down. I got up and turned it down a little. I knew he'd be disappointed so I said, 'Neighbours.' He nodded.

We sat there listening for a while, neither of us talking. Then he got to riffing Dizzie's solo out loud. 'Well I'll be damn!' I thought. I knew the solo real well myself, so I riffed right along with him. I kept listening for him to make a mistake. He didn't. When the solo was over we looked at one another, both of us smiling. It was like looking at somebody and thinking for a split minute that you was looking at yourself. We both laughed. He got up and came over to me and stretched out his hand.

'Skin,' he said. I slapped his palm real light and he said, 'Solid.' Then we shook hands, and he sat down again. I felt a lot better about his being there. In fact, I felt right then that he could stay there for the rest of his natural life, Amen.

We sat there for about an hour, riffing and listening: Bird, Miles Davis, Dizzie, Bud Powell . . . strictly the kick. He was mostly playing records with Bud on them, so he could listen to the piano. We was having a natural ball.

Then he turned to me and said, 'Do you turn?'

'Do I what?'

'Aw, man,' he said. He looked real disgusted. I'd heard what he said, alright, but I had to have time to figure out what he meant. Then I got it.

'You mean do I smoke?'

'Yeah, man. Yeah.'

'No,' I said, 'but you can go 'head if you want.'

I hadn't never seen anybody smoke marijuana. I'd heard it was bad, so I stayed away from it. But I figured that if he wanted to do it that was his business, not mine. I poured myself another drink and sipped it. He didn't move. When the record was over I got up and took it off. 'What you wanna hear?' I said.

'Play some J. J.,' he said. His mood had done changed, and mine had, too. 'God damn pot head,' I thought. But I liked him—after all, he was the first person I'd met who loved jazz as much as I do—so I was sorry I'd thought it. I found a record by J. J. Johnson and put it on. He still didn't move; just sat there looking down at the floor, like he was thinking. Then he cursed—real soft, but I heard it—and reached in his coat pocket and took out a reefer. He straightened out the ends of it and lit it.

I sat there watching him smoke—taking deep drags and then holding his breath so that no smoke came out—and I thought: what the hell; once won't hurt, will it?

'Gimme a drag,' I said. He handed it to me without a word and I took it. I smoked it just like he had, holding my breath so that the smoke stayed down. We both smoked it, passing it back and forth till it was down to a fraction. Then he put it out and put it in his pocket. 'Gotta save roaches,' he said, and smiled.

For a while I didn't feel anything; just the whisky. Then I got up to change the record—that is I started getting up, because it looked like I'd never stop rising up off that couch—and I knew it had hit me. I took the record off and put on 'Scrapple from the Apple' by Charlie Parker, then sat back down. While I was doing it I noticed that everything in the room looked like it had shifted just a little bit; like somebody had come in and moved everything a little up and to the left.

But it was sitting there listening to Bird and Miles playing in unison that I really got the feel of it. I got up and turned the volume up a little, then sat back down. I got up and turned it up some more. It was just like I'd heard them for the first time. I mean *really* heard them. I turned the record player up full blast. Wail, Bird. I tried to turn it up some more, but the damn thing just wouldn't go any louder. Wail, Bird. To hell with neighbours. To hell with everybody. WAIL, Bird!

We sat there and smoked a couple more sticks and got high as kites. After that he took to coming by my place nearbout every night, and when he ran out of pot it didn't matter. We'd get juiced and have ourselves an A-grade ball, listening and riffing.

I liked the pot. I like it a whole lot. When Ronnie—his name was Ronald Johnson—went back to New York he promised he'd write to me and send me some. Sure enough, about a week after he was gone here come a newspaper addressed to me, all rolled up. I unrolled it real slow, and there was a small package of pot pasted on the inside sheet. On the covering of the package he wrote one word: 'Wail.'

I didn't hear from him after that. I wrote to him and thanked him for the pot, and when he didn't answer I wrote again: nothing. So along about March of the next year I went on up to New York.

I got off the train at Pennsylvania Station and went outside to 34th Street and got a taxi. It was the first time I had ever been to New York. I told the driver where I wanted to go—it was a house on 127th Street near Lenox Avenue—and he took me through the city and through Central Park and then up to Harlem. I liked New York a lot, especially driving through the park. Harlem wasn't nothing like I thought it would be. I'd always imagined there would be lots of shambly houses and all that; but it was all built up, just like the rest of New York. And to this day I've never got over that.

So anyway, me and this taxi go on up to 127th Street and I pay the driver and start up the stairs. I'd checked my bag at the train station, so I didn't have anything to carry. The building was old and dirty and even in the daytime it was dark. I got to Ronnie's apartment and rang the bell. Nothing happened. Instead of ringing it again, like I thought of doing, I just stood there and waited. There was a circle in the upper half of the door and after a while it looked like it moved, so I tried to look through it. I couldn't.

'What do you want?' a man's voice said.

'Do Ronald Johnson live here?'

'What do you want?' the voice said again.

'Do Ronald Johnson—'

The door opened, and a man with hair that looked like it had been pasted down with axle grease poked his head out. He blinked his eyes and said, 'Who're you?'

'I'm Benevolence Delaney,' I said.

'You're *who*?'

I said it again. He kind of smirked and looked me up and down from head to shoes. Then he said, 'He's not here. If you want to see him you can . . .' He looked me up and down again. 'He's at the Y-Bar. You know where that is?'

'No.'

He told me where it was and I found it. It was almost as dark inside it as it had been in the apartment building. I went to the bar and ordered a shot, then looked around. We saw each other at about the same time. He was at the far end of the bar. He got up off his stool real slow, looking like he didn't believe what his eyes was showing him.

'Well I'll be gaaat-dam,' he said. 'My boy.' We shook hands and looked at one another.

'How you doin'?' I said.

'Aw, man,' he said. He looked me up and down just like his friend had done back at the apartment. I got the feeling he was embarrassed to see me; like I was a third cousin that was born on the wrong side of the river.

'You look good,' I said; but he didn't. He'd lost weight, and his clothes hung on him most like they do on a hatrack. When he talked his eyes kept shifting all around, like any minute he expected somebody to try and hit him.

'Ain't nothing shaking, huss,' he said. 'Nothing but dues, you dig? Kats won't let a man live. I had a gig up at The Track for a while—house band, you dig?—then my habit got me and I had to split but I kicked it and got another gig up in the Bronx. But them square mother-hubbers drug me so terrible I had to put that down. West Indians, you dig? I dig what they're sayin', man, but I can't make that time. How *you* doing, man? When'd you fall in town?'

He was talking real fast and looking all around, like I said, and I didn't hardly understand what he was talking about. I asked him what 'The Track' was and he told me it was the nickname for the Savoy Ballroom; only this time he didn't get irritant when I asked him. He was glad to see me, and said it. I told him I'd just got into town and he said, 'You got a pad?'

'No.'

'You could stay at my pad, but I'm sharing it with a stud.'

'I saw him,' I said. 'I reckon I'll get me a room in a hotel.'

'Solid,' he said. 'Let's fall down to the Dewey Square Hotel and get you a pad.'

We walked across town and caught a 7th Avenue bus and went down to the Dewey Square Hotel. I registered and then we went to a little square right near 116th Street and sat on a bench and talked. I asked him if he'd gotten my letters and he said yes. I thanked him again for the pot and said, 'You know where I can get some?'

'Some pot?'

'Yeah.'

'Ain't much shaking. The Man done put the finger on the kats and everybody's layin' low. My boy got busted.'

I looked at him and shook my head. I couldn't hardly understand a word that man said; but I learned to figure it out. He thought for a while and then he said, 'Come on, let's split.' We got up and walked over to 116th Street and 8th Avenue and caught the subway. We rode up to 145th Street and got off and went to a poolroom near the corner.

The poolroom was way bigger that the one back home, with about twelve tables to it. It was packed full of niggers. I followed Ronnie on back to the back of the place, edging by people, and when he stopped I stopped, too. It looked like he got real innerested in one of the games. The man that was shooting was real good. It looked like he was going run 'em all the way, eight-ball and all. I figured that Ronnie and me would be up soon, and I was kinda looking forward to a game. I noticed that nobody in the place was looking at anybody else; just at the pool tables. Then the man that was shooting missed. He cursed and lit a cigarette and moved back to the wall. He was standing right alongside Ronnie. I just barely seen it, I swear, I seen him slip a couple of reefers into Ronnie's hand and Ronnie slipped him some money. They didn't look at one another once the whole time, and not a word was said. Then Ronnie said 'Come on,' and we edged our way out to the street.

'That was real cool,' I said.

'*Got* to be, man,' he said. 'The Man done put niggers on the police force so they can put the finger on other niggers. And the squares are all happy out of their heads just because they got coloured cops. Ain't that a bitch?'

'Yeah,' I said.

'The only stripes I dig are *pinstripes*, man. I ain't got no eyes a-tall for them wide ones. Come on, let's fall down to my pad and get happy.'

We caught the 145th Street crosstown bus and rode over to 8th Avenue, and then we caught the 8th Avenue bus and went down to 127th Street and walked across town to his pad. His room-mate wasn't at home. It was the funniest apartment I'd ever seen. As you come in the door the first thing that hits you is a painting of Our Lord and Saviour Jesus Christ with a crown of thorns on His head. His face looked so sad it nearbout scared me. Underneath it there was a sofa with a leopard skin cover. There was a piano against the wall, and even looking at it you could tell the tone wouldn't be so hot; it was old. Through an open doorway you could see a stove with a pot on it.

'Siddown,' Ronnie said. I started to sit on the sofa, but that leopard skin was a little too much for me so I sat in an armchair with a faded green cover on it. I did my best not to look at that leopard skin.

Ronnie went into the kitchen and got to fumbling around. I looked around for something to pass the time and picked up a book. It was *Native Son* by Richard Wright. I read the first page of it and all of a sudden there was a wild sound above my head; a sound of trumpets. It made me jump, and when I looked up Ronnie was standing in the doorway laughing his head off.

'Wake up and live, Bennie!' he said. 'Things to *come,* man!'

I laughed and put the book down. Then I saw that Ronnie'd done had a speaker rigged up in the front room. The record player was in the kitchen. He came in and lit up a stick, or 'a joint,' like he said, and handed it to me. I took a few deep drags and handed it back to him, with the sound of trumpets like drumbeats in my ears.

'You short, black son of a bitch,' Ronnie said, and laughed. He was glad to see me alright. I could tell by his eyes.

So we sat there and got high and listened to records. Then he said his room-mate would be back soon, and since I didn't want to see him I left. I went down to Pennsylvania Station and got my bag out of check, then went to the Dewey Square. It was good to be in New York, and to be high again. It was real good.

I didn't see him for about a week after that. I'd go up to his place—he didn't have telephone—and either nobody was there or his greasy-head room-mate would tell me he didn't know where Ronnie was. I went to the Y-Bar several times, but I never saw him. So I got to looking around town on my own. I went down to Broadway a few times and looked at all the bright lights and the big Camel advertisement of a man with smoke-rings coming out his mouth. I took in a few movies, and it was sitting in a picture-show one night that I figured out where I might find him. The Dewey Square Hotel is on 117th Street, and right around the corner from it is a nightclub called 'Minton's Playhouse.' Ronnie showed it to me when he first brought me to the hotel. And so, when the movie was over, I went uptown.

My hunch paid off. Minton's was divided into two sections. There was a bar with a juke box in it, just like a regular bar. Then there was a swinging door and when it swung open you could hear live music coming from the inside room. Ronnie wasn't in the bar so I started into the back room. Somebody told me at the door that I'd have to pay more for my drinks in the back, but I said I didn't care and went on in. There was a row of tables on each side of a long room, and near the bandstand there was a dance floor about the size of a big playpen. It was dark inside, but most of the people were wearing dark glasses. I didn't know any of the musicians that were playing, but they were good. I sat at a table and ordered a drink. I didn't recognize Ronnie at first, because I hadn't ever seen him in dark glasses. I picked up my drink and went over and sat beside him. While the band was playing we didn't talk. When they stopped he said, 'Kicks to see you, man.' We shook hands.

'Where you been?' I said.

'Aw, man. I been goofing.'

'Oh, yeah?'

'Yeah, man. Dues, you dig? Gotta pay 'em."

'I been looking for you,' I said.

'I'm hip.'

The band started up again, so we stopped talking and listened. I noticed he was drinking a coke, and I touched him and asked him by signal if he wanted a drink. He frowned and shook his head. After a long while he turned to me and said, 'You got any bread?'

'I ain't got much,' I said. 'How much you need?'

'Three cents,' he said.

'Three *cents*?'

'Three bucks, man.'

'Oh,' I said. 'Sure, I got that much.' I started to reach for the money but he stopped me. 'Let's split,' he said. I paid the waiter and we went outdoors.

He called a cab and we drove about fifteen blocks uptown. We got out and went to a bar. He just stood inside the doorway and looked all around. He didn't see who or what it was he wanted, so we walked on to another bar. Same thing. We walked about two blocks and crossed the street: same thing. After about three more bars—I was getting kinda tired of this because I wanted a drink—he saw who it was he was looking for. You could tell it the minute he walked in the door. He looked like a great big heavy sack had just been lifted off his shoulders.

'Wait here a minute,' he said. To hell with that, I thought. I went to the bar and ordered a double. Ronnie'd done gone to a booth and was talking to a man in a leather jacket and sky-blue pants. They both got up after a time and Ronnie signalled to me—all he did was raise his head a little—so I finished the drink and all three of us went outside.

The other man walked just like Ronnie did: with that springy, bouncy step that looked like he was about to take off and fly. We walked on up the block—none of us saying a mumbling word—and around a corner and into a building.

We started up the stairs, me going last, and as we walked past the fifth floor I heard what I thought first was a pigeon cooing and next a baby crying. But it was neither a baby or a pigeon. It was a woman; and she wasn't crying. We walked up to the seventh floor and Ronnie and the man stopped. We was all standing on the stairs, Ronnie on top and then the man and then me. I thought they were going to somebody's apartment, because there was a door right behind Ronnie. But they weren't.

'You got the bread, Bennie?' Ronnie said.

'Oh!' I said. Then I remembered that I'd spent all the small bills I had. 'I ain't got nothing but a ten-spot,' I said.

'I ain't got change for that,' the man said.

'We can get change later,' Ronnie said. I gave the man the ten-spot.

Ronnie took off his jacket and hung it on the doorknob. Then he took off his belt and rolled up the shirtsleeve on his left arm. His skin was grey under the light. The man took a spoon and a little bottle of water out of his jacket pocket. The bottom of the spoon was black. Next he brought out a little brown packet from another pocket and tapped what looked like garlic salt into the spoon from the packet. Then he poured some of the water from the bottle into the spoon, crumpled the empty packet, threw it down the stairs and said, 'Gimme a match.' I lit a match and handed it to him. Ronnie had done wrapped his belt tight around his arm just above the elbow. He was flexing his arm back and forth, and the veins in his forearm were standing out like veins on a dead leaf. The man held the flame to the bottom of the spoon and moved it around so that it heated even. Then he threw the match away and took a hypodermic needle out of his jacket. He sucked all the melted liquid up with the needle, then handed it to Ronnie. Ronnie took it. You could hear him breathing hard. It looked as though he was looking for the right vein. He moved his arm around so that the light would hit it right, meanwhile flexing his fist. I heard the woman on the fifth floor half-shout and half-scream and call a man's name twice. Then her voice sounded like it was muffled in a pillow and the needle was in Ronnie's arm. When the needle hit him he moved back against the wall. But it was so slow that I swear 'fore God it looked just like the wall moved towards him and he was holding it up. When he finished he took the needle from his arm and handed it to the man. He unwrapped the belt and rolled his shirtsleeve down. He was breathing harder now, and beginning to sweat. He was moving now just like a man in a slow-motion movie. He put his belt back on and buckled it and put his jacket on. He went to the door and flung it open. It was then I seen that it was the rooftop, and not somebody's apartment. The other man all this time had taken his jacket off and was going through the same business all over again. I wanted to go outside to see if Ronnie was alright, but the man was fixing himself so I didn't disturb him. I just stood there and watched. All of a sudden there was a loud crash outside. It sounded like a man falling after he'd been hit with a blackjack. I wanted to go outside and look because I didn't know whether the roof was slanted and Ronnie might fall off or if he'd been hit by somebody and was hurt bad and all this time the man had the needle in his arm with the blood coming up dark red into it then going back into his arm real slow as he went tap-tap-tap on top of the needle, and then he was finished and his belt went on loop by loop and he went to the door and looked out.

'Man,' he said. 'That simple motherhubber done fell out.' He put his jacket on and zipped it up and started down the stairs. I stood aside to let him by.

When I got out on the roof Ronnie was laying flat on his back with this legs up like he was about to give birth. His mouth was open and in the dim light his forehead looked exactly like a window pane after a heavy rain. His eyes were wide open, staring up at the stars. I knelt down beside him.

'What's the matter, Ronnie? You OK, man?'

He didn't move. I remembered right then what I'd heard one time in the Army: *When a man takes dope don't let him pass out or he might pass out for good.* So I slapped him. Hard. He didn't move. I slapped him again. He was coming to. I picked him halfway up by the lapels of his jacket and leaned him up against a chimney.

'Ronnie!' I shouted, and shook him. 'Ronnie!' His eyes had closed when I slapped him the first time, and now he opened them. He looked like he was trying hard to focus; like he was looking at me from a distance of eighty miles.

'You OK, man?'

'Huh?'

'You OK?'

'I'm awright, Sugar,' he said. (It was the first time any man had ever called me 'Sugar' in my natural life. What the hell, I thought. Maybe he thinks I'm his wife or girl friend or something. In spite of the situation I couldn't help laughing just a little.) All of a sudden he was alright; or almost alright. He got to his feet by himself. Then he started to slump, so I grabbed him and helped him to the doorway. He shook my arm off. 'I'm straight, Sugar,' he said. I took out my handkerchief and wiped his face. We started down the stairs, and he slumped again. I helped him down a couple flights, then he shook my arm off again. He walked the rest of the way by himself.

When we got to street level he said, 'Git a cab, Sugar,' He sat down on the bottom stair and I went out and got a taxi. When I got back he was spitting. I helped him up and he walked to the taxi by himself. As we were about to start off he turned to me and said, 'Did you get your bread, Sugar?'

'Oh!' I said. I'd forgotten my change from the ten dollars. I started to get out of the cab, but Ronnie stopped me.

'Lemme do it,' he said. 'That's an evil motherhubber.'

He got out of the cab and walked back to the bar. I watched through the rear window to see if he was alright. He was walking just like a man who drinks a lot but can carry his load. In a minute he came back and handed me seven dollars. I thanked him a lot and we drove to his place.

I was sitting in a straight chair—I still couldn't take that leopard-skin couch—and he was sitting in the armchair. His room-mate wasn't there, and I didn't want to leave him until I was sure he was OK. It was about three in the morning by this time, and I was tired. He had one hand to his forehead, and he was beginning to nod. I didn't want to slap him any more, so I decided to talk to keep him awake. So I talked; just rambling on in general. Every once in a while I'd say, 'You listening, man?' and if he answered I'd keep on. If he didn't I'd go over and shake him and he'd say, 'I'm awright, Sugar, I'm listenin'.' So I'd keep on talking.

This went on for about half an hour. Then he got up and went to the piano. He sat there for a long while just looking down at the keys. Then he hit a minor seventh chord with his left hand. He didn't bang, but he hit it hard and kept his hand there. I could hear it echoing into infinity. He hit it again and leaned his head to one side with his left ear close to the keys. Listening. He hit it and hit it and hit it, leaning down lower. His eyes were squinched up real narrow, like he was trying to see the music as well as hear it. It was about then that I seen that what he was really looking at was the leopard-skin couch.

When he talked his voice was real husky, and sounded like he was surprised. 'You know what I see, man?' he said. 'When I look at that couch I see devils dancing in the moonlight. I see angels with skeleton's faces and witches with faces like dogs. And you know what else I see, man? I can see the face of God grinning like a happy nigger.'

He laughed, all of a sudden. Only it wasn't a real laugh. It was kind of a half-crying and half-laughing, as if he'd seen something and couldn't quite express it. Then, just as suddenly, he stopped and got up. I got up, too.

'I got to go,' I said. He looked at me, and his eyes looked just like he'd washed them with some kind of lotion: big and bright.

'Cutting out, huh?' he said.

'Yeah,' I said.

'Fall by tomorrow,' he said.

'I'll be by,' I said. We shook hands and I went downstairs.

It was warm out. I took my tie off and put it in my jacket pocket; then I took the jacket off and slung it over my arm and walked to the Dewey Square Hotel and went to sleep.

MARSHALL BRICKMAN

Marshall Brickman's accomplishments are diverse: television writer and producer; screenplay writer; motion picture director and producer; musician. He has co-written three movies with Woody Allen: *Sleeper, Annie Hall,* and *Manhattan.* On his own he has written and directed *Simon, Lovesick,* and *The Manhattan Project.* As a musician, he plays banjo and was a member of the 1960s' folk group the Tarriers. His recording of urban bluegrass music with Eric Weissberg became the soundtrack album for the movie version of James Dickey's *Deliverance* and sold more than two million copies.

Brickman says, "While I hung my banjo up years ago, I can't remember a project, a film, any important part of my life going by without recalling some jazz artist who wasn't, through benefit of LP's or CD's, an integral part of my own creative process—that is, I play lots of music while I write, and a lot of it is jazz."

The humorous *New Yorker* piece "What, Another Legend?" reflects Brickman's style of humor and was produced in that period when he was writing for *Candid Camera, The Dick Cavett Show,* and *The Tonight Show.* It gives a good-natured jab in the ribs to the anthropological jazz historians. The story makes it evident why Brickman and Woody Allen are so compatible.

WHAT, ANOTHER LEGEND?

Trans-Ethnic Gesellschaft is pleased to announce the release of another album in its Geniture series of recordings devoted to giants in American jazz. These liner notes are by the noted jazz critic and historian Arthur Mice, whose efforts first brought Pootie LeFleur to public attention.

POOTIE LEFLEUR, a legendary figure in the development of American jazz, was discovered—or *re*discovered, rather—last summer placidly raking leaves on the courthouse lawn in Shibboleth, Louisiana. Although one hundred and twelve years old and in semi-retirement (two days a week, he drops paper bags of water from his second-story window onto passersby below, for which he receives a small sum), Pootie has astonishing powers of recall, displaying the lucidity of a man easily fifteen years his junior. On a recent visit engendered by the production of this record, we got Pootie talking about the roots of the music he knows so well.

"Was there an ideal period when jazz was pure, untainted by any influence foreign to its African origins?" we asked.

"I spec' . . . um . . . *rebesac,* dey's a *flutterbug,* hee, hee, hee!" Pootie said, squinting very hard and making a popping sound with his teeth.

"And what of the blues? Don't the blues, with their so-called 'blue notes,' represent a significant deviation from standard European tonality?"

"I'se ketch a ravis, y'heah? A ravis, an' de *dawg,* he *all* onto a *runnin'* boa'd," replied the jazz great, leaning back in his chair expansively until his head touched the floor.

This album represents the distillation of over sixty hours of taped conversations with Pootie LeFleur (of which the above is but a fragment), plus all the significant available recorded performances by this authentic primitive genius, whose career spanned the entire jazz era, from Jelly Roll Morton to John Coltrane—including a three-month hiatus in 1903, when nobody in New Orleans could seem to get in tune.

Carlyle Adolph Bouguereau "Pootie" LeFleur was born into the fertile musical atmosphere of postbellum New Orleans. His mother had favorably impressed Scott Joplin by playing ragtime piano with her thighs, and his father was a sometime entrepreneur, who once owned the lucrative ad-lib franchise for all of Storyville and the north delta; for years, no New Orleans musician could shout "Yeh, daddy!" during or after a solo without paying Rebus LeFleur a royalty. The young boy taught himself to play the piano with some help from his uncle, the legendary "Blind" (Deaf) Wilbur MacVout, for two decades a trombonist with Elbert Hubbard, although Hubbard was an author and had no real need for a trombonist. When Pootie was five, he was given his own piano but misplaced it, requiring him to practice thereafter on the dining-room table.[1]

When Pootie was six, the LeFleur home was razed to make way for a bayou, and Pootie's father made the decision to relocate the family in St. Louis. Here Pootie tried his hand at composition. "The Most Exceedin' Interestin' Rag," the first effort which we have in manuscript, is clearly an immature conception; only two measures long, it contains a curious key signature indicated by a very large sharp accidental over the treble clef, and a flat and a half-moon drawn in the bass. The piece is melodically sparse (the entire tune consists of one whole note, with a smiling face drawn in it), but it does anticipate Pootie's characteristic economy by at least a decade. The material from this period (some of which is also available on "Pre-Teen Pootie," 12″ Trans-Ethnic Gesellschaft TD 203) reveals a

[1]Johnny St. Cyr recalled an anecdote about Pootie's habit of playing out scales and figures on the table. One night in 1938, Pootie, Kid Ory, Baby Dodds, and Tiny Grimes were at Small's Paradise having a late supper of miniature gherkins, and Pootie was occupied as usual tapping out a riff with his right hand. It finally became too much for Ory, and the famous tailgater put down his fork. "Stop that, Pootie," said the Kid. "It's annoying." Although attributed to many others, including Fletcher Henderson and Dorothy Parker, the remark was in fact made by Ory.

profusion of styles and influences. "Spinoza's Joy" has a definite Spanish, if not Sephardic, flavor, while "What Vous Say?" shows a hint of Creole.

According to Dr. Ernst Freitag and Gustav Altschuler's encyclopedic Dictionary of Jazz and Home Wiring Simplified (Miffin Verlag, 1942), the next few years were ones of extreme financial deprivation for the LeFleurs. Pootie's father had squandered the family savings by investing in a feckless enterprise called Fin-Ray Cola, a tuna-flavored soft drink, and in an attempt to bring in some money Pootie invented a new note, located between F and F sharp, which he named "Reep," and tried peddling door to door. Despite early bad luck, Pootie never lost faith in "my fine new note," as he called it, and some time later he hired a hall in Sedalia to test public reaction and attract financial backing. The playing of the note apparently made no impression on the casual Missourians, most of whom arrived too late to hear it.

It was about this time that LeFleur played for James P. Johnson, who urged him to go to New York or any other city a thousand miles away. The story of that trip is probably the most fascinating in the entire history of jazz, but unfortunately Pootie claims to have forgotten it. By now a leader and innovator in his own right, Pootie organized himself and three other musicians into what Nat Hentoff has called a "quartet," and secured an engagement at Buxtehude's, a speakeasy in the heart of Manhattan's swinging Flemish district. His first wife, singer Rubella Cloudberry, evokes those exciting years in her autobiography, "A Side of Fries" (Snead House, Boston, 1951):

> Well, don't you know, Pootie come in one night and say, "Pack up, woman, we goin' to the Big Apple!" And I say, "Hunh?" And so he say, "Pack up, woman, we goin' to the Big Apple!" And I say, "The big what?" So we stayed in Chicago.[2]

The stimulating, rough-and-tumble atmosphere of Prohibition sparked LeFleur's group (the Mocha Jokers) and others to marvellous feats of improvisation, typified by the moment during one din-

[2] Of course, when LeFleur did make it to New York, it was without his saxophonist, Crazy Earl Bibbler. Two days before the trip, Bibbler, an alcoholic, sold his lips to a pawn shop for twenty dollars.

ner show at Tony Pastor's when Bix Beiderbecke blew a brilliant version of "Dardanella" on a roast chicken.[3]

LeFleur's classical period begins with the reflective "Boogie for the Third Sunday After Epiphany" and ends with the tender and haunting "Toad" Nocturne. "Toad" opens with a simple piano motif in G, which is reworked into C, F, F minor, and B, finally retiring to E flat to freshen up. At the very end, following a tradition as old as the blues, everybody stops playing.

One of the hallmarks of LeFleur's career was his constant effort to adapt his style to contemporary trends—with the result that he was habitually accused of plagiarism. When the New Orleans style (or "Chicago style," as it was then called) waned, Pootie was eclipsed, but he reappears in 1939 as a member of the historic Savoy Sextet sessions, featuring Bird, Diz, Monk, Prez, and Mrs. Hannah Weintraub on vibes.[4]

With a penchant for overstatement typical of the period, Pootie tried augmenting the sextet, changing it first into a septet, then an octet, then a nonet, a dectet, an undectet, and so on, ending with the cumbersome "hundred-tet," which could only be booked into meadows. A major influence on him at this time was his attendance at a tradition-breaking rent-party jam session, during which nineteen consecutive choruses of "How High the Moon" were played in twelve seconds by "Notes" Gonzales—the brilliant and erratic disciple of Charlie Parker—who was later killed when his car crashed into the tower of the Empire State Building.

The next album in this series will cover Pootie's modern period, including the prophetic Stockholm concert, with Ornette Coleman on vinyl sax and Swedish reedman Bo Ek on Dacron flute, plus some very recent sides cut by Pootie at his own expense in the Record-Your-Voice booth at the West Side bus terminal in New York City.

[3] As retold by Miff Mole.

[4] Hear especially the second take of "Schizoroonia on Hannah Banana—The Flip Side of Mrs. Weintraub" (Ulysses 906) for a remarkable polytonal chord cluster achieved when her necklace broke.

JOSEF ŠKVORECKÝ

That many Europeans appreciate jazz much more than most Americans is well known. Jazz records not available in the United States are frequently found on foreign labels of much higher technical quality. So it is no surprise that jazz has also found its way into Czechoslovakian literature via the novels and short stories of Josef Škvorecký, a native of Nachod, Bohemia, Czechoslovakia, who immigrated to Canada in 1968 and is currently professor of English at the University of Toronto. He has won a Guggenheim Fellowship, the Neustadt International Prize for Literature, and is a Fellow of the Royal Society of Canada. Many of his works have been translated into English, including *The Cowards* (1958) and the novellas *The Bass Saxophone* and *Emoke* (1977).

"Eine Kleine Jazzmusik" has a 1940 Czechoslovakia setting and recounts the unsuccessful Aryan attempts to suppress jazz by putting severe restrictions on the instruments and the kinds of music musicians were allowed to play. The Masked Rhythm Bandits' fight to express their individuality by playing a kind of music that is intrinsically free is appropriately symbolic of the fight for political freedom that was being waged by the "non-Aryans" in Czechoslovakia at that time.

EINE KLEINE JAZZMUSIK

Translated by Alice Denesová

IT all began when Paddy—at that time he was still Pavel Nakonec—got his old man to buy him a jazz trumpet.

The fathers of us other boys soon had to follow suit. At a meeting in the Nakonec Villa, we mapped out everybody's job and decided that for a start we needed one of each jazz instrument. We did not then dream that we were laying the foundations of a band that has lasted till today and bears the name of its first and finest trumpet player and leader in undying memory: Paddy's Dixielanders.

But our fathers withstood the initial onslaught. And so, for the first rehearsal in Paddy's room, there gathered a most unlikely band composed of what had been to hand. There was Paddy's horn, a piano and a bass, but round that sound jazz core was grouped a tambour-like outfit of two violins, a mandolin, a Turkish drum, relic of a former castle band, which Franta Rozkosny, the caretaker's son, had discovered in the junk-room of the local chateau; and, lastly, a brandnew xylophone, the outcome of my saxophone campaign, which I tried to pass off to myself as a vibraphone.

My father, referring to my weak lungs, had come out flat against a saxophone. But as my mummy could not bear the thought of any of my wishes being denied, they bought me the xylophone.

Well, then, those were our beginnings. The noise that floated from the Nakonec Villa was a dreadful, caterwauling xylophone music, punctuated by artless kicks of Paddy's trumpet. The caterwauling was especially due to the distinctive violin duo which tried (unsuccessfully) to breathe the lightness of swing into the not quite mastered technique of the Malát school of violin playing. Their drawn-out squealing was interspersed with thundering bangs on the Turkish drum, the stubborn plucking of the mandolin, and my helpless and chaotic rappings on the xylophone. The result was absolutely inimitable.

It goes without saying that all this was a far cry from any kind of music, let alone jazz. It was a monotonous mezzoforte jam of noise which enraptured us and drove the neighbors insane. It was not jazz. But somewhere in that hotbed there germinated a seed which survived the atrocity of Paddy's xylophone band.

By late 1940 it had been transformed into the shining miracle of a big swing band with five saxophones, three trumpets, a trio of trombones, a complete rhythm section and the vocalist Suzy Braun.

This last-named piece of the inventory had been acquired for the orchestra by Paddy Nakonec. Suzy was an orphan girl whose parents had disappeared in Oranienburg concentration camp early in 1940. Neither Jewish nor German, she was a Czech in spite of her name. Mr. Nakonec had brought her to K. Her father had been a foreman on construction jobs projected by the Nakonec design office. Until that time Suzy had lived in Prague. The minute she appeared in K. she was an immediate hit. A large number of types from the grammar school and elsewhere began to grovel before her, but the one who grovelled closest was Paddy himself. He was, of course, at an advantage because Suzy had moved in with the Nakonec family and worked as a junior draughtsman in the office of Paddy's father.

Now it must be pointed out that Paddy was not an Aryan, or at best only half a one. His late mother's maiden name had been Sommernitz and her twenty years younger brother Harry Sommernitz was at present active beyond the frontiers of the Thousand Years Reich as a fighter pilot. From his father Paddy had inherited the Czech name, from his mother his Mosaic facial features. After they had kicked him out of the grammar school on account of this, he worked as a draughtsman in the office of his father's competitor Mojmír Ströbinger and lived in that odd condition in which persons of problematic racial origin existed at that time.

The more he doted on his jazz trumpet, the closer he was drawn to Suzy. And Suzy, our sweet Suzy, was in turn drawn closer to the band and discovered within herself a pleasant, agreeable husky contralto voice and a genius for rhythm and syncopation.

And so she sang, dressed in a black schoolgirl dress with a little white collar, swinging her hips, rotating her arms, and in her eyes sparkled the wicked, savage and sweet soul of jazz:

> My heart beats to a syncopated beat,
> must sing to feel I'm whole.
> Thrills run from my head right down to my feet,
> swing, that devil, has taken my soul. . . .

The town, at least its younger and, in exceptional cases, even its older inhabitants, was gripped by the music fever. In the Victorian café in the square one could hear names like Chick Webb, Andy Kirk, Duke Ellington, Mary Lou Williams, Count Basie, Bob Crosby, Zuttie Singleton, along with patently non-Aryan names, such as Benny Goodman, and first and foremost, of course, the name of Louis Satchmo Armstrong. Nights at the radio vibrated with syncopated gusts from Stockholm, where in those days of Aryan strains they rendered particular service to the spread of the poison that to us, if I may say so, meant life.

To us life, to "them" death. That is why our music got on their nerves and why we persevered the harder in playing it. Paddy entered into personal relations with the king of the Czech provinces, a man whose fame was based on the fact that even with a bandaged thumb he had served "a machine gun-like piano at a monster concert in Prague's Lucerna Hall" (to quote the impressionistic jazz critics of those days), and whose name was Kamil Ludovít. The late Fritz Schwarz, Kamil's first alto-saxophonist and tune arranger, wrote a special arrangement of the "St. Louis Blues" for us which was to be the highlight of our first band concert at the Municipal Theatre in K.

But it seemed that this concert would not take place, even though eventually it did.

It so happened that all the powers of the old set conspired against us: the headmaster of the grammar school and the chairman of the parent-teacher association, *Regierungskommissär* Kühl, and the district leader of the "Vlajka" (a fascist organisation), and the correspondent of the *Aryan Struggle,* Mr. Bronzoryp. But the special scourge of our movement among that group was Headmaster Cermák, who later spelled his name Czermack, of the State grammar school, an enthusiastic admirer of the Apostolic person of Emanuel

Moravec (pro-German Minister of Education in the "Protectorate" government) and a strict man of the new order. This energetic educator not only gave the Aryan raised arm salute when entering class, demanding the fast-as-lighting response of all present, if possible accentuated by heel-clicking, but he even made the Reverend Mr. Melon give the Aryan salute before scripture lessons. The Reverend, who was not as stupid as his name might lead one to believe, deftly expanded the Aryan gesture into a wide-armed Papal cross, each time putting on such an unworldly holy mien that not even the militant spirit of the incisive Czecho-German could raise a protest.

His neo-European efforts did not meet with any success in his institutions of learning. Legendary in this respect was the collection of scrap iron and non-ferrous metal from which arms were to be forged against the Bolshevik hordes in the East, as the headmaster put it in his broadcast over the school address system. The collectors optimistically appointed in each class turned up a balance of absolute nil at the end of the first week, a circumstance which obliged the headmaster to make the rounds of the classes in person, with hand raised in the Aryan salute and accompanied by the school porter who was carrying a bucket for the non-ferrous metal. And at that a disgraceful incident occurred in the Upper Sixth. After an urgent appeal by the head educator, which was a mixture of bland fanaticism, Hieronymus Bosch–like fantasy, veiled threats and crystal-clear rubbish, Franta Jungwirth, our band pianist, got up and with loud sobs wrenched a thickly encrusted nib from his penholder, dropping it into the porter's proffered bucket, presumably to contribute to the forging of arms against the Bolshevik cutthroats. Whereupon the headmaster was seized with a fit of rage which, luckily for Franta Jungwirth, led to nothing worse than a fortnight in the school lockup.

Headmaster Czermack took particular exception to the orchestra because he guessed vaguely and (accurately) that its members were at the bottom of the unpleasant surprises periodically put in his way. One morning, for instance, he had the fright of his life when awakening from a night's alternately greater-German dreams (in which his dearest wish came true: he was awarded the St. Wenceslaus Eagle) and collaborationist dreams (in which he used to swing), to see against the cold autumn sky outside his window a shaggy gorilla watching him with mean, little eyes and apparently about to break the window and fling itself upon his bed. This outrage had indeed been committed by the orchestra: the gorilla was part of the inventory of the natural science class and had been lowered by a clothes line from the window of the fourth form during the night.

Headmaster Czermack had a model son, an Aryan lad distinguished in German, Latin and tuft-hunting. He had an unpleasant experience of a different kind. A promising functionary of the *Kuratorium* (fascist Youth Organisation), he was strolling in the park one day, enjoying an illustrated account in the magazine *Signal* entitled *Das Ende eines bolschewistischen Panzers.* In the midst of his enjoyment, he was suddenly attacked by a band of masked men. A gag was thrust into his mouth and, in the bushes behind the statue of Karel Hynek Mácha, he was deprived of all bodily growth of hair in places visible and invisible. Afterwards he was bound to a tree and left to his fate; a large kitchen mirror had been fixed to the opposite tree. Two hours of looking at himself in this disfigured state filled the headmaster's son with such despair that as soon as he managed to cast off his bonds he did not hesitate to use the rope that had bound him for an attempt at suicide by hanging. But he selected an insufficiently strong branch which broke under his weight. This experience made him think better of it; he decided to live, instead, and crept off to the grammar school under the cover of twilight. Soon after, the theatre barber Kavánek could be seen hurrying into the schoolhouse with a bulky satchel under his arm. The next day Adolf Czermack appeared in a curly wig. Christina Hubálková, pretending to admire his curls, drove her inquisitive fingers into his wig and brought about his downfall. Adolf Czermack, leading light of the *Kuratorium,* headmaster's son and model scholar, was forced to feign a month's illness before the state of his head allowed him to surface again among his classmates.

So it was not surprising that shortly before the concert a circular went round the classes prohibiting all pupils from taking part in any theatrical, concert or other public performance after seven p.m., except on express permission from the headmaster. Headmaster Czermack was closing in on us for the kill.

But storm clouds were also gathering over the planned concert from other quarters. The journal *Reichszeitschrift für Volkstanzmusik* published an order by the *Reichsmusikführer* concerning popular and dance music. "In recent months," the document said (I am quoting from memory and cannot guarantee the exact wording, but I do guarantee the authenticity of the unmistakably Aryan spirit of the piece), "in places of entertainment in some areas of the Reich, the spread of music pervaded by the Jewish-Bolshevik-plutocratic infection of nigger jazz has been noticeable." The *Herr Reichsmusikführer* proceeded to list the names of several unfortunate Teutonic bandleaders (for whom this honor probably meant a free ticket to a concentration camp) whose anti-State cacophonic musical activity he contrasted unfavorably with the exemplary, race-conscious, melodic efforts of Peter Kreuder. He finally decreed with the utmost strictness:

1) in the repertoire of light orchestras and dance bands, pieces in foxtrot rhythm (so-called swing) are not to exceed 20%;

2) in the repertoire of this so-called jazz type, preference is to be given to compositions in a major key and to lyrics expressing joy in life (*Kraft durch Freude*), rather than Jewishly gloomy lyrics;

3) as to the tempo too, preference is to be given to brisk compositions as opposed to slow ones (so-called blues); however, the pace must not exceed a certain degree of allegro commensurate with the Aryan sense for discipline and moderation. On no account will negroid excesses in tempo (so-called hot jazz) be permitted, or in solo performances (so-call breaks);

4) so-called jazz compositions may contain at the most 10% syncopation; the remainder must form a natural legato movement devoid of hysterical rhythmic reverses characteristic of the music of the barbarian races and conducive to dark instincts alien to the German people (so-called riffs);

5) strictly forbidden is the use of instruments alien to the German spirit (e.g., so-called cowbells, flex-á-tone, brushes, etc.) as well as all mutes which turn the noble sound of wind-brass instruments into a Jewish-Freemasonric yell (so-called wa-wa, in hat, etc.);

6) prohibited are so-called drum breaks longer than half a bar in four quarter beat (except in stylized military marches);

7) the double bass must be played solely with the bow in so-called jazz compositions; plucking of strings is prohibited, since it is

damaging to the instrument and detrimental to Aryan musicality. If a so-called pizzicato effect is absolutely desirable for the character of the composition, let strict care be taken lest the string is allowed to patter on the sordine, which is henceforth forbidden;

8) provocative rising to one's feet during solo performances is forbidden;

9) musicians are likewise forbidden to make vocal improvisations (so-called scat); and

10) all light orchestras and dance bands are advised to restrict the use of saxophones of all keys and to substitute for them violoncelli, violas, or possibly a suitable folk instrument.

Signed: Baldur von Blödheim,
Reichsmusikführer und Oberscharführer SS.

In this situation we turned for help to our patron Kamil Ludovít, and in his Prague abode a plan was hatched.

Soon bills appeared on the hoardings of K., announcing that the popular orchestra of the Masked Rhythm Bandits of Prague would present a Program of Joyful Melodies from All Over the World to the local population. In answer to his inquiry, which was not slow in coming, Headmaster Czermak was informed that the Masked Rhythm Bandits was a musical body dispensing light music under contract to handmaster Kamil Ludovít of Prague-Zizkov, that he was therefore obliged to shut up.

But *Regierungskommissär* Kühl now took a hand. The *Kapellmeister der Maskierten Banditen des Rythmus* received a letter in German on notepaper bearing the letter-head of the *Regierungskommissär* in K., in which the signatory and representative of the *Reich* called on him to submit within five days a complete list of compositions to be presented at the forthcoming concert, including detailed information on tempi, keys, percentage of syncopation, distribution of instruments, as well as nationality and race of the composers performed. In case of failure to comply, the drawing of unspecified but easily imagined conclusions was threatened.

Another séance in Ludovít's flat yielded a program which—at least the way it looked on paper—would not offend even the most Aryan feelings of the Führer and Reichs Chancellor of the Greater German Reich himself.

The show was to open with a number entitled "Curtainraiser

Schottische," followed by creations by a certain Josef Patocka, Prantisek Cechácek and Günther Fürnwald, bearing such titles as "No Tears, my Darling" (*Keine Tränen, mein Liebling*), slow tune; "Our Bull Took Fright" (*Unser Stier wurde aufgescheucht*), quickstep; "In the Swimming Pool" (*In der Schwimmanstalt*), character piece; and "Evening Prayer" (*Gebet am Abend*), song.

On the program figured one or two slow-foxes and two foxtrots by well-known, tolerated music makers, as well as the "Song of Rzeshetova Lhota" (*Lied über die Rzeschetive Lhota*), which was listed as a novelty of the Prague season. Josef Patocka, Frantisek Cechácek and Günther Fürnwald were described as Aryans, in the first two instances Czech, in the third as greater-German Aryan (*grossdeutsch*). According to the program, the distribution of instruments was as follows: three trombones (in C), three horns (in B), six clarinets (in B), alternating in some of the mood compositions with five Sachs soundhorns. On what a Sachs soundhorn was supposed to be the program did not elaborate, judging accurately that the *Herr Regierungsrat* would not inquire for fear of appearing ignorant.

The submitted program was approved without any changes. Only in the "Song of Joy in Life" (*Das Kraft durch-Freude Lied*), Mr. Kühl noted in his own hand: *5% Synkopen auslassen* (omit 5% syncopes)!

However, Paddy Nakonec voiced apprehension as to the effectiveness of the disguises. He was afraid they would hardly protect us from the sleuthing capacity of Headmaster Czermack and insisted that this intruder No. 1 be rendered harmless by more drastic methods.

The headmaster's definite blockade was eventually brought about by Suzy Braun. Her feminine cunning unearthed one important detail, namely, that the day of the concert happened to be the day of an all-Protectorate Session of the *Kuratorium* of the Education of Youth in the Protectorate *Böhmen und Mähren,* at which the best organisational workers of all regions were to be decorated with the Shield of Honor of the St. Wenceslaus Eagle. With the aid of her girlish charms, to which a certain Herbert Starecek—an official of the *Kuratorium* Secretariat—was by no means blind, she got hold of some rubber-stamped *Kuratorium* notepaper and put it to good use in our cause.

And so it happened that the headmaster denied himself the pleasure of exposing the Masked Rhythm Bandits as pupils of his school. The letter that arrived from the Central Secretariat of the *Kuratorium* for the Education of Youth in the Protectorate *Böhmen und Mähren* informed him that in recognition of his services in the realm of fostering the Aryan Idea and the New Order within the Greater German Reich, it had been decided by the leadership of the *Kuratorium* for the Education of Youth in the Protectorate *Böhmen und Mähren* to bestow on him the Shield of Honor of the St. Wenceslaus Eagle, which would be presented at the ceremonial session of the *Kuratorium* for the Education of Youth in the Protectorate *Böhmen und Mähren* on Friday . . . at the Smetana Hall of the *Reprezentacní* Palace in the Royal Capital Prague.

That Friday was the day of the Concert of Joyous Melodies by the Masked Rhythm Bandits in K.

Headmaster Czermack obeyed the Aryan call of the all-Protectorate session of Aryans and departed on the afternoon train to Prague.

That same evening the Masked Rhythm Bandits opened their program in the Municipal Theatre in K. with the composition "Curtain-raiser Schottische" (*Wir fangen an mit dem Hopstanz*). Present connoisseurs had no trouble in recognizing in the schottische the "Casa Loma Stemp" which they rewarded with nerve-frazzling applause. The *Herr Regierungskommissär,* who was vainly trying to keep count of the percentage of syncopes in his box, began to scowl. He was beset by forebodings that the Aryan character of the joyous melodies might be violated. However, in the circle, filled to the last seat with members of a local *Wehrmacht* unit who had bought up every circle ticket in the advance booking by virtue of their superior race, pleasant excitement reigned.

Just then, as if elevated by the caressing rhythm of the syncopated tune, Suzy Braun rose to her feet in her black dress with the little white collar and a black lace mask over her eyes. Swinging her hips and moving her hands in gestures faithfully and naturally copied from every blues singer, seen and unseen, she began in her sweet and provocatively husky little voice:

Black shadows are falling
on the white man's city

train whistles are calling
life ain't got no pity.
Oh—ooooh—oh—ooh,
Give it everything you've got
C'me on, boys, play it hot!

At the last word, included also in the *Reichsmusikführer*'s list of offensive musical nomenclature, *Herr Regierungskommissär* turned pale and made up his mind to intervene. But a schizophrenic outburst of Paddy's horn which hit the eardrums of the breathless connoisseurs the following instant, cut the singer short and produced an enraptured sigh among the ranks of the *Infanterieregiment*. The singer continued in her melodic voice:

Manhattan glows
in a glare of light.
Nobody knows
that you don't treat me right.

The *Regierungsrat* rose but was so startled the next instant that he sat down again. In a unisono blast the brass gave forth a fortissimo bellow as if straight at his person. Everything went black before his eyes, and in the blackness sprung up another terrible word from the *Reichsmusikführer*'s decree: riff.

And Suzy Braun, transported by the squeal of the clarinets and roused by the sharp barking of Paddy's horn (so-called mute), raised her sweet, husky voice in the triumphant last chorus:

I'll shake off my sorrow
and forget my grief.
There may be no tomorrow
life is so brief.
Oh—ooooh—oh—ooh,
Give it everything you've got
C'me on, boys play it hot!

There rose a storm of barbarous rapture, especially in the circle where the sexually starved members of the superior race, led astray by the spirit of the negroid music and the charm of the racially inferior singer, forgot their sense of Aryan moderation and called for an encore by stamping of feet and lusty Teutonic shouts.

The *Regierungskommissär,* in view of the situation, decided not to intervene.

Meanwhile, thrilled with sweet anticipation, Headmaster Czermack sat in the half-empty Smetana Hall and listened attentively to a speech on the necessity and glory of the fight against Asiatic Bolshevism and on the historic destination of the Czech nation in the Greater German Reich.

The speech was given by a gentleman with a head like a well-polished billiard ball.

After the speech the session passed on to the granting of distinctions to deserving Aryans.

Meanwhile, the concert of the Masked Rhythm Bandits progressed exactly according to the advance program. That the character piece "In the Swimming Pool," by Josef Patocka, was in fact "Riverside Blues" by the nigger King Oliver and that the quickstep "Our Bull Took Fright," by Günther Fürnwald, was practically indistinguishable from the Jewish-negroid Tiger Rag was known only to the initiated part of the audience who were none the worse for it. But the overwhelming majority of the uninitiated were none the worse for it either, particularly those in the circle, with the exception of Counsellor Prudivy who recognized on the feet of one of the Rhythm Bandits the new shoes of his son Horymír whom he was wont to urge into playing excerpts from Smetana's operas on the piano, and whom he had just imprudently sent to the local Sexton for a lesson in bagpipe playing.

And we went on playing. God Almighty, who has created jazz and all the beauties of this world, only you know how we played!

It seemed to me that the theatre in K. had disappeared, disappeared along with *Regierungskommissär Kühl* and everything, and that there was nothing but the music. It seemed to me that I had escaped the paper score and was playing something that had never been written down and never might be. The sobs of the saxophones were like the sobs of angels or of a man in anguish. The horns wailed like Olympian choirs singing a hymn to the persecuted. And when Paddy rose and started on the great improvised solo in "Matters of the Heart," which was none other than Dippermouth's "Heartbreak Blues," I all at once seemed to hear the imploring and morally anguished voice of Mr. Katz, the teacher, calling, crying out and pleading. . . .

Headmaster Czermack was meanwhile following with impatience and rising nervousness as a gaunt, middle-aged youth in *Kuratorium* uniform called out the names of those about to be decorated on the podium with the Honor Shield of the St. Wenceslaus Eagle.

He waited to hear his own name called.

He waited, but that evening he waited in vain.

At the moment when he ascertained this distressing fact, the concert of the Masked Rhythm Bandits was coming to its climax with the novelty of the season, the "Song of Rzeshetova Lhota."

> Rzeshetova Lhota
> is my home.
> I'm on my way
> to see my Aryan folks. . . .

sang Suzy Braun to the music of the negroid Jew or possibly Jewish Negroid, W. C. Handy, known beyond the jurisdictional territory of the Greater German *Reich* (but also inside that territory, and even in the town of K.) under the title of "St. Louis Blues."

The Aryans of the Infantry did not understand the lyrics but applauded wildly all the same. But the connoisseurs in the stalls understood all right. Into the clapping and cheers mingled knowing guffaws.

And at that instant, somewhere in the darkened hall the indignant Aryan Mr. Bronzoryp stood up, for he had perceived that the race of which he was proud (though he had never asked himself whether his race was also proud of him) was being made the butt of ridicule. He pushed his way through to the wings. And we breezed into the last number of the evening until the eardrums burst, until words lost their meaning and it ceased to matter whether they were poetic and witty or lame and banal; only the music had meaning, only the score, the heart, the immortal soul of that provocative, soaring storm of music.

That brings me to the end of the happy part of the story. What is left to tell is the unhappy part.

In the rapture that enveloped us after the concert, for a long time we did not recognize among the shining faces of the connoisseurs who poured into the dressing room the fury-contorted Aryan features of Mr. Bronzoryp.

The no less fury-contorted Headmaster Czermack, whom the puzzled committee of the *Kuratorium* for the Education of Youth in the Protectorate *Böhmen und Mähren* had finally managed to convince that there had been no mistake but an inexplicable hoax, was getting into the night train from Prague to K., blood and murder in his soul.

The consequence of both these events were not long in coming.

If it had only been for us, it would not have mattered. Benny Prema got a severe reprimand and our guitarist Zábrana was suspended from the grammar school in K. but not barred from finishing his studies elsewhere. Myself and our pianist Jungwirth, the son of a railway official, were similarly afflicted, although in my case the verdict was later changed to debarment from all institutions of learning in the Protectorate *Böhmen und Mähren,* because in the meantime they had sent my father off to Belsen. This and similar measures resulted in the decimation and ruin of the historic swing band of the grammar school in K.

Paddy Nakonec, half-Aryan, half-Jew, paid for that little prank with his life. Mr. Bronzoryp, outraged in his Aryanmost feelings, denounced that half-Jew—who carried on like ten pedigree Jews, as the Aryan put it—as the instigator of the provocation.

Halbjude Nakonec was found guilty of violating the Aryan honor of the town of K., just as he had feared.

He was treated accordingly.

But that is not yet the end of the story. There was still Suzy, sweet Suzy Braun, the unofficial wife of the head trumpeter and shining light of our band, whom we all honored and secretly loved.

Then came the news in a note smuggled out of Pankrác Prison in Prague, that Paddy had been shot. And Suzy broke down.

But after a time she suddenly seemed to have got over it. She was seen in company one would have expected least, in the company of the Aryan Mr. Bronzoryp.

Word even had it that she was his mistress.

Naturally, the town condemned her.

On account of Paddy, the band condemned her too.

Nobody bothered to find out what was going on inside Suzy Braun, the sweet Suzy who was now absolutely alone in the world.

What an ass one sometimes is!

But that is not the whole story. Like Paddy, Mr. Bronzoryp did not live to see the end of the Protectorate *Böhmen und Mähren* either. One foggy morning he was found in his well-furnished, divorced man's quarters with a bullet in his skull. Beside the bed on which he had died, lay Suzy Braun, her hand holding a Browning, a weapon reliable Aryans were permitted to carry by special licence of the *Sicherheitsdienst.* She had shot herself through the mouth.

So she did, poor, dear Suzy, and her lovely mouth will never sing again in her husky little voice. Swing, that devil, has taken my soul. Because her soul was taken away by the angels. And her sweet body was laid to rest in the eternal hospitable soil.

So she died. Died, like Paddy Nakonec and Suzy's parents, like my father and Horst Hüsse and Mr. Katz, the teacher, like Dr. Strass, Mifinka and Bod, the Killer. So they are all dead, and we are living on.

Poor sweet Suzy. When I sit behind the music stand under the neonlit bandstand shell in the Park and play my tenor-sax part in compositions that Suzy no longer knew and never will, I remember her, dear lovely Suzy Braun, and all the others who are gone. Her sweetly husky voice seems to mingle with the song of the saxophone, and she sings again. And in tears, in sadness and joy over this life of ours, I sing with her:

> Rain or sunshine, come what may
> I'll keep my word until my dying day. . . .

Sleep well, sweet Suzy!

EVAN HUNTER

Hunt Collins? Richard Marsten? Ed McBain? Evan Hunter is all of these authors and has been publishing prolifically under these pseudonyms, as well as his own name, since 1952. His best known novel is *The Blackbird Jungle* (1954), which was made into a successful motion picture. He has also penned numerous short stories, plays, and screenplays. Many of his novels have been adapted for the screen.

Two of Hunter's novels are jazz-oriented: *Second Ending* (1956), the story of an addicted trumpet player trying to kick the habit, and *Streets of Gold* (1974), the account of blind pianist Iggie Di Palermo's discovery of jazz and his rise to fame on New York's fabled 52nd Street. The excerpt included here recounts the importance of Art Tatum as an inspiration for Iggie's piano playing and the rising influence of Bird, Diz, Bud, and bop.

FROM *STREETS OF GOLD*

THE bar was on Fordham Road, just off Jerome.

"It's full of niggers," my Uncle Luke said. "Let's get out of here."

This was February of 1944, and you could hardly walk through any street in New York without stumbling upon a place offering live jazz. I had asked Luke to take me to this particular bar because Biff Anderson was playing here this weekend. There were eight Biff Anderson records in my brother's collection, two of them with him backing the blues singers Viola McCoy and Clara Smith, four of them made when he'd been playing with Lionel Howard's Musical Aces, the remaining two featuring him on solo piano. His early style seemed to be premised on those of James P. Johnson and Fats Waller. Waller, I had already learned, was the man who had most influenced Tatum. And Tatum was where I wanted to be.

I was not surprised that the place was full of black people. I had begun subscribing to *Down Beat* and *Metronome,* which my father read aloud to me, and I knew what color most of the musicians were; not because they were identified by race, but only because there were pictures of them in those jazz journals. My father would say, "This Tatum is a nigger, did you know that?" (He also told me Tatum was blind, which was of far greater interest to me, and which confirmed my belief that I could one day play like him.) Or "Look at this Jimmie Lunceford," he would say. "I *hate* nigger bands. They repeat themselves all the time." I knew Biff Anderson was black, and I expected him to have a large black audience. But my Uncle Luke must have been shaken by it; he immediately asked the bartender for a double gin on the rocks.

"How about you friend here?" the bartender asked. He was white.

"I'll have a beer," I said.

"Let me see your draft card," he said, and then realized I was blind, and silently considered whether or not blind people were supposed to register for the draft, and then decided to skip the whole baffling question, and simply repeated, "Double gin on the rocks, one beer." *We* had to register for the draft the same as anyone else, of course, and—at least according to a joke then current—even blind people were being called up, so long as their Seeing Eye dogs had twenty-twenty vision. I didn't have a draft card because I wasn't yet eighteen. I'd have skipped the beer if the bartender had raised the slightest fuss; I was there to hear Biff Anderson play, and that was all.

The bar was a toilet. I've played many of them. It did not occur to me at the time that if someone of Biff's stature was playing a toilet in the Bronx, he must have fallen upon hard times. Nor did I even recognize the place as a toilet. I had never been inside a bar before, and the sounds and the smells were creating the surroundings for me. Biff must have been taking a break when we came in. The jukebox was on, and Bing Crosby was singing "Sunday, Monday, or Always." Behind the bar, the grain of which was raised and then worn smooth again, I could hear the clink of ice and glasses, whiskey being poured, the faint hiss of draft beer being drawn. There was a lot of echoing laughter in the room, mingled with the sound of voices I'd heard for years on "Amos 'n' Andy." The smells of beer and booze and perfume, the occasional whiff of someone who'd forgotten to bathe that month, the overpowering stench of urine from the men's room near the far end of the bar—though that was not what identified this particular dump as a toilet. To jazz musicians, a toilet is a place you play when you're coming up or heading down. I played a lot of them coming up, and I played a few of them on the way down, too. That's America. Easy come, easy go.

"Lots of dinges here tonight," the bartender whispered as he put down our glasses. "What're *you* guys doing here?"

"My nephew's a piano player," Luke said. "He wants to hear this guy."

"*He's* a dinge, too," the bartender said. "That's why we got so many of them here tonight. I never seen so many dinges in my life. I used to tenn bar in a dump on Lenox Avenue, and even *there* I never seen so many dinges. You hole a spot check right this minute, you gonna find six hundred switchblades here. Don't look crooked at nobody's girl, you lend up with a slit throat. Not you kid," he said to me. "You're blind, you got nothin' to worry about. You play the piano, huh?"

"Yeah," I said.

"So whattya wanna lissen to *this* guy for? He stinks, you ask my opinion. I requested him last night for 'Deep Inna Hearta Texas,' he tells me he don't know the song. 'Deep Inna Hearta Texas,' huh? *Anybody* knows that song."

"It's not the kind of song he'd play," I said.

"You're telling *me*?" the bartender said. "He don't *know* it, how could he play it? I don't recognize half the things he plays, anyway. I think he makes 'em up, whattya think of that?"

"He probably does," I said, and smiled.

"He sings when he plays," the bartender said. "Not the words, you unnerstan' me? He goes like uh-uh-uh under his breath. I think he's got a screw loose, whattya think of that?"

"He's humming the chord chart," I said. "He does that on his records, too."

"He makes records, this bum?"

"He made a lot of them," I said. "He's one of the best jazz pianists in the world."

"Sure, and he don't know 'Deep Inna Hearta Texas,'" the bartender said.

"There's got to be four hundred niggers in this place," Luke said.

"You better lower your voice, pal," the bartender advised. "Less you want all four hunnerd of 'em cuttin' off your balls and hangin' 'em from the chandelier."

"There ain't no chandelier," Luke said.

"Be a wise guy," the bartender said. "I tole the boss why did he hire a dinge to come play here? He said it was good for business. Sure. So next week *this* bum goes back to Harlem and *we're* stuck with a nigger trade. And he can't even play 'Deep Inna Hearta Texas.' Can you play 'Deep Inna Hearta Texas'?" he asked me.

"I've never tried it."

The bartender sang a little of the song, and then said, "*That* one. You know it?"

"I've heard the song, but I've never played it."

"You must be as great a piano player as him," the bartender said.

"How about another double?" Luke asked.

"Fuckin' piano players today don't know how to play *nothin'*," the bartender said, and walked off to pour my uncle's drink.

"*I* know 'Deep In the Heart of Texas,'" Luke said.

"Whyn't you go play it for him?" I said.

"Nah," Luke said.

"Go on, he'd get a kick out of it."

"Nah, nah, c'mon," Luke said, "Anyway, here he comes."

"Who?"

"The guy you came to hear. I *guess* it's him. He's sittin' down at the piano."

"What does he look like?"

"He's as black as the ace of spades," Luke whispered.

"Is he fat or skinny or what?"

"Kind of heavy."

"How old is he?"

"Who can tell with a nigger? Forty? Fifty? He's got fat fingers, Igg. You sure he's a good piano player?"

"One of the best, Uncle Luke."

"Here's your gin," the bartender said. "You want to pay me now, or you gonna be drinkin'?"

"I'll be drinking," Luke said.

From the moment Biff began playing, his heritage was completely evident. Johnson had taught Waller, and Biff had learned by imitating both, and when Tatum took Waller a giant step further, Biff again revised his style. He played a five-tune set consisting of "Don't Blame Me," "Body and Soul," "Birth of the Blues," "Sweet Lorraine," and "Star Eyes." This last was a hit recorded by Jimmy Dorsey, with Kitty Kallen doing the vocal. It was, and *is*, a perfect illustration of a great tune for a jazz improvisation. The melody is totally dumb, but the chord chart is unpredictable and exciting, with no less than nine key changes in a thirty-two-bar chorus. I still use it as a check-out tune. Whenever I want to know how well someone plays, I'll say, "Okay, 'Star Eyes.'" If he comes up with some fumbling excuse like "Oh, man, I don't like that tune so much," or "Yeah, yeah, like I haven't played that one in a long time," I've got him pegged immediately. It's a supreme test tune for a jazz musician, and Biff played it beautifully that night.

He played it beautifully because he played it *exactly* like Tatum. A tribute, a copy, call it what you will, but there it was, those sonorous tenths, those pentatonic runs, the whole harmonic edifice played without Tatum's speed or dexterity, of course, but letter perfect stylistically. I was sitting not fifty feet from a man who could play piano like Tatum, and I had been breaking my balls and my chops for the past seven months trying to learn Tatum by listening to his records.

"Let me have another one of these, huh?" Luke said.

"Hey, Uncle Luke," I said. "Go easy, huh?"

"Huh? Go easy?"

"On the gin."

"Oh. Sure, Iggie, don't worry."

The music had stopped; I could hear the laughter and voices from the bandstand.

"What's he doing up there?" I asked Luke.

"He's standing near the piano, talking to a girl."

"Can you take me up there?"

"Sure, Iggie. What're you gonna do? Play a little?"

"I just want to meet him. Hurry up. *Please.* Before he leaves."

"He's lookin' down her dress, he ain't about to leave," Luke said, and he offered me his elbow, and I took it and got off the bar stool, and followed him across the room, moving through a rolling crest of conversation and then onto a slippery, smooth surface I assumed was the dance floor, and heard just beyond earshot a deep Negro voice muttering something unintelligible, and then caught the tail end of a sentence, ". . . around two in the mornin', you care to hang aroun' that long," and the voice stopped as we approached, and my Uncle Luke said, "Mr. Anderson?"

"Yeah?" Biff said.

"This is my nephew," Luke said. "He plays piano."

"Cool," Biff said.

"He wanted to meet you."

"How you doin', man?" Biff said, and he must have extended his hand in greeting because there was a brief expectant silence, and then Luke quickly said, "Shake the man's hand, Iggie."

I extended my hand. Biff's hand was thick and fleshy and sweating. On my right, there was the overpowering, almost nauseating smell of something that was definitely not *Je Reviens.*

"You play piano, huh?" Biff said.

"Yes."

"How long you been playin'?"

"Twelve years."

"Yeah? Cool. Hey, Poots, where you *goin'?*" he said, his voice turning away from me. There was no answer. I heard the click of high-heeled shoes in rapid tattoo on the hardwood floor, disappearing into the larger sound of voices and laughter. Somewhere behind me, the jukebox went on again—David Rose's "Holiday for Strings."

"Dumb *cunt,*" Biff said, and turned back to me again. "So you been playin' twelve years," he said without interest.

"I've been trying to learn jazz," I said.

"Mmm," he said, his voice turning away. I heard the sound of ice against the sides of a glass. He had picked up a drink from the piano top.

"He's real good," Luke said. "He studied classical a long time."

"Yeah, mmm," Biff said, and drank and put down the glass again with a small final click.

"Why'n't you play something for him, Iggie?"

"That's okay, I'll take your word for it," Biff said. "Nice meetin' you both, enjoy yourselves, huh?"

"Hey, *wait* a minute!" Luke said.

"There's somethin' I got to see about," Biff said. "You'll excuse me, huh?"

"The kid came all the way here to listen to you," Luke said, his voice rising. "I went all the way uptown to get him, and then we had to come all the way down here again."

"So what?" Biff said.

"*That's* what!" Luke said. His voice was louder now. "He's been talkin' about nothin' but you ever since he found out you were gonna be playin' in this dump."

"Yeah?" Biff said. "That right?"

"*Yeah!*" Luke said, his voice strident and belligerent now. It was the gin talking, I realized. I had never heard my uncle raise his voice except while playing poker, and nobody was playing poker right that minute. Or maybe they were. "So let him play piano for you," Luke said. "It won't kill you."

"You think I got nothin' better to do than . . . ?"

"What the hell *else* you got to do?" Luke asked.

"That's okay, Uncle Luke," I said.

"No, it *ain't* okay. Why the hell can't he listen to you?"

"I just wanted to meet him, that's all," I said. "Come on."

"Just a minute, you," Biff said.

"Me?"

"You're the piano player, ain't you?"

"Yes."

"Then that's who. What can you play?"

"Lots of things."

"Like what?"

"Tatum's 'Moonglow' and 'St. Louis Blues,' and . . ."

"That's plenty. Just them two, okay? If you're lousy, you get one chorus and out. Now if your uncle here don't mind, I'm goin' to the *pissoir* over there while you start playin', because I got to take a leak, if that's all right with your uncle here. I can listen fine from in there, and soon's I'm finished, I'll come right back. If that's all right with your uncle here."

"That's fine," Luke said.

"Show him the piano," Biff said. "I'll cut off the juke on my way." He climbed down from the bandstand and walked ponderously past me toward the men's room.

"Black bastard," Luke muttered under his breath, and then said. "Give me your hand, Iggie," and led me up the steps and to the piano.

I played. I wish I could report that all conversation stopped dead the moment I began, that Biff came running out of the men's room hastily buttoning his fly and peeing all over himself in excitement, that a scout for a record company rushed over and slapped a contract on the piano top. No such thing. I played the two Tatum solos exactly as I'd lifted them from his record, and then I stopped, and conversation was still going on, laughter still shrilled into the smoky room, the bartender's voice said, "Scotch and soda, comin' up," and I put my hands back in my lap.

"Yeah, okay," Biff said. I had not realized he was standing beside the piano, and I did not know how long he'd been there. I waited for him to say more. The silence lengthened.

"Some of the runs were off, I know," I said.

"Yeah, those runs are killers," Biff said.

"They're hard to pick up off the records," I said.

"That where you got this stuff? From Art's records?"

"Yes."

"Well, that's not a bad way. What else do you know?"

"A lot of Wilson, and some Waller and Hines . . ."

"Waller, huh?"

"Yes."

"Takin' it off note by note from the records, huh?"

"Yeah."

"Mmm," Biff said. "Well, that's okay. What've you got down of Fats?"

" 'Thief in the Night' and 'If This Isn't Love' and . . ."

"Oh, yeah, the sides he cut with Honey Bear and Autrey, ain't they?"

"I don't know who's on them."

"That's all shit, anyway," Biff said. "That stuff he done with 'Fats Waller and his Rhythm.' 'Cept for maybe 'Dinah' and 'Blue Because of You.' "

"I can play those, too."

"Can you do any of his early stuff?"

"Like what?"

"Like the stuff he cut in the twenties. 'Sweet Savannah Sue' and . . . I don't know, man. . . . 'Love Me or Leave Me.' That stuff."

"No, I don't know those."

"Yeah, well," Biff said. "Well, that wasn't half bad, what you played. You dig Tatum, huh?"

"Yes. That's how I want to play."

"Like Tatum, huh?"

"Yes."

"Well, you doin' fine," Biff said. "Jus' keep on goin' the way you are. Fine," he said. "Fine."

"I need help," I said.

"Yeah, man, don't we all?" Biff said, and chuckled.

"A lot of Tatum's chords are hard to take off the records."

"Jus' break 'em up, that's all. Play 'em note by note. That's what I used to do when I was comin' along."

"I've tried that. I still can't get them all."

"Well, kid, what can I tell you? You wanna play Tatum piano, then you gotta listen to him and do what he does, that's all. Why'n't you run on down to the Street; I think he's playin' in one of the clubs down there right now. With Slam, I think."

"What street?" I said.

"*What* street? *The* Street."

"I don't know what you mean."

"Well, kid, what can I tell you?" Biff said, and sighed. "While you're down there, you might listen to what Diz is doin'. Dizzy Gillespie. Him an' Bird are shakin' things up, man, you might want to change your mind. Hey, now, looka here," he said.

"Hello, motha-fugger," someone said cheerfully.

"Get up there an' start blowin'," someone else said. "We heah to help you."

"Don't need no help, man," Biff said, and chuckled.

"Whutchoo doin' in this toilet, anyhow?" the first man said. "*Dis*graceful!"

Biff chuckled again, and then said, "Kid, these're two of the worl's *worse* jazz musicians. . . ."

"*Sheeee*-it," one of them said, and laughed.

"Been thrown off ever' band in the country 'cause they shoot dope an' fuck chickens."

All three of them laughed. One of them said, "We brung Dickie with us, he gettin' his drums from the car."

"The shades is he's blind," Biff said, and I realized one of the other men must have been staring at me. "Plays piano."

"Hope he's better'n you," one of them said, and all of them laughed again.

"What's your name, man?" Biff said. "I forget."

"Iggie."

"This's Sam an' Jerry. You sit in with 'em, Iggie, while I go dazzle that chick. I'm afraid she goan git away."

"Hey, come down, man," one of them said. "We here in this shithole to blow with *you*, not some fuckin' F-sharp piano player."

"I'm not an F-sharp piano player," I said.

"Hey, man, gimme a hand with this," somebody said. I figured that was Dickie, who'd been getting his drums from the car. "Come on, Jerr, move yo' black ass."

"Any blind piano player I *know*'s a F-sharp piano player," the other man insisted.

"*Tatum*'s blind," Biff said, "and he can cut your ass thu Sunday."

"He only *half* blind," Sam said.

"I can play in any key on the board," I said.

"There now, you see? Sit down with Iggie here, an' work out a nice set, huh? And lemme go see 'bout my social life. Play nice, Iggie. Maybe you can cover up all they *mis*takes."

"*Sheeee*-it," Sam said, and then laughed.

I listened as the drummer set up his equipment and the trumpet player started running up and down chromatics, warming up. Sam asked me to tune him up, and when I asked him what notes he wanted me to hit, he said, "Jus' an A, man," sounding very surprised. I gave Jerry a B flat when he asked for it, and he tuned his horn, and meanwhile Dickie was warming up on his cymbals, playing fast little brush rolls, and pretty soon we were ready to start the set. I'd never played with a band before, but I wasn't particularly scared. I'd listened to enough jazz records to know what the format was. The piano player or the horn man usually started with the head chorus (I didn't yet know it was called the head), and then the band took solos in turn, and then everybody went into the final chorus and ended the tune. I figured all I had to do was play the way I'd been playing for the past seven months, play all those tunes I'd either lifted from my brother's record collection or figured out on my own. Biff, after all, was a well-known and respected jazz musician, and he had told me that what I'd played wasn't half bad, which I figured meant at *least* half good. Besides, *he* was the one who'd asked me to sit in.

"You *sure* you ain't a F-sharp piano player?" Sam asked behind me.

"I'm sure," I said.

"'Cause, man, I don't dig them wild stretches in F sharp," he said. "You got some other keys in your head, cool. Otherwise, it's been graaaand knowin' you."

"Well, *start* it, man," Jerry said to me. He was standing to my right. The drummer was diagonally behind me, sitting beside Sam. I took a four-bar intro, and we began playing "Fools Rush In," a nice Johnny Mercer-Rube Bloom ballad, which I'd never heard

Tatum do, but which I played in the Tatum style, or what I considered to be the Tatum style. We were moving into the bridge when Sam said, "Chop it off, kid." I didn't know what he meant. I assumed he wanted me to play a bit more staccato, so I began chopping the chords, so to speak, giving a good crisp, clean touch to those full tenths as I walked them with my left hand or used them in a swing bass, pounding out that steady four/four rhythm, and hearing the satisfying (to me) echo of Sam behind me walking the identical chords in arpeggios on this bass fiddle. As I went into the second chorus, I heard Jerry come in behind me on the horn, and I did what I'd heard the piano players doing on the records, I started feeding him chords, keeping that full left hand going in time with what Sam and the drummer were laying down, though to tell the truth I couldn't quite understand *what* the drummer was doing, and wasn't even sure he was actually keeping the beat. It was the drummer who said, "Take it home," and I said, "What?" and he said, "Last eight," and the horn man came out of the bridge and into the final eight bars, and we ended the tune. Everybody was quiet.

"Well, you ain't a F-sharp piano player, that's for sure," Sam said. "But you know what you can do with that left hand of yours, don't you?"

"You can chop it off and shove it clean up your ass," the trumpet player said. "Let's get Biff."

They were moving off the bandstand. In a moment, and without another word to me, they were gone. I sat at the piano alone, baffled.

"What's going on here?" a voice asked. "Who the hell are you? Who's that band? Where's my piano player."

The voice belonged to a fat man. I could tell. I could also tell he was Jewish. I know it's un-American to identify ethnic groups by vocal inflection or intonation, but I can tell if a man's black, Italian, Irish, Jewish, or what*ever* simply by hearing his voice. And so can you. And if you tell me otherwise, I'll call you a liar. (And beside, what the hell's so un-American about it?) I was stunned. Some black bastard horn player had just told me to shove my precious left hand up my ass, and I didn't know why.

"You!" the fat man said. "Get away from that piano. Where's Biff?"

"Cool it, Mr. Gottlieb," Biff's voice said, "I'm right here; the boy's a friend of mine."

"Do you know 'Deep in the Heart of Texas'?" Gottlieb said. "The bartender wants 'Deep in the Heart of Texas.'"

"Beyond my ken," Biff said, in what sounded like an English accent.

"What?" Gottlieb said, startled.

"The tune. Unknown to me," Biff said.

"What?"

"Advise your barkeep to compile a more serious list of requests," Biff said in the same stuffy English cadences, and then immediately and surprisingly fell into an aggravated black dialect, dripping watermelon, pone, and chitlings. "You jes' ast you man to keep de booze comin', an' let *me*—an' mah frens who was kine enough to come see me heah—worry 'bout de music, huh? Kid, you want to git off dat stool so's we kin lay some jazz on dese mothahs?"

"What?" Gottlieb said.

"I'll talk to *you* later," Biff said as I climbed off the stool and off the bandstand.

My uncle Luke had drunk too much. His head was on the table, touching my elbow, and I could hear him snoring loudly as Biff talked to me. On my right, the girl with the five-and-dime perfume sat silent and motionless, her presence detectable only by her scent and the sound of her breathing. The trumpet player had left around midnight. The bass player and the drummer had followed him at about one. We were alone in the place now, except for the bartender, who was washing glasses and lining them up on the shelves, and Gottlieb, who had tallied his register and was putting chairs up on tables, preparatory to sweeping out the joint. As he passed our table, he said, "This ain't a hotel, Mr. Jazz," and then moved on, muttering.

"Cheap sheenie bastard," Biff said. "He's got his bartender watering drinks. You okay, Poots?" he asked the girl. The girl did not answer. She must have nodded assent, though, the motion of her head and neck unleashing a fresh wave of scent. Biff said, "Fine, that's fine, you jus' stick aroun' a short while longer. Now, you," he said. "You want to know what's wrong with how you play piano?"

"Yes," I said.

"You're lucky Dickie's a gentle soul. Dickie. The drummer. Otherwise he'da done what Jo Jones done to Bird in Kansas City when he got the band all turned around. He throwed his cymbal on the floor, and that was that, man, end of the whole fuckin' set. 'Scuse me, Poots."

"Well, *they* ended the set, too," I said. I still didn't know that Bird was someone's name. This was the second time Biff had used it tonight, and each time I'd thought he meant bird with a lower-case *b;* the reference was mystifying. For that matter, I didn't know who Jo Jones was, either. But I figured if he'd thrown a cymbal on the floor, he had to be a drummer, whereas all I could think about the use of the word "bird" was that it was a black jazz expression. (Come to think of it, it *was.*) "And I'll tell you something, Mr. Anderson, your bass player pissed me off right from the start. Excuse me, miss. Making cracks about F-sharp piano players."

"Well, le's say he ain' 'zackly de mos' tac'ful of souls," Biff said in his watermelon accent, and then immediately added in his normal speaking voice, "But he's a damn fine musician, and he knows where jazz *is* today, and *that's* what he was trying to convey to you."

"I'm no damn F-sharp piano player," I said.

"He didn't know that. Anyway, that ain't what got him or the other boys riled."

"Then what?"

"Your left hand," I said.

"I've got a good left hand," I said.

"Sure," Biff said. "If you want to play alone, you've got a good left hand, and I'm speakin' comparative. You still need lots of work, even if all you want to play is solo piano."

"That's what I want to play."

"Then don't go sittin' in with no groups. Because if you play that way with a group, you're lucky they don't throw the *piano* at you, no less the cymbals."

"Mr. Anderson," I said, "I don't know what you're talking about."

"I'm talking about that bass," he said.

"That's a Tatum bass," I said. "That's what you your*self* played. That was Tatum right down the line."

"Correct," Biff said.

"So?"

"Maybe you didn't notice, but I was playin' *alone.* Kid, a rhythm section won't tolerate that bass nowadays. Not after Bird."

"What do you mean, *bird*? What's that?"

"Parker. Charlie Parker. Bird."

"Is he a piano player?"

"He plays alto saxophone."

"Well . . . what *about* him?" I said. "What's *he* got to do with playing piano?"

"He's got everything to do with everything," Biff said. "You tell me you want to play Tatum piano, I tell you Tatum's on the way out, if not already dead and gone. You tell me you want to learn all those Tatum runs, I tell you there's no room for that kind of bullshit in bop. You know why Sam . . ."

"In *what*, did you say?"

"Bop, that's the stuff Parker's laying down. And Fats Navarro. And Bud Powell. Now *there's* the piano player you ought to be listening to, Powell; he's the one you ought to be pickin' up on, *not* Art Tatum. You want to know why the boys shot you down, it's 'cause you put them in prison, man, you put them in that old-style bass prison, and they can't play that way no more. These guys're cuttin' their chops on bop. Even I'm too old-fashioned for them, but we're good friends, and they allow me to get by with open tenths and some shells. Sam wants to walk the bass line himself, he don't want to be trapped by no rhythm the *piano* player's layin' down, he don't even want to be trapped by the *drummer* no more. Didn't you hear what Dickie was doing behind you? You didn't hear no four/four on the bass drum, did you? That was on the cymbals; he saved the big drums for klook-mop, dropping them bombs every now and then, but none of that heavy one, two, three, four, no, *man.* Which is why they told you to stick your left hand up your ass, 'scuse me, Poots, to *lose* it, man. They wanted you to play shells in the left hand, that's all, and not that pounding Tatum rhythm, uh-uh. You dig what I'm saying?"

"What's a shell? What you mean, they wanted me to play shells?"

"Shells, man. You know what a C-minor chord is?"

"C, E flat, G, and B flat," I said.

"Right. But when Powell plays a C-minor, all he hits are the C and the B flat. With his pinkie and his thumb, you dig? He leaves out the insides, he just gives you the shell. He feeds those shells to the horn players, and they blow pure and fast and hard, without that fuckin' pounding rhythm and those ornate chords and runs going on behind them all the time, and lockin' them in, 'scuse me, Poots. Piano players just can't *play* that way no more.

"*Tatum* does," I said. "And so does Wilson."

"A dying breed," Biff said in his English accent, "virtually obsolete. *Look,* man, I was with Marian McPartland the first time she heard Bud play, and she said to me, 'Man, that is *some* spooky right hand there,' and she wasn't shittin'. That right hand *is* spooky, the things he does with that right hand. He plays those fuckin' shells with his left—the root and seventh, or the root and third—because he's got tiny hands, you see, he couldn't reach those Tatum tenths if he stood on his fuckin' head, 'scuse me, Poots. Some of the time he augments the shell by pickin' up a ninth with the right hand, but mostly the right is playin' a *horn* solo, you dig? He's doin' Charlie Parker on the piano. There are three voices dig? Two notes in the shell, and the running line in the right hand, and that's it. Tatum runs? Forget 'em, man! They're what a piano player does when he can't think of nothin' new, he just throws in all those rehearsed runs that're already in his fingers. That ain't jazz, man. That's I don't know what it is, but it ain't jazz no more."

"You people going to pay rent on that table?" Gottlieb said.

"What're you thinking, kid?" Biff asked. "I can't tell what you're thinking behind them shades."

"I just don't understand what you're saying."

"You don't, huh? Well, here it is in a nutshell, kid. The rhythm ain't in the left hand no more—it's passed over to the right. The left hand is almost standin' still these days. And if you want to keep on playin' all that frantic shit, then you better play it all by yourself, 'cause there ain't no band gonna tolerate it. That's it in a nutshell."

"I still want to play like Tatum," I said.

"You'll be followin' a coffin up Bourbon Street," Biff said. "Look, what the hell do I care *what* you play? I'm just tryin' to tell you if you're startin' *now,* for Christ's sake, don't start with somethin' already *dead.* Go to the Street, man, Fifty-second Street, dig what the cats are doin'. If you don't like it, then, man, that's up to you. But I'm tellin' you, sure as this sweet li'l thing is sittin' here beside me, Tatum and Wilson are dead and the Bird is king, and jazz ain't never gonna be the same again." He suddenly burst out laughing. "Man, the cats goan drum me clear out of the tribe. They got strong hostility, them boppers."

"I want to hear them play," I said.

"Get your uncle to take you down the Street. Diz an' Oscar—Pettiford, Oscar Pettiford—got a fine group at the Onyx, George Wallington on piano. Go listen to them."

"Will *you* take me there, Mr. Anderson?"

"Me? I don't know you from a hole in the wall," Biff said.

"Oh, *take* the fuckin' kid," Poots said.

DONALD BARTHELME

Much of what Donald Barthelme has written is controversial by virtue of its anti-traditional style and its mocking, satirical content. His characters and situations lack reality but promote truth. First published in the *New Yorker* in 1963, Barthelme has since written the novels *Snow White* (1967) and *The Dead Father* (1975) and many volumes of short stories, including *Great Days* (1979), from which "The King of Jazz" is taken.

"The King of Jazz" is a parody of the jam session, likened to an old cowboy shootout. Since the most important aspect of jazz is improvisation, it is natural that serious jazz musicians practice long hours and strive to excel at the art, strive to be the very best, strive to become the next jazz legend—the next Charlie Parker or Lady Day—yes, strive to become *greater* than Bird or Billie.

Jazz, of course, is communication and involves an audience. Comparisons of musicians are made via word-of-mouth, the record reviews, and the many magazines and jazz books. Who is the current king of jazz and who will be king tomorrow? Being the very best at anything is important to most of us, but at times, Barthelme implies, it can become a bit foolish.

THE KING OF JAZZ

WELL I'm the king of jazz now, thought Hokie Mokie to himself as he oiled the slide on his trombone. Hasn't been a 'bone man been king of jazz for many years. But now that Spicy MacLammermoor, the old king, is dead, I guess I'm it. Maybe I better play a few notes out of this window here, to reassure myself.

"Wow!" said somebody standing on the sidewalk. "Did you hear that?"

"I did," said his companion.

"Can you distinguish our great homemade American jazz performers, each from the other?"

"Used to could."

"Then who was that playing?"

"Sounds like Hokie Mokie to me. Those few but perfectly selected notes have the real epiphanic glow."

"The what?"

"The real epiphanic glow, such as is obtained only by artists of the caliber of Hokie Mokie, who's from Pass Christian, Mississippi. He's the king of jazz, now that Spicy MacLammermoor is gone."

Hokie Mokie put his trombone in its trombone case and went to a gig. At the gig everyone fell back before him, bowing.

"Hi Bucky! Hi Zoot! Hi Freddie! Hi Thad! Hi Roy! Hi Dexter! Hi Jo! Hi Willie! Hi Greens!"

"What we gonna play, Hokie? You the king of jazz now, you gotta decide."

"How 'bout 'Smoke'?"

"Wow!" everybody said. "Did you hear that? Hokie Mokie can just knock a fella out, just the way he pronounces a word. What a intonation on that boy! God Almighty!"

"I don't want to play 'Smoke,'" somebody said.

"Would you repeat that, stranger?"

"I don't want to play 'Smoke.' 'Smoke' is dull. I don't like the changes. I refuse to play 'Smoke.'"

"He refuses to play 'Smoke.' But Hokie Mokie is the king of jazz and he says 'Smoke'!"

"Man, you from outa town or something? What do you mean you refuse to play 'Smoke'? How'd you get on this gig anyhow? Who hired you?"

"I am Hideo Yamaguchi, from Tokyo, Japan."

"Oh, you're one of those Japanese cats, eh?"

"Yes I'm the top trombone man in all of Japan."

"Well you're welcome here until we hear you play. Tell me, is the Tennessee Tea Room still the top jazz place in Tokyo?"

"No, the top jazz place in Tokyo is the Square Box now."

"That's nice. O. K., now we gonna play 'Smoke' just like Hokie said. You ready, Hokie? O.K., give you four for nothin'. One! Two! Three! Four!"

The two men who had been standing under Hokie's window had followed him to the club. Now they said:

"Good God!"

"Yes, that's Hokie's famous 'English sunrise' way of playing. Playing with lots of rays coming out of it, some red rays, some blue rays, some green rays, some green stemming from a violet center, some olive stemming from a tan center—"

"That young Japanese fellow is pretty good, too."

"Yes, he is pretty good. And he holds his horn in a peculiar way. That's frequently the mark of a superior player."

"Bent over like that with his head between his knees—good God, he's sensational!"

He's sensational, Hokie thought. Maybe I ought to kill him.

But at that moment somebody came in the door pushing in front of him a four-and-one-half-octave marimba. Yes, it was Fat Man Jones, and he began to play even before he was fully in the door.

"What're we playing?"

"'Billie's Bounce.'"

"That's what I thought it was. What're we in?"

"F."

"That's what I thought we were in. Didn't you use to play with Maynard?"

"Yeah I was on that band for a while until I was in the hospital."

"What for?"

"I was tired."

"What can we add to Hokie's fantastic playing?"

"How 'bout some rain or stars?"

"Maybe that's presumptuous."

"Ask him if he'd mind."

"You ask him. I'm scared. You don't fool around with the king of jazz. That young Japanese guy's pretty good, too."

"He's sensational."

"You think he's playing in Japanese?"

"Well I don't think it's English."

This trombone's been makin' my neck green for thirty-five years, Hokie thought. How come I got to stand up to yet another challenge, this late in life?

"Well, Hideo—"

"Yes, Mr. Mokie?"

"You did well on both 'Smoke' and 'Billie's Bounce.' You're just about as good as me, I regret to say. In fact, I've decided you're *better* than me. It's a hideous thing to contemplate, but there it is. I have only been king of jazz for twenty-four hours, but the unforgiving logic of this art demands we bow to Truth, when we hear it."

"Maybe you're mistaken."

"No, I got ears. I'm not mistaken. Hideo Yamaguchi is the new king of jazz.

"You want to be king emeritus?"

"No, I'm just going to fold up my horn and steal away. This gig is yours, Hideo. You can pick the next tune."

"How 'bout 'Cream'?"

"O.K., you heard what Hideo said, it's 'Cream.' You ready, Hideo?"

"Hokie, you don't have to leave. You can play too. Just move a little over to the side there—"

"Thank you, Hideo, that's very gracious of you. I guess I will play a little, since I'm still here. Sotto voce, of course."

"Hideo is wonderful on 'Cream'!"

"Yes, I imagine it's his best tune."

"What's that sound coming in from the side there?"

"Which side?"

"The left."

"You mean that sound that sounds like the cutting edge of life? That sounds like polar bears crossing Arctic ice pans? That sounds like a herd of musk ox in full flight? That sounds like male walruses diving to the bottom of the sea? That sounds like fumaroles smoking on the slopes of Mt. Katmai? That sounds like the wild turkey walking through the deep, soft forest? That sounds like beavers chewing trees in an Appalachian marsh? That sounds like an oyster fungus growing on an aspen trunk? That sounds like a mule deer wandering a montane of the Sierra Nevada? That sounds like prairie dogs kissing? That sounds like witchgrass tumbling or a river meandering? That sounds like manatees munching seaweed at Cape Sable? That sounds like coatimundis moving in packs across the face of Arkansas? That sounds like—"

"Good God, it's Hokie! Even with a cup mute on, he's blowing Hideo right off the stand!"

"Hideo's playing on his knees now! Good God, he's reaching into his belt for a large steel sword—Stop him!"

"Wow! That was the most exciting 'Cream' ever played. Is Hideo all right?"

"Yes, somebody is getting him a glass of water."

"You're my man, Hokie. That was the dadblangedest thing I ever saw!"

"You're the king of jazz once again!"

"Hokie Mokie is the most happening thing there is!"

"Yes, Mr. Hokie sir, I have to admit, you blew me right off the stand. I see I have many years of work and study before me still."

"That's O.K., son. Don't think a thing about it. It happens to the best of us. Or it almost happens to the best of us. Now I want everybody to have a good time because we're gonna play 'Flats.' 'Flats' is next."

"With your permission, sir, I will return to my hotel and pack. I am most grateful for everything I have learned here."

"That's O.K., Hideo. Have a nice day. He-he. Now, 'Flats.'"

PAMELA PAINTER

Pamela Painter's story collection *Getting to Know the Weather,* published in 1985, won the Great Lakes College Association New Writer Award a year later. Since then she has published stories in *Ploughshares, Harper's, Mademoiselle,* and *Kenyon Review,* among others. She is the founding editor of *Story Quarterly* and teaches in the Harvard Extension and the Vermont MFA programs. In 1988 she received an NEA Fellowship.

Painter says that "The Next Time I Meet Buddy Rich" was inspired by her having met "a brazen, young man—a drummer, as it turned out, who wanted to be as good as Buddy Rich." She wrote the story and later had the opportunity to meet Buddy, who was gracious enough to visit with her and discuss drumming. A second meeting with him some months later resulted in his autographing the manuscript of the story she was revising. Although Rich later was given copies of the story, Painter says "I'm still not sure he ever read it." When she last saw him about one year before his death and asked him what his personal feelings about jazz were, he said, "Hell, I don't know about that. For me it's playing two hours here, then going down the road to Muncie, Indiana, to the next gig. Nothing more."

Although Painter confesses she doesn't know much about jazz, she says, "I've loved jazz since I first heard it—and it has always been part of the periphery of my life." She and her husband, Robie Macauley, listen to jazz recordings when they retire for the night.

THE NEXT TIME I MEET BUDDY RICH

WE pulled into town just as the sun was coming up, dropped some stuff off at the rooms they gave us, and took the drums and other instruments over to the club. The debris of empty glasses, full ashtrays, disarranged chairs was still there from the night before, heavy with stale air. I unrolled my rug, set up my drums. Felt for the piece of gum Buddy Rich once gave me—now stuck at the bottom of the floor tom-tom. Vince hooked up the sound system and then we headed back to the hotel.

I carried in my practice set, calling to Gretel to open the door. Finally I used my key. Sounds of the shower running droned from the bathroom. Her clothes were scattered over a chair, suitcases sprawled open on the floor. Then the water went off and Gretel appeared in the doorway with a towel around her, a folded rim keeping it in place, flattening her breasts. Her hair was piled on her head and held by one barrette. Beads of moisture gleamed on her shoulders, her legs.

"No more hot water," she said, as she pulled the barrette from her hair, shaking it loose. "I'm getting tired of these places. This is too far away from the club considering we're going to be here two weeks."

"We can move. We have before."

"It's the whole scene," she said pointing to the suitcases. "Where's it going? I know what you want. But sometimes wanting isn't enough."

I lay down on the bed and closed my eyes. I saw her standing in the towel. I took the towel away and looked at her full breasts, her stomach, a different texture of hair.

"Sorry," she said. "You want to listen now or later?"

"Later." I put the towel back and opened my eyes. She was looking out the window. I felt sorry for her living this way, but the words to change it all, to take me back to Erie, just wouldn't come. "Let's have a nice dinner after the club run tonight. Chicago doesn't close down like Kansas." She shrugged her shoulders. She was right. If you weren't playing, it was hard to care what you did out here. One room after another. A hundred tables in a hundred towns. The bed slid as I got up. I licked some of the water off her right shoulder. She didn't move.

"OK, later," she said. And I understood that everything would have to wait. That was OK too. She had been traveling with me for the past year, ever since we decided we'd eventually get married. We never mentioned settling down, but I could tell she was tired of being on the road. The band probably wouldn't be together much longer anyway with Jack pulling toward hard rock. Then I'd take my uncle up on his offer of being a plumber for him again. *That* I didn't want to think about.

So I arranged my practice set, fitting it around my chair. Settling it into the sparse pile of the rug to make it steady. "Bring me back two ham on rye," I told Gretel when Jack and Vince knocked on the door.

Vince understood. Five years I've been breaking my ass to get the big break, trying to make it happen. One night in Columbus I was talking to a drummer who was almost there, would be in a few years—by thirty you have to be. That's what I asked him. "How do you get there?"

He wiped his hands under his arms and said, "You practice your ass off all your life and the better you get the worse you seem to yourself and you're ready to give up; and then one day when your hands aren't getting any faster you say the hell with it. When you next sit down at a set of drums after you haven't touched them for days, weeks, like a vow you'd made—suddenly you're doing all the things you've been trying to do for years—suddenly there is a 'before' and 'after' and it's the 'after' where you are now—and goddamn you don't know why, you just know that you're finally there. Then it's only a matter of time."

And now my time was running out. The band close to breaking up. Kids, pets, hard rock up against the slower stuff. I looked down at my hands. Clean, now. The prints clean, sensitive to the smooth surface of the sticks. I hated being a plumber although I was good at it. All that grease, fitting pipes, welding. I straightened my back. Time enough for planning that later. Time to practice now. I pulled back the plastic curtains to let in the last of the hotel's sun. Then I started to play. Slow at first, just letting my wrists do the work, looking out past the sunken single beds, past the cheap print of some flower, using a little pressure, feeling how my wrists were somehow connected with the tension in my feet. Just feeling it happen like I was watching myself in the mirror. Trying for the sounds of Buddy Rich.

The next time I meet Buddy Rich it'll be at a 76 station in some crazy place, like Boone, Iowa, not at a concert, and he'll be all burnt out waiting for a cup of coffee and I'll go up to him and say—what I'll say I haven't worked out yet but it'll happen and I'll say it then.

I met Buddy Rich for the first time at Rainbow Gardens in Erie, Pennsylvania. I was playing a spot called The Embers and it was our night off. We went really early, to get good seats up close so I could watch him play, watch his hands and feet and the way his body moves. He's a karate expert—once said that the martial arts apply to drumming; they key your mind up for getting into it, coordinate your hands and feet. I want to ask him about this when I meet him next.

The Rainbow Gardens is an oval-shaped arena, a stage at one end and a big wooden dance floor in the middle of a bunch of tables. Loads of people and glasses and cheap booze. It was during intermission, on my way back from the john, that I saw him. He was sitting off to the side, just happened to be there—probably after changing his shirt. Not drinking, just leaning back in his chair. Looking out as if to say, "OK, show me something intelligent."

I walked past thinking, "That can't be." Somehow you think of stars as either living on stage or in their dressing rooms. No real life, no tired hands. Then I walked past again and got enough nerve to say, "Buddy Rich?" and he didn't say "no," so I went on and said, "I'm Tony—I'm a drummer and I play with Circuit of Sound." The words kind of rushed at him like a spilled drink and just as effective. "I think your band is really great," I said. He seemed to lean further back in his chair. He had on a long-sleeved grey shirt and grey pants. His fingers were tapping on the table, tapping like they were just doing it by themselves. I fumbled in my wallet for a card with the name of my band on it. "Would you autograph this for me," I said. I gave him a pen.

His first words were, "Who do you want it to?"

"Tony," I said, "and good luck on the drums."

He looked at me kind of funny and then wrote, "Best Wishes." I nodded, disappointed. Then I thanked him and went back to my seat, knowing I had blown my chance. Where are the questions when it matters? I wished I could grab him by the collar and say, "Hey, I'm different. I'm not like all the rest of the people who don't understand what Buddy Rich is unless you're in solo. Who don't understand that you, Buddy Rich, are here for the band—while all these people are here for Buddy Rich." But I didn't say it. I drank down eight ounces of Schlitz—chugging it to drown my embarrassment, and dying a second time because I finally realized that he thought I meant good luck to him on the drums. As if he needed it. Shit.

I let about ten minutes pass. Watching him just sitting there, wanting to know what was going through his mind, wanting to know what was keeping his hands moving or still. What's in his mind when he's playing. He had a back operation in July and a night later he was on the bandstand, behind the drums. Later, on a talk show he said they should have done the operation while he was playing, then they wouldn't have needed an anesthetic.

Finally, I couldn't stand it anymore. I chugged another Schlitz and stood up. I hadn't talked to my date since I sat down and all I could do now was tap her under the chin—grateful that she understood.

"I talked to you a few minutes ago and nothing came out right—including asking for your autograph," I said. He seemed to appreciate my honesty because his eyes stayed on me longer and again I told him how great he and his band were and he said, "sit down," so I pulled out a chair across the table from him. Then I started to pinpoint all the different songs that I really enjoyed off his albums—some of them almost unknown. I counted on that. Like "Goodbye Yesterday," like how it talks to me instead of playing.

"It shows how close the musicians work—you know the music is in front of them, but no arranger, no charts could do it for you—it's the energy of the group that pulls it together, that makes it talk." I told him this and more about "Preach and Teach," and he was nodding his head and not leaning back anymore. Now he leaned forward on his table, looking at me. "You know," I said, "with you, it's not just jamming. It's structure pushed to the end in sound." We sat in silence for a few minutes thinking about it.

"Yeah, you do understand," he said. Then he kind of grinned that wide smile of his. "Hard to talk about, isn't it. Easier to play."

"If you're you," I said. "I'm still trying."

"You know," he said, "interviewers are always asking me about the future of music. Hell I don't know about that. For me it's playing two hours here then going down the road to Muncie, Indiana. It's the next night for me. Nothing more." His hands were still now and I saw them for the first time.

"You don't have any calluses," I said.

"Hell no I don't." He grinned again, spreading his fingers on the table. "If the pressure's right the sticks don't rub." Smooth. Magic.

Just then I noticed some kids standing off to the left of us waiting with their pencils and papers—finally having figured out who he was and who I wasn't. So I stood up to give them their turn and he reached out and grabbed my wrist. "Don't go," he said, "I'm not done talking to you." So I sat down. My wrist was burning and I knew that the next time I played, the next time my right hand had to make itself heard, it wouldn't be the same. "Sit down," he said, "I got a few more minutes before I have to play to this airport hangar." He gestured around the arena, the high steel-beamed ceiling, the cold aluminum walls painted yellow, pink, blue. It would never be the same for me again.

He held out his hand for pencils and paper and a guy stepped forward, a couple more shuffling behind him. Wondering who I was, sitting there like a friend.

"I really like your "Sing, Sing, Sing,'" he said to Rich. Rich looked up at me sideways and winked and told him, "I'm going to play 'SSS' and 'Wipeout' in a medley just for you." The dumb ass should have known it was Krupa's theme song. I suddenly had a feeling for what Buddy Rich had to deal with, wanting to be liked and understood and yet running into people who kill off any generosity you feel for the public out there. Like the ones who come to hear his band—they're all looking for the drum solo—you can see their eyes light up as if the stage lights suddenly got switched around.

They don't understand the dynamics and togetherness. They know the finished product in a half-assed way, but not how it comes about. Even the critics in the early days would say he plays too loud, or throws rim shots in where they don't belong. *Now* they know what they're hearing.

We talked for a few more minutes—then he said he had to go. Gave me a stick of gum—Dentyne. He stood up and leaned over the table and did a quiet roll with his hands to my shoulder. "I think you'll make it," he said. "I'll be hearing you some day." And he was gone. I guess I heard the rest of the concert. But now being there meant something else to me. And when I hit home that night the stick of gum went into my drum. Was there now. A small pink lump. I look at it just before I begin to play.

Gretel still wasn't back so I practiced a while longer. Then I moved to the bed and lay back, still hearing the sounds, my own sounds this time, and I lay there for one hour. Not sleeping but waiting for show time to come round. When she arrived with the sandwiches I ate them. When Vince called to check the program I talked. But I was hearing other things, I was making my own program for tonight.

Finally, I must have slept for a few hours because pretty soon Vince was pounding on the door yelling, "how we going to make it without our practice?" I knew what he meant. He plays a cool sax—sliding notes around like melted butter then pulling them together with a tension that tells in his back, in the way his arms move toward his sides when he gets up for his solo run. We might have made it, Vince and I; maybe he'll keep something together. "Meet you in the lobby," I yelled.

We took three changes of costume and all went in one van over to the club. We were starting out tonight in tuxes, then switching to sequined jump suits that remind me of kids' Dr. Denton pajamas, ending up in jeans. All a part of the act. Jack was driving and putting on his cuff links at the same time. He's a good guitarist and upfront man. Can talk to anyone—sifting his smile out over the audience behind his velvety voice. Carol, the vocalist, and he were a good pair. She was filing her nails. Gretel was out shopping.

The stage loomed in the back of the place away from the bar and the lighting was OK. Bad was bad. OK was good. There were a few early drunks sitting around before going home to the wife and kids and mashed potatoes—they'd be moving along as soon as the sound built—it always happened. I took a run on my drums—did some rolls—soft then faster and faster. I hit each drum firm, getting that crisp beat, starting with the snare and ending up with the floor tom-tom and then one closing beat on the bass to cut it off sharp. I set out two sets of new sticks because I've been breaking one or two a night. Then I rolled up my pant legs and sat there sipping coffee. Vince was off talking to the waitresses, trying to line something up for later—much later. It's hard—you have fifteen minutes here and there to make contact, change clothes, and sound like you're not coming on too strong. He's good-looking in a seedy sort of way and even then he's about 90 percent unsuccessful. I just let it happen if it's going to. Sometimes classy groupies show up two, three nights in a row and you know they want to be asked out. Sometimes they think you'll be a temporary drug source, but they got us all wrong. If we find it we use it, but we don't travel with the stuff. Or play. If cops are even a little suspicious in some of those one-horse towns they'll rip your van apart in the middle of a cornfield—drum sets, suitcases, instruments, speakers, music. It happened once when Jack had some coke from another musician at a gig. But it wasn't on us. Who the hell wanted to be looking for bail in Boone, Iowa.

We were about ready to play, so I changed into my high-heeled shoes for a better angle. We started out with show songs, dance music—moving toward two shows a night. My solo is in the second. I usually start light, play something basic that people can tap their feet to. Then I build up by getting louder, and faster, bringing it back down to nothing then building to a finale with a very fast single-stroke roll. My sticks are moving so fast you can't see them. People relate to a set of drums before any other instrument—I guess because it's obvious what a drummer does—it's so physical.

We started playing and people began coming in. The usual crowd—single people needing movement and noise, countermen, clerks from the local record and sheet-music stores. Bored couples. And a drummer or two. I've met one or two in at least half the towns. Some I looked forward to seeing, some I hated running into again.

We didn't get any requests yet. That'd come later in the evening after a show, after Carol went into her act. A few songs. Talking at the tables, telling women about the men they're with, always on their side. Gretel wasn't here yet. I missed her. But it wasn't reason enough to make her want to stay.

While we were playing "Preach and Teach" something felt different. I moved into a double stroke roll. Not too loud, just testing. It was a feeling. And then I was going faster and my sticks were almost floating across the drums, washing the high hat, the cymbal and snare with rushes of sound. Solid sound. And suddenly I knew I had to stop right there. It was happening and I wasn't going to let it happen yet. Gretel still wasn't here. And I was afraid of what it meant for both of us. But I had to be sure so I changed into a quiet single stroke, hearing the sounds I've heard on my Buddy Rich albums, and my hands were going places they hadn't been before, moving to beats I'd dreamed of playing, sounds I'd played in my sleep, and tonight they were mine. They were in my muscles and fingers as if they'd always been there—even though I knew they hadn't, but this time I hoped they weren't ever going away.

I slowed way down as Jack went into his bass solo and then we took one more run at the chorus before ending. Then I sat there feeling the sticks in my hands, rolling them between my fingers like magic wands. I felt my back relax and curve into a tighter arc as I sat there marking that place and that time. The bar stretching off into the distance of lights and neon noise. Gretel now at our table center front. Gretel in her beaded Indian blouse. My brown coffee mug on the floor beside a bottle of Schlitz. Me at the drums, at twenty-six.

We took a break and I changed into my jump suit fast. Then I joined Gretel at the table. I wanted to tell her but first I wanted her to hear it—without words getting in the way. Anyway she avoided my eyes so I ordered a beer. The tables were filling up. Sounds, smells starting to multiply into that magic of late-night movement. A girl at the next table raised her glass to me. She had beautifully manicured nails—painted green. I nodded politely.

"I went to the bus station today. Checked out the fare to home," Gretel said, finally looking at me. Her eyes were tired. She used to look more alive slaving in the Head Start program where she was working when we met. "But I didn't get the ticket yet."

"Is that what you want?" I asked. My stomach felt like a drum tuned too tight. I knew what she wanted but now I wasn't sure I'd ever get the whole thing together. I covered her hand with mine.

"I don't know what I want anymore," she said. "This just isn't enough even if we wanted the same thing. You big and famous on the drums. Us." She looked around the noisy room and I followed her glance to the stage, to the light glinting on the steel rims of the drums.

"We *are* us," I said but she didn't hear.

"I mean what makes someone give up. I feel like giving up and you're still out there playing." There were tears in her eyes and she blinked fast to spread them away.

"You want to know where being on the road ends for us?" I asked. She pulled her hand away, but I caught her fingers, could feel the turquoise ring I'd given her. "You're afraid I won't know." I knew she was because I had the same fear—living on a dream till the real end of everything. It was almost enough to walk me out of that club, my arm around her, the sticks and drums left behind. Almost enough.

She nodded. "And I know I'd keep asking. Wanting two things at once. Like I don't want to go now but I think I'm going anyway. For a while. Maybe I'll be back in a week. Round trip." She wiped her eyes and laughed up at me. It was a laugh too weakly struck to carry but, God, I loved her for that smile. Then she clinked her glass with mine.

"I might get home before you do," I said. I missed her already. Her waiting for me at tables. Sleeping, turning when I turned. Her trivia games on the road as we zigzag across Route 80 just to break the monotony, getting off to the county roads for a while.

"Don't say that, Tony. I don't want to expect you."

She was right. There was nothing for me to say that I could say. Vince and Jack were back on stage, tuning up. The others were coming back fast. I gave her hand a squeeze. "I have to play. We'll talk later."

"I'll be back for the last show," she said. The light played on the beads of her blouse as she sighed. Softer than drums. Her lips smiled. I kissed her fast. I loved her, but I left to play.

Close to the next break I looked out through the haze, the smoke now thick with words, perfume sprayed on too heavily in the ladies' room. Through the conversations, words going as much past the other person as our music, past people not used to listening to anything beyond their own pulse. And with the drums I had two. I looked out through this, looked for the few who made it all come together, for the one person alone, here for listening. The one who was watching my hands go to where they're supposed to be, craning his neck to watch my feet make the beat.

These people were the ones I leaned toward, the ones I played to. They knew it, and I knew they knew it. And sometimes during a break I would go and sit at their tables. I listened to things Buddy Rich much have heard a million times. But I'm not tired of it yet, maybe because it wasn't true—that I'm the greatest. But I liked to hear it and I talked back, I looked at them straight. It was the same way I played. Sometimes they couldn't handle it—me coming to them, my hand on the back of a chair ready to join them if asked—maybe they didn't have the next three questions memorized—so I moved on. I loved them just the same, but I moved on, doing us both a favor. A time and a place and all that crap. I've been there.

That night I sat with Harry Ratch, an ex-drummer turned history teacher. He told me that once in St. Louis he sat in three nights for Flip Belotti when he had an emergency operation. Harry was the high school hero. History went down pretty easily for the next few months.

I ordered a beer, keeping my limit of two while playing. Harry Ratch was drinking beer too. He was past the physical fitness of a drummer—it was hard to be overweight in this business—but I could tell by the way his arms moved, his shoulders moved, that he once sat behind a set. Suddenly I saw myself ten years from now sitting in The Embers in Erie, Pennsylvania. Talking to some young kid. Telling him about the time I talked to Buddy Rich. Pulling my back straight to hide the tire around my waist. Hoping he'll offer to let me take a turn at his drums. Wishing I hadn't had three drinks already.

It hadn't happened yet. I focused back on Harry Ratch. He told me that Flip Belotti said the thing for beginners is to always practice. "If you're right-handed, do it with your left. There's always practicing to be done when you're not behind the drums." Harry was passing this advice along to me. I accepted it graciously. It made sense. I told him I hoped to see him again in the next two weeks. Maybe he could sit in on a couple of numbers. For a moment his eyes lost their sad history.

"I'll be here," he said sitting back. "I'll be here." It felt good to make someone's night.

I broke my sticks in one of the first numbers and started working with a new pair. Then we began to play the medley that led into my solo. Again I just moved into the drums. I held off till the last moment, catching the beat at the last possible second, almost afraid to know if it stayed, afraid to trust my knowing. But man it was there.

I could feel it again and I listened to my wrists making music I was born to hear. I was loose and tight at the same time. My wrists were loose and my forearms were keeping the pressure under control. I was arching over the set. I looked for Gretel and she was watching. And she knew. I was playing the answer. Her eyes were sad and happy at the same time; her hands flat on the table, still. And I was moving back and forth toward the sounds I needed to make, toward the sound Vince heard because he stood up, and—still playing—he turned and saluted me with his sax. I knew he was hearing what was happening to me as my legs were tight against my jeans and my feet were wearing shoes I didn't feel and I thought: this is what I always wanted to know from Buddy Rich. What do you feel? When I'm as fast as you are, will I feel what you feel, will I know?

These questions went through my head like lightning, their smell remained, and now it was what I knew that stopped me thinking. That pulled my sounds out of the forest of tables and noise like an ancient drum in some tribal ritual. It was my night. I heard the voices in the club lose their timbre, saw heads turn. There was no going back to Erie, only nights like these to keep me whole.

People were standing now. And Harry Ratch must have felt in his heart that he was helping me to what he never made. I was glad he was here to help me move, and then there were no more voices. One by one the band was dropping back and out, and only Vince and I were left—his fluid notes winding around the sticks I was moving but no longer felt. We were making circuits of sound. He turned facing me, leaning into his sax, giving his pledge with the notes he made before he too dropped out and I was left. I was dripping wet and winging it. The spotlight hung before me like a suspended meteor. I played as if waiting for it to hit.

WILLARD MANUS

A New York native currently living in Beverly Hills, California, Willard Manus is the author of numerous plays, screenplays, short stories, articles, and reviews. He has also written several novels. *Mott the Hoople* (1967) is the best known, and *The Fighting Men* (1982), a story inspired by the Vietnam conflict, is his most recent. "Hello Central, Give Me Doctor Jazz," is a section of *Connubial Bliss,* a novel he is working on.

Manus has been interested in jazz from his youth. He says that "jazz—Afro-American music, to be more accurate—lies at the heart of American culture, perhaps even is the heart, the source, the mainspring of whatever is unique and native about that culture."

The model for Sol in "Hello Central, Give Me Doctor Jazz" was a childhood friend of Manus who "played bass and was the first kid on the block in those post–World War II years to get into bebop. Very quickly he became proficient enough in the new music to play with some of bebop's pioneers (Bird, Davis, and so on). He was the first of our bunch to leave the neighborhood, live in the Village, experiment with drugs, be part of those musically revolutionary days." He says, "My story is meant as a tribute to him and as a requiem to all those great musicians like Sol whose self-destructive tendencies overwhelmed their creative gifts."

HELLO CENTRAL, GIVE ME DOCTOR JAZZ

D*AUPHINE STREET BLUES* on the record-player, the savor of *won-ton* and fried rice on the tongue, and a stick of joy making the rounds.

When it came time for Teddy's date Sugie to take a hit, she looked down at the joint and asked why it smelled funny.

"It's just ordinary tobacco laced with a little honey," I said.

"Honey?"

"Hash-oil to you."

"Never smoked any of that before."

"Of hash and love, the first is best."

Sugie sucked the smoke down into her lungs and held it there. Then: "Wow (cough) I don't believe it. I'm high already," she said, coughing again.

"It sure does hit home," Karen said.

"That's right," Sidney agreed, also coughing. "Where'd you come by it, Len?"

"My wife gave it to me as a splitting-up present," I explained.

"Glad you finally got something out of the marriage, man."

More laughter, coughing, and ingesting of honey-laced smoke.

Another stick went round and so did the music, Sidney playing one side after another, a band or two at a time, taking us on a trip back through time. He had kept all his brother Sol's old "race" records from the 20s and 30s, labels such as Regal and Savoy, musicians like Curley Weaver and Dog N Whistle Red playing the blues, the Down Home Blues and Good Morning Blues and How Long Blues . . .

Some yellow dog gal stole
my man from me
Some yellow dog gal done . . .

Through it all, I kept checking Sugie to see how she was taking it. She looked mystified, as if she couldn't quite fit it all together, being here with all these jangly, joking, middle-aged white folks. Teddy hadn't prepared her for anything like this and was content now to just kick back and get high and grin at Sidney as he brought out his kazoo and started tootling away on it.

Hello central, give me Doctor Jazz
He's got what I need, I'll say he has . . .

What a record collection Sidney had: Forest City Joe and Sleepy John Estes, blues masters, jazz masters, the forgotten and the famous, the Lady Days and Memphis Minnies, and he took us down the river with them, right back to Buddy Bolden and King Oliver, with long loving stops along the way with such moderns as Charlie Parker and Diz and that Jackie McLean record with Donald Byrd on trumpet and somebody doing some startling things with the instrument, using the bow high up in the harmonic position, like a Bartok concerto, and then suddenly producing a pizzicato sound like Segovia's.

"Who's that on bass?" Teddy asked.

"Who's that? Schmuck, don't you recognize Sol when you hear him?"

I had the chills; ice water was running down my back.

"It's been so long since I've listened to Sol," Teddy said. "I forgot just how good he was."

"Remember that night when we went downtown with him to the Cafe Bohemia?" Teddy asked. "Oscar Pettiford was there and the Adderly brothers. Sol walked up on stage and blew every one of those motherfuckers to bits."

"It was like being born again," Sidney said. "There was my brother, cutting all those black dudes, proving that a jewboy from the Bronx had as much soul as they did."

It was all coming back, all those bittersweet memories of Sol. He'd been the first of the gang to leave the Bronx, splitting Lydig Avenue for a pad on MacDougal Street. He'd been the first of us to discover bebop, the Royal Roost, Birdland, that whole new postwar jazz world out there. He'd also given us our first hits of marijuana in those early days, days of excitement and experiment, life changing right before our eyes, going from C-minor to D-flat. A few years later Sol copped the *Downbeat Magazine* award for Best New Musician of the Year and I got married to Rhoda Sutphin, an activist high up in the ranks of the Progressive Party (Win with Wallace) who convinced me that brotherhood and socialism were right around the corner.

"When was the last time you saw Sol?" I asked.

Sidney shrugged.

"When, goddammit?"

"Look (cough), I don't remember. Maybe a year ago."

Teddy hadn't seen him for two years, but believed he was still at Cloverdale.

"What's the matter with you guys? How could you abandon him like that?"

"Where do you get off saying that?" Teddy asked heatedly. "If you cared so much about Sol, why'd you go off to California?"

"That's right," Sidney said. "You were the closest to him."

"Look—"

"Forget the excuses, Len. You split, not us."

"I just had to get away from New York."

"We know all about that. But the bottom line is, you walked, we stayed."

"What happened to Sol isn't our fault," Teddy said. "He hasn't been the same since you and Rhoda broke up, and you know it."

Teddy was right: Sol's only good years had been when he lived with Rhoda and me. He'd check in with us before and after his stretches in the Federal penitentiary at Lexington, Kentucky. Rhoda's halfway house, he'd called our pad. And written a tune about it: "Rhoda's Roost." Good enough for Coleman Hawkins to record. I'd heard it recently in L.A. one night, on KKGO. I'd suffered damnation there, thinking of Sol, wondering about him, remembering the break-up with Rhoda, the first and most painful of my two failed marriages.

Somewhere there's music
How high the moon . . .

Sol was the first one I told about the break-up. He understood when I told him there was just no way I could stay in New York any longer, not with Rhoda living around the corner with her boss, one of the editors of the *National Guardian*. I had put as much continent as I could between them and me.

Teddy was the only one of my friends who tried to talk me out of going. He didn't want things to change, ever. That was the thing about Teddy, the fantastic thing, the terrible thing. We'd been a team ever since childhood, going to school, playing ball, chasing pussy together. We'd had some good times, but he didn't want them to stop rolling. He really thought he could hold back time, keep it from changing us. Teddy was a romantic, clinging to an ideal but impractical notion of life.

He still wouldn't let go of that notion. Look at him. At 53, he was amazingly trim and slim, with bright and shining eyes and cocoa-colored skin that still held its firmness. And here he was, doing what he'd done every Saturday night since his teens, diddly-bopping around town with a pouch of records under one arm, a sweet young *thang* on the other. Get high, get laid, and then get up Sunday morning to play ball. This is your life, Theodore Gordon.

How could he go on repeating himself, replaying the same old movie, content at his age to be putting the make on a silly 19-year-old like Sugie who could talk only about clothes and herself and the latest Michael Jackson video?

That was it (cough). That was where it was at, not only for Teddy but for much of the country. We were arrested in time, frozen in immaturity like a fish in ice. Look at us, the whole crazy society, watching mindless lying tv; listening to bubblegum rock-n-roll. From top to bottom America was a kindergarten, a nation of overgrown juvenile delinquents, craving distraction, sensation, cheap thrills. Look at the novels we read, the food we ate—hot dogs and hamburgers, Cokes and Egg McMuffins. Kiddie food for a nation of people like Teddy Gordon who refused to grow up—

"Somebody please shut him up!" Teddy said angrily.

I looked at him with surprise. "What do you mean? I haven't said a word."

"Are you kidding? You've been running your mouth like mad."

"I've never seen it fail," Sidney offered. "We talkers turn dumb when we get stoned. But a quiet man like Len does just the opposite—his tongue starts flapping like a broken tape recorder."

"OK, I'm high, but that doesn't mean I'm not right. Admit it. We're a nation of arrested adolescents. Childhood means everything to us; it's in our blood, our literature. Name me five American writers who can write memorably about anything except adolescence."

"How about Harold Robbins," Sidney said.

"Wise-ass! Where are our Malapartes, our Malrauxes, our Solzhenitsyns—?"

"All working for J. Walter Thompson," Sidney answered.

By two a.m. Teddy and Sugie were in the next-door bedroom together, getting it on, but Sidney, poor Sidney, was making no progress at all with his date. Karen seemed too uptown for Sidney, strictly a Houston Street man. But that didn't stop him from trying. He was all over her, groping, grabbing, begging. Suddenly I felt out of place, redundant. Unwanted.

Down the stairs I went and out into the New York night. Once in the car and heading uptown I knew I would have to keep driving and see Sol. It was mid-day before I finally reached Cloverdale and found him. He was sitting in the oak-tree shade on a hilltop overlooking the amphitheatre below. All the flesh on his body had been hammered down to a flat transparency. The veins in his hands showed like the filaments in a leaf. He seemed weightless and immaterial. I was afraid that the wind might lift him off the ground and blow him away.

All those years on drugs, the stretches in prisons and clinics, had taken their toll. The skin on his face was dry and scarred, showing jagged gashes for eyes and a mouth. Only his nose was intact, that magnificent, curved, Semitic beak.

"You picked the right Sunday to visit," he said, smoking a Sweet Caporal, the dark, fragrant New Orleans cigarette that he claimed was the closest thing to a legal high. "We're having a concert soon."

"Really! You going to play?"

"I don't know. I dragged my bass there," he said, indicating the half-shell stage, "but I don't know if I'm up to it. They've had me on heavy doses of Thorazine. I think I've lost my chops, man."

"Don't say it. They'll come back."

"I don't know. Right now I feel as if I'll never play again. What the hell for, Len?"

"For yourself, who else?"

"Been playing for myself all my life. Be nice to play for somebody else for a change."

"I'm here. Play for me."

"Are you really here? I thought we'd lost you to the Big Orange, bro."

"I'm back, Sol."

"Have you heard from Rhoda?" he asked.

"I got a Christmas card from her last year, telling me she's found religion. She's living in Colorado, on some ashram or other."

"What the hell, as long as you're happy."

The inmates were beginning to file across the lawn toward the concert stage, voices floating lightly on the warm breeze.

"So you're back," Sol said. "You broke up with Number Two and came back. You got a job?"

"It's been tough finding one, at my age. But there should be one out there, somewhere."

"You've got guts, Len, always had. I'm a coward, though, always taking the easy way out, getting strung out on some chemical or other."

"That's all behind you."

"Is it? Do people really change?"

"You're off smack, aren't you?"

"Yeah, and on Thorazine. Or methadone. What's the difference?"

"For one, what the doctors give you is legal. Two, you can still play, can't you?"

"Can I? I wonder, Len."

"You won't know until you try."

Sol went into one of his silences. He sat motionless, staring down at the scene below us, the Sweet Caporal burning down to a nub between his nicotine-stained fingers.

The line of inmates swelled, became a crowd. Most of the patients at Cloverdale were alcoholics. Moving on woozy legs, supported by attendants and nurses, they were followed in turn by the dopefiends, who oozed along in ghostly, somber procession, eyes shielded from the light. Next came the schizos, all bright smiles and banter as they herky-jerked along, followed by the paranoids and psychotics, the child-rapists and fetishists, God knows what. Cloverdale had them all, enough psychiatric case histories to fill a medical encyclopedia.

"They're what every jazzman dreams of," Sol chuckled. "A captive audience."

It was a perfect day for a concert. The New England air smelled warm and milky-sweet, like a farmgirl's thighs.

"Trouble is," Sol went on, "we haven't had a chance to rehearse. Some of the musicians just checked in this week."

"That shouldn't bother you guys. Wing it."

"Maybe I won't be able to."

"Come on, Sol, stop worrying. Give it a shot."

"Why should I risk embarrassing myself?"

"Because you're a musician. So go and play music."

"I'm nothing, man. I'm an ex-junkie living out his days in a mental institution."

"Hey, I've got news for you. You can come and live with me again. There's room at the inn."

"Thanks, but it wouldn't be the same without Rhoda."

"Forget Rhoda. Rhoda's dead history."

Sol looked thoughtful. "That's right," he said. "It's all dead history. We lived in fame and went down in flames, right?"

"Some of us walked away from the crash. We may be walking wounded, but we're alive."

"Are we? I sometimes wonder," Sol said.

He got up, though, he pulled himself up and started down the hill, but slowly, hesitantly. When he reached the stage, Sol picked up his bass and started warming up with some flamenco-like runs, alternating plucked notes with slide-pitches. His fingering was stiff and he looked small and frail down there, child's body draped around the upright instrument, clinging to it as if for support.

His fellow-musicians began to join him on stage. I recognized the trumpet player, a tall studious-looking black man with thick glasses and close-cropped grey hair. He'd been a sideman with some of the best bands of the 60s and 70s until a series of mental breakdowns choked off his career. Another familiar face was that of the pianist, Petronius Priest. Fifteen years ago, he'd been the best-known, most innovative jazz pianist of his time, a true original who'd won international acclaim for his artistry. A singular figure in a derby and goatee, playing his crabbed single-line notes and crazy chords with wicked humor, he'd slipped eventually into a pattern of infrequent playing and increasing dependence on alcohol. In recent years he'd spent more time up here than outside, the drink gnawing at his career and life.

The pick-up band started the concert with Ellington's *Across the Track Blues,* but awkwardly, at the wrong tempo, with Petronius and Sol bungling all the breaks. Their next effort, an up-blues version of *Gingerbread Boy,* was even worse. I had to close my eyes. But then the trumpet and saxophone began to cook, playing intricate ensembles that were as important as the solos. It was breathless, darting music and as it moved into improvised counterpoint, becoming dense and daring and headlong, I felt my spirits begin to lift.

These oldtimers weren't as sharp as they had been once upon a time. Petronius' solos were bare and perfunctory, and Sol's playing still sounded tight and self-conscious. But it didn't matter. They were playing, dammit. Playing with passion, delicacy and succinctness. Playing jazz.

In a while, Sol began to relax. Instead of clutching desperately at the bass, he now enfolded it within his arms, embracing it like a loving woman. He played with closed eyes, in total communion with the instrument, picking out ripe, dark, full-bodied chords that hung shimmering in the sunlight like bunches of grapes. Then he went into a long, lyrical piece, leading the way for the others. It had a lilting, descending melody, tempo changes and brief but complex ensembles. I knew it inside and out, having been there when he wrote it, "Rhoda's Roost."

Sol delivered several short, cascading solos, only to defer to the trumpet, who took every phrase and turned it away from where it appeared to be going, an inspired flight that Sol moved up in intimate, organic fashion, jazz improvisation at its best, and all of a sudden I found myself on my feet, shouting at Sol and his fellow dopefiends, "Do it, do it for us" as the tears stung my eyes and trickled down my cheeks.

BETH BROWN

A graduate of Bryn Mawr College with a degree in music and philosophy, Beth Brown also holds an MFA in fiction writing from Goddard College. Currently, she is working on a Ph.D. in music composition at the University of Pennsylvania. She is a pianist, singer, jazz composer, and arranger.

Brown has published several collections of poetry: *Lightyears: 1874–1976* (1982); *Blue Cyclone* in the *Pennsylvania Review* (1982); *Kaze* (1985); and *Satin Tunnels* (1988).

"Jazzman's Last Day" is taken from her MFA thesis. She says, "The inspiration was a train ride. Actually, I fell into a daydream about a jazz trumpeter. The story was influenced by what I knew concerning the life of Lee Morgan who was shot from the stage by his own wife."

JAZZMAN'S LAST DAY

BLOODEYE rises over a structure of bones. It is the jazzman's last day. As the mattress springs back to its original shape, he is revving up his shaver. The blue cold of morning is breaking away at 10 p.m., and the temperature rising to 35 still degrees. Under the ice, the sea at the waterfront swings out and throttles back in a great circle of tension and intentionality, going nowhere. Snowstorms blowing in off the coast threaten to eat the city. Most of Tuesday is still a possibility. There may be an earthquake or a tidal wave, muses the jazzman, patting lukewarm water on puffy eyes.

Every man's wetdream: Bess is on her way over. He hangs up the phone. Bess could be a mechanical doll, the way she makes her voice clipped and monotoned when she calls. It's her way of taking care of business. But he knows she'll run in out of the storm like a wild orange bird, reeking of Avon, to ask him first of all for stockings. He laughs so hard at the thought of her, he has to lie down for a minute. Most evenings, he can count on her to be waiting in the back of the club for him to finish the gig so she can drink his money. She turns heads, gets top dollar from that sonofabitch clubowner, warms his walkup like a heater at night. Worth every nickel, says the jazzman.

Blow *truth*, baby! A name like Truth is a burden. He earned the name one night in the last high screaming notes of a 5-minute solo when he was soaking his shoes in sweat and the walls slapped his improvised melodies back and forth until he could've wrapped that whole room in sound and stuck it under his arm like a birthday present for his old lady. A man in the front row yelled Blow truth baby. The same man became his agent for a month until he faded out with all the bills he could stuff into his pockets. The jazzman still has those posters with JIMMY "The Truth" JACKSON printed at the top and a picture of him with his trumpet in his left hand disappearing around a streetcorner followed by a droophead stray dog.

His dreams still play the time when he picked up the broad with the wired bra when the zipper on his pants stuck, before Bess the posters and marquee lights and a chance to make it. He could shuffle the deck & pull the aces or sneak a sevenspade out of his jacket and lay down hand after winning hand. He'd walk for blocks, cutting a path in the crowd with the smooth roll of his stroll, the smell of his cologne and his old lady's hips. When he picked up his trumpet & licked his lips, a huge ball, deep blue, of silence would explode in a room packed with audience.

Bird's silence. Between his lips and the mouthpiece. A waste of that shapeless stuff. No audible breathing in the room except his slow intake broke the air. The smoke from cigarets and roaches paused in gray & blue clouds around faces that melted into one giant listening ear. He would try to reach the corners of the room, rock the spiders down and weave his sound into their webs. He could play with that silence by rolling it into a bluer, smaller ball & balancing it between his lips and the mouthpiece. Or he would swim in it like a wave. He waited, made them wait, waited with them, to begin. . . .

2. The snowstorm clogged the transit system above ground. People are walking sideways into the wind clutching at scarves. Jimmy pushes downtown. White people are black outlines traced on the snow. Dark wanderers stand at their feet like blackbirds begging crumbs with the pigeons. There isn't anyplace to go or anything to do except fight the cold and dance on the ice. Afternoon light leans on the buildings spilling gray ashes of shadows to the street. Land smells of waste & tears. There are no special provisions for the jazzman's life in any of these buildings: no offices, no BUREAU OF THE JAZZMAN'S FATE. Nothing but welfare and the foodstamp lines. A woman with a mouth like a

hot spot of red sealing wax is waiting for her phone to ring & drinking her fifth cup of the black coffee people are always singing about, hoping Jimmy will make it over & they'll get into something. Hoping the Truth will stop in.

3. For the jazzman, evening has always been a wail growing softer and lower as the night progresses, diminishing to a moan. Morning is mute. Light only sobs. The reflections off his trumpet have the only human voices & he can speak with them in fast riffs which take all night of sitting on the edge of his bed with his trumpet in his hands to understand. He is pleased with himself when he finishes practicing. It is the only schooling he will ever obtain, outside of the Lessons & Conversations with master musicians after gigs when he is taught how to hope. The master's task doesn't require many words—the right gesture will say everything. The masters showed him how to bring his trumpet to his lips & pause, filling a room with the blue ball of anticipation.

Bess doesn't come to this restaurant. Jimmy is avoiding her. Midnight walk smokestack talk. The sky is stitched with a legacy of birds moving out of sight into darkness. The sounds of the night are rich with speech. Neon signs keep up their end of the conversation with short, pastel exclamations.

What else is there to do but lay out the choices? Years of speaking emotions & ideas make it easier for him to listen to unspoken messages that bend his blood backward in his veins like dark portwine. The thought of his body buckeyed on some street corner flashes like a news item for Tuesday: death of an epigram child of a wombless mother.